PRAISE FOR KEREN LANDSMAN

"A fascinating and original urban fantasy… Landsman demonstrates virtuoso writing ability, building a fascinating plot, an impressive combination of sources of inspiration and rare emotional depth, which make reading a sweeping experience and the book suitable not only for fans of fantasy and science fiction but for every reader."
Israel Hayom

"The Heart of the Circle is an important step forward for the Israeli genre scene, and in its portrait of young people struggling with both their outsized emotions and an unjust situation, it delivers a powerful, engrossing story."
Abigail Nussbaum, author of *Asking the Wrong Questions*

"Keren Landsman did not write a good book, she wrote an excellent book."
Saloona

"Oh wow. Wow, this book. How am I supposed to write anything now?"
N.S. Dolkart, author of the *Godserfs* trilogy

"A bold new voice in Israeli fantasy… an enchanting debut."
Lavie Tidhar, World Fantasy Award winning author of
Osama and *Central Station*

Keren Lansdman

THE HEART OF
THE CIRCLE

ANGRY
ROBOT

ANGRY ROBOT
An imprint of Watkins Media Ltd

Unit 11, Shepperton House
89 Shepperton Road
London N1 3DF
UK

angryrobotbooks.com
twitter.com/angryrobotbooks
Love is a battlefield

An Angry Robot paperback original, 2019

Cover by Francesca Corsini
Edited by Noa Menheim, Gemma Creffield and Christopher Slaney
Translated by Daniela Zamir
Set in Meridien

ISBN 978 0 85766 811 0
Ebook ISBN 978 0 85766 812 7

Printed and bound in the United Kingdom by TJ International.

9 8 7 6 5 4 3 2 1

To Yoav, Barak and Keshet,
without whom I would never have become a writer.

1

The day after the murder we sat in a circle at the Basement. Their food sucks, the alcohol selection leaves much to be desired, but there are books lining every inch of the walls, the smell of wood, and music you don't have to scream over to have a conversation. We were sheltered from the outside world, with only familiar faces around us. It was hot and damp, typical for mid-July, the air-conditioner powerless against a room packed with people wearing sullen pouts. We sat on the side couch, next to the shelves crammed with books, sock puppets and burned out candles. My shirt was sticking to my back; Daphne placed her head on my shoulder and I sniffed her curls. I wrapped my arm around her, letting her nestle in my embrace. They were all so sad, everyone saying, "We have to stop the next murder," but no one had any ideas. I was drained of tears.

Rhyming chants from the high schoolers' protest on the street above us infiltrated the pub between songs.

"They're going to get their asses kicked," someone behind me said.

"They have to learn to fend for themselves," came a reply. I stopped listening.

"Your curls are tickling me," I said to Daphne.

She hugged me, looked up and said, "One day your beard will tickle me."

The first murder was agonizing. Incessant tears and self-blame. It took some time to realize we couldn't have stopped it, that none of us could have changed what had happened. We have since developed a routine. Getting out of the house helps. Being around people helps even more.

I touched my chin. "Beards itch."

Letting out a sound between a laugh and a sob, she lowered her head back onto my shoulder. Her curls got into my nose again. I stroked her hair without saying a word.

This time we didn't know the murdered girl. A photo of her was placed on the bar top, next to the other photos, surrounded by little candles. The faces in the various photos began to blend together. They were all smiling at the camera, heads aslant with mischievous expressions that made them look younger than they really were, all against a slightly blurred background. Brown eyes, black eyes, blue eyes. Hair in different colors, different styles. Men. Women. When the first murder happened we cried for a week in the city square, refusing to leave until the prime minister promised she would personally investigate. After the second murder, our tears were silent. The third – we stopped crying.

There was the pathetic attempt at revenge organized by a few pyros after the first. They got caught before they reached their target. Speaking for the cameras, the spokesperson for the police Prevention of Future Crimes Unit explained theirs was a sacred duty. The bodies dangled from the gallows behind him. Daphne cursed him for a whole hour, then cried herself to sleep.

I closed my eyes. Someone switched the music to depressing peace songs. *Give Peace a Chance.*

Matthew, my brother, plopped himself on the armrest next to me. "If I hear that song one more time, I'm going to break someone's fingers."

He was wearing the same clothes I saw him in yesterday, before he left for work. A T-shirt with 'Stop the Violence' printed on it, jeans in desperate need of a wash, and sneakers.

"What are you doing here?" I whispered to him. "It's dangerous. You remember what happened last time."

"If you get stabbed, you're going to want someone around you who knows how to use a tourniquet."

I rubbed my hand where the scar still hurt. "If you get your arm broken because of me, Mom would never let me forget it."

"Don't worry, I've already landed a permanent position at the hospital. Not even a shattered arm could get me kicked off the ward." He winked, and I could feel the fear lurking inside him.

Daphne straightened her back towards him. "Hey, Matthew."

Matthew walked passed me and hugged her. "Hey, babe."

I leaned back, waiting for them to break up their hug.

Matthew unzipped his backpack. "Mom sent sandwiches. And before you say anything, I know." He handed me one. It was wrapped in a paper napkin with my name scribbled on it.

I took it from him. White bread with chocolate spread.

Matthew took out another sandwich and handed it to Daphne. Our mom had started treating her like family from the moment she abandoned the fantasy that Daphne would magically transform from a close friend into a girlfriend. I knew Mom had expected Matthew to fill the spot I didn't want, and I knew he tried; moreover, I knew how much Daphne had hated turning him down. She said he wasn't her type, that he was like a brother to her, but I knew it was because he wasn't like us, and neither of us had the heart to tell him.

"I know," Matthew repeated, "but she's just trying to help."

I knew it was Mom's way of showing support from the first time she had sent Matthew to the pub with food for us, ignoring every social convention. She knew what kind of pasta each of us liked, and even made separate salads because I couldn't stand cucumbers and Matthew hated onions. But the announcement that another person was murdered in one of our rallies must have thrown her off balance. It wasn't like her to forget I don't eat chocolate.

I handed Matthew the sandwich. "You want one?"

His beaming smile almost made me grin. "I thought you'd never offer." He wolfed it down in three bites.

"Want me to order you something?" Daphne asked while nibbling her sandwich.

"I can't eat. I'm too, too…" I waved the idea away.

"It's the Reed Diet," Matthew said while chewing. "Stage one – go somewhere that has lots of really sad people. Stage two – be too overwhelmed with everyone's feelings to eat. Stage three – vanish into thin air."

I feigned a pout. His attempt at a joke might have worked had he himself not been overcome with fear and loss.

He poked me. "Come on, I'm just kidding."

"You forgot a crucial stage," I said, holding up a finger.

"What?"

"Be born a moody," I replied and smiled. He knew me well enough to know it wasn't a real smile. Just as I knew him well enough to read him without having to *read* him.

"I hate that term." Matthew scrunched up his napkin. "It's offensive. I don't understand how you can use it."

"It's called reappropriation," I said, wearing my pedagogical face. "You take a derogatory term and turn it into a–"

"Oh, hush already," Daphne interrupted me, slapping my knee. "I'd seriously advise hitting 'unsubscribe' to all those overbearing online groups of yours." She shot Matthew a look. "Saw anyone you like?"

Matthew grimaced. "No, but I'll take what I can get."

I looked at Daphne and sighed. "You really think this is an appropriate time for this?"

"Poor Matthew," Daphne giggled, ignoring me.

Matthew stuck the crinkled napkin in his backpack and said, "The girl behind you is cute."

I sighed again, louder this time, and turned around. Forrest and Aurora were making out on the couch behind us, his fingers running through her hair. Daphne and I met them during our college days and the four of us have been friends ever since. He was a chubby redhead and she was built like a beanstalk, almost devoid of feminine features. They had been marching close to us only seconds before the murder, Forrest making sure I was drinking enough because it was a hot day.

Matthew was probably referring to the girl wearing the 'Peace Starts Within' shirt, who was visibly ignoring all the men trying to chat her up. Next to her sat a scrawny, pasty looking guy who seemed vaguely familiar; I was busy trying to remember where I knew him from when the woman sitting on his other side looked up and our eyes met. I froze.

"Ivy," I said.

"Where?" Matthew sprang up.

She was wearing a blue shirt with a white ribbon, hair pulled back into a ponytail. She looked away and said something to the guy sitting next to her. Her brother.

"He's cute," Daphne said.

"Don't go there. He's not for you."

Daphne kept looking at them.

"He's Ivy's brother. You don't want anything to do with him."

"If I was going to judge every person by their brother…" Daphne said, cocking her head towards Matthew with a smile.

"Excuse me," someone standing above us said. It was Ivy's scrawny brother. I tried to recall his name. The last time I saw him he was about to be released from the army. Then it came to me. Oleander.

"I saw my sister was making you uneasy. I asked her to leave." Oleander smiled at Daphne, clearly ignoring my presence.

"Lovely," I blurted.

Oleander held his hands out and said, "I'm just trying to help."

"Help who?"

"I'm not my sister."

The emotions between Daphne and Oleander shot through me like an electrical current. Daphne slapped my thigh again. "Let it go. It's been years." She placed her half-eaten sandwich on my knee. "Don't eat that. You'll have the worst stomach ache tomorrow." I wanted to stop her, but she just shot me a look, got up and left. I knew that look all too well. Drop it, it said. Let me live my life. Once Daphne joined them, the conversation behind me livened up.

"I can't believe Daphne can actually find someone to hook up with in this mess," Matthew said, waving both hands in the air. "What do I have to do to find someone?"

"You think I'm the right person to answer that question?" I scooted over, letting him stretch out next to me.

Matthew fell silent, the twinkle in his eye fading. He looked down and picked at the threads coming out of the strap of his old backpack. It was standard military issue, the symbol of the medical corps printed on its side. I knew what he was about to ask, and I knew I had to let him ask it before I answered.

"Mom's asking," he said and paused. "Well, I'm asking, but also Mom."

I waited.

Matthew took a deep breath. "How close were you when it happened?"

"Close enough," I replied. That wasn't the real question.

"Because it was…" Matthew paused again, grabbed the strap of his bag and looked at me. "It was really scary this time."

It was. I knew because I was there. I saw the knife. I felt the life seeping out of the girl. I held Daphne whose knees buckled when all those futures came crashing down on her.

"We're worried. All of us. Including me. I don't… I don't know what I would have done if it had been you." He took my hand in his, like when we were children and he had to console me whenever the neighbors spat on me as we passed by them. Eventually Dad decided we had to move, and we picked up and left the north for a more centrally located city, full of all kinds of people and feelings.

"Maybe you could…" Matthew's voice cracked. "I know this is important to you and Daphne. It's important to me too. But… maybe you could…"

It was the same conversation we had had dozens of times: My parents want me to stop attending the rallies, I explain to them that without the rallies nothing will change, they don't listen, and I ignore them. But my big brother was scared, and I couldn't just shrug him off.

"I'm just really worried," he said, fixing me with his pleading eyes. "You have to be careful."

I put my other hand on his.

"Please," he begged, his voice wavering. He was supposed to ask us to stay home. Daphne had told me he would. To not attend the next rally. To sit this one out and look after ourselves, like everyone else who had stopped showing up at the rallies. There were fewer and fewer marchers each time, and more and more candlelight vigils afterwards. The police claimed they couldn't prevent the murders if we insisted on marching, but at the same time they released announcements about the arrests of potential murderers, people who none of the damuses I knew deemed dangerous.

Matthew didn't say anything but "Please." Nothing more. And left his hand in mine. I squeezed it and wondered whether we were too old to hug.

"OK," I answered the question he hadn't asked.

"Thanks." It wasn't the dialogue Daphne had predicted. She could only foresee probabilities, of course, but she saw this conversation with a certain degree of clarity: Matthew asks us to stop attending the rallies, I object, he whips out two arguments, I find a compromise, and we manage to work things out.

It would have been easier had Daphne been there with me, but she was busy flirting with Oleander. I could feel her easing up, becoming softer. It felt nice to be swept along with her. To feel her open up to another human being. I closed my eyes.

Matthew picked up the sandwich from my knee and unzipped his backpack. His fear was abating. All he needed was to see us, to know we were OK. Taking something out of his bag, he let out a small, quiet sigh, leaned back and stretched out his legs.

I opened my eyes. A weighty book with small print lay open on his knees. It was too dark to read, and he was shining a small flashlight on the pages.

I lifted the book cover. "*Approaches to Laparoscopic Knee Surgery,*" I read out loud.

Matthew nodded. "And it's more complicated than you'd think."

"Good to know. I won't try it then."

Without looking up from his book, he dug into his backpack and fished out a paperback with a colorful cover and a mini clip-on book light. "I thought this might help."

It was the adventure book we used to read as kids. Five children walk into a toy closet and find a magical kingdom where it's summer all year round. I opened the book, feeling the light fragrant breeze carried from between its pages, so much more palpable than the dying breaths of air the tormented air-conditioning exhaled. This book was the reason I had decided to become a moodifier and go into the emotional design business when I grew up. I dove into the world in which children could make a difference and defeat evil all on their own.

Halfway through the book I sensed an unfamiliar consciousness. I looked up. Matthew was still immersed in his textbook. Around us people were either making out or sitting in small groups with their heads bowed. A few of the high schoolers had joined us, proudly boasting their fresh bruises and scolding the "geriatrics" for hiding in a pub instead of standing outside with them and stirring up a riot. Behind me, Forrest and Aurora were in a heated discussion, fragments of which floated my way. She, as usual, was insisting on carrying out the revolution from within the political system by infiltrating the major parties. He, as usual, supported armed resistance and forming squads to patrol the streets, ensuring our safety. They were going at it in high-pitched tones until someone mentioned the Sons of Simeon, and they both instantly turned against him.

"Excuse me?" asked a woman with short hair, standing above me wearing a floral summer dress and tightening the fabric around her thighs. "Mind if I sit here?" The tension she exuded stood in stark contrast to her bright tone.

I shrugged. "Free country."

"So they keep saying."

She was so tense I could barely feel her. I scooted over. She sat down on the ottoman next to me. "I'm Reed, and this is Matthew."

I nudged Matthew with my leg. He looked up, smiled, and went back to his book. I didn't sense a change in him. He probably won't even remember her.

"I'm Sherry." She held out her hand. A silver charm bracelet was looped around her wrist.

"I'm a moody."

Matthew muttered something under his breath. I ignored him.

"I know you don't actually need the sense of touch to do what you do," she said, looking me straight in the eye, "and I'm trusting you won't try anything. Besides…" She turned her hand palm down, fingers spread outwards. A pebble. "We have rules, right?"

We shook hands. The charms crushed against my skin. They were a nice, cool contrast to the humidity hanging in the room.

"That's a nice charm."

"My mom makes me wear it," she said and shrugged. "You know what moms are like."

I nodded. "My mom would want me to wear a hazmat suit whenever I go out."

Sherry grinned and brushed the hair off her face. Too short to tuck around her ears, it bounced right back. She looked at Matthew and asked, "Are you a moody too?"

Matthew looked up from his book and said, "No, an orthopedist. Reed takes people's pain away, and I make them feel it."

We both laughed at his stupid joke. Sherry shifted her gaze between the two of us and smiled politely. "I'm a cop."

My smile froze. "You were at the rally?"

"Every single one in the last two years, since…" she fell silent.

"Since Flint," I finished the sentence for her. At that rally, a bomb had been tossed into the middle of the crowd, detonated by an unknown pyro. It was the Sons of Simeon's first murder. Nothing was ever the same again. They saw themselves as the heirs of Simeon Ben Shetach, the Sanhedrin murderer during the reign of Alexander Jannaeus.

"I'm one of those nutcases who volunteer to actually go the rallies instead of staying at the station and getting the reports after the fact." Sherry bit her bottom lip. "I'm also involved in the surveillance of potential murderers."

"You're supposed to tell me not to worry, that this time you'll get him for sure," I said, trying not to sound bitter. I didn't mention that her volunteering didn't help us. That the police hadn't managed to prevent a single murder, and that the cops mostly stayed on the sidelines and never made any arrests.

Matthew kicked me. "Be polite."

"He's very polite," Sherry said quietly. "Most people here won't let me anywhere near them once they find out what I do for a living."

"We're nicer than most," Matthew said, smiling at her.

Before Sherry could answer, Daphne appeared above her, almost tripping over the ottoman. She crouched between us, opened Matthew's backpack and took out what was left of her sandwich. "I'm taking Oleander back to our place," she said and winked at me. "Don't come home too early."

I was torn between my desire to keep her away from him and the urge to wish her a flaccid night. "Just keep the noise down, OK?"

"Sure thing," she said, and got up.

Sherry smiled. "It's good to see that at least for some of us life goes on as usual."

Crossing his legs, Matthew said, "It's just a shame those some of us aren't into me." He sounded bitter but smiled, and we moved on to small talk, ignoring all the political debates around us, which were simmering to a boil courtesy of the late hour and the alcohol. Forrest launched into a diatribe about how 'if we don't help ourselves, no one's going to help us,' while Aurora kept countering with 'armed resistance would just set public opinion against us,' and the usual 'we have to understand their motives, we have to find common ground'.

Sherry glanced at me. "You disagree?"

I tried to show as little emotion as possible. "After the votes for Change from Within failed to reach the threshold? To get even one seat? No."

Sherry held her hand flat, palm facing upward. "We have a chance with the major parties. Flint managed to get into parliament."

"And got killed. And no one even investigated it seriously. It's been two years and not a single lead."

Matthew shifted in his seat. I looked at him and asked, "What?"

"Nothing." He shook his head.

"I'm not running for parliament."

"Good," he said, tightening his lips into a grin. "God forbid you should make a decent salary."

I tried being annoyed at him, but it was impossible. "Never mind the salary, what would I do with a car?"

Sherry looked at him, then at me, and said, "And a driver." She smiled, and for a moment she looked pretty.

"We'd never find parking. The poor guy would have to circle the neighborhood all night."

We got to talking about our apartments, and from there to even more trivial, mundane matters. Sherry had three cats, each of which had run away to a different neighbor during one of the heavy storms last winter, and she told us how she frantically knocked on every door in her apartment building late at night to try bring them home. Matthew asked whether I could have tracked them down by attuning to their feelings, which eventually led to the story of how I caught the mouse that had set up camp in one of our kitchen cupboards last year.

By the end of the evening, when Matthew gave me a ride home, I felt a little less dismal.

2

The following morning I dragged myself to the shower with eyes half closed, trying to remember whether my shift started at eight or nine. Lately I had to pick up more shifts to cover my part of the rent, which the landlord had once again raised after reading some article about the unreliability of people like us.

Oleander came out of the bathroom in a cloud of warm vapors, dressed in the old T-shirt I received at the end of basic training and had loaned Daphne years ago. He had curly light brown hair and bright, smiling eyes. I thought of Ivy and her funny stories about her fights with her younger brother, scuffles that were mostly carried out in reflections so their parents wouldn't see what they were doing to each other.

I rubbed my eyes and yawned. I had gotten maybe four hours sleep, and even those were muddled by one disjointed nightmare after another. It would be days until the feeling of the knife being pushed in between my shoulder blades faded. At least this time I hadn't been in the closest circle. Back then it had been weeks of waking up in tears, and no pill could make me lie in bed for more than two hours straight.

"Hey," Oleander said, his voice pleasant and deep.

"Hey." My own voice produced its usual morning rasp.

"We didn't make too much noise last night, did we?" He seemed too wakeful and chipper for seven am.

"I really need the bathroom," I replied.

Daphne opened the door to her room, dressed in a nightie. Oleander's feelings for her sizzled up and struck me with such force I could barely keep myself steady.

"Good morning," Daphne said, smiling. Her passion came flooding into me.

I rubbed my forehead. "Would you please, please stop thinking about sex? Please."

Daphne feigned an innocent expression. "Who, me? I'm thinking no such thing!"

The next wave made my knees go weak.

I fixed her with a look. "Please, wait half an hour until I'm gone." My voice, which was supposed to sound leveled and confident, came out a miserable snarl.

"Fine," she replied with a dramatic eye roll. It was enough to get a small smile out of me. I wondered if she had planned it that way. "And you're going to want to take an extra shirt today."

I sighed. "Again?"

"I'll wait for you," Oleander said to her before finally stepping away from the bathroom door and disappearing into her room.

I cleared my throat. "Daphne, are you sure about–"

"Haven't we already discussed this?" she interrupted me, looking somewhere over my shoulder, as she always did when searching for the fastest way to end the argument.

"This is not a good idea. He's her brother. You know what–"

"He's a one-night stand. Nothing more."

"It's just that… I don't want this to be another Alder."

"Neither do I," she said, flicking the hair from her eyes. "But Oleander isn't… it's not… he's nice, and thoughtful, and…"

And a damus. "Alder was nice and thoughtful," I said, trying to keep my tone steady, soothing even. I'm just asking, I told myself. I'm absolutely not going to barge into her room and physically kick Oleander out of my house.

"Oleander isn't another Alder," Daphne blurted. "And I'm not the same eighteen year-old girl terrified of her commander. Have a little faith in me." Before I could answer, she added, "And he's not Ivy."

"I just think that…" I said, searching for the right words, "that maybe there's a better way of coping with what happened than…"

"And I think that maybe instead of burying yourself in work, you should remember we could all die tomorrow, so you better live a little," she said, her voice slightly deflated.

I was too tired and miserable to produce a supportive and understanding answer. "Unlike you, I'd rather go through life without catching an STD from every man who passes by and having to get monthly antibiotic shots."

"Of course you won't catch anything, you'd have to actually do something for that," she retorted with a smile meant to lighten up the message.

"I do enough."

"What do you do? Dishes?" she snorted. "That's one odd fetish." She arched her eyebrows so ridiculously high, I couldn't help but smile.

She returned the smile. "Feeling better?"

"How do you do it?"

"Magic," she said, kissed me on the cheek and went to her room.

I stepped into the bathroom. The showerhead spurted in two opposite directions, neither of them directly above me. I had to hop left and right to get wet. The mold painted a greenish-brown fringe on the shower curtain. We really do have to replace it, I thought, even though it was the first thing we bought for the apartment together. The bloody handprints design gave us a laugh.

I was happy we were out of hot water. The icy drops helped me focus, get my act together. After each murder, Daphne was on the lookout for one-night stands, and I always booked enough double-shifts to exhaust myself to the point of passing out at night. It didn't work, but it was the only solution I managed to come up with.

Not listening to the news was the one thing we agreed on. Turning a deaf ear to the many pundits, to the hollow speeches broadcast from parliament, to the attempts to rouse our worn-out, divided community with endless debates.

Beneath the water, I closed my eyes and tried to find myself amidst the overwhelming pain.

3

The bus was late, as usual, and almost every seat taken by the time it arrived. The other three people waiting at the station boarded from the front. I could board with them, and no one would notice. This time there weren't any visible bruises on my face to reveal what I had been up to last night. I could board from the front, and pay with cash instead of using my smart card. I could pretend I was from another city and simply didn't have a Tel Aviv bus pass. Easy-peasy. As long as an inspector didn't board, I'd be fine.

But I couldn't bring myself to do it. I waited until the back door opened, dodging the looks of everyone sitting in that part of the bus. I held my pass against the reader, and it beeped, as usual, arousing murmurs from the rest of the passengers. I fixed my gaze on the floor, proceeded to the section bordered in white and stood by the window. I looked out, ignoring the whispers buzzing around me. The passengers closest to me were radiating palpable aversion. One passenger's repulsion was so strong he was physically sick. I considered heightening his nausea. I pictured him throwing up on the woman sitting next to him.

Three teenagers huddled in the back seat were talking about the rally. One of them said 'They took down another one,' and his friend laughed and told a joke I had heard a million times before.

They were being intentionally loud. I could feel their need for violence, driven by fear and loathing.

The radio was blaring with the regular series of interviews: a man who claimed he had alerted the police before the rally but no one paid him any attention – followed by the police spokesperson's response that the man was lying; then came the ambulance driver who had evacuated the wounded and complained they weren't being paid enough to transport 'those people'; two politicians from rival parties debated who was to blame for this recent murder, and a nurse from Gershom Hospital, to which the wounded had been admitted, harped about the overcrowding and the shortage of skilled nurses.

"Let them die," one of the teenagers behind me scoffed, and the other two laughed.

I compressed my anger into an explosive force.

"The Sons of Simeon are doing them a favor," one of them said.

The bus came to halt at the next stop. The rear door opened. A woman in a floral dress boarded; her bus pass beeped, alerting the passengers of another presence similar to my own. The hem of a purple skirt was peeking out from under her dress, revealing her occupation: relieving people of their emotions for a fee.

We exchanged a silent glance.

One of the teenagers laughed. "Look, they can't even get along with each other." His words were steeped in panic. The song playing on the radio now over, the host of the morning talk show was interviewing the deputy minister of defense. They talked about the rally, the deputy minister demanding that the prime minister take active measures to ensure public safety from this 'domestic threat'. She spoke about all the innocent people who could have gotten hurt were a riot to break out due to 'internal intrigues that have nothing to do with normal, law-abiding citizens.' She didn't say a single word about the Sons of Simeon. They didn't interview one true representative of our community. Not even the chairwoman of The Coalition for Peacebuilding, who was always peddling her tired mantra about peaceful coexistence inspired by the promotion of diversity. No one believed in those slogans any more, not even radio hosts, apparently. At least this time they didn't interview Linden, the leader of the Sons of Simeon, or Prof. Yeshurun, a splasher and self-proclaimed expert on the community who jumped at any opportunity for self-promotion, even when it came at our expense. The only good thing I could say about him was that at least he was the first to shun the airhead rapist who used his powers to prevent his victims from calling out for help.

Before the transition to the newscast, the host once again played the statement made by Sons of Simeon, claiming responsibility for the bombing. "Another blow has been dealt today in God's name. Today the Sons of Simeon wiped another medium off the face of the Earth, as our Holy Scripture commands. We have struck at the heart of the depraved city of Tel Aviv, and we shall continue to strike wherever they lurk until every last medium is annihilated."

I choked back my tears, put in my earphones, and cranked up the music. Outside, people were walking, talking, nodding, stopping to toss a few shekels into the open guitar case of the musician on the street corner. I scrolled down the most recent posts. Someone had started another thread about patriarchy and using our powers, and I immersed myself in typing an appropriate comment, one that would be angry enough to get my message across, but not inflammatory enough to get me blocked again.

The bus stopped.

A man with a thick, carefully styled beard, dressed in a tank top and hiking boots, boarded from the rear door. His pass beeped as he swiped it against the reader. He looked at me and then at the woman standing next to me in the white section, and pressed his thumb to his index finger, making a small circle. Looking for a psychic. The woman gave off a quick surge of fear.

I could have let her treat him. She was going to anyway, once the bus pulled over at her stop. But I couldn't ignore the tremor that shot through her. I tried to imagine myself doing what she did, day in, day out. Having to touch every person I crossed paths with just to make ends meet, having to feel what they felt, to do for them what they wouldn't allow themselves to do within the confines of civilized society. I sent her a short protection wave, looked the man straight in the eye and scratched my temple with my middle finger. Empathy. Daphne would flick her hair back and touch her forehead with her pinky to signal foresight.

The woman exhaled her pent-up breath. The man approached me and extended his hand. I took out my earphones.

"Remember me? We were in elementary school together. Danny, right?" He was engulfed in a cloud of cheap deodorant.

I didn't have to shake his hand to feel him, nor did I have to ask what he wanted from me. His outstretched hand gestured consent. He was leaking sadness.

I shook his hand. "Reed, actually," I said, managing to feign a smile.

I took away the top layer. Not a lot, but enough to get him through the day. I saw the relief in his eyes. He exhaled as the pain subsided. I held his hand for another moment, thinking he might be interested in something more than a quick fix. The bus started moving again and the woman in the floral dress lost her balance. He reached out and helped her steady herself, turning his attention entirely away from me.

I shifted my gaze out the window again. I had to scatter the foreign emotions swirling inside me so I wouldn't absorb them. Usually I'd disperse them among the bus passengers, maybe even toss a few out the window if the bus was at a standstill for long enough. This time I directed all of it at the three teenagers sitting behind me. I made sure the emotions really seeped in. The one who was in the middle of yet another joke fell silent, and the other two stopped giggling. I felt the sadness sink deep inside them. They didn't and wouldn't understand where it came from, and I didn't care. When the bearded man looked the other way, the woman caught my attention and clasped her hands together, a gesture of gratitude and solidarity. I returned the gesture and separated my hands once the man turned his gaze back to us.

By the time the bus reached my stop, one of the three teenagers had managed to overcome the emotions I had planted in him, and started muttering something about how if he ever had a kid 'like that' he'd make sure the midwife strangled him at birth. I got off the bus without looking back. I made sure no one was following me. Although it was broad daylight, and there were no telltales of my true nature, one could never be too sure.

My phone beeped with a message from Aurora about the upcoming meetings of the Coalition for Peacebuilding's youth support group, Youth for Youth, or as we called it, Yoyo. Aurora wanted me to serve as a counselor again. I tried drafting a reply that wouldn't offend her but at the same time made it perfectly clear that I wasn't going to do it. One of the main advantages of living in Tel Aviv was the high concentration of people like me; a city full of the "lunatic fringe," as the deputy defense minister liked to call us. One of the disadvantages was that I was constantly expected to volunteer, as if I was some loser with no life, as if I hadn't done more than my fair share already. I'd been volunteering since high school, and I'd had enough. Enough of people who kept demanding more of my time, who completely disregarded my private life, who didn't understand why I couldn't pick up another shift, take on another group, devote what little spare time I had to the community. The community could take care of itself for once.

At least she hadn't mentioned Ivy's presence at the Basement.

Someone touched my shoulder. Damn, I'd been too caught up in drafting the text to notice, and had let my guard down. I condensed my fear, and focusing it in case I'd have to strike, turned around. The bearded man from the bus was standing behind me, holding out an open palm, fingers spread in front of me. A splasher. I dissolved the intended blow.

"I wanted…" he began, a small wave of hesitation creeping towards me before he continued. "When are you usually here?"

I tightened my grip on the straps on my bag. "I'm on my way to work."

"Right, of course." He gave a side-glance to make sure no one was eavesdropping. "I meant what time do you usually go to work, when can I find you here."

"I understood the question," I replied, holding his gaze. "I have a job. A real one." And it wasn't relieving strangers of their feelings. I wasn't that desperate. Not yet.

"Of course." He placed a heavy hand on my shoulder, squeezing. "If this is about money…"

I shook him off.

He blinked, taken aback. "I thought…"

"I know what you thought," I interrupted him, "and if you don't stop with those thoughts, you'll get back everything I took with interest."

A wave of fear crashed into me. "I'm sorry," he mumbled, stepping back. "I didn't mean it."

But he did. Just like every other person who held out an open palm in front of me.

I gave him an icy glare. He took another step back.

"I'm going to work now," I intoned, "and I expect never to see you around here again."

He was taller than me, and yet seemed shrunken when he turned around, almost breaking into a run.

Once he was out of my line of vision, I leaned against the wall behind me and closed my eyes. There was no reason for me to feel this way. No reason to want to run home and take a shower just because someone extended an open palm expecting me to relieve emotions that were too difficult to bear. I took in Tel Aviv's humidity. I had to let go, get on with my day and immerse myself in work. I had to break away from the wall and keep going. At least it wasn't my actual job. Unlike the woman from the bus.

I opened my eyes and started walking.

At the Sinkhole, Daniel was already cutting lemons behind the bar. He looked up the moment I walked in. It was one of the only cafés in town that didn't have a separate entrance for people like me, or a segregated sitting area where the tables were painted white. I stored my bag in the employee lockers in the back.

Remy, the boss, was standing in the kitchen yelling at the new cook, whose name I still couldn't remember, for adding too much salt to everything and burning the toast. I got the feeling that she barely spoke any Hebrew and was used to this type of browbeating. She nodded every now and then, when Remy came up for air between sentences. Remy walked around with a bandana around his head, and in interviews the first question he asked every potential employee was "Who's the best singer in the world?" Whoever didn't know that the correct answer was Bruce Springsteen found themselves on the receiving end of a twenty-minute lecture about the real boss.

I joined Daniel behind the bar. He was oozing loss and fear, similar to Matthew last night. Avoiding his gaze, I took a lemon out of the plastic container, picked up a knife and started cutting. Slow steady strokes, like he once showed me.

Daniel didn't say a word. We stood side by side, cutting lemons. His feelings gushed whenever he pierced the lemon, and ebbed when the blade hit the cutting board. Remy's usual song list was playing in the background, current affairs kept at a safe remove from the bubble of the café.

"You want me to relieve you of that?" I asked quietly, cutting another lemon slice.

"Of what?" Daniel asked, considering me, his voice a little louder than the quiet space called for.

I put down the knife and looked him in the eye. "Of what you're feeling, you want me to take it away?"

"And then what?"

"And then you won't be in as much pain as you are now."

He had brown eyes lined with wrinkles, a short, reddish and slightly scraggly beard, and freckles on the tip of his nose, which paled in the winter and darkened in the summer. And right now he was scared. He knew we were at the rally, but hadn't called after the stabbing to make sure we were safe. I assumed Matthew had updated him. Daniel and Matthew had met by chance when Matthew came to pick me up from work one day, and bonded despite their differences. I knew they had a pact to inform one another about our rallies. I never asked for the details.

Daniel wasn't the crying type. Nor was he the kind of person who raised his voice, or scolded, or expressed any kind of emotion other than that calm, pleasant affectation expected from bartenders. I felt his inner conflict, the desire to say 'yes' and let me disarm his pain, his fear, leaving nothing but the simple joie de vivre floating beneath the stiff veneer.

Once, during what seemed like an endless shift, both of us so tired we could barely keep our eyes open, he asked me how I could tell the difference between a person's immediate feelings and his inner core. I explained to him that it's like the crust of a hot chocolate gone cold, and he asked, completely deadpan, if I enjoyed stirring chocolate milk. We doubled over, bursting into such a hysterical fit of laughter that the boss came shouting at us to keep the noise down.

"No," Daniel finally said and pursed his lips, careful not let out anything more. He picked up his knife and started playing with it. "I'd rather feel it. I'd rather be angry, and afraid, and deal with it alone."

He started stabbing the cutting board repeatedly, and I placed my hand on his, stopping him. "You're not alone."

Daniel curved his mouth into a small smile, barely crinkling the corners of his eyes. "Neither are you."

I returned the smile.

"Don't do that," he said, fixing his gaze on his lemon. Fear. Stab. Slice. Fear, stab, slice.

"Don't do what?" I asked, taking a fresh lemon out of the container and cutting into it.

Stab. Slice. "Don't smile if it's not real."

I reined in my feelings, building a fence around them. It became a little easier with every murder. I guess there's nothing you can't get used to. "So you shouldn't do it either."

24

Daniel paused, the knife hovering above the rind. I counted. At seven he finally said, "Sometimes saying things helps. With words. Not just feeling them." He cut through the lemon and pushed the slice aside.

He was entirely focused on the lemon, slicing it as he had done with hundreds if not thousands to date. Daniel, who did nothing but work at a beachfront café all day and then go home and raise his twin girls, wanted me to talk to him about my feelings. He was a normie. If I tried telling him that I lacked the words to explain feelings, he simply wouldn't understand. Only a moody could, and I didn't know a single one I was willing to confide in.

Stab. Slice. Stab. Slice. Push slices aside. No. I was wrong. He didn't want to talk about my feelings. He needed to talk about his.

"Sometimes it helps to give words to feelings," I said quietly.

"I just…" Daniel said, dragging out the last word. "What would I do if one of my girls turned out to be…" He put down the knife and wiped his nose with the back of his hand.

I studied his profile. His girls were too young to undergo an official detection, but I didn't need the diagnosis. While sorcery only develops fully at puberty, you can detect early signs in children. "They're normal," I said. "Just like you."

I wasn't expecting the emotional flood that followed. Fear and relief poured out of Daniel, easily knocking down my fences. Don't cry. Don't cry. Don't think about the fact that one of my only friends is happy that his girls aren't like me. Daniel leaned over the bar.

I blinked back my tears. The same stifled tears from last night. "OK?"

"Sure." Daniel picked up his knife. "Anything else you want to talk about?"

"Daphne brought someone home last night and he's incredibly annoying."

Daniel laughed. "You always hate the men your roommate brings home."

Stab. Slice. We picked up the pace, working quietly, methodically. After a while customers began to trickle in, and I had to start memorizing who wanted his coffee black and who wanted milk on the side, who wanted his herbal tea to go and who wanted his omelet with extra parsley, hold the oil. Please and thank you.

I concentrated on maneuvering people into leaving bigger tips. Just a bit more than usual. It was easy. The trick was to make them feel comfortable, a little happier, so when they got the bill they'd be a little more generous with their waiter. Not enough to make them notice it, but more than enough to fill up the tip jar. At least when you maneuver normies, the residual headache isn't as bad. A few of the customers were wearing protective charm bracelets. They couldn't actually keep me from maneuvering them. But they did symbolize lack of consent, and I didn't want to get into trouble. I focused on those who weren't wearing the charms. Mostly the café regulars. I assumed they came for that little morning boost. A shot of emotional caffeine. I never asked.

Towards the end of the shift, the pain was shooting up from my ankles to the middle of my back. My feet had become numb floor tiles. Focusing on the physical pain helped me edge out the emotional anguish. The same kind that assailed me whenever I allowed myself a moment to consider it.

Daniel was also working a double shift. I got the feeling that he had decided to keep an eye on me, that maybe he'd even offer to walk me to the Basement later. But I had no intention of going there tonight. Daphne's latest distraction would help her work through whatever she was feeling, and I hated sitting there alone with the background music, and the moodies trying to disarm the grief of whoever sought relief, and the endless political discussions. I might go stand with the high schoolers. It would be an opportunity to let out some of my anger and frustration in a scrap we'd undoubtedly lose. None of us dared to practice our abilities in public. At best, it would end in a prison sentence – life without parole.

I was busy cleaning one of the tables outside, clearing the half-empty mugs, when I turned around and bumped into someone.

My tray came crashing to the ground, the leftover coffee spilling all over my dark shirt. "Sorry," I mumbled, and bent over to pick up the tray and mugs. I would have to remember to thank Daphne for her morning prediction.

"No, it's my fault. I shouldn't have…" the person I had bumped into said, and crouched beside me. He reached out for one of the mugs.

"Don't worry, it's fine," I replied, gathering the mugs back onto the tray. At least they didn't break this time. I looked up, smiling without really registering the person in front of me, and went back to searching for the spoons that had scattered across the floor.

"Reed?"

I instantly lifted my head, our foreheads almost touching. "Blaze." His name flew out of my mouth. He had aged. Soft stubble adorned the lower part of his face and his hair was shorter than it had been when we last met. His eyes were still brown and deep, and his smile subtle, almost hidden. He was wearing a suit, the jacket open over a light-colored shirt that brought out his dark skin. His shirt was now sporting a coffee stain; and he probably didn't have a damus at home for wardrobe advice.

I poked around inside him. There was joy there, and excitement, and a little sadness as well. He got up and extended his hand. I placed the tray on the table behind me and shook it. Not too firmly, not too softly. For years I'd been practicing what I'd say to him if we ever met again, and all those rehearsed lines had now disappeared. All I managed was to shake his hand and feel its warmth. His skin's slight coarseness.

I smiled at him. His own smile widened, and all at once it was the Blaze I knew. A wave of joy drifted out of him in my direction, and he pulled me in for a tight embrace. I couldn't help but hug him back, my pain was abating with the embrace, making way for a myriad of new emotions. I kept them bottled up, so they wouldn't seep out. The happiness, the way his touch felt. The simple joy of meeting him again.

I took in his scent. I couldn't think straight. It's Blaze. He's here. And he's hugging me. That's all my brain managed to process. He took a step back and gestured towards the man standing beside him.

"Lee, meet Reed." Lee was tall. Very tall. Too tall for my liking. Other than that there was nothing special about him. Just an ordinary guy in a dress shirt and jeans. He was unreadable; a moody with impenetrably high walls. He didn't even send out his feelers in our customary greeting.

"Reed, this is Lee, my boss." Blaze's smile was too tight, his words too distinct. Without reading him, I could tell he was oozing tension. I smiled at Lee and held out my hand. After a moment's hesitation, he shook it.

"So you're Reed?" His voice was low and melodic, like in an infomercial. He curled his lips into a teeth-baring smile. "You're a waiter? Because Blaze told me you're a writer." He had a faint American accent.

I straightened my back. A sharp wave of pain shot through me, mimicking the one that throbbed in my back and legs. "Moodifier," I said, any trace of my smile now gone. "A freelancer," I added, before either of them could mention that there wasn't much moodifying work in waiting tables.

Blaze placed his hand on Lee's arm but looked directly at me. "It's so good to see you," he said with a half-smile, the same kind that had once made me yell at him that if he wasn't genuinely happy to see me, he shouldn't fake it. The memory stung.

"Nice to see you too. I didn't know you were back in Israel," I said, trying my best to keep my emotions from merging with my words.

"We landed a few days ago. I meant to call, but then we saw the news and…" he said, his voice trailing off.

We. Plural. And his hand was still on Lee's arm. Whatever they had clearly went beyond employer-employee.

"Was the Confederacy having an empath for an empath deal? Dump one, get the other free?" I smirked at Blaze.

Lee pursed his lips. "Do you read all of Blaze's friends, or should I be flattered?"

"Friends?" I said, still keeping my feelings from creeping into my voice. "You didn't know? Blaze can't be friends with empaths."

Blaze seemed to recoil, an almost imperceptible movement. I regretted saying it. I didn't actually want to hurt him. "I have to get back to work," I said, gesturing behind me at the café.

Blaze tightened his grip around Lee's arm. "We have to get back too, we're late."

Lee's smile remained steady. "Wait, let's grab a coffee to go," he said. Blaze was trying to say something. Lee fixed me a look and said, "One black with two sugars, and one soy milk cappuccino with sweetener."

"You aren't…" Blaze said, looking at me and shaking his head.

I managed to edge out the insult and smile at Lee. "It's fine. Be back in a sec with your order."

I re-entered the café, which was now teeming with customers. I squeezed my way to the bar. Daniel was pouring milk into two mugs at the same time. "It's supposed to look like a cat. What do you think?" The shape that appeared in the foam could have passed for a nebula.

"Sorry I'm not a splasher," I said, leaning against the bar. "The best I can do is make a customer happy that his order came out, however it looks."

Considering his scrambled latte art, Daniel said, "You're the least useful sorcerer I know."

Someone at one of the tables was mumbling something about places that hired "those kinds of people." A person sitting at the table next to his reassured him that I was "actually all right." One of our regulars.

Daniel put down the milk jug, took a toothpick and drew a mustache in the foam. "Maybe you could make the milk happy that I'm designing it? Because that would definitely help."

When I didn't answer, Daniel's face fell. "What happened? That should have at least got a smile out of you."

I handed him Lee's order ticket. "Make it on the house."

Daniel tilted his head towards Blaze and Lee who were standing outside, talking with their heads bowed, creating an island of intimacy in the middle of the street. "Friends of yours?"

I shook my head. "One's an ex and the other's just some asshole." It was a lot easier than explaining that one was the greatest love of my life, and the other a vain moody who was apparently above sharing.

"In whose coffee should I spit?" he asked and winked at me.

I managed to wrest a smile before elbowing my way through the customers and convincing myself not to maneuver Lee into feeling that he was being talked about behind his back. Empaths didn't maneuver other sorcerers, let alone other empaths, no matter how much of an obnoxious dickhead that other empath happened to be.

As I approached, I picked up on their feelings. There was nothing romantic about their whispers. Blaze was emanating anger. Lee was still unreadable.

"You have to get closure with your ex before–" Lee was whispering.

A small wave of rage rose from Blaze, tinted with self-blame and some undertones of warmth and affection. I couldn't tell at whom the warmth was directed. Me? Lee?

Blaze noticed me, straightened up and curved his lips into a smile that stood in jarring contrast to everything I felt from him.

"Your coffees are on me," I said, handing them the mugs. *Your ex*, he had said. They were talking about me. Of course they would be. "Everything OK?"

"Sure," Blaze replied a little too quickly. "Lee's a bit cranky. He hates jet lag."

Lee looked at him before shifting his gaze to me, his expression unaltered. "While he," Lee intoned, "hates the Middle East." He waved at the street. "With the heat and humidity, it's no wonder everyone here is murdering each other."

I flinched.

"Did you know her?" Blaze asked, radiating a detached interest.

I shook my head. "They always choose the loners. The ones with the least protection around them. And however hard we try..." my voice trailed off.

"There's no police, or, something?" Blaze asked.

Lee snorted.

"What?" I tightened my grip on the tray. Lee was blocking me like only another moody could. Nothing could pass through those walls of his.

Lee took a sip of his coffee and said, "The police here is a joke. In the States we have the Crimes Against Sorcerers Unit."

"Lee..." Blaze said in a cautioning tone.

"I'm glad the Confederacy has a unit that fights crimes against sorcerers," I said with a successfully impassive tone. "Do they operate inside or outside the reservations?"

"At least back home we had some protection," Lee replied, lowering his cup from his mouth.

"At least here we're allowed to get married, and to talk, and to walk the streets freely," I said, sending Lee a well-aimed arrow of anger into the tiny crack I detected in his wall.

Nothing but a small spark in his eyes indicated that my anger had made it through. "And get killed," he said with an icy voice, "freely."

"Enough," Blaze raised his voice, causing two people on the sidewalk to stop and look at us before shuffling along.

Lee lifted a submissive hand.

I picked up my tray as if erecting a barrier between me and the rest of the world. The murmur from the nearby tables died down, and people were staring intently at their plates.

Lee clenched his jaw. "I'll go pay." He stormed into the café, leaving Blaze and me on the sidewalk. I didn't bother reminding him it was on the house.

"I'm sorry," Blaze said, slouching his shoulders. I felt the sigh of relief he was trapping inside himself. "He's mad at me for something completely unrelated to you. And the murder... it's... it's tough on him."

"I'm sure it is," I blurted, injecting as much sarcasm into those four words as possible.

"You don't get it," he said, looking past me at the people starting to fill the street. "His father is... they're activists. Death threats are an everyday thing in his family. We came here, among other reasons, to get away from that."

"You picked one hell of a destination," I said in a softer voice.

He sipped his coffee, grimaced, peered into the cup, and the liquid started to bubble. Classic pyro, preferred heating up his coffee on his own to asking for a new one, even though reheating it changes the chemical makeup and completely ruins the texture and flavor. The fact that he did it out in the open, in plain view, only showed how detached he was from us and our daily lives. At least there wasn't much left in the cup so no one could see it frothing.

I wanted to tell him that I missed him, that his absence had been felt, especially these past few years. I wanted to apologize for the way I started the conversation, but it was too late.

"I need..." he said, staring at his feet. "I need to tell you something."

"Sure," I replied. He was going to tell me that he and Lee were an item. I could take it. It had been ten years after all, and I'd also had my share of relationships. I looked him in the eye. "It's OK, you know."

"What's OK?"

I gestured towards Lee, who was standing at the bar talking to Daniel. "That you have someone. It's OK," I said, trying to smile. "It's important to move on."

Blaze let out a brief chuckle. "Yes, he's the best friend I've ever had," he said, and quickly added, "other than you, of course."

"Of course." So Lee was a friend. "You two aren't a couple?"

"No, no." Blaze tightened his grip around the cup. He was radiating some serious tension and fear. I couldn't understand why. "We went out twice, it was a disaster." Blaze was breathing slowly. I felt the fear mounting inside him. "I'm not with Lee. I'm with River."

"River?" It sounded like a name that meant something, a name I would've remembered. I didn't know any Rivers.

"Lee's River. I mean, Lee is River's brother."

"OK." It stung, but not as much as I had expected. Whether it was Lee or his brother didn't make any difference to me.

Blaze exhaled, the tension leaving his body like a deflating balloon. He smiled, this time genuinely. "I don't know why I was so worried. Of course you're fine with it. You've always accepted me for who I am."

"Of course," I said, maintaining a calm expression. "So when do I get to meet this River of yours?"

"As soon as she lands," he said, still smiling. "Lee and I took an earlier flight to find an apartment and all that. I mean, it's not as if we're living together. I mean, we are, but…"

He kept on rambling, talking about the apartment he had rented, and that if River didn't like it, they'd move into the apartment that Lee had found for himself, and he talked about the rent, and signing the lease in front of the landlady, who sounded a lot more tolerant than my landlord, and the packing and shipping, and kept repeating how happy it made him that I accepted him for who he was.

But all I could think about was those few words, 'as soon as *she* lands.' River was a woman. Not a man. I felt the universe whirling around me. Blaze was dating a woman. I thought back on all those times we were together, an endless sequence of images. How could he possibly be interested in women? I knew him. He had never expressed the slightest interest in the opposite sex. He was the reason I felt so comfortable with myself in high school. He was like me. I wasn't alone.

His phone rang. He apologized for taking the call before stepping aside.

I followed him with my gaze, feeling a deep, sharp burn. I focused on a stranger walking by and pushed some of the pain his way. I still had an entire shift to get through with Blaze's smile flashing before me, and with the customers whispering about how they saw the local sorcerer arguing with some guy in the middle of the street, and…

"I know how you feel." Lee was suddenly standing beside me, looking at Blaze who was pacing the opposite sidewalk.

"And I don't mean that metaphorically." He shifted his weight from one leg to the other. "I mean that you're leaking all over the place." He had green eyes shot through with brown specks. "Do you need help blocking yourself?" His voice was different. Soft.

I shook my head. He was right. I reined in my feelings. The surprise. The anger. The disappointment. I could take Blaze choosing Lee over me. I couldn't take Blaze choosing a woman.

Lee folded his arms across his chest. He seemed fidgety, his eyes still following Blaze on the sidewalk. His voice was so quiet it sounded like he was talking more to himself than to me. "Blaze was dating like crazy, and always seemed miserable, and he didn't want me because, well," he said and gestured at me. "It took me two years to ask him out. After our second date, which was great, we went back to my place and River was there, she came to borrow something, I don't remember what, and I could feel Blaze shifting all his attention from me to her." He chuckled. "You can imagine. Right?"

"You don't mean metaphorically."

"He even offered to walk her home. And I'm standing there, knowing exactly what he's planning," he said, shrugging. "And since then they won't shut up about how it was love at first sight."

I closed my eyes, focusing on my breath. I can take it, I can get through this. I felt Lee touching my shoulder. Had he been Israeli, that gesture would have symbolized that he was willing to take away my pain. He didn't say anything, and I didn't want his help. I fenced my feelings, hemmed them in. I opened my eyes. "That's what you were fighting about?"

"Blaze didn't want to tell you because it 'isn't the right time.'" He grimaced. "As if there ever is one."

It hurt. More than I could bear. Blaze was still on his phone across the street. I looked back into the café. Daniel waved at me that he was fine and didn't need help. I knew Lee could feel Daniel's peacefulness as well as I could, which meant I had no excuse to go back inside.

Lee rubbed his forehead, his hair falling over his face. "I'm sorry," he said. He seemed more genuine, vulnerable. "If we had known you worked here, we never would have come. He shouldn't have told you like this."

It stung. I didn't want his pity. "It's been a decade. People change."

"So there's hope for us yet?" The grim smile returned to his face. "One day we'll find out we were actually always attracted to women, and we'll get married and have kids?"

"My mom would love that," I said, twisting my face into a sneer. "She suggested I make a pact with my roommate. That if we don't find a partner by the time we're thirty, we'll marry each other." I sighed. "I have five more years of freedom."

Lee laughed. "Can't be, you and Blaze are the same age. Twenty... seven?"

"Eight." I shot him a grumpy arrow. He produced a huge smile, and suddenly I understood what Blaze found in him. His smile lasted no more than a second; he drew it back in once he saw Blaze approaching.

Blaze shifted his gaze from me to Lee. "Everything OK here?" He was tense, the fear still radiating from him.

"Sure," I said, leveling the tray. "I was just grilling Lee about you."

Lee shot me a glance from the corner of his eye. I ignored him and smiled at Blaze. "More specifically, I was trying to find out how you reacted when you saw River naked for the first time and discovered she was missing something." I looked at Lee and said, "I assume he was quite in shock, am I right?"

I shot Lee a soothing arrow. He nodded. "It was awful. How would I know what my sister has between her legs?"

Blaze shifted his gaze between us and started laughing. Lee was the only one who managed to keep a straight face, until he too finally broke down and burst into laughter, and my pain was pushed to the back of my mind, repressed, waiting for the night, when I'd be alone and safe.

4

I made it home after midnight, my legs paralyzed and my back firing well-aimed bursts of pain with every wrong move I made. Daphne was asleep. The lights were out, but I could still see the upside-down pots on the dish rack. It wasn't her turn to do the dishes, but she had washed them anyway. The living room couch looked inviting. Soft, piled with throw pillows. In the dark you couldn't see the mysterious tomato-sauce stain, whose origin neither of us could recall, or the loose tile next to the couch, which shifted at the slightest movement. We always joked that was where the landlord was hiding the millions he was making from raising our rent.

I crawled to the shower. The hot water helped a little, not enough. I closed my eyes and washed off the sweat. The memories of Blaze started creeping back in.

With my eyes closed I could evoke his image from nearly thirteen years ago, when we first met. He was going for a smoke behind the gym and bumped into me while I was walking out of a class for the millionth time, tired of the teacher trying so hard not to look at me. Trying to show how grown up I was, I bummed one of his cigarettes. I took one drag and nearly suffocated in front of him, and he laughed. I was coughing so hard my eyes welled up.

I squeezed out soap and lathered up. How many times had I pretended he was standing next to me? How many times had I rehearsed what I would say? Until that one time when I worked up the nerve to mumble something about how I thought he was handsome, unable to look him in the eye because I was afraid he wouldn't return the look, or that he'd make an excuse, or say he was "fine with that," like everyone else before him, which was to say – not into me, but not offended by the proposition. Without saying a word, he leaned into me, and when I dared look him in the eye we were so close I couldn't breathe, and my feelings poured out and flooded him, and he smiled and said, "I didn't know it was like that with empaths," and then kissed me and my mind went blank.

I noticed my heart was racing. I stood perfectly still, and put out my feelers. Daphne was still asleep. I was safe behind my walls.

I opened my eyes, edging out the memories. I scrubbed my back, my arms. The present came crashing down on me, enveloping me in pain. For a few hours I had managed to forget. Blaze had that effect on me. Back when we were together, Matthew used to joke that I was flying so high someone might come and snatch me, and Blaze hugged me and said I had nothing to worry about, that he'd keep me close to the ground. I remembered his arms around me, the scent of his new aftershave mixed with the faint smell of sweat that I loved like only a seventeen year-old could. That was before Blaze went away, and before the first rally. Before everything. When the world was still intact, and normal, and the military draft and society's ignorance was all that kids like us had to worry about, as opposed to knives and incompetent cops. I couldn't tell whether I missed Blaze, high school, or that period of relative safety. I only knew I was longing for something that no longer existed.

I dried myself off, put on the worn-out sweatpants that served as my pajamas in the summer, and went to my room. My clothes were scattered all over the floor. I couldn't imagine picking them up and throwing them in the laundry basket. I was exhausted, but my thoughts kept racing. The rally. One image chasing the next. The feelings of emptiness among the empaths. The framed photo on the bar top, the shared pain and certainty that there was nothing we could do. That we couldn't win.

I tried to conjure up another image of Blaze. To recreate that moment in the shower when he took over every part of me. Too late. I couldn't sink into the sensation again. I grabbed onto the edge of Daphne's consciousness. Her mind was full of fog, and I took some for myself. It wasn't the usual temporary fog of a sound sleep. It was something stronger, meant to knock her out for hours. I took enough to fall asleep, and let the blanket of oblivion cover me.

5

I was running. Everything around me was black. Daphne stopped me and said, "They're coming," and suddenly red and blue lights flashed around us, and Daphne shouted and collapsed, and I drowned in her tears.

I woke up in a panic, drenched, my mouth dry. I cursed. I was so busy disarming the memories of Blaze that I hadn't dealt with the memories from the murder. Of course they would creep into my dreams. I was behaving like a teenager, not an adult. I checked Daphne. Her waves were roiling. I didn't know whether it was the result of her dreams or whether the emotions from my own dream had seeped into her. The feelings emerging in a dream have a longer range than waking feelings, due to our inability to control a dream. I tapped into a neighbor who was sound asleep and extricated some of his calm, transferring it to Daphne in the hope that it would give her a more pleasant sleep. I picked up on a little girl who was stirring in her sleep and gave her some of his calm as well. I kept canvassing. My dream hadn't seemed to disturb the sleep of any other neighbor.

I drank some water and returned to bed. The key was to approach feelings cautiously, and not let them overwhelm me until I couldn't deal with them.

I closed my eyes, replaying the rally. Moment by moment, feeling by feeling.

We were marching on Shmuel HaNavi Street, holding hands, singing about love and acceptance. There were normies marching among us. At least three damuses made sure to maintain a present in which no one was being harmed. I linked arms with Daphne. I didn't sing. I hate singing. Daphne sang and I only joined in the chorus, when the singing turned into chants. Daphne laughed. She was happy. All the damuses were happy, so sure that nothing would happen. Not this time.

The moodies were marching on the fringes of the crowd, making sure no one infiltrated. This time no one would die. There were cops everywhere. Someone joked that there were more cops than protesters. I heard one confess that it was his first rally, and that he hoped nothing would go wrong.

An errant thought wandered into my memories. I wondered whether Sherry had been there. Whether I'd met her at the rally. It wasn't important. It's not like she managed to stop it. I edged out the thought and focused on the real memories.

I felt sleepiness taking hold and shook it off. Not yet. I couldn't allow myself to fall asleep just yet.

There was some commotion on the sidelines. Once again, a group of the Sons of Simeon trying to disturb our march. The cops were pushed back as a few of us rushed to the area of the riot to stop it in time.

I remembered the exact moment someone yelled 'Knife!' It was behind us, nowhere close to the riot, and someone said the commotion on the sidelines was just a distraction, and a wave of fear and anxiety passed through us, pouring out of the cops and amplified by the crowd, completely curbing the moodies' ability to act. There were too many feelings gushing around, and we couldn't put our walls back up in time. I remembered myself standing there, unable to understand how we failed to feel his homicidal outburst. To track him down.

And I felt the damuses falling like flies. One after the other, pulling the moodies down with them into a bottomless pit of overwhelming fear when the futures collapsed. One of the damuses searched in vain for the assailant, and the elementalists channeled every force of nature around us, but even they couldn't track him down; it was all too late.

I screamed when the knife went in between her shoulder blades. The pain ricocheted from her to all of us, amplified by the moodies; it spread in waves, ripples of pain breaking up the rows of marchers, stopping us dead in our tracks.

And then we saw the medics running to her, but it was too late, they couldn't stop the bleeding, and we all felt the life draining out of her.

And Daphne collapsed on me and cried. She couldn't stop. I held her, unable to take her sadness away because I was flooded, and everyone around us was crying and shouting, and one of the cops looked at me. He was pale, and I felt his fear. It was his first rally, and suddenly I understood that they had sent only rookie cops, inexperienced, and that there was no one to protect us. That we were on our own. Always on our own.

Tears were running down the corner of my burning, aching eyes. I turned around and buried my head under the pillow, keeping out all noise. It wasn't my fault. None of us were at fault. It didn't help. The pain was almost unbearable. I fell asleep crying.

6

A drilling noise crept into my dream, a soundtrack to the
hallucinations about running away from blood-dripping knives
and a cigarette falling to the ground and a face laughing at me with
a toothless mouth.

I managed to open my eyes. The alarm clock on my phone
was on its third grating cycle. I hit snooze. It was eight am, and I
couldn't find a reason to get out of bed. I tapped into Daphne. She
was still sleeping. I could have borrowed a little more from her,
but I felt that her sleep was already dissolving. She'd wake up if I
dipped into her.

The alarm started screeching again. I cursed it and hit snooze.
How did it get to be eight-thirty?

It shrilled again. Five minutes to nine. I rubbed my eyes and
sat up straight, yawning. I felt the exhaustion in my joints, as if
every ligament between my bones was made of rubber. I stretched.
Another shrill. I picked up the phone to turn off the alarm clock
once and for all. But it wasn't the alarm clock this time. It was an
unlisted number calling.

I stared at the screen. It was probably another sales rep
peddling useless life insurance. Daphne told me that the damuses
who worked for insurance agencies didn't actually give them
real information, only jumbled up the futures they saw so that

43

competing agencies wouldn't be able to poach clients. I knew they weren't going to stop calling until I picked up and threatened them with a lawsuit.

"Yes?" I asked, my voice hoarse.

"Just so you know, this was my idea, not Lee's." It was Blaze. My heart skipped a beat, and settled. "He was against it, but I know you're good at what you do. You were amazing at it in high school, and I'm sure that–"

I let out a loud yawn; Blaze stopped mid-sentence.

"I'm sorry," I mumbled. "I pulled a double shift yesterday and I'm beat."

"Should I call back later?"

I wanted to say yes, but I knew I wasn't going to fall back asleep. "It's fine. What can I do you for?"

"We need a moodifier for a pretty simple gig. You said you're a freelancer. If you have the time, we could really use your help." He sounded, well, normal. As if we were just two acquaintances who'd been working together for years, as opposed to exes who hadn't spoken to each other in a decade.

I rubbed my eyes. "How long will it take?"

"Four hours, maybe five."

Rule of thumb said that clients could never really estimate how long a moodification job would take. If Blaze estimated it at five hours, it would take at least ten, if not fifteen.

"Let me check my schedule." I lowered my phone and stared at the blank wall. My bank account would be grateful for the cash flow. My work portfolio would be grateful for another project. The downside would be working with Blaze, but I was a big boy and could handle it. I picked up the phone again and said, "I have an opening, but I'd need to see the job first to give you a more accurate time estimate."

"Great," Blaze replied. I could hear the smile in his voice. Just like old times, I returned it. We agreed to meet in an hour. His office was a thirty-minute ride from my house, requiring two buses, and I was still trying to push through the haze of sleep. I managed to drag myself to the bathroom, brush my teeth and shave. Daphne once told me that on the day I died I'd have a short beard. I'd been shaving every morning since.

I went into Daphne's room, just to make sure she didn't have to get up for work yet. There was a full bottle of sleeping pills on her bed-stand. I wasn't worried. She knew exactly when she was going to die, and it wasn't destined to be by sleeping pills. I trusted her not to try anything while we were sharing a house. She knew how much her death would devastate me. She saw it, and promised she would spare me the sight.

Thin rays filtered into the room through the half-open shutters. Her laptop was switched off, the heart sticker twinkling in the faint light. The day we moved in together, I had bought her a pack of three-hundred stickers, and she laughed and promised to use every last one of them. In return, she bought me the cheesiest poster she could find, and dared me to put it up.

Daphne was partially covered, her legs poking out of the blanket and her head buried under her pillow. There was a note next to the alarm clock: "First meeting at eleven, last at eight with the Canadians. Don't wake me before ten." I moved the pillow and stroked her hair.

"I'm going out," I said quietly. "Don't be afraid when you wake up. Everything's OK. See you in the evening."

Daphne didn't budge. She was breathing slowly, the fog of her sleep dispersing with each breath, but still thick enough to hide her from me. When she woke she'd see what kind of present we were in, whether equilibrium had been restored, and she'd see that I was here, telling her everything was OK. She once explained to me how she could remember events that had taken place even when she hadn't been there. She could rewind her present and see the divergences and currents that had led up to them.

I covered her legs, walked out of the house, and braced myself for the heat and humidity of mid-July. By the time I made it to the office building, my shirt was sticking to my back. I hoped my deodorant hadn't completely worn off.

After walking through the inferno of summer, the lobby felt nice and cool. The guard glanced up at me. I responded with the customary half salute. He didn't ask me for an ID, didn't order me to stop, and didn't even rifle through my bag. He just went back to the documents in his hand and ignored me. There wasn't even a separate door painted white.

Lining both sides of the fourth floor corridor were cheap flowerpots containing musty soil and cigarette butts. A sign saying "ArtDot – Designing the Present" hung askew on one of the doors. It was colorful and slick as befit a graphic design company, and I assumed the crooked angle was deliberate.

The door opened into another long corridor, leading to more drab office rooms. Small signs with department names were fixed to the wall next to each door. The scent of sorcery emanated from the end of the corridor. I followed the trail to a cubicle with the sign "Accounting" hanging next to it, and peeked inside.

Blaze was sitting behind a green desk, typing into a light-blue laptop sporting the ArtDot logo. He was wearing a dress shirt similar to the one I had seen him in yesterday. His black hair spilled in curls over his forehead. He reached for the penholder, missed it, looked up and saw me. The smile that spread across his face struck me. I smiled back. Detaching myself from the wall I was leaning against, I stepped inside. Blaze held open his arms, but it was better not to hug him. He had once been the person closest to me. Too much time had passed.

I reached out for a handshake, and felt the swift, deep insult. He didn't let it reflect in his expression. He just shook my hand and smiled, said he was glad I had come and led me to Lee's office. Lee was sitting in the opposite cubicle, behind a "Quality Control" sign. His desk was an exact replica of Blaze's, but in his penholder there were also two peacock feathers. He was typing and staring at the computer screen with such concentration, I wondered whether he was on any meds. I didn't know a single person who was able to focus on texts like that. On the wall behind him hung a crayon drawing of stick figures floating in a star-studded sky, inscribed in childish handwriting to Uncel Li.

Blaze cleared his throat. "Got a minute?"

Lee looked up from the screen and sent me a small warm ball.

"I didn't know you had nephews," I said, pointing at the drawing.

"A gift from the neighbors' daughter." There was a softness to his smile. He bent under the desk and resurfaced with a stack of books. Five proof copies.

"These are children's books. They require very little emotion," he said, furrowing his brow. "The last moodifier made a complete mess of it."

I leaned in and opened the first book to a random page. A wave of nausea hit me. I pushed it out and moved onto the next page, which flooded me with anxiety. I closed the book with a thud. "They're all like that?"

Blaze nodded. "Can you do it?" he asked, exuding tension. I wondered what exactly he had told Lee about me before he called to offer me the job. "We have the author's notes, should you need them."

I drummed my fingers on the desk. "I can give the first one a go, and if it's too complicated you'll have enough time to find another moodifier." Moodification was tricky enough without having to deal with the emotions already incorporated into the page by another moodifier. I had to read the text closely, had to parse the author's intention and add my own interpretation. Then I had to weave the emotions into the print itself, amplifying the reader's experience while remaining loyal to the original story, rather than emotionally bombarding the reader to the point of rendering the story irrelevant.

"Let's go for it," Lee said and turned to Blaze. "Please draft a standard contract, and this time no bonuses we can't pay." His walls were too high for me to read him. Blaze's reaction was filled with shame. I wondered who Blaze had promised all those bonuses to.

Lee set me up at a small desk and asked to watch me work on the first book. I got the feeling that he wanted to make sure I knew what I was doing. Maybe he didn't trust Blaze's recommendation. As he sat down beside me, all I could sense from him was a small trail of curiosity. I blocked him so I could concentrate.

The first page was full of dread. I dismantled it slowly, making sure to start from the edge and work my way up the page. The previous moodifier had inserted the emotion into the paper with a long spiral, and I had to unravel it throughout. At least I didn't have to look for a capacitor. Emotions trapped in paper dissipated by themselves when you unraveled them.

When I was done, the page was devoid of emotion, nothing but a drawing of a girl holding a toy tractor and a boy peering at her from the corner.

I looked up. Lee was as focused on me as he had been on his computer screen earlier.

I didn't know exactly how much he knew about moodification. "I have to unravel the old emotions before I can weave in new ones."

"Is it OK if I continue to watch?"

"Sure." Something about the look in his eyes made me smile. Too many weeks had passed without an interesting project. Weeks of working on nothing but flyers and posters for movies no one went to. It was fun working on children's books for a change.

I returned to the page, feeling Lee's eyes on me.

It took me the whole day to finish neutralizing four pages. The moodifier before me had been aggressive, weaving one layer of emotions after another into the page. You would have thought he was working on an adult novel that required such emotionally rife layers. Blaze popped in every now and then to ask if everything was OK and offer me something to drink. I was too busy to pay him any attention, too occupied even to be polite.

Lee spent most of the day hovering over me, observing my work. I felt his fluttering touch accompanying me as I unraveled the design. I paused only once to explain the process to him, after which he smiled and left the room.

He came back with a woman in a dress so tight she could have been sewn into it. Something about her told me she would have preferred to be in a T-shirt and sweatpants.

Lee introduced her as the manager of ArtDot, Odelia. I didn't sense sorcery from her.

"Lee says you know your way around this stuff." Her tone was direct. "And that you're better than the last empath who worked here."

Lee raised an eyebrow. "Technically, I'm the last empath who worked here."

Neither of them used the common slang. Lee was American, maybe he wasn't familiar with the local dialect. I wondered whether Odelia, like Matthew, refrained from using the term moody because it was considered derogatory.

Odelia shot him a look. "Yes, and when you get tired of this place you'll go back to the Confederacy and work for us from there. Don't think I don't know." She then turned to me. "You're Israeli, right? I assume this means you won't be flying off in two months because you can't handle the humidity?"

I nodded.

"Good," she said, handing me a stack of papers. "This is your contract. Review it, consult with whomever you like, and hand it in signed by the end of the week."

She turned to Lee. "The Cohen assignment should be on my desk by the end of the day, and this time we're in the same time zone."

As she walked away, Lee said, "Don't worry, she's not as tough as she sounds. The last few times we were here..." He fell silent mid-sentence.

"But this is the first time Blaze has been back since he left," I blurted. It took me a moment to realize what he was saying.

Lee didn't answer.

Oh. "So this isn't the first time," I said quietly. "He just didn't want to meet me." The embarrassment Blaze radiated when I saw him and his attempt to find me a job suddenly made sense. After all, he could have easily tracked me down during his previous visits. My parents hadn't moved. I knew him well enough to understand what had happened here. On his first visit home, he couldn't work up the nerve to call me, and it only became more difficult with every visit. The combination of guilt and shame drove him to invite me to ArtDot the moment he ran into me on the street, hoping I'd stop being mad at him.

"It's just the nostalgia that stings. For both of you. It's not real," Lee replied with a similarly quiet voice. "He's not the same person he was when he left, and you're not the person he misses."

Lee sent me a small wave of old anger, followed by a stronger wave of comfort. Of course. He had been hurt by Blaze too. He patted me on the shoulder and said, "What's important is that you're here, and that you'll be brilliant, and Blaze will be jealous, but it'll be too late because he switched teams." He leaned into me. "And if you ever convince him to switch back, just remember you owe me."

I couldn't help but smile. "I won't forget," I replied with a deadpan expression.

Lee went back to his desk, and I shoved the contract into my bag. I wasn't going to consult with a lawyer. Daphne would suffice. She'd be able to tell me whether signing the contract was a good idea, or whether it would pose difficulties in the future. I was hoping it wouldn't. Odelia seemed nice, and I much preferred working on books to the final projects of film students whose ideas were bigger than their budget. Maybe this job would finally allow me to cut down on my shifts at the Sinkhole. And Lee was nice. The fact that working at ArtDot meant working with Blaze didn't even bother me that much. The world was slowly making sense again.

I called Daphne on my way to the bus.

"The contract's fine," she said straight off the bat. "And you're not coming home. Oleander is here."

"I'll schedule the next antibiotics shot," I said, trying to mimic my mom's voice.

Daphne giggled.

"I'd love to take a shower before my evening shift."

"Matthew has a shower," she replied. I heard whispers in the background. "Better if you go there."

It was a not-so-subtle hint. We said goodbye, and instead of taking the bus home I walked to the hospital complex. Matthew lived in the staff residence of the Rabbeinu Gershom Hospital, a cramped tenement resembling a pile of blocks constructed by an unimaginative child who had quickly abandoned it for a more colorful game.

He opened the door wearing a pair of flip-flops, shorts and an old blue T-shirt with a *Doctors Without Borders* logo. His studio apartment was furnished with a single bed, a fold-out couch, and a sink. The counter was barely large enough for the kettle, two mugs, and piles of disposable containers from the hospital staff kitchen. The shower curtain was drawn, revealing an unexpectedly clean surface.

"Had someone over tonight?" I asked, collapsing onto the couch and dropping my bag onto the floor.

"That's so none of your business," he replied, switched on the kettle and fished out a mug from the depths of the sink. Dishes clattered, crashing against each other.

"Everybody has someone," I said, and took the ArtDot book out of my bag.

Matthew turned and gave me a little smile. "Daphne driving you nuts?"

"Oleander. She's insisting it's just a fling, but he won't get out of her—" I sighed and leaned back. "Her room."

"Room. Sure." Matthew placed two mugs on the counter.

"I don't mind that she has someone, I just wish she'd find a steady partner already."

The kettle whistled. "Long term isn't for everyone."

"I thought girls were supposed to want a life-long relationship. I'm the one who should be playing the field."

Matthew laughed, sat down beside me on the couch and handed me a mug. "You're jealous."

51

"I'm not," I replied just a little too quickly.

Matthew arched his brow and didn't say a word.

I took a sip. It was herbal tea, a blend that imitated the flavor of coffee without the caffeine which I couldn't handle on such emotionally taxing days. Matthew knew I wasn't back to my old self yet.

"I'm not jealous," I said, looking at the swirling tea leaves. "I'm happy for Daphne. And I'm happy for Blaze, and I'm happy for you."

I felt his attention condensing. "Blaze?"

I nodded, staring at the small whirlpool in my teacup. "He came back for a while. Said he missed it here."

"And…?"

I looked up at Matthew. "He has a girlfriend."

"Blaze??" Matthew gasped.

He was so surprised, I couldn't help but smile. "That's how I reacted. But with less coffee in my mouth."

"Is he happy?"

"I think so."

"Good. He deserves to be happy." Matthew took another sip.

I recounted my entire conversation with Blaze, mentioning Lee only in brief. In return, Matthew told me that the girl who spent the night at his apartment was Sherry, the cop we met after the murder.

"I saw her at the hospital and offered to buy her coffee with my staff discount," he said, and sipped the last of his coffee. "Then we went out for a drink, and then…"

"And then…" I said, parroting his voice.

"It wasn't like that. We talked. She's… very different from anyone I know. Her life is different." A sliver of softness lurked beneath the feelings he was radiating.

"Just talked?" I asked, trying to keep the surprise from seeping into my voice.

Matthew nodded. "About her life. About the rallies she had attended. She's trying to set up a special task force to help protect you guys."

"Great. Basically twenty-four-hour surveillance," I said, scowling.

"It's for your own good. You do get that, don't you?" Matthew placed his empty mug on the floor next to him. "What else can they do?"

"How about increasing their presence at the rallies?" I couldn't help but raise my voice. "So that next time Daphne and I march–"

"Next time?" Matthew interrupted me, his body stiffening.

"What I meant was…" My thoughts were racing, trying to find another way to complete the sentence.

"What you meant is that you're going to march in the next rally, even though you promised me."

"No, no at all." I immediately backtracked. "Once everything calms down, then we'll march…" It was too late.

"Are you trying to get killed?" he asked, his voice a deep growl. "Because if you are, there are some great pills I can prescribe. It'll be a hell of a lot faster."

"I'm not trying to get killed." I tried to keep my voice down.

"You promised," he said, and stood up. "You promised me you'd stop. So I wouldn't have to be scared out of my mind."

I stood up in front of him. "You don't have to be scared at all. I told you, we'll wait until–"

"Enough! Stop lying to me." He pounded his chest. "Me. You're lying to me. Right now. To my face."

His feelings were swirling around me. I didn't smooth them out. I had never touched Matthew. Not since I realized I could manipulate people's feelings.

Matthew's hands balled into fists. "Don't you get that I'm worried about you?"

"I can feel how much you worry about me," I said.

"Then stop marching." He had lowered his voice, but the rage still rang out. "It would at least make Mom a little less miserable."

I was going to reply when my phone rang.

"Take the call," Matthew blurted and folded his arms across his chest.

It was Aurora. "You didn't text me back, and it's getting close. It's only an introductory meeting. Mostly splashers, you know what the class of '97 is like, not much diversity to speak of, and…"

"I'm a bit busy," I interrupted her. "Is it urgent?"

There was a lengthy silence on the other end of the line, and I heard Forrest whispering in the background, "Ask him."

"Ask me what?"

Matthew's anger was washing over me in such giant waves that I barely managed to ignore it.

After another moment, Aurora said, "We're having a circle, behind the shelter on Hashmonaim Street, you know."

I hummed in response.

"We could use the backup of a psychic. We only have two, and they're young."

"I'm at my brother's," I said.

Matthew arched his eyebrows.

"Yoyo," I whispered to him.

"Reed? It would really help if you could make it," Aurora pleaded. "You're just what we need. I don't trust anyone else…"

"You mean you couldn't get hold of anyone else."

"I really do need you," she said quietly.

Matthew was still angry at me, and still worried. What he needed was a reminder that I could fend for myself. It had been a long time since he joined me at a circle. "Want to tag along?"

Curiosity rippled through the wave of his anger. He shrugged and remained silent.

I lifted the phone back to my ear and said, "I'm coming with my brother."

Aurora whispered something to Forrest, and then said, "Look…"

My hands were sweating. All I wanted was to take a shower, get to the café, finish my shift and be done with this day. I didn't want to volunteer in another of Aurora's little projects, I didn't want Matthew to be angry at me anymore, and I didn't want a stranger in my house. If Aurora didn't let me bring Matthew, I'd just say I wasn't coming and go home. I might even maneuver Oleander into leaving Daphne alone for a bit.

"He's one of us. For real," I said, raising my voice.

Matthew's anger started to abate. I didn't know if it was because of his curiosity, or what I had said to Aurora.

"Fine, come. Both of you," Aurora finally said, and hung up.

I put the phone back in my pocket. "Let's go."

After a twenty-minute walk we found ourselves standing on a side street in a part of town I preferred not to visit after dark. Scavengers were rummaging through the dumpsters, dragging shopping carts brimming with empty bottles and cans, old clothes and scraps of cardboard. Two moodies were standing on the curb, scantily dressed in purple. They didn't need to hold a sign saying 'Memory Dissipators,' their purple miniskirts were enough of a signal for the drivers who slowed down when they passed by. I extended my consciousness towards them. One was completely blurry. The other was clear and sharp and she looked up once she sensed me. She sent me rejection and withdrawal. I left her alone. When I wandered even farther, I could feel a third girl, slightly hazy, sending a bolt of passion to someone. I immediately withdrew.

I put out my feelers and poked around for the circle. There was a faint trail of sorcery, leading to a yard between two buildings, the passage blocked by broken pieces of furniture, empty cardboard boxes and trash.

I took a step forward. Matthew was rooted to his spot, wearing a perplexed expression. I tugged his hand. "Come."

Behind the makeshift barrier we found a group sitting in the backyard, a few on the ground, some on folding chairs. I could guess each one's element by where they had chosen to sit. I knew only Aurora and Forrest, both with their backs to me. There were five teens of various elements, all huddled together, all looking up at Aurora with adoration. I skimmed through each one's consciousness, picking up the familiar fear. Word on the street was that the Sons of Simeons' psyches were calm and free of anxiety.

Not that there was any real chance of finding them here, among us. And yet, I was used to checking.

One of the girls was tossing fireballs into the circle, while Aurora, sitting beside her, levitated them. I thought about how Blaze used to make little fireballs and scorch my notebooks when he got bored watching me do my homework. I stopped the wave of longing. He was with someone else now, and it had been years; I had to focus on the here and now and not wallow in the past.

I felt my way to the moody. She was a girl with purple hair that faded into pink at the tips. She was standing on the sidelines and turned to me the moment I sent her a short wave. Three others turned and looked up when she approached us.

I drew my middle finger to my temple. The moody skimmed through me. I assumed she had heard the same rumors I had. I felt resistance and rage bubbling under a thin film of fear, yet her expression was one of indifference. Chewing a pink wad of gum, she blew a bubble and popped it.

Aurora stood up and turned to me. Her glasses looked different. Forrest brushed his hand through his hair. His shirt sported dark underarm stains.

They all extended their hands, each with their associated gesture. There were two short pebbles; one fair-skinned, the other dark. Even their clothes were in contrasting colors. Three pyros – two men and the girl bouncing fireballs. Apart from Forrest there were two other splashers. Including Aurora, there were five airheads. I didn't recognize any of the adults. Probably new Yoyo volunteers who joined long after I'd quit.

The last one was a thin teen in cargo pants and a face riddled with acne. He raised his hand and brought his pinky to his forehead. A damus. I shifted my weight from one leg to the other. Damuses who weren't Daphne always made me nervous. It felt like they knew me too well. Better than I knew myself.

We were all waiting for a signal from the moody. Aurora nudged her, and she jolted. "I confirm he is of pure intentions."

Taking a step forward, Aurora said, "Welcome. Blessed be he who joins the circle."

We were in Tel Aviv, in the middle of summer, sweating and breathing in the humidity, standing behind piles of junk. The buses were honking nearby, spewing clouds of soot into the air, but those words were echoes of a faraway era. These were our rituals, and for a moment I experienced Matthew as an unwelcome outsider. An unacceptable distraction.

"Blessed be thy invitation." I tried to utter the ancient words with the accurate intonation. I took a step forward.

"Will your kin bear witness to the circle?" Aurora motioned towards Matthew with a sweeping gesture.

Rejection cut through me from the direction of one of the sorcerers I'd never met. I didn't get the chance to examine it more deeply before it disappeared.

It felt silly, saying the ritualistic words to Matthew. The same person who used to throw ketchup-drenched French fries at me when we were kids. But noblesse oblige. I turned to him and reached out my hand. "The circle summons you to bear witness."

"Am I supposed to take your hand?" he asked. The last time he had observed a circle was years ago, and back then there were only six of us and we didn't bother to say more than the bare minimum.

I nodded. Matthew took my hand. His grip was steady. He was used to holding a scalpel in much more stressful situations. I led him to the edge of the yard, to a spot from which he'd be able to watch us at a safe remove.

"Thanks for coming," Aurora whispered to me once I left Matthew behind and came back to the circle. "I was getting worried that we'd have to settle for something less challenging for them. They're so frightened."

"Good. They should be frightened." Traces of Matthew's anger had seeped into my voice. "They're trying to murder us."

Aurora held my arm and stopped me. "You need a refresher on supporting teens?"

She was right. I blocked Matthew and tapped into the compassion I always had for our young ones. "Sorry."

Aurora shrugged. "It's OK. We're all nervous. You must be feeling it more than any of us."

"You've been talking to Daphne."

"I know what the rallies do to you guys without having to ask," she said, straightening her glasses.

You guys. Once again that imperceptible line between elementalists and psychics. But I knew she meant no harm, and I couldn't be angry with her. I looked into her eyes and asked, "Are those new glasses?"

"An old pair. My new ones got broken in the rally."

"A pyro?"

"Someone just stepped on them."

"You should start wearing contacts."

"That's what I've been telling her," Forrest said, suddenly standing behind Aurora with his hand on her shoulder. "Ready?"

Forrest introduced me to the group. A few of the teens exchanged whispers. One of the pebbles fixed me a stare. I stared back, and she lowered her gaze, blushing. I wondered what they had heard about me. It had been years since I last served as a counselor at Yoyo. By now the kids from my last group had already completed their military service.

The elementalists stood in a group before me. The first time I participated in a mock battle was in the military. Daphne and I fought together against every elementalist on the base. There were more than fifty of them, and they still complained that they were outnumbered.

The moody stood next to me, and the damus slightly behind us. Her name was Gaia and his name was Guy. You didn't have to be a moody to sense how much they liked each other. Guy blushed every time he looked at her, and her expression softened when she thought no one was looking. Gaia considered me with her gaze. "Do you even remember how to fight?"

I rolled up my sleeve, exposing the fresh scar. It was still pink, shiny with newly formed skin. I waited until I could feel her pain dissolve, then rolled my sleeve back down. "Anything else you want to ask?"

Gaia blew a pink bubblegum bubble and popped it. "Bring it on."

"Follow me." I pulled a few of her feelings in my direction and felt her incorporating herself into me. Not fully, that would be impolite. She only sent me her aggression. Guy cleared his throat behind me. I felt his nerves grating.

All at once the world was ablaze; a wall of fire stood between us and the elementalists, the flames flaring when the airheads threw oxygen into it. The earth split beneath my feet and filled with thick mud. The pebbles and splashers were working together. If we moved, we'd slip. It was an interesting tactic.

Gaia held her breath. I felt her panic. The splashers linked their arms together behind the screen of fire.

Behind us, Guy was moving between futures, keeping the elements they were casting at us at bay. The fire didn't touch us. He was young, and not as good as Daphne. She could move so that we wouldn't even feel the heat. He only managed to keep the fire from scorching us. My and Gaia's job was to neutralize the other sorcerers.

The force swirled around me, and it took serious effort to penetrate it. Maneuvering sorcerers was much more complicated than maneuvering normies. I could feel the headache coming on. It wasn't the kind that would pass within a few hours, like after a shift at the Sinkhole.

I fumbled my way out and led Gaia with me. I showed her where to push on the other consciousnesses, making sure to avoid touching Matthew's. I knew his psyche inside out. Gaia's hesitation read loud and clear; I sent her an irritated wave and pulled her in my direction again. There was no time for decorum. The other side had given its consent, and we had a job to perform.

The pebbles crumbled the earth beneath me. I tripped, and Gaia pulled me back up. They were smart enough to direct their attacks at me and not her. Hail reigned down. Guy groaned, intercepting it. Gaia's hesitation dissipated, making way for anger. Childish, petty, but enough to drive her into action. We pressed all the elementalists' fear buttons, increasing the insecurity inherent in some, and the confusion in others. A rivulet of joy flowed from Gaia to me. I wondered whether it was the first time she allowed herself to let loose like that.

Our opponents tried their best to fight, hurling everything they had at us, but their power was dwindling. Something wet hit my face. The splashers must have put some serious effort into their attempt to create rain in the middle of the summer. The air was heavy with humidity, which the pyros' fire was supposed to evaporate.

Their impossible effort was our opportunity to break through the wall. We projected our combined consciousness, planting nausea, dizziness and headaches inside them.

The fire dissipated and the mud underneath our feet hardened. Four people were crouching on the ground in front of us, throwing up. A pebble was lying on her back with her eyes closed. I felt her lightheadedness. Forrest nodded at us, and I returned the gesture with a small bow.

"Wow," Guy said.

Gaia looked at me, panting. Her relief washed over me, as well as a little of the expected headache. I blocked her out. My temples were throbbing.

She chewed her bubblegum. "I thought the famous Reed Katz would be a little less–"

"Scarred?" I asked, raising an eyebrow.

"Old." She popped a pink bubble and smirked.

I smiled at her, overcome with nostalgia. The young faces. The transformation of young individuals into a tight, empowering group. No. I wouldn't be volunteering again. "You can come over," one of the splashers called out to Matthew. "We're done."

I expected him to join me, but instead he ran towards the back of the group of elementalists, where some were still doubled over, vomiting, and the pebble was prostrated on the ground, breathing slowly with her eyes closed. He leaned over her, held her wrist and spoke to her quietly.

I approached them and crouched next to Matthew.

"You did this?" he asked, staring at me with his jaw clenched.

"It was part of consensual battle."

"Can you stop it?"

Forrest came and knelt by the other side of the pebble. "No."

Matthew looked at him.

"Moodies don't maneuver sorcerers," Forrest said. I nodded in affirmation.

"You maneuvered her," Matthew said, "you maneuvered all of them." He gestured at the group.

"It was part of a consensual battle," I reiterated. "If I did it now, it would be…" I searched for the right word. Immoral? Obscene?

"It's simply not done," Forrest completed my sentence. "Thanks for looking out for us. We know what we're getting into when we take on psychics."

Matthew turned to me again. "Did you win?"

"That's usually the case." I felt very mature when I managed not to say, 'I told you, you don't have to worry about me.' My headache was beginning to drill holes in my temples.

Matthew looked at me. "You were hit by fireballs, there was exploding hail, and you, you didn't do anything… and…"

I shrugged, trying to appear indifferent. I poked around Matthew, searching for pride. His little brother had beaten elementalists right in front of him. But all I found was fear. "You think you can stop whoever comes after you," he said.

I nodded.

"And if you're wrong? If someone attacks you and you miss, just once, I'll be an only child." His whisper sounded like a whistle when he said, "You didn't do anything," he repeated. "There were explosions, and you just stood there."

I felt fear mounting inside the teens around me. I had to reassure not only Matthew but them as well.

I placed my hand on his. "I had a damus on my side, who made sure we'd remain in a present in which nothing could hurt me. And I had a moody to empower me, and we both saw to it that none of the elementalists would want to hurt the damus."

"But you don't always walk around with a seer by your side, and—"

"Daphne has my back. And I have hers. I don't go outside before she assures me that I'll make it back in one piece."

"At the rallies they do hurt sorcerers," Matthew said, his tone stern.

"Only elementalists," I said, and immediately felt Forrest recoiling behind us. Damn it. I tried to rephrase. "They can't hurt—" I was going to say 'moodies' before I remembered how much Matthew loathed the term. "Empaths, or seers. We psychics know when they're trying to hurt us, and we…" I stopped, and tried again. "No one can survive an attack by an empath or a seer. That's why they never go after us head-on."

Matthew bit his lip. "If you die, I'll kill you."

I smiled. "Even worse – if I die, Mom will kill me."

Matthew examined each elementalist, making sure none of them was severely injured. He offered one a pill to help relieve her nausea, and she thanked him. She was polite enough not to tell him that she'd feel better once her power of sorcery regenerated. Guy followed Matthew like a shadow, studying everything he was doing.

I wrapped it up by shaking hands with the older sorcerers. Aurora had managed to convince two of them to start volunteering at Yoyo. She still hadn't talked to me about Ivy.

The splasher hesitated before telling me her name. "River," she finally said.

I smiled at her. "Nice to mee—" I stopped mid-sentence, my smile freezing. Then I noticed the color of her eyes. A deep green – identical to Lee's, minus the brown specks. There was a resemblance in the nose and chin as well.

"Yup, that River," she said, and folded her arms across her chest in a defensive gesture. Her accent was much more subtle than Lee's. "I wasn't sure it was you. You looked different in the photo Blaze showed me."

I didn't have to ask her what photo she was talking about. It was my seventeenth birthday. We were walking around Meir Center, and Blaze made me eat three chocolate-filled doughnuts. When we realized that both our faces were smeared with chocolate, we decided to hop into one of the photobooths that were scattered across the mall. We divided the four photos between us, and after he moved to the Confederacy, I hid mine in the bottom of my drawer and hadn't looked at them since.

"My brother thinks you're very good at your job."

"Thanks." I tried to smile. She looked like a Photoshopped model. I searched for the flaws, but other than a beauty mark on her chin and nearly translucent eyelashes, I couldn't find any. And she was a splasher. That must have bothered Blaze. Their elements did clash, after all. I couldn't help but notice that she was beautiful. She looked like an upgraded version of Lee.

"It would be nice if you popped by for a visit sometime." She smiled politely.

I started phrasing a reply in my head, but before I could talk she continued: "You'll come, we'll talk for ten minutes, eat something, and Blaze will stop worrying about you and me killing each other the moment we meet." She uncrossed her arms and let them drop to her sides. "I don't want to be your friend. I have enough friends. I just want my boyfriend to feel comfortable about us meeting here."

"Fine," I said and held out my hand. River shook it.

Matthew finished his impromptu patient round and approached us.

Gaia was walking alongside, her chin slightly protruding. "Where are you heading to?"

I shrugged. "Back to the hospital dorms, I guess. My brother probably has two hundred pages to memorize by tomorrow."

Matthew let out a brief, joyless laugh. "Three papers on non-invasive approaches to cruciate ligament repair to present first thing tomorrow morning."

"Fascinating," I said, feigning a yawn.

Matthew poked me in the shoulder. "You're right, hearing about moodifying posters for graphic design students is so much more interesting! And such an invaluable contribution to society!"

I smiled. His anger at me had nearly disappeared. But the fear was still rooted deep inside. I assumed it was never going to fade. All the battle did was dull it a little.

"Wow, senior citizens lead such fascinating lives." Her voice was drier than the air had been when the pryos tried to dehydrate it during the battle. "We're going to the beach, want to come?" she asked, her tone nearly as prickly as her gaze.

Matthew moved uneasily, an almost imperceptible motion.

"Sure," I said before he could turn down the invitation. "But first I have to remember where I parked my wheelchair," I added, parroting her sarcasm.

Gaia popped another pink bubblegum bubble. "Awesome."

The *we* she was talking about turned out to be all the teens from the circle, as well as Forrest and Aurora, the latter deep in conversation with one of the other airheads about manipulating condensation in a closed vehicle during winter. We shuffled along the sidewalk in a group animated with chatter, and squeezed together into the rear of the bus. It was the first time I didn't feel lonely standing on the white square. I hadn't realized how much I had missed that feeling – being with others like me, with hopeful, passionate youngsters still unscathed by reality.

Gaia glanced at Matthew as he stood beside me on a white square.

"You can sit, like them," she said in a slightly barbed tone.

Matthew shrugged. "Reed can't sit, so I won't either."

She stopped chewing her bubblegum.

"My dad always sits," Guy muttered with his eyes to the floor. "Our parents don't."

It was partially true. Since my mother's knees had started acting up she stopped standing next to me on the bus, but she always made sure to sit in the seat closest to the white section.

Gaia fixed her gaze on me and sent me a wave of admiration. It was too strong, its colors too bold. It was so full of awe, it almost hurt. I softened it and sent it back to her. She mimicked what I did and sent me another wave, one less painful this time. I sent her a subtle confirmation. She returned the confirmation in an even more delicate, almost feeble wave. I bolstered it and sent it back to her.

"Did you take a first-aid training course?" Matthew asked Guy.

Guy nodded. "Last summer."

"I could see you know what you're doing," Matthew said, smiling.

"I wanted to take an advanced medics course, but they pushed my draft date forward. I'm enlisting in the winter. I'll probably forget all my medical training by the time I get out." He didn't have to explain. Damuses were enlisted to the intelligence corps. Always.

Matthew rubbed his chin, and his eyes suddenly twinkled. "I have an idea," he said.

By the time we made it to the beach, Matthew and Guy had already come up with an elaborate plan, according to which Guy would continue his studies during his military leaves, and even take courses that would help prepare him for his bachelor's degree. Aurora and her group ran to the shoreline. Matthew, Guy, Gaia and I stayed together and strolled the beach. Gaia and I exchanged a few more emotional waves. She threw at me almost every emotion she managed to produce, and almost all them misfired in terms of intensity and color tone.

We were working on polite indifference, and had almost managed to get to the accurate shade Gaia was trying to project – all while popping bubblegum bubbles in my face – when I noticed the sky flushing red. I glanced at my watch. "Shit."

"What is it?"

"My shift starts in an hour."

"Time flies when you're having fun," Matthew said, slapping me on the shoulder.

"Or when you have Alzheimer's," Gaia remarked and giggled when I looked at her. Instead of saying anything I sent her a well-aimed feeling of a stifled sneeze. She sent it right back, more compressed.

"Where do you work?" she asked.

"In the Sinkhole," Guy answered for me. "You know, that old café with the bad eighties' music."

"Just don't let my boss hear you say that," I said. I didn't tell him I'd rather he not peer into my other timelines. He wasn't an experienced damus. He was just a teenager.

Guy squinted at a point beyond my shoulder like damuses do when they're skimming through futures, and said, "In the one scenario I actually do say that to Remy, he lectures me for an hour… no, two." Guy smiled from ear to ear and turned to Gaia. "And you get annoyed that your omelet's getting cold because he won't take the dish out until he convinces me."

Gaia gave him a kiss on the cheek and said, "Then don't argue with him."

They held each other's hand. I stifled a snarky comment.

Matthew patted me on my shoulder and asked, "Shall we?"

I went to say goodbye to Aurora. She was wiping her glasses and looked at me, blinking. "Would you, maybe… at least consider it?"

My head started pounding again. Damn it.

Aurora gestured with her head at Guy and Gaia who were walking along the shoreline, arms linked. "They need you. I need you. Please."

"I'll think about it."

Aurora smiled and put her glasses back on. "Thursday, in two weeks, half-past five, in the center."

I furrowed my brow. "I haven't said yes yet."

"I didn't say you did. Merely mentioning when the next meeting is," she said, playing it coy. Then she lowered her voice and said, "Gaia would be in your group. If you decide to take on a group, that is."

I looked at the moody. Her hair was flowing in the wind, Guy gently brushing it off her face.

"I'll think about it," I repeated quietly.

Aurora nodded. I walked Matthew to his bus stop. As we pulled away, I felt a delicate, well-constructed arrow of gratitude from Gaia. I smiled to myself.

7

The sound of someone clearing his throat broke my concentration, and the feeling coiled back into the page. I swallowed my sigh. I had been working on that page for nearly half an hour, and had yet to pull apart the top layer of jealousy the previous moodifier had planted. The story was about a boy whose toy tractor was stolen by a girl, but with the amount of emotion that went into the pages one would have thought it was a Russian epic novel.

I looked up from the book. Lee was standing on the other side of the desk in a light suit over a dark dress shirt. No one dressed that formally in Israel.

"River told me you met yesterday," he said with a hint of a smile.

It was difficult to be mad at him when he looked like that. "It doesn't bother you that I maneuvered your sister?"

Lee shrugged. "If you're going into a battle with an empath you should know there's no getting out." I wasn't used to other sorcerers using the official term. The slang must be different in the Confederacy.

I smiled and stood up. "Next time just tell me and I won't go so easy on her."

Lee smiled. "She's a tough cookie, she can hold her own." A faint sluice of discomfort trickled out of him. Maybe from needing to express himself in a foreign language.

"We don't have to speak in Hebrew," I said in my hesitant English. "We all study English at school here." The delicate line forming between his eyebrows was the only sign of how grating he found my accent. Matthew's was nearly perfect, while I could never master the different vowels.

"I know," he said. "It's me. I don't like to feel foreign. Being an empath is tough enough…" his voice trailed off, as if he realized he was divulging a lot more than he had intended.

I sent him a small wave of commiseration instead of answering. He lowered his walls a bit, letting the wave wash over him.

"A lot going on in there?" I asked quietly.

"Here?" he said, pointing at his temple. "Always."

He shouldered his backpack, an old, frayed thing that clashed with his neatly pressed suit. "See you later," he said, and walked away, leaving nothing but a faint trail of emotion and aftershave behind him.

I sat back down behind the desk. His words lingered, echoing above me. I could imagine how he felt. In my post-military trip with Daphne, we learned that even in places where sorcerers were fully integrated into society, empaths were still considered personae non gratae. Daphne could walk among a crowd without even once being asked what she was, whereas I was exposed to everyone's emotions the moment they figured me out.

I stood up again and rushed after him. Lee was sitting in his chair, rummaging through one his desk drawers.

"Want coffee?" The words came out of my mouth without thinking.

Lee straightened his back and looked at me. He sent me an inquisitive wave.

"Soy milk cappuccino with sweetener, right?" I said offhandedly before adding, "I'm a waiter, remember?"

Lee considered me, running his eyes across me. I brushed my hand through my hair, my fingers getting caught in a mass of tangles. I was wearing a T-shirt and the only pair of clean jeans I had in my closet. At least I wasn't in flip-flops today.

"I'm sort of your boss. It's not such a good idea…" Lee started to say.

I felt Blaze's consciousness before I heard his footsteps approaching. He placed his hand on my shoulder, saying, "I heard you ran into River yesterday."

I wanted to shake him off. I also wanted him to press closer against me. I couldn't move. "I didn't know it was her."

"She told me," Blaze said, patting my shoulder and laughing. "So what are you two up to?"

"Reed was asking me out for coffee," Lee said, and got up. "And you need to finish the Sirkis report before I can review it." He walked around his desk and gestured towards the door. "Shall we?"

Blaze removed his hand from my shoulder, and I followed Lee without looking back. Once we were out in the corridor Lee turned around and said, "We don't have to go for coffee. You looked like you needed an excuse to get out of there. We can just wait here a few minutes and–"

"We don't have to. I want to," I interrupted him, and realized it was true. I did. "Even when you're from here, you feel like a stranger most of the time." I put my hand on his arm. "It's good to meet someone who understands."

Lee placed his hand on mine and stood perfectly still. I didn't have to read him to know what he felt.

The coffee in the cafeteria on the ground floor of the ArtDot building turned out to be a murky, burnt concoction.

Lee stirred in his sweetener. "It's a real art," he said, took a sip and grimaced, "to ruin a cup of coffee so…"

"Methodically," I mumbled. The foam decorating my cup looked dismal and lonely. I added another spoon of sugar and tried again, but it just made it too sweet.

Lee pushed away his cup. "I'll wait until it condenses. Then we can pretend it's a mysterious field ration."

I laughed. Lee smiled. "I meant what I said earlier," I said.

Lee fiddled with a packet of sweetener.

"If you'd rather we spoke English, that's fine," I said in my horrendous accent.

"There's just one problem with your idea," he said, holding up a finger. "I feel you don't understand me quite as well when I speak English."

And all at once his mask came off, revealing the lonely person in need of another soul. I felt my expression soften in response. He touched my forehead with his finger and said, "Your walls keep leaking."

I brushed away his finger. "It's intentional."

He kept his finger linked in mine, his warmth contrasting with the cold plastic table.

"Here in Israel we let other empaths read us superficially. Whoever chooses to block himself entirely…" I searched for the right words to explain the complexity of recent years, "…probably has something to hide."

Lee nodded. "Like this?" he asked, and slightly opened his walls. Just enough to let me feel that he was embarrassed and excited at the same time. I nodded in approval, making sure my reaction remained buried deep down. He was excited, because of me! I also had to curb the smile blossoming inside me.

"Back home we keep it all bottled up," he said. "If you leak it means you're not good enough, and people should keep their distance from you. You might accidentally flood others."

I gently caressed his consciousness through the opening he had left. "No one will take advantage of it. Don't worry."

"It feels like…" he hesitated, and blurted out the words, "like the first time."

I blushed and immediately retreated. Lee burst into laughter. He leaned in, winked at me and said, "Don't worry, I'm sure you'll be gentle."

I laughed, conscious of my reddening face, knowing that he was able to feel the trail of emotion I was trying to hide from him, and I didn't care. Not one bit.

8

Dinner at Blaze and River's meant I had to swap shifts at the café, giving up the fat Thursday night tips. Matthew managed to get out of it by saying he had to pull an all-nighter at the hospital. Daphne came with me instead, for moral support. For hours I thought about what to bring, and finally Daphne and I decided on two bottles of wine.

We stood outside their front door, holding the bottles. It was one of those new buildings put up on the border of Jaffa. They boasted a lavish outlay, cheap rent, a lobby filled with mirrors, and complete alienation from the neighborhood. Daphne and I hated them.

The small door sign read 'Blaze and River' in English, above an illustration of a couple standing in the rain, the man holding a bouquet of flames above their heads.

Daphne took my hand. "I'm so sorry there isn't a rally tonight. We could have gone and gotten ourselves killed instead of being here."

"I'm even sorrier," I sighed.

Daphne giggled and knocked on the door. Before it opened, I felt an inquisitive wave pouring out from behind it.

Lee was standing in the entrance, wearing faded jeans and a short-sleeved T-shirt with a print of a unicorn peeing a rainbow, a complete departure from his usual office attire. He reached out to the wine bottle I was holding and said, "Just the right thing."

Daphne held out her bottle. "And what about this one?"

Lee took it from her. "We could have used five more."

"What happened?" I whispered.

"River wants everything to be perfect." He gave me and Daphne a once-over and said, "At least you followed her dress code." Daphne was in a light pink dress, and I was wearing casual dark pants and a dress shirt I found in the back of my closet.

"Reed and I have a plan," Daphne whispered. "We're going to organize a rally and invite an assassin."

"Sounds marvelous," Lee replied, and stepped aside to let us in. It was an overly decorated apartment; the kind that whoever designed it probably wasn't thinking actual people would inhabit it. Everything was in black and white and clashing angles. It was far nicer than my neon orange room, and significantly less comfortable. The walls were covered in framed posters of movies and musicals.

In every corner of the house were see-through aquariums filled with water, all devoid of fish. A few had white snowflakes swirling in the water, refracting the light into tiny rainbows, while others displayed whirlpools winding in and out of each other. One of them even had soil and seedlings swaying rhythmically. It was a beautiful water spell.

River finished setting the table. She was wearing a black and white dress, her hair meticulously tousled in the latest fashion.

I paused by an aquarium that displayed small steam bubbles popping to the surface in random circles.

"There's no fire," Daphne said, voicing my thoughts.

"Blaze doesn't like elemental art," Lee remarked.

"Blaze doesn't not like elemental art," River said as she approached us. "He just doesn't like doing things he's not good at."

I introduced her to Daphne. River smiled politely, radiating the usual unease people experience near damuses.

"You did these?" I pointed at the aquariums.

River nodded, her smile slightly softening.

"It's very nice." I wasn't just being polite. When it came to elemental art, the upkeep was tricky. A small wave of pride hit me from Lee's direction. He was looking at River, proud of his sister.

We heard the sound of flushing water, and after a moment Blaze appeared in the living room. Everyone stood, smiled and said how happy they were to see each other.

River led us to the table. Lee poured everyone wine. When he got to me, I put my hand on top of my glass.

"You aren't drinking?"

I shook my head. "Don't like it."

Smiling his thin, impassive smile, he said, "I'll drink for us both."

"Lee," River blurted with an admonishing tone.

Lee looked at her, feigning innocence. "Well, at least one of the empaths here has to let loose, don't you think?" He winked at me and took his seat.

I smiled reluctantly. He could be charming when he wanted.

River was a high-energy physicist with a subspecialty in multiple timelines, and I managed to nod and seem interested when she described her work, without understanding a word of what she said. She and Blaze spent close to fifteen minutes recounting the blunders they had made when trying to reconcile their contrasting powers. I tried laughing at the right places and ignoring the stinging pangs whenever they completed each other's sentences.

The conversation moved on to our families; Daphne avoided talking about her father, and I just filled in the silence with anecdotes about our family dinners. We learned that it was only Lee and River's dad who was American. Their mom was Israeli. Daphne muttered something about people who jump ship and become expats, and I felt a guilt tremor from Blaze's direction.

"So," Lee said, leaning in, "how long have you been having these circles?"

I pushed all the peas on my plate into a single pile. "I don't participate in them on a regular basis. Only when Aurora and Forrest decide, or…"

Blaze snickered and blurted, "Lee is just looking for an excuse to maneuver River."

Lee rolled his eyes. "I don't need an excuse to maneuver my sister."

"Maybe not," River said, cutting the asparagus on her plate with long strokes, "but you better make sure I'm unconscious when you're done. How many of your sweaters have I already destroyed, five?"

"Six," Lee grunted. "And I was actually very fond of the red one."

"Then next time don't maneuver me at Christmas," River said. She put a piece of asparagus into her mouth and smiled.

I laughed. Despite myself, I was starting to enjoy this dinner.

After the meal, River and Blaze stretched out on one of the couches, holding hands, like Guy and Gaia on the beach. Daphne sat down in the armchair. Lee and I exchanged glances. "Want to help me with the dishes?" he asked me.

When River started to get up, Lee raised his hand, signaling her to stop. "Blaze is dying to ask Daphne about foresight, and you're dying to show how knowledgeable you are on the subject. We, on the other hand," he gestured to us both, "are dying not to be in the same room as our ex."

River leaned back. Blaze didn't say a word. I felt their uneasiness.

"Come," I said to Lee, and picked up all the plates and cups into a single pile that I balanced in one hand. Lee sent me a wave of admiration. I winked at him. "A waiter, remember?"

He smiled and led me to the kitchen.

Behind me, I heard Blaze saying, "You know that foresight contradicts physics?"

I could imagine Daphne's polite smile. I knew how much she hated it when people asked about her foresight. It was always the same questions, asking her to read their future or demanding that she change it in their favor.

I heard her saying, "Yes and no. Only if you think about time as a strict progression of cause to effect. But that's not how time works. I don't see things in a linear manner. I see all the possibilities…" I stopped listening. I knew that speech by heart.

Like the rest of the apartment, the kitchen was meticulously designed, with a polished black marble countertop, red and gray cabinets, a stainless-steel fridge and an oven with a black glass door. It seemed that everything they saved on the rent was put in to the design. I placed the pile of dishes on the counter, and Lee opened a hidden door that revealed a dishwasher.

I leaned against the counter and asked, "So, you come here often?"

Lee fed the glasses into the dishwasher. "You want coffee?"

I smiled. "If you knew me better, you'd ask if I'm up for a quick round of strip D&D monsters."

His face broke into a wide smile. "If you knew me better, you'd know I only talk about the 3.5 edition and ignore everything they came out with afterwards."

"No wonder we're both single," I said, and we burst into laughter.

Daphne's voice drifted in from the living room. "There's a reflection of you and River fighting over one of the dinner courses, and over there there's a reflection of the couple who used to live here busy making out, and there's one where the door doesn't even exist, it's just a metal frame. I can see everything. I choose not to, otherwise I'd go mad."

Despite her relatively calm voice, I felt her distress. Out of habit, I smoothed out her feelings.

"She lets you maneuver her?" Lee asked quietly.

I nodded. "We have an agreement." Which we had made during our army days.

I heard Blaze asking, "So if I ask you what I should wear tomorrow, you'd be able to tell me?"

"No," River interjected. "Because it's insignificant. She already explained it. Minor events don't carry enough weight for her to see them unless you're very close to each other."

I felt Daphne's patience wearing thin. I needed to go rescue her. It was my fault she was stuck there. The right thing to do would be to return to the living room and redirect the conversation.

Lee looked at me and smiled. "So what are the rules to strip monsters?"

I stuck my hands in my pockets. "One player opens the Monstrous Compendium and reads a name out loud. The other player has to describe the monster's characteristics. If he gets it wrong, he loses one article of clothing."

Lee's smile widened. "Kobold."

Meanwhile in the living room, Daphne was explaining to Blaze and River about the different types of visions. When and why a flooding vision appears, and how damuses' memories work.

I tried to remember the characteristics of Kobolds, which was difficult given Lee's beaming smile and the fact that he kept drawing closer to me. Just half a step, enough to make me conscious of the way I was leaning against the counter, and wonder whether I had something stuck between my teeth.

My phone rang, breaking my concentration. It was Matthew.

"Are you there?" he asked, sounding agitated. There was some kind of commotion in the background, people and beeping machines. He must be at the hospital.

"Yes, but don't worry. I'm actually not having a bad time." I made sure to keep my voice low.

"You're OK? Really?"

"Sure, it's just a dinner."

Lee pretended to remove his shirt and pointed at me. I stuck out my tongue. He laughed quietly.

"There was an attack at the café. They say there are casualties." There was fear in Matthew's voice.

"I…" I tried getting my thoughts straight. An attack. Casualties. And Matthew calling me right away. "I have to go."

Lee's expression immediately hardened. I knew I was radiating urgency. I rushed to the living room.

"There's a taxi two blocks from here," Daphne said to me. "Run southwards."

Pointing at Daphne, I said to Lee, "Look after her. She'll need you to take away the depression if it starts dragging her too far down."

River and Blaze stood up. "What happened?" Blaze asked.

I shook my head, saying, "I don't know. Matthew said there was an attack at the café. I'm going to make sure everything's OK."

I looked at Lee again.

"Look after her. Got it. Go," he said and stepped closer to Daphne, bridging the distance between them.

I ran down the stairs. Once outside the building, I almost turned north, towards the Sinkhole, until I remembered Daphne's comment and ran south. Two blocks from Blaze and River's building, a taxi driver was leaning against his car, smoking a cigarette.

"Can you take me to the boardwalk?" I didn't want to maneuver him, but I knew that if he said no, I'd do it.

"Sure," he said, tossing the butt onto the curb. "Get in."

The taxi reeked of cigarettes. During the ride, I learned that the driver was named Johnny, after the singer Johnny Cash, and that he was about to quit smoking. In fact, that had been his very last cigarette. I felt the fib beneath the words even without giving him a deep read. I went along with the conversation and maneuvered him just a little, just so he'd drive a bit faster than he normally would. I texted my parents, telling them that I was fine and I wasn't at the Sinkhole when it happened. I sent another text to Aurora.

The driver dropped me off near the Sinkhole and set off for his next fare, his soul already craving more nicotine.

People were moving around me. I felt the sorcery here and there, dotting the crowd. I ran towards the café. Blue and red lights flashed all over. I picked up fragments of conversation while elbowing my way inside. The chairs were scattered across the floor.

Four people in white were loading a stretcher into an ambulance. Daniel was lying on it, an oxygen mask strapped to his face.

"Excuse me," one of the police officers said, stopping me. "No unauthorized entry."

"He's my friend," I said, pointing at Daniel. "I have to be with him." I didn't dare maneuver a cop. It could end with a criminal record.

Remy was sitting by a table, one of the men in white taking his blood pressure. "Let him through," he called out to the cop. "He's OK."

A female police officer started lecturing him about protocol. He raised his voice and said, "I'm telling you to let him through. Now."

The cop let me pass. I ran to Daniel and held his hand. IVs were hooked up to both his arms. He was pale, lying there with his eyes closed. The edges of his shirt were slightly singed. The medics lifted the stretcher into the ambulance. One of them, a woman with long black hair streaked with blue, turned to me and said, "You're riding with us?"

I nodded. I didn't want to let go of Daniel's hand.

The medic put her hand on my arm and said, "He's stable. Don't worry."

I managed to smile, and squeezed into the back of the ambulance, still holding Daniel's hand. Machines beeped and hummed, and the team called in to the hospital over the radio.

We got out of the ambulance in front of the ER, and Daniel was wheeled through the heavy, sealed doors of the trauma room. I was left outside with the promise they'd keep me informed, doing my best to seal myself from the pain around me. I stood in the ER, abandoned, and called Matthew. He said he'd be there in a few minutes.

A nurse in uniform approached me with a stack of forms in her hand. The tight tug in the bottom of my stomach indicated she was a sorcerer. I drew my thumb and index finger into a small circle. She held out her hand, fingers stretched, palm down. A pebble. "Come, you need to sit," she said. "I'm Lilia. You?"

"Reed Katz," I mumbled as she handed me the forms.

She explained what had happened while I went over the forms, unable to concentrate. A man had walked into the Sinkhole and lobbed fireballs all over the place, hitting three customers, as well as Daniel and the boss. The primary injury Daniel had sustained was deep tissue burn. I looked at the report, the words blurry squiggles. I had to wipe my eyes twice before I could read anything.

I filled out the emergency contact details. Daniel's partner, who was pregnant, was on a genealogy trip to Poland with her two girls and her mother. I remembered her first name, but not her last or phone number. I filled out what details I could and handed the form back to the nurse.

"Can't remember the rest," I said. I couldn't breathe.

I felt Matthew in the corridor before I saw him. He was in scrubs. He ran to me and took me into his arms, and I broke into tears.

Lilia made sure Matthew would stay with me before she returned to the trauma room. Matthew led me to a bench. He was pale, and couldn't stop leaking worry. "When they said there was a casualty, I… I didn't know what to think."

I wanted to calm him down, but didn't know what to say. For the first time ever, I looked straight at him and said, "If you give me a few moments to get my act together, I can take it away from you."

Matthew raised an eyebrow. "Take what away from me?"

I took a deep breath, and said, "The fear you're feeling right now. It won't disappear on its own. I can take it away from you. I'm fine. You don't need to be scared anymore."

"Are you fucking…" he said, and stepped back from me. "I don't need you to take away what I'm feeling. I don't need you to tell me not to worry about my baby brother when there's some lunatic throwing fireballs at people where he works." He raised his hand and gestured towards the trauma room behind him. "All I need is the casualty not to be you. That's all."

"It wasn't me."

"This time."

Lilia appeared through the heavy doors. We stood facing each other, while Matthew resumed the formal bearing of a confident surgeon. He grilled her about Daniel. Among the jumble of Latin words the only thing I understood was that the damage to his internal organs wasn't as severe as they had first thought, and that he would be hospitalized for at least a week and a half, but could expect a full recovery.

Until that moment, I hadn't realized how much tension I'd been holding in. I collapsed back onto the chair, leaned my head against the wall and closed my eyes. Matthew sat down beside me.

"I'm sorry I can't take it away from you," he said softly, and placed his hand on my knee.

I felt a lump in my throat. I looked up at him. "You do plenty. I'm just not used to…"

"To being on the other side," he completed my sentence.

I nodded.

He looked at the doors to the trauma room and said, "You have no idea how scary it is."

"I'm starting to realize."

"I'm sorry I can't take it away from you," Matthew repeated silently.

My phone rang.

"Reed?" It was Lee.

"Everything's OK," I said. "It's Daniel, the guy who works with me. He'll be fine."

"I'll go see what's going on inside," Matthew said, got up and disappeared through the doors.

"I can't find Daphne," Lee said.

I felt the lump in my throat tightening. "What happened?"

He mumbled something I couldn't make out. I fixed my gaze on the wall in front of me. Green, the plaster peeling at the bottom.

People kept passing by me, concealing and revealing more peeling parts.

"River and Blaze were busy in the kitchen, and I tripped on my way back to the living room, and she just left, walked out of the house, and when I ran after her she was gone. I think she chose the future in which we can't track her down. I can't pick up the trail of her feelings, and I don't know where she is."

I heard cars honking in the background. Lee was still standing out on the street. "I'm sorry, I didn't think…" he said.

"It's OK." A long crack snaked along the wall in front of me. I focused on it. It started between two floor tiles and curved to the left, emerging under the peeling green paint. Daphne hadn't told me how she would die, only how she wouldn't, and she promised it wouldn't happen while we were still sharing a house. There were worse things than sudden death, and all the possibilities that could make her run out of a house full of people who could keep her safe were popping into my mind one by one.

"If Daphne doesn't want to be found, we won't find her. She'll come home eventually, don't worry."

"Is there anything I can do?" His voice was brittle, cracked with concern.

You can come over. Help me dissipate my anxiety and sadness. No. We weren't close enough, and I didn't want that invasive feeling that accompanies the touch of another moody inside me.

"Go home. Get on River's nerves for me."

"If you change your mind…"

I hung up and leaned my head back against the wall.

I felt the wall pressing against my skull. The pain in my neck. I couldn't take it anymore.

9

Daniel was taken out of the trauma ward two hours later. I went in to see him. He was asleep; the machines next to him beeped incessantly. The nurses hovered around him, letting me hold his hand and cry on the inside, without a single tear creeping out.

Matthew made me take a sedative and called me a taxi home. He said I looked like I was about to uproot the bench from the floor, and promised to update me if there was any news.

I returned to a dark, empty house. I switched on the kitchen light. I was hungry, even though the sandwich from the hospital was still giving me heartburn. I remembered only vaguely how the evening had begun, that it was fun, and entertaining, and cozy. My phone beeped with a message from Aurora. I answered as briefly as possible.

I needed to take a shower and go to sleep, but the distance between the kitchen and shower seemed untraversable. I shuffled to the living room and plopped myself onto the couch, burying my face in the pillow. The tears I had been choking back for hours wouldn't come out. I felt the pill fogging up my mind.

Psychiatric medication worked differently on moodies. I was entirely conscious of the chemicals breaking down in my system, detected every altering effect. It didn't prevent anxiety. Not for me. It suppressed all feelings, dialed them down. Matthew once explained to me the neurological aspect, saying that studies have shown that we don't actually feel the effect of the drug, but merely imagine it. He used big words and was so patient I didn't have the heart to disabuse him of that notion. In all the studies he talked about, empaths were asked about their feelings. I knew I was incapable of accurately describing my emotions. Every moody I knew spoke with words too crude and basic to describe the many tendrils of emotions we felt. Of course the studies would be wrong, they were based on our inaccurate answers.

The sound of the door opening woke me up.

Oleander walked into the apartment, supporting Daphne. "Some help?" he said.

I rushed to them. Daphne was flooded. I couldn't distinguish between her many emotions, and they were all pouring out of her in such a strong current that they covered Oleander.

I reached my hand out to Daphne, and she leaned on me. "What happened?"

"She had too much to drink. You know alcohol can do that to us." He sounded worried, but it was too dark to see his expression, and the deluge from Daphne made him unreadable.

He said *us*, and meant him and Daphne, but I immediately thought of Ivy, when she told me that their father used to yell at them that if they could both see everything, how is it that they couldn't prepare a decent meal, or tidy up their room like he had wanted them to, or succeed at school by his standards.

Daphne put her hand on my cheek and asked, "Where's the blood?"

"Everything's fine," I said, trying to smile. I looked at Oleander. "I'll take care of her."

"No, no," Daphne said, hanging onto me. "Oleander's here. He needs… he…" She crinkled her brow, as if trying to remember.

"Oleander is leaving," I said assertively, "and you're going to bed."

"No!" Daphne yelled, digging her fingernails into my arm.

I instinctively flinched, taking a step back, and Oleander caught her before she fell. "You want me to help you get her into bed?"

"No, no, Reed and I don't…" Daphne's voice trailed off and her gaze wandered somewhere past my shoulder. All at once her feelings condensed. The sadness gushing out of her made my eyes well up. "I need to get to Matthew, I have to–"

I felt a knot twisting in my stomach. "Matthew?" I made Daphne look me in the eye. "What's going to happen to Matthew?"

"The same as everyone else," she replied, stroking my cheek. "You die. And Matthew dies. You all die. I'm left all alone. Just me."

The pit in my stomach grew wider, darker, sinking deeper with every word she uttered. I hated her death prophecies. They always attacked her when she was already rattled. It was probably brought on by the evening at Blaze and River's and my disappearance. Had I been there, I would have disarmed it in time and prevented the prophecy from being issued. It was my fault she was having a vision. "She's always like this when she's drunk," I said, managing to hide the pain her words had inflicted. "She becomes a terrible pessimist. Tomorrow morning she'll wake up with a vision about cats running out of yarn to play with."

Daphne stared at me, saying, "Where's the blood? There should have been blood on your face."

That was a new one. She'd never prophesized that I'd get injured before I died. Her consciousness was blanketed with mist. I couldn't penetrate it with the pill still in my bloodstream, wreaking havoc on my powers.

"Come, Daphs, let's get you into bed," I pleaded.

Daphne turned to Oleander and mumbled slowly, "You're dead. I told you I loved you, and you died. Poof." She flung her hand up, snapping her fingers.

Oleander looked at me and said, "Let me help, please." Without waiting for me to answer, he wrapped his arm around her shoulder. "Let's go to bed now, OK?"

Daphne nodded and rested her head on his shoulder. "I miss you so much, and I can't die, and you're already dead."

"I'm here now," Oleander whispered to her.

We supported Daphne to her room, Oleander on one side, me on the other. When we lowered her onto the bed, she moaned and closed her eyes, drifting away from me.

I looked up at Oleander, his face awash with the yellow glow of the street lamps outside. The deeper she fell into sleep, the more Oleander's feelings disentangled from hers, and I could finally read him. Pain and guilt.

"When do you die?"

Oleander jolted, staring at me. "It's impolite to ask a seer about his death."

I shrugged. "It's impolite to let your girlfriend get hammered."

"We're not…" he started saying, then shifted his gaze back to Daphne. "We're not that close yet."

"But you will be?"

"If she wants. There are a few possible timelines. I let her choose which one we'll travel." He kept staring at Daphne, and I got the feeling he was taking in an image already deeply imprinted in his memory, not a woman he had met only a few days ago. "It's just… I didn't want you to kick me out of the house."

"We've had some bad experience with your family," I said, trying to keep my voice flat.

"I'm not my sister," he replied quietly. "I would never hurt Daphne."

I gave him my nicest smile. "Of course not. If you did, I'd turn your brains into mashed potatoes."

"You wouldn't hurt me," he said, returning the smile, "she would." He touched his forehead and left.

10

Before I was entirely awake, I felt Daphne's hangover. It poured over and touched the edge of my consciousness. I fortified myself before it could affect me, and got out of bed only after making sure she was completely blocked. I had received a text from Lee asking if everything was OK. I texted back a reassuring message.

Daphne was lying in bed staring at the ceiling. I sat down beside her on the edge of the bed.

"Was I horrible last night?"

"Don't worry. Oleander helped me get you into bed."

Daphne covered her eyes. "Oh no. Oh god."

I put my hand on her shoulder. "That bad?"

She moaned, and I giggled quietly. She lowered her hands from her eyes and said, "What did I say?"

"You can see for yourself."

She shook her head. "I hate looking at myself drunk. It's so embarrassing."

I recounted as much of last night as I could. Daphne cringed, practically shrinking into a ball as I spoke.

"I can't believe you let me behave that way." She scooted over to make more room for me on the bed. "Some friend you are."

"I didn't make you drink." I lay down on my side. "It was an awful night."

Daphne stroked my cheek. "Daniel will be OK. At least you didn't make an ass of yourself 'cause you saw…"

"Tell me."

"I can't see it clearly, just fragmented images. People injured. A lot of blood. I think it happens at a rally."

The grief seeping out of her was almost unbearable. I raised my inner walls. "All of us?"

Daphne brushed her hand through her hair, her black curls spilling from between her fingers. "Everyone I know. Lying on the ground." A wave of guilt flooded Daphne and poured over to me. That's why she ran away from Blaze's house. That's why she went and drank herself into a stupor. I would have done the same had I gotten a vision of her bleeding on the ground.

"Do we all die?"

"I'm not sure." She wiped her tears. "Everyone's hurt real bad, and I see graves. But I don't always see…"

"The same certainty as last time?" I asked quietly.

She nodded.

Back then I was sure I was alone, feeling lost and confused, and she found me when I was aiming my gun; she was so quick the bullet didn't even graze me. After leaping to such a faraway edge, the visions stirred up a storm in her mind rendering her nearly dysfunctional, and I spent weeks restoring her equilibrium. The following morning I asked our commander to forbid everyone from touching their weapons, without confessing I distributed Daphne's pain among all the soldiers in our company. The company commander had us running laps all day instead, and everyone hated me for it. But since no one shot themselves, I decided it was worth it.

"So do the same thing now," I said, keeping my voice from trembling.

"I can't. All I see just makes things worse," Daphne whispered, and the wave coming out of her drowned me. Her tears welled up in my eyes. "They changed something. Damuses, I think. It wasn't supposed to end like this," her voice petered out.

"There has to be something we can do," I said after clearing my throat, sounding almost normal. "If you see it, the damuses on the police force see it as well. Or maybe you're the first to see it, and if that's the case we have to alert them, say something."

"Anything we do might have an unexpected effect." Her grief overwhelmed me. She was mourning a future I hadn't experienced, hadn't known.

I sniffled. "Think, Daphs, you can solve this. There has to be something. Even just a clue. We don't have to find the entire solution now, just make things a little better."

"Maybe…" Daphne stared past my shoulder. "No, wait," she said, biting her lip, her eyes fluttering over futures I couldn't see. "Matthew's new friend."

"Sherry."

Daphne nodded, the cogs in her mind working towards a decision. "Talk to her."

"And say what?"

"Whatever you can."

My mind was racing. Daphne's focus on a single future would attract the attention of the other seers. "Are they looking at us?"

She shook her head. "Not yet, but…"

"You don't want to attract attention." My decade-long relationship with Daphne boiled down to that one sentence. Whatever plan we devised would immediately be known to every damus. Not only the seers that worked for the police, but also those who shifted reality to a present in which we all got hurt in a rally.

Daphne nodded.

I put my hand on her hip. "Don't worry. I'll take care of it."

Daphne smiled, her eyes shining with pent-up tears. "You want to talk about Ivy?"

"No. I think we talked about her enough. Want to talk about Oleander?"

"No," she said, smiling. "I think you don't want to hear about what we really do. We and all our reflections." She winked.

I rolled my eyes, and she laughed. She's a damus. If she saw something dangerous, she'd stop it. I had to trust her. I kissed her forehead. She recoiled and held her aching head. "Want some help with that?" I asked.

"You have bigger problems." Just as she finished the sentence, my phone rang in the next room. I rushed to answer.

It was my mother. "You forgot about us?"

A phone can't transmit emotions, and yet my mother was able to make my insides turn to stone all the way from a different city. I took a deep breath. Exhaled. Slowly. "No."

"Good." Her tone sent shivers down my spine. "So you're coming?"

Friday. Lunch. Of course I was supposed to go. I could cancel, but that would entail an explanation, which meant lying to my mom. She wasn't an empath, but she could spot a lie from a mile away.

"Half an hour," I said.

She hung up. I put the phone back on the dresser, on top of two splayed-open books. I went back to Daphne's room. She sat up in bed and gave me a once-over. "Oh no."

"What?" I asked, shaken.

"I'm sorry," she groaned. "You won't die before you get to your parents." She smiled and I started laughing, which made her burst into giggles.

11

The table on my parents' balcony was covered with pots, serving plates and beverages. There was enough food there for a busy shift at the Sinkhole, even though it was just the four of us. We sat on the balcony, disjointed fragments of conversation filtering in from the nearby buildings. A baby started crying in the apartment above us. His feelings were primal, hunger and frustration. At the same time, I was picking up his parents – helplessness tinged with anger. I stared at the cold tomato soup my mom had made. Gazpacho, she called it. It tasted distinctly of cucumbers, even though she swore there was nothing in it but tomatoes. I could relate to the baby.

"We need to make a decision about Rosh Hashanah," my mom said while plopping another spoonful of steaming potatoes on Matthew's plate.

"I'm on call," he said, taking a schnitzel from the serving plate.

"You couldn't possibly know that so far in advance," my dad muttered under his breath.

Matthew raised his eyebrow. "On holidays, the army requires round-the-clock availability from doctors. It's the busiest time of the year in terms of car accidents, and…"

"OK, OK," my mom interjected, waving her spoon and silencing him. "And what about you, Reedy? You're also busy on the holidays?"

Drawing my attention away from the grumpy baby, I met her gaze. The sun shone brightly behind her, making her hair glow auburn, a shade darker than her usual color. "When did you start dying your hair?"

My mom looked at my dad, then back at me and said, "That has nothing to do with my question."

A small gloating wave hit me from Matthew's direction. I shot him a look. He was hiding a thin smile. "Mom! It's really nice that you're spiffing yourself up."

I nodded enthusiastically. "That color looks good on you."

Pointing at me, Matthew said, "See? Even the family artist thinks so."

A stifled laugh came from Dad's direction. Mom stared daggers at him. He cleared his throat and straightened his back. "Reed, Mom's asking whether you have plans for the holidays, not what you think about her hair, which happens to look perfectly natural. I hadn't even noticed she did anything to it," he said. I could feel the slight anger inside him, mixed with resignation. Had they let me, I would have read them both in depth, just to understand how the convoluted relationship between them worked. I couldn't imagine myself in such a long relationship, with such complex feelings.

I shrugged. "Depends on Daphne. You know what her family is like."

"Excellent," Mom said and smiled, piling another spoonful of salad next the pallid drumstick on her plate. "Then come with us to Heather's."

I shot up. "No."

Mom rested her hand on the table. "Why not?"

"Mom…" Matthew said in a low voice.

She turned to him and said, "Heather is a very nice woman, always going out of her way to make you feel welcome. And whenever I mention her name–"

I pounded my fist on the table. "I'm not going to spend an entire evening with someone who insists on pouring a glass of wine for Elijah the prophet every Passover. I have no intention of bringing my best friend there only to have Heather explain to her that it's just a myth."

"But–"

"No!" I raised my voice. "She might as well put out a glass full of blood. That murderer butchered dozens of sorcerers…"

"It's just a myth," Mom shrilled, "no one actually thinks–"

"I'm never going back there!"

Silence descended on the table. I didn't want to feel them. I focused on the feelings of the baby, who was no longer hungry and was starting to fall asleep, enveloped in his parents' warmth.

My dad broke the silence. He lifted his fork and knife and cut a piece of potato. "I think that if Reed doesn't want to go to Heather's, he doesn't have to."

I was hit by a wave of betrayal. It was coming from Mom. She shot Dad a look. He looked up from his plate and met her glare.

Matthew turned to me. "Are there testimonies from seers that go that far back?"

"It doesn't matter," Mom interrupted him. "What matters is that–"

"No," I answered Matthew's question. "But our stories are more credible than…"

"Than ours?" Matthew raised an eyebrow.

I nodded. There was an invisible yet clear line running down the table isolating me from them. The silence hung heavy in the air.

"Cool," Matthew finally said, smiling. "One day you'll have to tell me the psychics' theory of how the universe was created." He stabbed a piece of schnitzel on his plate.

All I felt from him was pain and empathy, no curiosity. And yet I returned the smile and said, "All matter was compressed into a single point, and then there was a big 'bang!'…"

Matthew chuckled and dunked his piece of schnitzel into a puddle of ketchup.

Mom sighed, finally breaking her gaze away from Dad and fixing it on me. "Fine, if you don't want to come, don't come. That's absolutely fine. We're already used to going there without our children."

Matthew offered her a perfectly polite smile, and said, "Great. Then Reed will come to the hospital and we'll eat in the cafeteria together. Their idea of a festive vegetarian dinner is textured soy protein."

"Sounds amazing," I said, and dunked my spoon in the cucumber-flavored tomato soup. "Maybe you two want to join us?"

My dad let out a gurgle of laugher that felt more genuine than Matthew's affected smile, and we managed to get the conversation back on track.

When we left, Matthew wrapped his arm around my shoulder and pulled me close to him. "I got a car for the weekend. You want a ride home?"

"Very much so."

We got into the small vehicle, which appeared to be white underneath the layer of dust. Matthew started the car. "You don't have to let Mom climb all over you. And you don't owe her any explanations. Just say you don't want to go to Heather's."

"It's more complicated than that."

"You're the one making it complicated. Stop reacting to her feelings. Just react to what she actually *says*. Like me. You can't solve the competition between her and her sister-in-law, and you can't give her any explanation she'll be able to repeat later."

"Maybe I should go to med school. I could use the on-call excuse."

Matthew slapped my knee. "It's not an excuse. I work my ass off during the holidays."

I snorted. "At least you get to avoid family dinners."

Matthew smiled.

"You want to come over to my place?" I asked, moving the seat back. It was fun not taking the bus for once.

"I have plans," he replied, his smile quickly disappearing.

"Someone who's 'so none of my business'?" I tried mimicking his voice.

He shot me a sideways glance. "Yes. And before you ask, we're just going to a movie. I can't be away from the hospital for more than a couple of hours. My plans include a movie with Sherry, and back to the ER at midnight."

Daphne's vision involved a rally. Rallies only took place at the beginning of the month, which meant at least two more weeks. Once I talked to Sherry she'd want to hear all the details, and she'd forget about Matthew. I could wait with the conversation until after Matthew returned to the ER.

We spent the ride in meaningless chitchat, and when Matthew wasn't looking I copied Sherry's number from his phone to mine. I'd call her at midnight. That was the plan. If we were all going to get horribly wounded anyway, at least I could give Matthew a nice evening.

The giggles were the first thing I heard when I walked into the apartment. The door to Daphne's room was open. I felt her consciousness, light, lively and free of pain, and I felt Oleander's presence. I walked toward her room. She was sitting on her bed, dressed in a hideous T-shirt and jeans. She clearly hadn't been expecting Oleander's visit. Only another damus could hide himself from her.

Daphne looked up when I leaned against the doorframe. "You're back early."

"Felt like an eternity," I sighed. "No more hangover, huh?"

Daphne gestured at Oleander. "Someone came over with a painkiller, an egg sandwich and lot of OJ."

"That's nice of you," I said to Oleander, edging out my usual fear. Then I turned to Daphne again and asked, "Any hot water left?"

Daphne nodded. "And leave some for me, OK? I want to take a shower before we leave."

"Where are we going?" I asked.

Daphne giggled. "*We're* not going anywhere. Oleander and I are."

I bit my lip. "Daphs…"

"Don't worry, I looked at it. Made sure we don't end up at the ER or the police station. We're both going to have a nice evening. We earned it." My phone rang. It was Lee.

"Go," Daphne said, tilting her head towards my room. "I'll let you know exactly where we are. OK?"

I went to my room and shut the door behind me, hearing the giggles resume on the other side.

"Thanks for letting me know everything's OK," Lee said.

"Sure." I unbuckled my belt, cradling the phone between my ear and shoulder.

"I wanted to ask…" Lee said, "I don't…" he paused again. "I don't know anyone here, and it's Friday."

I straightened up. "You're looking for a date?"

"Not with you."

"Ouch," I blurted.

Lee laughed. "Don't take that the wrong way, but two empaths together? We'd drag each other down into a black pit of depression. And I'm not looking for a date date. I just want to go out, and I don't know the area well enough."

I plopped myself on the bed and closed my eyes. Just the distraction I needed. "There are a few places that aren't too terrible. I can take you."

I could hear the smile in his voice. "I'm glad I'm not being offensive. You don't look like someone easily offended."

"Your accent is appalling," I poked back at him.

He laughed. We agreed to meet, and something in his voice made my smile linger even after I hung up.

When I came out of my room, Daphne's door was closed. I felt her exuberance replenishing. I took a shower, leaving her enough hot water, and rummaged through my closet until I found a decent looking shirt.

Daphne opened the door to my room while I was trying to decide whether to tuck in my shirt or leave it out.

"Out," she said, looking at me.

I pulled the shirt out of my pants.

"It's more than a one-night stand," I said, gesturing towards her room.

"A two-night stand," she replied, shrugging. "Don't forget," she added.

I remembered, "Talk to Sherry."

She smiled.

"Have fun," I said, returning the smile.

"Fun? God forbid. I wouldn't know what to do with it." Her smile shriveled, and her pain trickled towards me. She waved and walked out of my room.

12

Lee lived close by, a ten-minute walk from my house, in a low-rise last stuccoed in the eighties. The sign on his door read only *LEE*, no last name, above a doodle of a robot holding a fluffy baby chick in its hand.

He opened the door dressed in shorts and a tank top in a color similar to the light blue I was wearing.

I pointed at the door sign. "Lovely."

"Thanks," he said, taking a step back. I walked into the apartment and was hit by the smell of tobacco mixed with faint notes of sage. I tried not to wrinkle my nose.

There was nothing stylish about the apartment; it was the complete opposite of Blaze and River's place. The living room couch was frayed, and there was no TV in sight. The walls were covered in posters of old Sci-Fi movies with giant squids and damsels in distress. Standing in for a coffee table were two upside-down crates, laden with notebooks filled with doodles. There were stacks of books on the floor, leaning against the corner of the wall.

"A drink?" he asked, gesturing towards the fridge. "I have some non-alcoholic stuff. I think." He froze mid-movement and turned back to me. "What happened?"

I returned the stare. "Nothing." I wasn't expecting the force of my internal wave, and strained to produce a smile; I couldn't help but wonder whether Lee was one of the wounded people Daphne saw in the rally.

He considered me, took a step forward and pressed his finger against my forehead. With me in shoes and him barefoot, he was only half a head taller. "Here. What happened here?"

I bit my lip.

"Want some help with that?" he asked softly.

I shook my head, unable to cope with his offer.

Lee didn't respond, he just kept looking at me. I made sure my walls weren't leaking. "I don't want you in my head," I said quietly, "no offense."

"None taken," he replied with the same soft voice. "If you change your mind and want someone who gets it, just say the word."

Lee smiled a small, almost imperceptible smile, took a step back and turned around, severing the intimacy between us. He went into his room, giving me time to pull myself together. I approached one of the posters. It wasn't a movie I'd ever heard of. When I looked closely, I noticed it wasn't printed, but had been done by hand. Lee's signature appeared at the bottom. It was the same hand that had illustrated Blaze and River's door sign. I wondered how painful it was for him to make it.

A small wad of paper hit me. I turned around. Lee was wearing long pants, holding another wad in his hand. "Are we staying in or going out?"

We walked to the Beer Belly, a relatively new sorcerer-friendly pub with an alcohol selection that easily outdid the Basement's. I had the feeling that Lee would appreciate a place with good alcohol, and preferably one that didn't have a permanent photo display of murder victims on the counter.

We talked. Lee had studied history and graphic design in college and met Blaze in an elective on the history of sorcery. He wanted to be a historian, but couldn't get a scholarship and settled for graphic design instead. Moodification design didn't appeal to him at all. He landed at ArtDot while looking for a place that didn't shy away from people like us, and one that would let him wander from branch to branch according to the workload. When he heard about an opening for an accountant, he brought in Blaze.

I knew Blaze had a scholarship to study elemental math in Boston. He managed to get discharged from the military to pursue his scholarship. I told Lee how I had considered going to the airport after him to persuade him to stay in Israel, with me, but we had just gotten over a big fight and I was in the army and I believed my parents when they told me he didn't love me, that he was just using me to take away his difficult feelings. I didn't go to say goodbye to him, and he left. Blaze and I spoke only a little after that, and the relationship petered out.

Lee filled in the gaps for me: there was next to no demand for Blaze's expertise in academia, and after a few years he gave up and went to study accounting in order to make a living.

Lee didn't touch me. He didn't send me anything. He only stood there, looking at me with his lips pursed, and then said, "I don't want to keep talking about him."

"Then what do you want to talk about?"

"Explain your hand gestures to me." He steepled his fingers. "That's our sign for sorcery. What's yours?"

I interlaced my fingers, palms up against my heart. "That's the sign for general sorcery." Then I pressed my thumb to my index finger, forming a circle. "And that's for psychic sorcery."

Lee burst into laughter. "Back home that means 'Want to have sex?'"

I laughed. The American gesture for psychic sorcery was pressing your hand against your forehead with outspread fingers. I remembered the question that was on my mind when we first met. "Don't you have nicknames over there?"

Lee raised his brow and sent me an inquisitive wave.

"We don't use the official terms, just the slang," I explained.

He nodded. "It's the same back home, but only north of the Mason-Dixon line. It's considered impolite to use slang in the South. One time in Richmond I accidentally said *starter*. You should have seen the guy's face…" He paused, noticing my confusion. "What is it?"

"Starter?" I asked, sending him a baffled wave.

"As in firestarter," he said, holding his hand in a clenched fist and spreading his fingers. "Fire."

"Pyro," I said, holding my hand with my fingers turned upwards.

"Surfers." Lee arched his hand, palm down. "Water."

I nodded. I showed him our sign for water sorcery – palm down, fingers mimicking a wave-like motion. "Splashers, we call them." I winked. "Or Splashies, if you really want to annoy someone."

Lee giggled. He balled his hand into a fist. "Rock. I know that one."

I shook my head. "We haven't been calling them rocks since the eighties. We call earth sorcerers pebbles now," I said, holding my hand flat, palm down, fingers spread outwards.

Lee held his hand flat in front of his chest and moved it side to side. "Levitators? Floaters? You know, air sorcery."

"We call them airheads now." I raised my hand, stretching my fingers out and pulling them back in twice.

Lee linked his thumb and index finger and pressed them against his forehead. "Clairvoyants."

"Seers," I said, pressing my pinkie against my forehead. "We call them damuses."

"Damuses?"

"Like Nostradamus, abbreviated."

Lee lowered his hands to his sides and looked at me. "And us? Empaths?"

"Moodies." I wondered whether to explain to him where the name came from.

"As in mood. It's nice." He gestured half a salute with his palm out. "Back home we're called vampires, because we feed off other people's emotions."

I twisted my mouth into a grim smile. "They have no idea what it feels like deep down."

Lee nodded. "No one does."

We exchanged glances. "Sorry for bumming you out. Want to go home?"

"I don't want to be alone."

"Then come," I said, pulling him by his arm. I edged out the fear caused by Daphne's vision, the sliver of pain Lee and I shared, and led him into the pub.

It was hot and noisy inside, and I could lose myself in the music. I felt the sorcery crackle in the air. Lee smiled and took a deep breath. "Now I feel at home," he yelled into my ear. Our loneliness was diluted by the crowd.

We danced for a while and drank, only a little, and once Lee felt completely at ease, he allowed himself to blend in with the crowd. I felt him disappearing with the others. I could feel his walls as long as he was standing relatively close. Every once in a while he shot me an inquiring arrow, and I sent back a little ball of reassurance.

There was no talk of the political situation, and no one mentioned the rally. It was the perfect escape. All I felt like doing was having a cold drink and sinking into a world in which sorcery was permissible. I could breathe.

Around midnight, the music became louder. My head started pounding. Lee appeared out of nowhere and leaned against the bar beside me, holding what looked like a glass of orange juice. He was radiating confusion and disorientation with a thin veneer of artificial happiness. He rested his head on my shoulder and, breathing on my neck, said, "It's nice here."

I put my hand on his head and gently pushed him away. He seemed like a completely different person from the calm and collected Lee I had come to know.

He took another sip of his juice and handed me the glass. "Want some? There's a lot of fun stuff inside."

I shook my head and gestured at the glass of Coke in my hand. "I'm good."

"Someone told me there's another floor for people who want something a little different. Want to come with me?"

The lower level. Of course. I hadn't forgotten about it, I simply chose to block it out. I'd been there only a few times, and always ran back upstairs after a few minutes. "It's packed with a lot of people with a lot of very strong emotions. You'll be flooded. You're sure you want to go down there?"

Lee stroked my shoulder, his hand sliding up my neck in an intimate gesture. "Only if you come with me."

I put my hand on his. "Sure, I'd be happy to, but not when you're like this."

Lee leaned into me, giving off the smell of sweat, smoke and booze, and whispered, "It's only when I'm like this that I can do these kinds of things. I don't have the nerve otherwise. I keep it all inside. If I wasn't like this right now, I couldn't tell you I like you."

"I like you too," I replied, and sent him a small, warm wave of affection.

"But not like this?"

I shook my head. "Try again when you're sober."

Lee tore himself away from me and straightened up. "That'll take a while. I'm going to see what's downstairs."

"OK," I nodded with affected formality.

"See you in a bit," he said, smiling. I returned the smile.

He hurled at me what was clearly meant to be a ball of gratitude, but that was mixed with confusion and discombobulation. I laughed. I had no idea what he was on. But he was obviously happy. Lee turned around and walked away, disappearing into the mob crowding the bar.

I took a sip of my Coke. I needed to call Sherry, but all I could think about was Lee caressing the back of my neck. I decided that when he returned, I'd agree to go downstairs with him. If he still wanted me to.

"Hey," a hand on my shoulder startled me. Sherry. I turned around. "Your roommate sent me." She was wearing plain pants devoid of any feminine embellishments. She didn't look like someone who had just been out on a date – a meeting with a friend, at most. Poor Matthew.

"I was just thinking about you. When did you two speak?" I asked.

"Late afternoon. She told me to come around midnight."

Daphne had probably called her sometime after I left to meet Lee and before she went out on her nightly escapade with Oleander. It was just like her to make me do all the work. "What did she tell you?"

"Nothing," Sherry said, shaking her head. "But I made sure she's credible, and one of the seers I trust told me to do what she says."

The noise around us grew louder, and suddenly I realized why Daphne had sent Sherry over to talk to me. There were too many people around for a damus to pick up on our conversation. Large crowds disrupted a damus's ability to read us, just like they prevented me from tracking Lee.

"All she said was to come over and talk to you. Does this have anything to do with the recent rally?" she asked, waving the bartender over.

"I don't think so."

I wasn't sure how to tell her about Daphne's vision. 'We're all going to die' sounded a bit overdramatic. The world was relatively quiet for the bomb I was supposed to drop on Sherry. I didn't even know her rank in the police. Maybe she was just a beat cop, and telling her would be entirely useless. Maybe Daphne was just trying to get me out of the way to do whatever she and Oleander were doing, which could be sitting around laughing at the pathetic moody wasting his Friday night on a cop.

"Maybe you guys have an idea who…" I stuttered. "In the rallies, I mean. It's…"

"You don't listen to the news?"

"I try not to," I replied, shifting uneasily. My mind was still wrapped up in Lee, in the touch of his finger on my nape.

Sherry's drink arrived. She swirled the liquid in her glass and stared at me. "Matthew said you always march."

I nodded. "With Daphne. It's… you know."

"He said you were really close to the explosion last time."

I looked at the ice cubes as they whirled inside the dark liquid in my glass. "Not as close as I was two months ago."

"And yet, you went back," she said. "It's important to you."

"Of course it's important to me," I said, glaring at her. "Isn't it important to you? Why are you even on the police force if you don't care about our future?"

"Our future is very important to me." She tightened her grip around her glass. "That's why I'm here. To understand what exactly–"

"Understand what?" I interrupted her.

Sherry took a step closer to me. "I want to understand why Daphne called me. Why she asked me to come here, and why–"

"Daphne asked you to come here to stop people from dying in the rallies," I said. I was getting all riled up. "After Flint, no one did anything, none of you."

"We're all doing the best we can," she said.

"And it's not enough. They keep breaking through our barriers. Each and every one of them. The damuses' barriers, the moodies', even those your worthless cops set up. Do they have inside information? Someone who informs them where and how they should strike? Why aren't you doing anything?!" I was panting. "Daphne sees the square filled with people injured or dead, we're all going to die in the next rally, and meanwhile the police are twiddling their–"

"And what are you doing? Apart from worrying your brother and walking around with a giant bullseye on your back?"

"Do you have any idea how it is to feel someone dying? To feel someone's pain? Someone's hatred? You… you…" I searched for the right words. "I have to be there. I have to do something. If I can help, even just a little…"

"Motherfuckers, burn!" someone yelled in the crowd.

And just like that, the place caught fire.

Sherry and I turned. The flames danced all around us, and my thoughts crashed into each other. Smoke inhalation. I had to run outside. Lee was stuck downstairs. I had to get him out. He had no idea what was happening, and he was completely high.

"You wanted to help? Now would be a good time," Sherry said firmly. She climbed on top of the bar and yelled, "Fire! That way!" she gestured the pyromaniacs' sign dramatically. At least three people noticed her.

"Burn!" someone else yelled out of the crowd, and this time I could feel them. At least five separate consciousnesses, all driven by hatred. I put out my feelers. There were no other moodies in the crowd. Or maybe they were all downstairs. I couldn't tell.

"Water!" Sherry yelled. No one was moving.

People were bursting into flames, and I couldn't understand where our pyros were to stop it. They could have put out the fire. Unless…

Unless the pyros here weren't *ours*.

"Reed!" Sherry called out to me.

The crowd's panic flooded me. I knew only one way to help Sherry make the crowd follow her instructions. I penetrated the hateful consciousnesses and filled them with pain. People were burning. Without thinking twice, I took away their pain and hurled it at the assailants. I heard agonizing shrieks and the place filled up with thick smoke and the smell of burning flesh. Sherry was yelling out orders next to me. She didn't sound scared. I could feel the panic bubbling inside her, buried deep under the well-practiced discipline. It was unlikely that I could maneuver every person in the pub, but I could take the fear away from at least some of them. Just to help them stop it. To put out the fire. I withdrew the pain and panic oozing from the burning people and shoved it into the hateful consciousnesses. People were starting to follow Sherry's orders, putting out the fire and helping the wounded. I continued to extract pain and frustration from the others inside the pub and cast it into the assailants' consciousnesses. The air started to clear. Probably airheads helping to cleanse the place, maybe even stifling the flames. It was a continuous effort, the kind of pressure I hadn't experienced in a long time.

I couldn't stop. Not now. I took all I could, concentrating only on transferring the pain from the wounded. Too many people. Too much consciousness. I had little sorcery left in me. My grip was slipping. My head was going to hurt like crazy tomorrow.

"Reed, are you OK?" Sherry asked, looking down at me from the bar.

"Sure," I said as the world slipped from my grasp and turned black.

13

I woke up in a bed that wasn't mine, dressed in a cotton nightgown, covered in an itchy wool blanket. I heard repetitive, high-pitched beeps. The room was cold. My head was throbbing. Someone was next to me. I could sense so little of him that I couldn't figure out who he was. I opened my eyes. Matthew was sitting on a chair by my bed, cradling his head in his hands. He was breathing slowly.

I looked around me. The letter G was printed inside a circle on the blanket. I was at the hospital, hooked up to three monitors, each showing different lines, only one of them beeping in a steady rhythm. I gasped.

Matthew woke with a start. "Don't you dare move," he said, putting his hand on my shoulder. "You hear me? Don't move."

My throat hurt. "Can I have some water?"

Matthew nodded. "I'll go get some. One sec." He didn't move, just stroked my forehead. His eyes were red.

Lee knocked on the open door, still in the same clothes he was wearing when I last saw him. His shirt was wrinkled. "Can I come in?"

"Reed wants water," Matthew blurted, and turned back to me. Lee turned around and went out.

I didn't have time to think about something to say before Lee returned. "Couldn't find cold water. It's lukewarm," he said, walking into the room, holding a plastic cup with a straw.

Matthew kept his eyes on me. Lee walked around the bed and stood beside me, smelling of smoke. Matthew still wouldn't look at him. I took a tiny sip. Lee remained standing on the opposite side of the bed.

"Where's Daphne?" I asked. My voice came out hoarse.

"She's not picking up," Matthew said. "I texted her that you're in the hospital, but she still hasn't read it."

Of course not. She was probably still out with Oleander. Or asleep. How did she not see what was going to happen? "What time is it?" I asked.

"Four am," Lee answered.

I looked at him. "I can't feel anything from you," I said, trying to sit up.

Matthew reached out and stopped me. "Lie down," he said, his voice trembling. "You're depleted."

Lee bit his lip. His face was an impenetrable mask, but a tiny spark in his eye hinted that he was angry. At me.

I shrank into a ball. It was one thing to talk with Sherry about how I was willing to do anything to help, and quite another to stand on a chair and maneuver every person in the pub. No one did that. The thought weighed so heavily on me I could barely breathe. Lee knew. He knew what I had done. What could I possibly say to him? I'm sorry? I didn't mean it? People would have died if I hadn't done it?

The ceiling was a solid, dull yellow. I turned to Lee, searching for words. "I… I know it isn't right…" But that's not what I wanted to say.

Lee closed his eyes and turned his head. I knew what I would have felt had I been able to poke around inside him – giant, impenetrable walls.

The door opened again. It was Sherry. She entered the room, her expression revealing nothing of the emotional state she must have been in. "How are you feeling?" she asked, shutting the door behind her.

"Fine," I replied with the steadiest voice I could produce. For Matthew's sake as well.

"It'll take you at least four days to regenerate. When coming in contact with normals, you're obligated by law to disclose that the interaction might–"

"Lead to severe side effects," I completed her sentence. We were all familiar with the legalese. A depleted sorcerer draws his powers from the normies around him at a pace and intensity that aren't healthy for them. The result is joint aches, fever, susceptibility to infections and sometimes even heart attacks.

"I thought empaths couldn't be hurt," Matthew remarked in a scathing tone.

"Reed wasn't hurt. Only the normals and elementalists were injured," Sherry replied and pursed her lips. She looked at me and said, "In fact, thanks to Reed's actions, a lot of people were saved." She approached my bed, and her gaze softened. "I know you have a… code. About maneuvering without consent."

"It's not just a code," Lee spoke up for the first time. "It's a matter of basic morality with regard to others."

"I'm happy you broke your code," she said, putting her hand on my shoulder. "If you hadn't been there, it would have ended very badly."

"Do you know who it was?" Lee asked, clearly trying to redirect the conversation.

"You're asking the wrong question," she said to Lee. "What you should be asking is why anybody would want to hurt you guys. Why five pyros with no criminal records would walk into a pub and set themselves on fire, when they know perfectly well they wouldn't come out of there alive."

"Because they're psychopaths," I said. "Because they think that–"

"That we should all be killed," Lee completed my sentence, and our eyes met.

"Calling them psychopaths is just letting them off the hook," she said, breaking the silence between us. She started pacing the room, Matthew following her with his gaze. "These are people who seem perfectly sane... And then–"

"Like Ivy," Matthew said.

Sherry paused and shot me an inquisitive look. "Ivy?"

I licked my dry lips. "We used to be really good friends, and... she..."

"She flipped. Went nuts," Matthew said. "She told Reed that everything he was, all their friends, they were all just a terrible mistake, and that she intended to do everything within her power to make up for it." He looked at me. "Right?"

"Sort of," I replied. There was more to it. At first the simple explanations made her feel better. Feel meaningful. Her ability was no longer a threat, but a blessing. It was only later that the doubts appeared, and the self-hatred started to seep in, amplified by the sense of helplessness because now she wasn't simply a mistake in her father's life, but a mistake of the universe itself. "She joined Sons of Simeon when they were just a fringe movement. A small, messianic cult we still thought couldn't do any actual harm. We haven't been in touch for years."

Sherry drummed her fingers on her thigh. You could almost hear her thoughts taking form in different patterns. How much of this had she already known? When I thought about our conversation in the pub, I realized she was simply gleaning information, and wasn't volunteering anything I hadn't already known. No different from now. "We need more details," she finally said. "I'm assuming that's why your roommate, the seer, wanted me to meet you. So you could fill in the blanks. What exactly did she see?"

Lee was standing in the corner, curling into himself so as to become unnoticeable, avoiding Matthew's gaze. He was out of place. He didn't belong here, and yet he was standing by the door when I woke up.

He deserved to know what was about to happen.

I felt my stream of emotions turning into a raging torrent. My walls had crumbled, and I couldn't put them back up. I didn't have enough sorcery inside to pull it off. I was almost completely depleted. The only thing I could feel was myself. The only good thing about being this enervated was that at least there was no risk of my emotions affecting others.

I described what Daphne had seen as succinctly as I could, trying to stick to the facts and not my interpretation of them. When I finished, Lee was leaning against the wall, pale. Matthew buried his head in his hands. Sherry was standing with her arms folded across her chest.

"OK," she said.

Matthew looked up at her.

"I'll look into it with the seers at the precinct. We have some very good people on the force. So far they haven't reported anything that sounds like what you're describing." She started pacing the room again. "I'll talk to them, and then to your roommate again. We need to understand the discrepancies between what she saw and what the police seers are seeing."

"How is that going to help?" Lee asked in a stifled voice.

Sherry stood and turned to him. "Details we haven't seen before. Missing information. Now we know who they're going to target next time, and we can use it. It's an opportunity to find out more."

"Find out more what?" Lee asked. "You already know there are psychos after us. You already know that—"

"I don't know why, and I don't know who. But now I have a lead, and it's coming from a reliable source," she said, pointing at me.

"You… you…" Lee stuttered, straightening up. "You can't be serious. It's madness. It'll just end with more casualties. Reed might—"

"I'm stopping the next murder," Sherry interrupted him, her voice quiet and assured. "You worry about Reed, I'll worry about the rest of Tel Aviv. Cool?" She turned to me and said, "Tell Daphne I said thanks. I'll be in touch."

She exchanged a silent glance with Matthew and left.

Lee pulled up a chair and sat beside me. From the other side of the bed, Matthew held my hand again.

"You might want to keep some distance," I told him, even though it pained me to say that to Matthew.

"Nonsense," he muttered and tightened his grip on my hand. "I'm in contact with depleted sorcerers on a daily basis. You wouldn't believe what people do to impress their friends. They push their sorcery to the limits. I'll be fine. It's just a legal warning. You have to rest."

"I am resting." I couldn't feel anyone. I was trapped inside my own brain. "We need to talk about–"

"Nothing," Lee said, touching my shoulder. "We don't need to talk about a thing. You need to get better."

Matthew leaned in to me and said, "Sorcery regenerates with rest, right? So rest."

My emotions were too chaotic. I couldn't muster up enough sorcery to calm myself down. I felt a well-aimed arrow from Lee. My mind blurred.

"Now he'll rest," Lee said. I was too tired to turn and look at my brother.

Matthew said something, but I couldn't make out the words. I fell asleep.

14

Daphne came to visit the following day. She came alone, dressed in a pressed black skirt and a cream-colored blouse I liked. Her face was riddled with guilt. I couldn't be mad at her. I could only imagine how terrible she must have felt when she found out what had happened.

"I hope your date ended better than mine," I said, sitting up in the hospital bed while she pulled up a chair and sat down beside me.

Daphne crossed her legs, her heels tapping against the floor. "It was great. We snuck into the drive-in."

"Daphne…" I tried to sound reprimanding but I knew she could see the smile I was hiding.

"I know, I know. It's horrible. I'll be arrested." She touched my hand. "How are you feeling?"

"I'm not." I bit my lip. "It's so weird. Like when the dentist numbs you. You keep touching your mouth without actually feeling it, you know? It's like that."

"I think I get it."

Lee would for sure, and I wouldn't have to explain it to him. "Did anything change since yesterday?"

She shook her head. "Exactly the same."

I rubbed the edge of the blanket between my fingers. "I told Sherry. I thought it would be enough."

Daphne grabbed my wrist to quiet my nervous gesture. "It doesn't work that way. You know that. We have to wait."

I was glad I couldn't feel her. She must have been dripping loss.

I leaned back against the pillows. "OK, then tell me something to distract me."

"I have a better idea," she said. She opened her bag and fished out a decorated tarot deck. "Want me to read your cards?"

I laughed and straightened out the blanket across my lap. "Go for it."

My future showed a critical choice between two paths, without explaining the nature of the choice, the paths, or what the decision might lead to. Daphne smirked when she saw the next card – a skeleton clad in black, clutching a scythe.

"I'm going to die? Because I've already heard that from a more credible source."

Daphne shook her head. "It means you're facing either a beginning or an end."

"Amazing."

"Or death. But it has to be death by completely *natural* causes. Let's say homicide, because you forgot to take out the garbage when it was your turn and I had to fight with the creatures lurking inside the dumpster."

It got a laugh out of me, and after a few more meaningless rounds Daphne shuffled the deck and we started playing Spit, debating which card was higher, since none of the cards was numbered, and we couldn't divide them by colors; and also, Daphne kept cheating.

15

Matthew spoke to the attending physician, and the two of them decided to change my medication regimen to a stronger combination of painkillers and sleeping pills, so I spent hours drifting mindlessly in and out of consciousness. Matthew promised it would speed up my recovery, but I could barely keep my eyes open.

One day, as I was slowly waking, barely able to shake off the fog of sleep, a worried presence wafted into the room. I could feel it. It had to be Matthew. I fought off the last remnants of sleep.

The door opened.

"Hey," Matthew said.

"I came to check on our patient," Sherry said.

I wanted to say I was OK, but I was too sedated to open my eyes, to talk. Everything was heavy, impalpable.

"Still asleep. He won't talk about… what we discussed."

"Yeah, he's the type that wants everyone to live in peace and harmony."

"And let him serve them cappuccinos and cookies," Matthew said, a smirk in his voice. I heard a screeching sound, and then Matthew saying, "You want to sit?"

"Thank you."

There was a long silence. I managed to float slightly out of the sticky fingers of sleep.

"And how are you doing?" Sherry asked.

I tried to remember if anyone had inquired into Matthew's wellbeing since we'd arrived. No. Not that I could recall.

"Not great."

Silence again. "I know how it feels. Being like this."

"Injured and hooked up to every IV on the ward?" Matthew sounded as if he was trying to make a joke.

"Sitting next to my sister's bed and praying to every god out there that she'll live." Sherry sounded… fragile. I didn't think she had it in her.

I made sure to keep my eyes closed. It wasn't the right time to show them I was awake and listening.

"You want something to drink? To eat? Our mom keeps bombarding Reed with–"

"I think you need to talk to someone."

"I think my brother needs to stop making me spend every night at the hospital."

"I think being the older brother of an empath is almost as difficult as being the older sister of a seer," Sherry said quietly. "I had no one to talk to either."

A chair screeched. "What's it like to be the sister of a seer?"

"Lonely," Sherry replied.

I heard sniffling.

"When my sister was little she always warned me before I broke something, and she used to find everything I lost." Sherry fell silent for a few moments, and when she started speaking again, her voice was quieter. "Soon after I started middle-school, I was invited to a school party on the weekend. She threw a tantrum, wouldn't let me leave the house. I got really angry at her, wouldn't speak to her, I yelled, I threatened to tear up her favorite book. The following Sunday, three kids didn't show up to school. Two were in lock up. One was in the hospital. You don't think it's going to be your baby sister who has to protect you. Have you ever wanted to thank Daphne for something she changed, and couldn't find the words?"

Matthew let out an audible sigh. "Of course." I tried guessing the instance he was thinking about.

Sherry took a deep breath. "Does Daphne know when she'll die?"

"Reed says she does. Down to the exact moment."

"All seers know. It's funny. They have infinite possibilities, but only one TOD. And you tell yourself she can't be right. She's so beautiful and successful, and has so many friends. It can't be that she'll go just like that." Sherry was speaking so quietly that I had to calm my breathing to hear her. "And then she calls you, in the middle of the night, crying. She made some stupid mistake and now she's lost, and she feels completely blind. So you run out of the house barefoot, and race over on your delivery moped, and call the police to tell them that your baby sister is spaced-out at some party at the Yarkon Park, and they say they'll send over a squad car, but you know that won't happen because who cares about a few drugged up sorcerers in the park. And by the time you make it there, it's already too late."

Sherry paused and took a deep breath. "I don't know whether she did it on purpose. I think maybe she did. When I got back home from the hospital my aunt was waiting for me. She's also a seer. She said my sister knew I'd come, that she knew how much I loved her, and that she was with god now."

I knew how I would react if someone told me something like that. But Matthew was better than me at masking his emotions. Sherry would never know.

"My grandma always said that seers are here to fulfill a unique calling in this world. This was a woman who had two daughters and a granddaughter who are seers. Maybe she's right. I don't know. The fact is that when my sister's calling came to an end, she…" Sherry's voice died down. "The cops who questioned me at the hospital also came to the *shiva*. They asked if I wanted to volunteer on the force and help them get to those kinds of parties before it's too late." The chair screeched again. "That's what being a seer's sibling is like. They manipulate us so we won't know when their end is near, and they keep changing our lives even after they're gone."

When Matthew started speaking, his voice was more brittle than I'd ever heard it. "I was about six years old when I realized Reed was… different. Mom brought him back from kindergarten, he was a sobbing mess. I remember he could barely explain what happened. He still didn't speak that well, he was only two, maybe two and a half. And I had just gotten home from school, and I was hungry, and I wanted my mom's full attention. I remember thinking how much, how much I…" His voice was strained. "I didn't want him. How good I had it before he was born. How much I wanted him to disappear." He sighed. I couldn't breathe. "And then he looked at me, and stopped crying, and said, 'Mat no sad. Ree bye bye.' And he let go of my mom's hand, and walked to the door. Just like that."

"Sounds awful," Sherry said quietly.

"It was. I ran after him and said everything was OK, that he didn't need to leave, and my mom never understood what I did to make him stop crying. Years later she was still telling everyone how I always knew how to soothe him." Matthew fell silent. "How did I feel when I found out Reed was an empath? I felt like a six-year-old who made his baby brother want to disappear."

One of them sniffled. I assumed it was Sherry.

"All in the past. Now I'm the successful older brother, and he's the one getting his ass kicked in rallies because he has ideals."

"Yup, all those sorcerers with their silly fight for equality," Sherry said sarcastically.

Matthew let out a brief laugh. "Come on, you know what I mean."

"I do."

After some moments of silence, Matthew sighed. "That's what being an empath's sibling is like. We know by heart all the signs of clinical depression, remember exactly what medication they take, know how to spot if something in their room looks off, have the mental hotline on speed dial, avoid contact when we're too sad or too happy because it makes them go off the rails."

"Luck of the draw. I think you drew the sibling with the better powers."

"I drew the sibling who doesn't eat cucumbers," Matthew said, and Sherry chuckled. I couldn't understand how he managed to pull it off.

"So-" Matthew said.

"I-" Sherry started.

They laughed together, and Matthew said, "Do you want, maybe... I know you're busy, and..."

"No," Sherry said. "Not now," she quickly added, and I knew it was too late even without feeling Matthew.

"It's OK, I get it," he said, his tone more reserved.

Sherry sighed. "No. You don't."

They both fell silent.

"I can't afford it, I'm not like you," Sherry said, and something of her harshness seeped into her tone. "I might be the sister of a psychic, but I'm not a normal like you."

"Being a normie isn't really a privilege-"

"It certainly is," Sherry interrupted him. "You just can't see it because you didn't have a sister who navigated your entire life and determined its course years ago."

"You can try to resist, try to change that course," Matthew said softly.

"Resist?" Sherry laughed bitterly. "Turning a blind eye to the daily injustices carried out against people like me? She gave me the tools to make a difference, and I can't throw that gift away for a one-night stand."

Matthew was silent.

"I'm sorry," Sherry said. "But it's not going to happen. Not now."

"I understand," he mumbled so quietly I barely heard him.

"Don't look so discouraged. You're a real catch. What about Daphne?" Sherry asked, her tone gently probing.

This time Matthew's laughter was more genuine. "When a seer tells you 'it's not going to happen between us,' you don't try again."

Sherry joined in on the laughter. "I'm sorry."

"It's OK," Matthew said with a dramatic sigh. "I'll be here when you need to patch up your wounded."

"I know," Sherry replied, something about her tone suggesting profound knowledge.

They were silent, and after a while the nurse came in to get the IV dripping again and I fell asleep.

16

A couple of days later, I started feeling better. My range had expanded, and I could already feel the people beyond the walls of my room. The hospital was located smack in the middle of Tel Aviv, and I was constantly exposed to swarms of normies. I felt the gentle percolation of sorcery trickling from them to me, and wondered whether I could trace its source and enhance it to speed my recovery. But it was just a thought, I wasn't aware of any good way to pull it off.

Matthew wouldn't let our parents come visit me. He told them I was in good hands, and that being around me when I was depleted wasn't safe for them. I assumed he wanted to spare me the emotional strain. I was incapable of dealing with my mother when she was truly worried. To make up for her absence, she sent over massive amounts of food, which I promptly passed down to the nurses.

Lee, Daphne and Matthew pulled shifts at my bedside. Matthew took over the mornings, between rounds on the ward and visits to the ER; Daphne spent the afternoons with me, between work meetings, and Lee would show up in the evening and open a sketchbook or a proof copy of a book, or just leaf through sales reports. He didn't speak to me unless I initiated a conversation. He just sat by my side. I didn't mention what he said to me in the pub, and he didn't bring it up either.

Daniel had been transferred from the ICU to the internal medicine ward in the adjacent building. His parents barely left his side. We texted back and forth, pretending we were still at the Sinkhole in a dragged-out nonsensical dialogue to alleviate the boredom of those long days.

Blaze and River wanted to visit, but Lee vetoed the idea. I had the feeling that he consulted Matthew behind my back. I was secretly relieved. I knew I couldn't cope with Blaze's guilt-ridden face and the lovey-dovey gazes between him and River. They sent me a box of chocolates, which Matthew took to the nurses' station after showing it to me.

At the end of the week, Lee, Daphne and Matthew arrived together. Matthew had just finished his shift, Lee had a deadline to meet and couldn't concentrate at the office, and Daphne got bored when I wasn't around. Their excuses were so sweet that I didn't mention the fact I could already sense the anxiety seeping out of each one of them. We played Privileged, a card game in which players are dealt cards representing different biological and cultural categories, and their ability to progress in the game is determined by the identity their cards form. Lee was in the lead by a landslide.

"How's Sherry?" I asked Matthew while he was dealing the second round. I was a young urban Christian-Arab. Could have been worse.

Matthew fanned out his cards without looking up at me or anyone else.

Daphne started giggling. "What, you're having a hard time with her 'Call me when you get off your shift'?"

Matthew blushed and buried his face in his cards. "She's not interested in anything serious. I'm not interested in anything serious. And you, stop trying to play matchmaker."

Lee snorted, and I shot him a look.

"What?" He raised an eyebrow. "At least someone's getting something out of this giant mess you've got going in this country."

"It's your country too, you know," I remarked.

"Pass." Lee tossed two cards on the table and drew two from the deck. "I have enough countries, and some of them even have snow and none of the insufferable humidity you've got here."

"They also don't have suicide bombings," Daphne muttered under her breath, and we all fell silent.

"You know why," Lee said, staring at her, his faint smile gone. "Because where I'm from when someone tries to hurt the community, he won't make it through the night with his sanity intact. And if he's one of us, he simply won't make it through the night. Fire is a very effective punishment."

"Yeah, judge and jury be damned. Brilliant idea." Matthew was holding his cards so tightly they started to crinkle. "An excuse to blow people up is just what this country needs."

"You know what they say, you can't make a revolution without breaking a few kneecaps," Lee said.

"Enough," I said loudly, attracting stares. And then again, in a softer voice, "Enough."

Lee clenched his jaw. "All I'm saying–"

"I don't want to hear it," I said, my hands almost shaking. "I don't want to hear how we should be hanging anyone who steps slightly out of line, I don't want to hear how we should kill all the fanatics, and I certainly don't want you to suggest breaking the kneecaps of anyone who doesn't follow our rules." I glared at Lee. "Or maybe you meant we should be breaking the kneecaps of moodies who maneuver an entire pub so no one will die?"

"No, that's not at all what I meant," Lee said, looking at me. Then he flashed a tiny smile. "I'm actually a pacifist. I think we should only kill people who don't play when it's their turn." He placed an even card on the pile. "White man from the city center. Who wants to bet against me?"

"Would someone be willing to build me a train to advance my employment prospects?" Daphne asked, and tossed down all her cards. "This game doesn't exactly work your imagination."

I put down my character cards. As an Ethiopian child from the south, I didn't stand a chance.

17

They changed my meds again; the pain had lessened, and my mind was sharper. When Matthew was busy on the ward, I took advantage of his workload and snuck in to visit Daniel. He was lying in bed on the general ward, surrounded by balloons and chocolates. He smiled when I walked in, and I was flooded with his joy. There were two more beds in the room, both with disheveled sheets. Toiletries were strewn on one bed, and a partially packed bag on the other.

"I don't have roommates," I said, approaching his bed.

"Let's switch," Daniel said. He pressed the button on the side of his bed, which heaved him into a seated position, and sighed. He was still hooked up to the IV that was trickling something into his vein, but at least it was just one IV.

"Do you really want to lie in a ward packed with sick sorcerers?" I put my hand on the side of his bed. "Fireballs everywhere, icicles suddenly materializing in the middle of your room…"

Daniel smiled. "Not really." His pallor brought out his freckles. I asked him about his family, and he showed me photos and a video his daughters had sent him. He had decided not to tell his girlfriend about what happened until she returned from her trip. I didn't question his decision.

"He was yelling 'Death to sorcerers,' you know?" His gaze was full of worry. "I thought… I thought those kinds of things only happened in the suburbs, or other cities. Maybe Jerusalem. It's supposed to be safe here for… well, you know."

Of course I knew. I envied Daniel's innocence. "Here, there and everywhere," I sang. I thought about how Lee had suggested breaking the kneecaps of anyone who strayed from protocol, and yet he still called himself a pacifist. I needed to ask Daphne whether they were targeting me, or just wanted to wreak some havoc.

"You know why… I mean…" he fumbled, clearly worried about me.

"I'm fine, don't worry." I managed to wrest a smile. "Just a few nutjobs looking to stir things up. Like always. Once it starts raining, they'll calm down and crawl back to their holes."

"Matthew was here. He said you have a problem with your…" Daniel paused, biting his bottom lip, "your thing."

I didn't know Matthew had visited Daniel, but it made sense. We were in the same hospital, and Matthew's heart was bigger than his whole body. "There was one day when I couldn't feel anyone. It passes."

"It must have been difficult for you," he said, a smile creeping onto his face, "without your hot chocolate."

I couldn't help but burst into laughter. Daniel laughed along with me.

"He said you're… depleted?"

I nodded.

Daniel scratched his head. "What does that even mean? I didn't know you had a limited reserve or anything like that."

"It's not exactly a reserve." I tried recalling an explanation I once heard. "Sorcery is actually produced from the awareness – the wisdom really – of normal people. We have a kind of magnet that pulls that wisdom in, and then we're able to navigate it to influence things. To steer it. But we need a minimum amount of sorcery within us already to draw in more powers. If we use up

126

everything in us, we can't create any more sorcery. We get depleted. That's what happened to me." And when we're depleted, the magnet becomes so strong that we could drain whoever happens to be around us and cause some serious damage to normies. But I couldn't bring myself to say that out loud.

Daniel fished a piece of candy from the heaping bowl next to his bed. "So you're actually taking away my sorcery?"

"Sort of. But you don't use it anyway." I leaned against the side of his bed.

"I'll let you as long as you use it for good. By which I mean – learn to make latte art."

The two of us were doubled over with laughter when his parents walked in.

Daniel introduced me. Despite their smiles, their disdain read loud and clear. Only Daniel didn't notice it. The sting was sharp and sudden. For some reason I was sure that if Daniel was able to accept me for who I was, his parents would too. They merely nodded, leaving my outstretched hand unshaken.

"Nice to meet you," Daniel's mother said.

"Good to finally meet one of Daniel's colleagues," his father added and shifted his gaze to the door. "I thought they were only allowing family visits for now."

I managed to smile and say, "I just popped in to say hi." I turned to Daniel, "Thanks for the company."

He protested, but I shuffled back to my ward.

There was no one in my room. The deck of playing cards was resting on top of the dresser. I crawled into bed. Lee had left me a proof copy he had nearly finished editing. I picked it up. It was a story about two boys who find themselves caught in a battle between two powerful sorcerers.

I started reading, pushing the faces of Daniel's parents to the back of my mind. What did I care what other people thought, I said to myself, repeating the mantra while flipping through the pages. Who cares what two strangers, who simply happen to be genetically related to my friend, think of me.

My phone rang just when the boys had learned of the existence of a magical diamond that could transport them back home.

"Hey, Gaia here," the voice on the other end of the line said.

"Reed here," I replied.

She laughed, then stopped abruptly and said, "I heard what you did."

I reclined on the bed and stared at the ceiling. "On the news?"

"No. The news was just your ordinary bullshit. Blah blah blah, evil sorcerers disrupting public order, blah blah blah." I could imagine her exact expression when she uttered those words. "But my friend was at the Beer Belly and said you maneuvered the entire crowd by yourself, and I told her there's no way, because we don't maneuver without consent, and that there are consequences, but she said she was sure of it, and that it was an emergency so it was OK that it was without consent."

"Is your friend a moody?" I couldn't help but ask.

"God no. I don't have those kinds of friends."

Those kinds. Even she had internalized society's rejection of our kind.

"She's an ariel," Gaia continued without paying attention to my thoughts.

"An ariel?"

She tsked in annoyance, and I waited for her to call me an old geezer. "Come on, *The Little Mermaid*? The movie? Motion pictures? You are aware of that invention, right?"

She managed to get a smile out of me, despite the pain and loneliness. "Yup, I've heard of it. I understand it requires that other new invention the young'uns came up with – electricity."

She giggled. "That's right."

"So your friend, the splasher–"

"The ariel," she corrected me. I wasn't even going to try to remember the new slang. "She said it was awful," Gaia continued with a quieter voice. "She said people were bursting into flames right in front of her. And that there was some woman who was barking orders at them, but it just made everyone freak out even more, and that then she suddenly felt better. Just like that. Said she felt calm and in control, and really focused, and that she was suddenly able to follow that woman's orders. Not that it helped much, since she was on neutral."

"On neutral?" I asked, once again lost in the maze of her chatter.

"You know, she hadn't exactly expected to find herself on the battlefield. But that's not what I wanted to say. What I wanted to say is that after it was on the news, I asked Aurora, and she said it really was you, and she also said she'd let you know I asked about you, and then I told her not to, but then I changed my mind, so she said she'd give you the message, and that's it. So I called."

"Thanks for calling," I said, in what I hoped was a calm, mature yet non-geezerish voice.

"Thanks for…" she began, and immediately paused.

"For not dying?"

"Something like that."

"You're welcome," I said and smiled.

"You're the coolest geezer I know," she blurted out.

"Cool? You still use that word?"

Gaia burst into laughter. "I just wanted to make sure you could understand what I'm saying."

"I understand, it's just that my hearing aid has been acting up."

She laughed again, and I asked her about school, and she immediately broke into another animated ramble about taking her matriculation exams earlier so she could start pursuing her bachelor's degree.

I whistled. "I wasn't half as ambitious when I was your age. I just wanted to survive high school."

"I'm short on time," she said.

I recoiled. Her boyfriend was a damus. Maybe he had given her a vision in which she died? I didn't even know how to begin to ask.

"My mom did her PhD when she was thirty. I have to beat her. And a PhD takes four years, so if I get accepted into an accelerated program, I can get everything done from my bachelor's to the

PhD in six years, but I'm still not completely sure I want to do it in neuropsychology. Maybe a different field? So I have to leave enough time for a potential change of heart, get it? I have to start preparing, like, now. You know?"

"No. I think you lost me at neuro-something."

She laughed again, and called me a geezer again. "You didn't have any plans at my age?"

I tried thinking that far back. There was that bucket list I had made in high school, all the things I wanted to do before I died. "Some plans were made. They just didn't go with what the world has turned into since I graduated high school."

"But you do have a degree, right? Aurora told me."

"Yes, but in art. I don't really know anything about neurons and science."

"I'll explain it to you," she said, her voice softer. "I'll explain to you everything about neurons, and you'll explain to me again how to focus what I send out. Although I'm really good at it now, I've been practicing like crazy."

"I'm sure." I closed my eyes. "In the next Yoyo meeting you'll teach me about neurons, and I'll see just how good you've become."

"I don't believe it," she said, her tone scolding again. "You call the organization Yoyo?! You're such an old fart!"

I couldn't stop laughing.

After she hung up, I sent Aurora a text saying, "You won. I'll take on a group."

18

After the doctors made sure I was no longer depleted or posed a "threat to the normal population", as stated on my release forms, I was discharged from the hospital. Matthew took me home. Our parents were waiting in my and Daphne's apartment; the smell of cooking wafted through the air. I felt both my parents' anxiety from the other side of the door.

"Everything OK?"

I wondered whether I was still pale or just looked miserable. "Mom's literally trying to cook away her sorrow," I said.

"You don't need an empath to know that," he said, standing close to me. "All they know is that there was a riot, none of the specifics. We haven't told them about Daphne's vision. I want us first to have more details from Sherry's investigation and maybe from what Daphne sees. It wouldn't have been fair to them."

"Thanks," I said, putting my hand on his.

Matthew opened the door.

The smell of frying hit me first, followed by the aroma of soup. There was also something in the oven. Standing in the kitchen, Mom turned around to us, clutching a wooden spoon. She rushed over to me, her face beaming.

"Reedy," she exclaimed, held her arms out and hugged me.

Even though more than fifteen years had passed since I had shot up past her eye level, being taller than her never ceased to amaze me. I hugged her back. Her worry was genuine and fierce, drowning out any other emotion. She didn't cry. She never cried. She wouldn't release me from her embrace. Dad waited patiently behind her. I felt his tension. Instead of showing it, he pulled that funny face of his, the one that used to make me laugh when I was a kid and said, "Enough, Sharon, you're smothering the kid." I saw her wiping her eyes when she finally let go of me.

"There's mashed potatoes," she said, pointing at the kitchen with her wooden spoon, "and corn schnitzel, and I also made pea soup…"

"Help!" Daphne yelled, darting out of the living room and jumping on me, pushing my father aside. "Your mom's force feeding me!"

I hugged her.

"Well, look at you," Mom said to her, waving her spoon, "all skin and bones."

Dad patted Daphne's back and said, "You look wonderful, don't listen to her."

Daphne finally released me, letting me hug my dad. I felt the fear in his embrace. They were constantly scared. Because of me.

I broke away from him. Still smiling, we patted each other on the back, and I told them silly stories from my hospitalization, like how the doctors kept insisting I was thirty and I had to correct them over and over that I was twenty-eight. Daphne spoke about Matthew's mysterious date, and our mom's attempts at a subtle interrogation were so ridiculously obvious that he finally broke down and said he had merely popped by the police station to check whether there was any progress in the investigation, and that Sherry just happened to be there.

"Sherry," Mom said in an incredibly flat tone. "That's a nice name. Similar to Sharon."

"Sharon, don't start," my dad muttered under his breath.

I leaned back in my chair with a stomach full of home cooked grub, happy that everyone's anxiety and fear were channeled into this invasion of Matthew's privacy.

Dad's phone beeped on the table with an incoming message. I quickly peeked at it. *A third arson attack.*

I looked up and blurted, "Third?"

Matthew and our parents exchanged glances. Daphne was playing with her spoon and wouldn't meet my gaze.

Dad finally sighed and said, "There were a few incidents in businesses that employ… uh… people like you."

"How many businesses were hit?"

Putting down her spoon, Daphne said, "The police identified at least five. There were seven."

"Is it organized?"

Daphne shook her head. "I asked Oleander as well, he doesn't see anything out of the ordinary."

"Sherry doesn't think it's organized either," Matthew added, and clammed up when I looked at him. He shrugged, suddenly resembling an overgrown child. "They think they are isolated events. Vigilantes. Maybe spurred on by what happened a few days ago."

Obviously neither he nor Daphne would say anything worrisome around our parents.

My mother and father's fear was mixed with anger – their self-righteous liberal rage.

I looked at Daphne. "Does it have anything to do with what you saw a few days ago?"

She shook her head again. "I can't see," she replied, her voice slightly stifled. Matthew buried his head in his plate.

"What did you see a few days ago?" my mother intervened, leaning in across the table.

Before Daphne could answer, Matthew said, "Reed's hospitalization." He looked at me, and I quickly nodded.

My mother shifted her gaze between me and Daphne. Instead of following up on Matthew's answer, she looked at my dad and said, "I think it's time for dessert."

My parents got up, and my mom put her hand on Daphne's. "When you want to tell us, we'll listen."

We had dessert, and before they left my mom hugged me a little tighter than usual, and my dad held my arm for several moments before letting go. And that was it.

19

The moaning woke me up from a troubled sleep. I couldn't remember the dream, only that it was heavy with passion, and when I was completely awake I managed to distinguish between the internal and external components. Daphne had company. She was barely making a sound, but he was very loud. Oleander no doubt. I stared at the ceiling and cursed the day I didn't kick him out of the apartment. We had a very clear agreement. Neither of us would do anything in the apartment without giving the other a heads up. Plain survival. I didn't want to experience what she felt towards other men, and she didn't want to see what I did. I blocked everything out as best I could and took a deep breath, cleansing my thoughts from the foreign desire. When I was feeling more like myself again, I got dressed and ventured out of my room.

There was a pile of dirty dishes in the sink – Daphne's way of hinting that I had skipped too many turns doing the washing up. I turned on the kitchen radio to drown out the noises from Daphne's room and immersed myself in soaping and rinsing.

When the song ended, the newscaster said, "You're listening to Eppur si Mauve! with Mauve Ben-Yitzhak. Following the recent riots, we've invited to our studio Professor Yeshurun, spokesperson for the Hands Across Israel association, to shed some light on the situation."

"Good morning," Yeshurun said. "I'd like to start by mentioning that we at Hands Across Israel work to reduce the divisiveness and polarization in our society. Extremists are trying to pit us against each other, and we must remember that what we share is greater than what divides us. I am, of course, under no circumstances justifying violence against my brothers and sisters. However, we cannot ignore that to a certain extent, we did bring this on ourselves."

The plate I was rinsing almost slipped from my hand. I caught it before it crashed into the sink.

"By which you mean?"

"Well," I could hear his smug smile. "We demand equal rights, but few of us actually abide by the rules we ourselves have set. We see people exploiting their powers to move up the social ladder. While I make no excuses for the measures taken by the Sons of Simeon, one can understand that they are motivated by trepidation. The fear that sorcerers will join forces in an attempt to usurp the place of government."

"But for that we have the police special task force," Mauve said, "and the Tobianski Act."

"He was exonerated posthumously, and that law is barely enforced," I blurted angrily at the plate. There was still pasta glued to it.

"I'll just remind our listeners that the Tobianski Act allows for the immediate execution of any sorcerer suspected of major criminal activity," Mauve continued. "Although it is rarely applied. If I'm not mistaken, the last time it was enforced was in the case of the Cash Splasher, a water sorcerer who attempted to rob a Brinks armored truck by drowning it, and was shot during his arrest."

"That's right," Yeshurun said, and it sounded like he was going to add something, but Mauve interrupted him.

"I'd like us to talk about the new announcement released by the Sons of Simeon," she said. 'From the center of sin city to the farthest corners of the land, we shall not rest until this country is purged of the depravity impeding salvation. We shall no longer stand for the tyranny of the foretellers of the end times.' The announcement is signed by their leader, Linden."

The string of pasta finally detached from the plate and sank to the bottom of the sink.

"Yes–" Yeshurun began to reply.

"We can assume from this announcement that he intends to off all the seers." The silence in the studio was palpable. "Right? The foretellers of end times are seers. Like in the verse, 'Blasted be the bones of those who foretell the end times.'"

"Indeed, from the Talmud," Yeshurun said and cleared his throat. "As such, it's also important to clarify that seers are not, in fact, sorcerers. They are simply people afflicted by the misfortune of remembering their lives from their moment of death backwards. They do not manipulate the elements, or even neutralize other people's defenses, like real sorcerers do. Some call them 'timeline operators,' or even 'time-impaired.'" He sounded like my university lecturer in Elements and Psyche 101. It was the one course Aurora had regularly skipped, leaving me to take notes for both of us.

Yeshurun continued. "In the past, people feared that all the seers would join forces to shift the world into a timeline in which they have the upper hand. Excuse me, 'timeline' means–"

"They wouldn't do that!" I told the radio. Ridiculous. Seers have to go to work and pay rent just like everyone else. It's not even feasible. I still remembered Daphne's explanation about how even if all the damuses in the world entered the strongest fountain of sorcery together, they still wouldn't be able to move us into a present so distant from reality. Daphne hated the whole 'united seers' conspiracy almost as much as I hated the 'every war in history broke out because of the empaths' conspiracy.

"With all due respect, the definitions are beside the point right now," Mauve said. "The real question is why the goings-on inside your community should concern us normal citizens?"

"Protecting the normies is pivotal," Yeshurun replied. "And indeed, there is no reason for internal disputes to seep outside the community. And if I may, I'll add that in my opinion, given the recent events, our community needs to do some serious soul searching."

"And I'll add," I said to the pot I was holding, filled with shapeless mush, "that someone needs to rip you a new one."

"Soul searching?" Mauve asked.

"Indeed. The community is in crisis. People are turning against us. We must ask ourselves what we have done to steer them off the peaceful path of comradeship. We must embrace them, understand what motivates them, and help them. We must use our gifts for the good of humanity at large. Hands Across Israel is committed to social outreach, to bringing the communities closer together, to advocate for diversity and…"

I slammed the pot into the sink and changed stations. Just music, no interviews with two-faced, spineless assholes more interested in sucking up to the normal audience than actually helping our community. I was rinsing the third pot when Daphne stepped into the living room behind me, all smiles. "Thanks."

I blurted a noncommittal "mhm."

"You're not angry, are you?"

I shot her a glance and lowered the sudsy pot into the sink. "You're supposed to make sure I'm awake," I said, then nodded towards her room and added, "that's exactly the kind of thing I don't want to–"

"I know, I know." She lifted her hand in a pacifying gesture. "We were just kissing, and suddenly it got kind of steamy. It surprised me too."

I rolled my eyes and went back to rinsing the pot. "You're acting as if you've never…" I said, falling silent mid-sentence.

"As if I've never been with another damus," she replied. Her smile faded.

I turned the faucet off.

"OK," I said quietly.

"OK," she repeated, waiting.

"I'm sorry," I said.

"We're good," she replied, looking past my shoulder. When she shifted her eyes to meet mine again, her emotions were softer. "I love you too."

I stuck out my tongue at her.

The door to her room swung open. Oleander came out wearing nothing but jeans, calling out, "Do you know where I left my…" He stopped when he saw me, and said, "Hey, I didn't know you were here."

"I live here," I replied sarcastically.

Oleander smiled and looked at Daphne. "You weren't kidding when you said he was protective." He took a step forward and held his hand out. "What's up?"

I didn't bother shaking his hand, but he made a point of keeping it up there, waiting. Daphne started to smile with genuine amusement. Oleander's smile widened, and the cheeriness radiating from them both finally made me cave. I wiped my hands and shook.

"Next step, peace in the Middle East," Daphne said, giggling.

Withdrawing my hand, I picked up the pot from the sink. "Sure, just let me finish the dishes first."

Oleander nodded. "Dishes first, and then you're cutting some watermelon for me too."

"Hey," I said, pointing my finger at him, "just because I let Daphne look at my futures doesn't mean you're allowed to."

"Sorry," he said, his short beard bristling as he smiled.

"The most popular word among damuses, huh?" I scowled.

"Actually, for me it's the phrase 'I'm not my sister'," Oleander said and tilted his head towards Daphne. "You wouldn't believe how many times I've said it over this past week alone. Read me if you don't believe me."

So I did. I skipped over his attraction to Daphne and dug deeper. He didn't share his sister's mercurial nature, none of the deep sorrow, the elation when he tapped into his powers. He was… serene. Nice. Whole. And yet I could detect the usual mix found in all damuses – the feeling of omnipotence suffused with despair. Daphne once told me it stemmed from their ability to influence everyone's death but their own.

"Happy now?" he said quietly, no longer smiling.

I nodded. I looked at Daphne and asked, "You planned this?"

"I did," Oleander answered. "I wanted to find the fastest way to get you to stop sulking whenever I'm around." He hugged Daphne, and added, "I still don't get why you hate me so much. Apart from the obvious, that is."

Nestled in his embrace, Daphne said, "Reed doesn't like damuses, other than me, obviously."

"Reed doesn't like other people answering for him," I said, trying to sound lighthearted.

The emotions leaking from Oleander changed shades. From lightness to solemn profundity. I wondered what exactly he saw when he said, "I told you, I'm not the one who's going to hurt her."

I looked him straight in the eye. "And I told you, if you do anything to her, I'll turn your brains into mashed potatoes. Empathetic maiming is no urban legend."

"Enough with the pissing contest!" Daphne hissed, and shook Oleander off her.

He looked at her with surprise. "I don't get it. He saw for himself that I'm nothing like my sister. He saw that I won't do anything to you."

Daphne didn't say a word, and their emotions were shifting. Daphne's pain intensified. Oleander was drifting from confusion to anger to acceptance. She had probably shown him Alder, back when I wasn't there to protect her.

"You're very lucky to have found Reed," Oleander said to her quietly.

Daphne averted her gaze from us.

"I'm sorry, I didn't know," Oleander said to me.

He really didn't. He couldn't have. And he was nice, and he was good for Daphne. I could tell she was happier when he was around. It wasn't his fault that he was a damus, nor was it his fault that his older sister had betrayed me.

I put the pot down on the dish rack and turned to the fridge. "You guys want some watermelon?"

20

Three hours later, we'd already devoured most of the watermelon, the leftovers my mother had left us in the fridge, and I even managed to beat Oleander at poker. Daphne was laughing her head off next to him on the couch.

"I can't believe I lost," he said, cradling his head in his hands. "And to a moody no less."

"I'm sure there are timelines in which you won," I teased back.

Oleander shook his head without looking at me. Daphne was in stitches.

They both looked at the door. I felt Lee on the fringes of my consciousness. His walls had started to pull away.

"Go," Daphne said, gesturing. "We'll tidy up in the meantime."

I got up and darted outside.

Lee was walking along the low stone wall outside our building, looking straight ahead. I caught up with him and pulled him onto the wall with me.

"I didn't want to get in the way," he said, his eyes lowered, shrinking into his consciousness. "You… and… everyone."

Breathe deeply. Ignore the fact that he can block my attempt to understand what he wants. "You wouldn't be getting in the way," I replied. The rustles of late evening surrounded us. The rattle of a distant car, a TV set cackling from a nearby living room.

"That's how it feels."

He was wearing a T-shirt with a print of a robot on a running track. The style was similar to the drawing on his door sign.

I looked up at him. "You drew that." I pointed at his shirt.

He nodded.

"And the shirt with the unicorn?"

A hint of a smile flickered across his face. "It was my final project in my fashion design course."

I held onto the tiny trace of emotion he was projecting. "You're really talented."

It was the wrong thing to say. He blocked me out again. "I just…" I started, but he raised his hand and looked at me.

"I came to say I'm sorry," he said. "I know you had no choice. I shouldn't have reacted the way I did when you woke up. I still think about it. If I hadn't been downstairs when it happened… If I had been with you…"

I didn't want sad Lee, apologetic Lee. There was enough sorrow in my life. "So we'd be hospitalized together, it would have been the most romantic thing in the world." I tried to make my voice sound sarcastic and patronizing. It worked. Lee smiled.

I wanted his smile to last. "Yup, there's nothing more romantic than being stuck in the same room with a moody who also happens to be my ex's ex!" I raised my hand in front of him in an over-the-top imitation of his own gesture.

Lee laughed.

"I'll make a deal with you," I said, smiling.

He nodded inquisitively, his eyes still twinkling with laughter.

"You tell me why I can't compliment you on your mad artistic skills, and in exchange I won't tell your sister that we're a couple."

"We're not a couple."

I arched my brow. "We're sitting alone, in the dark, outside a perfectly air-conditioned apartment full of food and friends. Hmmm…"

"Hmmm…" he parroted me, smiling. Lee's smiles were gigantic when he really let them out, and something fluttered inside my chest when they were directed at me.

"So…?" I asked, extending him my hand.

"Back home we don't shake," he said, gazing down at my outstretched hand. "If empaths…" he paused and corrected himself, "if moodies shake hands, they're supposed to exchange something."

I shrugged. "You don't scare me."

Lee hesitated for a moment and shook my hand. I wasn't expecting the outpour of his emotions. He lowered his walls just enough for his excitement to gush out – and anxiety, worry, fear and self-blame. Immediately, he put his walls back up again.

I was panting.

"I'm sorry," he said, and withdrew his hand.

"Don't you dare." I grabbed his hand and sandwiched it between both of mine, looking him in the eye. "Enough. Stop running away from me. And no more blocking me out. I won't have it."

"I don't get why you care," he replied, something in his tone suggesting that he felt undeserving of affection.

I myself didn't quite know the answer. But it was Lee. Mr. Contradictory. Grinning from ear to ear, I said, "I happen to be interested in the unique inner workings of the artist's mind. You're my subject. That's all. So why can't you take a compliment?"

He didn't return the smile. Instead, he yanked back his hand and crossed his arms. "It isn't real art. It's just…" He raised his finger to his temple, "It looks different in my head. And it comes out just, blah. Flat."

Feeling. He was an empath who couldn't imbue his art with feeling. That was actually something I could fix. I straightened up and met his gaze. "Want to see a magic trick?"

With him leaning against the stone wall and me standing perfectly straight, we were the same height. He didn't respond. I decided it counted as consent. I touched the print on his shirt.

"I need you to focus," I told him, peering into his eyes. In the faint yellow glow of the street lamps I could barely see the green in them. His eyes looked dark. "What did you want to show when you drew this?"

"I was sad. Also a little happy. He's trying to achieve a goal, and he isn't going to make it."

I searched inside me for the right thread. Sad, and a little happy. The pursuit of an unattainable goal. I found a flicker of an old memory, when I wanted to build the world's tallest tower, and Matthew and I toiled over it until we ran out of Lego pieces. We started dismantling the bottom of the tower to use the pieces to make it taller, and when it fell apart I broke into sobs and Matthew said 'Now we can build a Lego sea!' and I laughed through my tears.

I spread my hands across the print in the center of the shirt, to catch the emotion and insert it into the fabric. I made sure not to lose the edges of the drawing, and to get it in from both sides, so that when wearing the shirt you could continue to feel the same emotional thread as when you were looking at it.

When I was finished, I lowered my hand from Lee's chest. I studied the drawing. It radiated the emotion Lee had described, but not perfectly. "It'll come off after a few washes," I said, touching the edges of the print. "If you want me to strengthen it, just say so. There are a few products we can use."

Lee didn't answer. I looked up at him. He was staring at me. "How did you do that?" His voice sounded different. Deeper, slightly hoarse.

"Moodification designer, remember?" I smiled.

Lee brushed his hair off his forehead and looked at me. "I want to take you home and force you to do that to everything I've ever drawn."

"Or you could just ask." I put my hands on my hips, trying to make out what he was feeling. He wasn't happy. He wasn't sad. I noticed tears welling up in the corners of his eyes. He tried to wipe them while fixing his hair.

I looked down and said, "Coming?"

Lee sniffled. "OK." I got the feeling he meant to say something else. I looked at him. He bore into my eyes, standing perfectly still.

"OK," I said, unable to tear my gaze away from his.

Lee exhaled. It sounded like a quiet sigh. "Thanks," he said, and stood up.

"You coming?"

"I want…" He faltered and tried again, his voice softer this time. "I want to go home, take my shirt off and look at what you did."

"And then put on something else and come back?" I tried to sound lighthearted and casual, but there was a lump tightening in my throat when I thought that he might not return.

Instead of replying, he hugged me. I was caught off guard, and by the time I loosened up enough to hug him back he had already released me from his embrace. "Sorry," he mumbled.

I was still engulfed in his scent. I wanted to tell him to stop apologizing, stop blocking me out. I wanted him to be high again, to not care what anybody thought, to brush his finger across the back of my neck. I wanted him to look at me again, and have to pretend to be fixing his hair so I wouldn't notice I had made him tear up. But there was nothing I could say that wouldn't scare him off. That was Lee and I had to remember that. That was Lee, and he was afraid of intimacy, afraid of his own feelings; and I wanted him to stay.

Take a deep breath. And again. Find the right words to say to him.

"I want you to come," I said, gesturing behind me. "If you're going to take off your clothes, I'd rather you do it where I can watch."

"You don't strike me as someone who gets off on watching." The thin smile returned to his face. He was hiding something else underneath that sentence. He didn't think I'd want to watch him. Which obviously just made me start picturing him naked, sending my heart aflutter.

I winked at him and started walking. I didn't dare look back. After a moment, I heard his footsteps behind me, and he soon caught me up.

Together, we entered the apartment.

"Look at what I brought," I announced.

Oleander and Daphne were drying the dishes. Oleander approached us and extended his hand to Lee. "Nice to meet you."

Lee didn't respond.

"It's fine," Oleander said. "I trust you."

A slight trickle of surprise seeped out of Lee, and he shook Oleander's hand.

I tugged Lee's arm. "Let's go see if they left us any watermelon."

"I've got a better idea," Oleander said, smiling. "Let's all go to the amusement park."

"The amusement park?" Lee asked with genuine bewilderment.

Oleander nodded and turned to Daphne. "What do you say?"

"Yes!" she exclaimed, pointing at the hook with the car keys dangling from it. "I'm driving!"

I raised my hand and said, "I wasn't going to suggest otherwise."

As usual with Daphne behind the wheel we didn't hit a single red light or the least bit of traffic on the way. We listened to music, and Lee edged out his tension. We sat in the back, avoiding any accidental physical contact. I snuck him a look every now and then, and noticed that he did the same, a gentle smile playing on his lips whenever our eyes met. I sent him a small wave of affection, just to see how he'd react. He sent back a similar wave, shaded with a delicate hue of excitement. My heart leapt inside my chest again.

Daphne parked the car behind the amusement park, on a dark dirt road.

"That's a lot of walking to do to get to the main entrance," I grumbled.

"What do you think you've got two damuses here for?" Oleander said, winking. "Follow us."

They led us to a metal gate. At the mere touch of Daphne's hand, it opened with a grating screech. Lee turned slightly pale, and I felt the nausea he was hiding inside him, almost perfectly sealed.

"Is this legal?" I asked.

Daphne shrugged. "Is it my fault the park employees forget to lock the back entrance?"

"It certainly isn't," Lee replied and raced ahead of me. "Come on!" he said, reaching out to me. I took his hand.

Lights were twinkling everywhere, and corny pop music was playing over the speakers. Kids were squealing, running around between the rides.

Oleander rubbed his hands together. "Where do we begin?"

"The Ferris wheel," Lee replied.

"The pirate ship!" Daphne said.

"How do we get on the rides without tickets?" I asked.

"What do you think you've got two damuses here for?" Oleander said with a smirk.

I held my tongue. "I'd like to go for the legal option."

Oleander grunted. "There's nothing fun about the legal option." He considered me for a moment and said softly, "We'll pay for the food, OK? And Daphne and I will make sure no one gets punished for leaving the back gate open. I promise you no one will get hurt from us sneaking in without paying."

"Fine." I shrugged and looked around. I couldn't see a single ride I wanted to go on. It was all too bright and loud. Daphne was bubbling with excitement, Oleander was on a mission, and even Lee let me feel the faint twinge of joy stirring inside him. I was the only buzzkill in the bunch.

"I know," Lee said, wrapping his arm around my shoulder, "the tunnel of fear." He pointed towards the signs. "And I won't even say a word when you'll start bitching about their horrible moodification design work."

"I don't bitch all the time," I mumbled, and Lee burst into laughter. He pulled me closer to him and lowered his hand; my shoulder instantly grew cold where he was no longer touching it.

We started at the tunnel of fear, which indeed suffered from horrendous moodification design. It hadn't been properly maintained, and the feelings seeped between each "haunted" attraction so you knew when something was going to jump out at you. The pirate ship jerked and jolted us around so badly that even Daphne got queasy. We made a stop for snacks and boarded the Ferris wheel with our pockets bursting with an impressive variety of sugar derivatives.

"Want to share a cabin?" Oleander tilted his head at the line.

I glanced at Daphne. She shook her head in a gesture that would have been imperceptible to a less familiar eye. "I don't think so."

Everyone else had to squeeze into the cabins in groups of four, but when our turn came there were two empty ones. Oleander and Daphne boarded one cabin, and Lee and I took the other.

"Is it OK that I tagged along?" Lee asked quietly.

"Tagged along?" I raised an eyebrow.

"With you and your friends. I just showed up out of nowhere and…" his voice trailed off.

"I invited you, remember?" I smiled at him.

"I thought maybe you were just being polite."

Light and breezy. I have to keep it light, and breezy. I put my hand on his. "Very polite. I'm not at all undressing you with my eyes right now."

The sparkle was back, and instead of replying he sent me a warm, gushing wave. The smile was still on my face when we got off the Ferris wheel. Daphne's hair was completely disheveled, and Oleander's silly grin betrayed what they had been doing on their bench the entire ride. I was happy there were enough people around us to dilute the effect of Daphne and Oleander's feelings. I couldn't cope with their emotions on top of what I was feeling towards Lee that very moment, and what I suspected he was beginning to feel towards me.

"What now?" Oleander rubbed his hands together.

"You need another round on the Ferris wheel?" Lee winked at him.

"No, do you?" Oleander winked back.

Lee started laughing. "You're nicer than most seers I know."

"More than Oliver?" Oleander smirked.

"Oliver?" Lee's brow furrowed.

"You know, Oliver, the psychologist." Oleander sounded amused. "The damus you're always hanging out with?"

"I don't know any damus psychologist named Oliver," Lee replied.

Oleander's forehead creased.

Daphne smiled apologetically. "It's a different timeline. Oleander got mixed up." I didn't sense any confusion from her, only a flash of fear.

Lee's smile withered. "Does it happen to you a lot? That you're in the wrong timeline?"

"It happens to all of us," Daphne answered for him, the tension inside of her mounting.

I touched Lee's arm. "Damuses often respond to something that isn't there," I said, and sent him a small wave of reassurance.

"Yeah, but not people who aren't there," he said, without taking his eyes off Oleander. "If he's seeing someone who isn't here, and he's not inside a fountain of sorcery, it has to be brought on by Salvia."

"Salvia?" I asked quietly.

"Salvia divinorum," Lee replied, and waved two fingers in the air. "It blows your mind." He looked at Daphne, "See for yourself. You should know."

Daphne cleared her throat. "We don't look at each other's timelines."

"Bullshit," Lee snarled. "Seers always check the people around them to make sure they aren't dangerous. You're the most calculated people I know."

I wanted to tell him that they didn't always check, but the sudden pain pouring out of Daphne silenced me.

"Salvia is the only thing that makes you wander between timelines instead of staying connected to the current one," Lee continued.

"Alcohol can do it," Oleander retorted, and straightened up. "And other substances as well. Almost anything that affects our perception of reality can cause it."

Lee shook his head. "No. I've seen people on Salvia. This is exactly how they react."

Oleander crossed his arms over his chest. "Really? You want to tell Reed where you've seen people on Salvia?"

Lee recoiled, immediately retreating behind his walls.

"Enough," I raised my voice. "Enough with this stupid argument." I gestured towards Daphne and said, "If Daphne says everything's fine, everything's fine." I put my hand on Lee's arm. "Come on, let's take another spin on the Ferris wheel."

He shifted his gaze from Oleander to me. "No," he said, and sent me a wave of caution, covering it with a layer of warmth. "I think I'll call it a day."

I was hoping he was going to hug me again, and I was planning on returning the hug, but he only waved and walked away, disappearing into the crowd. I felt his consciousness pulling away from me.

"Reed," Daphne said, touching my arm.

I shook her off. "I think I'll call it a day too."

"If you hurry you can catch up with him," Oleander said.

I stared at him. "I meant it when I said I don't want you looking at my futures." I turned to Daphne. "Are you coming home tonight or sleeping at his place?"

"His place."

I held my tongue and nodded. "See you tomorrow." I left them standing there, the loneliness gnawing at me as I made my way out of the crowded amusement park.

There was only one person waiting at the bus stop outside the park. Lee. He was sitting on the small bench, his legs stretched out, looking at the ground.

"May I sit?"

He straightened up and moved over.

I sat beside him. The same distance between us as in Daphne's back seat. And on the bench on the Ferris wheel. But this time there was a giant, indivisible wall between us.

"There are two options," I said quietly, before he managed to say anything. "Either you tell me why you were so scared by what Oleander said, or we go back to being just two people who work together and maybe have a coffee once in a while."

"I don't think we were ever just two people who work together," he said, just as quietly. The noise from the amusement park was grating in the background.

I remained silent.

"I don't want to scare you off. I don't know…" Lee said, and bit his bottom lip. "I don't have many friends."

I knew what he meant. I had Daphne and Matthew, and that was it. I could always feel people's lurking suspicion when they talked to me. Convinced that I was maneuvering them without their ability to resist.

"Blaze said you guys are friends," I pointed out.

"Blaze is fucking my little sister. He better be my friend." His voice was harsh, and his American accent suddenly more pronounced. I made an effort not to pull away.

Lee slowly exhaled. "Sorry."

"Continue," I replied to what he didn't say.

He lowered his gaze and looked at the tips of his shoes. I scooted slightly closer to him. "I promise not to run away."

Lee looked up at me. "I used to do a lot of dumb shit."

I shrugged. "Who hasn't."

"I'm talking shit that lands people in jail. Or in the hospital. Or in coffins."

"We don't do coffins here," I said.

His lips curved into that faint smile of his. "I think," he said slowly, "you actually won't run away."

I smiled back at him. "Tell me."

"How much of it do you want to know?" he asked.

"As much as you want to tell me," I said, and quickly added, "how do you know what Salvia does to people?"

Lee leaned back on the plastic wall of the bus stop. "Remember being a teenager? When you start really experiencing what it is to be… like us? When it feels like everyone's constantly watching you. Everyone knows exactly what you are, and you can't even walk down the street without arousing suspicion?"

I nodded, even though he wasn't looking at me.

"I can barely remember anything between the ages of sixteen and twenty. Just images and people. It's all…" He twirled his finger in front of his temple. "Garbled. I ran away from home and…" He shook his head. "One time my parents found me and had me committed to a psychiatric facility with round-the-clock supervision. The kind with armed guards outside your room, and for every attempt at slashing your wrists they send out a damus to force you to deal with the consequences of what you tried to do." He smiled nervously. "The good old days."

"Sounds fun," I said. The facility I had spent three weeks in as a teenager was a lot slacker, and I was so good at faking the 'right' kind of behavior that the head psychiatrist didn't even understand why I was there.

I edged out my apprehension. "Go on."

"You're not running?" He shot me a look.

I shook my head.

"When I got out of there, I met Morty." He straightened his legs. "He had a whole group of followers. Most of them weren't even like us. Just people who were after a painless death, without admitting it to themselves."

I hid my pain when he uttered those last words.

"He tried to save us." He gave a small smile. "He believed that if you give people the right treatment, they can overcome depression, loneliness. He took each death personally." Lee was breathing slowly. "When he found out I was an empath, he asked if I was willing to participate in his experiment. He made a list detailing substances and emotions, how to maneuver me and what the results were. It was perfect. You're floating carelessly. You're not worrying about the next fix, or about a combination that could kill you."

His voice was tinged with longing. I swallowed my fear, my aversion, and hid them deep inside me. So he wouldn't be able to guess what I was thinking. Not now. Not like this.

"I saw damuses on Salvia in Morty's group," Lee said, looking me straight in the eye. "It made them break away from the current timeline. It's scary as hell to be around them when it happens, it gives us the worst feeling of nausea. And they can drag other damuses along with them. I've noticed you're protective of Daphne. If Oleander's doing Salvia, he might persuade her to try it."

"And then what would happen?" I buried my fear for Daphne deep beneath my other feelings, making sure Lee could only pick up on the lighter, more pleasant emotions. So he wouldn't shut me out again.

"Best case scenario she'll just be happy, completely detached from any timeline, and feel like a normal human being for a few moments. Worst case scenario, she sees people in other timelines, like Oleander does. Worse than worst case scenario, the detachment from the present will cause her to relive something difficult from her past, and that can really crush certain people."

I fought off my desire to run to Daphne and physically pull her away from Oleander. "But if she wants to do something like that, she'll make sure I won't be able to stop her."

Lee nodded. "That's the problem with damuses. If they want to get fucked up, you can't stop them. We can only be there for them afterwards." He put his hand on my thigh. "What you're doing for Daphne, how you take away her turmoil when she's having a hard time, she knows you're always there for her."

"Not always," I whispered. That old twinge of pain was throbbing inside me. For once, it was my own pain, not Daphne's. Instead of talking about it, Lee sent me an enveloping wave of consolation. I closed my eyes and leaned back, letting the wave wash over me. When it ebbed, part of my pain had dissolved. I opened my eyes.

Lee was leaning back next to me, looking straight ahead at the road. I sent him gratitude. He closed his eyes, savoring it.

"Have you ever done Salvia?" I asked quietly.

He shook his head, eyes still closed. "It doesn't sit well with empaths." I looked at the road and took in a lungful of car exhaust, Tel Aviv humidity and the subtle scent of Lee's aftershave. "I've never tried anything stronger than Goldstar," I said.

"That's more piss than beer," Lee said, smiling to himself.

I kicked his leg. "I won't judge your preferences if you don't judge mine."

He laughed and turned his head to me. "Deal."

A bus pulled up against the curb. "Shit," he blurted.

"What?"

"This one's mine." He got up. "It was good talking to you." He smiled at me, genuinely, wholeheartedly.

"Right back at you." I returned the smile. I looked up and registered the bus number; it wasn't headed in our direction, but downtown. I assumed he was going to River's.

The driver opened the front door. Lee gestured towards the back one. The instant wave of disdain flowing out of the driver almost drowned us both, and we raised our walls almost simultaneously. The driver opened the back door. I groped for Lee's consciousness as the door closed, and sent him a wave of affection. He grabbed onto the pole and looked at me through the window. I raised my hand to say goodbye and sent him another wave, ignoring all the other emotions flowing at me from the bus passengers. He sent me back a tight arrow of warmth and endearment.

The bus pulled away from the kerb, and I remained on my own, surrounded by traces of Lee's emotions. I replayed our conversation in my head. Everything he had said, and the underlying truth. His apartment smelled of sage. He was still dabbling, but probably nothing as hardcore as in the past. At least he was still functional. And his concern for Daphne had been perfectly sincere.

I exhaled slowly and stared at the deserted road, my mind racing.

21

I woke to the blaring shrieks of both the alarm clock and my phone. I tried turning off my phone and answering the alarm clock before I had regained enough of my senses to understand what belonged to which device. I turned off the clock and slid the icon on my phone to accept the call.

"You awake?" It was Daphne.

I rubbed my eyes. "What's up?" Certain parts of me were still inside a dream that featured a lot of Lee and very little of reality.

"Oleander had an idea, I need…" She paused. "You're not dressed."

"It was hot last night." I tightened the blanket around my stomach, edging out my shyness. We'd known each other for a decade, and I knew for sure that she had seen me naked in visions, if not also in reality. "What were you saying about Oleander's idea?"

"What exactly happened after you two left us yesterday?" I heard the smile in her voice.

"Nothing." I tried sounding as matter-of-fact as possible. "What did you two get up to after we left?"

"It wasn't what you're worried about," Daphne replied. I closed my eyes, hoping she was seeing me right now, registering my relief.

"Oleander suggested that we try seeing my vision together, hone in on it."

I rubbed my forehead. "The vision of the wounded?"

"He saw very little, and only after I described exactly where he should be looking."

"What do you need me to do?" I yawned.

"Help me trust Oleander." Her voice sounded smaller somehow. "Because what Lee said bothered me too. I've already guessed something wasn't quite right with him, but I kept thinking that it was because…"

"Because?"

"Because he's going to die in two months."

"What?!" I gasped.

"I knew from the beginning that our time was limited. Otherwise I never would have let it get this far."

"Daphs…" I tried sounding soothing, supportive. I never asked Daphne about her end. I could feel the jagged fear merely looking in that direction stirred in her, and whenever I felt it I hugged her without saying a word. Ivy was different. She wouldn't stop talking about her end, about her plan to 'go out with a bang,' and then laugh when I looked at her with horror.

"I'm fine. It was a conscious decision."

"So when he said he wasn't going to hurt you…?"

Daphne sniffled. "He won't. I made sure he won't. In any timeline."

"And yet, you don't trust him enough to look at the vision together."

"I haven't known him long enough, and despite what he says he's still Ivy's brother, and I know how other damuses behave when their end is near. But I have to trust him enough to focus the vision, to get a better sense of what's going happen, so we can…"

"It's OK." I sat up against the headboard. "I need to stop by the Sinkhole to get my shift schedule, but I'll come right after."

"Should I get someone to help you wake up?" she said.

I stuck out my tongue, making sure she was watching. "Stop trying to fix me up."

"There's hot water if you want to take a shower."

We said goodbye, and I stretched out and closed my eyes. It felt nice being naked in bed, nestled in the traces of my dream about Lee. I had no way of knowing when Daphne was looking at me and when she wasn't. I swept my gaze across the empty room. "Daphs, if you're looking right now, then stop." I burrowed under the blanket, stealing a few more moments of quiet before going on with my day.

After a shower and cup of coffee I walked out into the blazing street and started counting the hours until I could take another shower. My back was sticky with sweat. Daniel was still in the hospital. I could visit him on my way to Oleander's, after I stopped by the café. He'd appreciate it if I brought him a croissant or a sandwich. I could also bring some frothy milk in a take-out cup and tell him it's happy milk. Hopefully it would make him laugh.

People passed by me, talking to each other, laughing, yelling. Cars were honking at pedestrians who took too long on the zebra crossing. A bus sped out of a station, and two kids with school bags yelled after it. I was so used to the sights and smells, primarily of soot and exhaust, that it took me a moment to realize what was wrong with this picture. I could hardly feel any focal points of sorcery around me. Not on the street, not inside the shops. Everything was quiet. I recalled that I hadn't felt any yesterday either, and the driver had displayed more intensive loathing than usual, but I was so wrapped up in me and Lee that I didn't give it any thought. Now reality was staring me in the face.

A couple passed by me. I felt the sorcery emanating from them. "It's like in the suburbs," the man muttered, and the woman nodded. Neither of them slowed down enough to make eye contact with me.

I spotted two smashed shop windows on the way. One was of a hair salon, the other a toy store. "Death to sorcerers" was

spray-painted on the salon door. The only sorcerer in the toy
store was the airhead cleaner, and all she did was levitate tiny
paper planes every now and then. It made no sense. Strewn
on the ground in front of the two shops was some torn police
tape that the wind had blown over. People on the street were
radiating fear underneath the usual commotion of the day:
thick, solid fear. I picked up my pace. At the bus stop no one
was standing in the square of white paint, even though I felt the
sorcery wafting from one woman. She boarded the bus through
the front door and paid with cash, avoiding eye contact with
me. I did the same.

The closer I got to the Sinkhole, the more vulnerable I felt.
I clenched my fists. The Sinkhole was my safe space. The one
place where no one cared what I was. Where the boss got mad if
someone fiddled with his playlist, and Daniel asked me to make
coffee foam look like a cat, and the cook always added either too
much or not enough salt to the food. It was my home.

The chatter around me was picking up. One of our regulars
spotted me and crossed the street, dragging his girlfriend along. I
hastened my steps.

I had been expecting police tape, blood stains on the sidewalk,
a busy crowd of onlookers. But the Sinkhole looked like its
usual self. No malicious graffiti sprayed on the door, no smashed
windowpanes, no torn pieces of police tape. Nothing out of
the ordinary. The tables were still crowding the sidewalk. Remy
waved to me as I walked into the café, the cool breeze from the
air-conditioner a soothing welcome. Only a few customers were
inside, but it was still early.

Remy was wearing his regular outfit of jeans, a sleeveless flannel
shirt and black bandana tied around his forehead. "Good to see
you. How are you feeling?"

"Better." I attempted a smile. The warmth radiating from him
was sincere.

"Good." He was slightly shorter than me, stocky and
bullnecked. He had black beady eyes, and an almost crimson tan.

I glanced around. Remy followed my gaze. "What are you looking for?"

"Burn marks," I said without thinking.

"You won't find any," he said, waving at the counter. "We painted over everything. Burn marks are bad for business."

I'm safe here. The Sinkhole is my home. No one will hurt me here.

"I'd understand if you decided not to return," he said, the tension inside him palpably increasing. "We need you, especially now with what happened to Daniel and all, but I'd understand if you don't want to come back. It's your call."

I tried to parse the source of his tension. I wasn't sure if he actually wanted me back.

"I'd love to help," I said. "But if you think it would stir up more problems…"

His eyes lit up. "Great. I knew I could count on you. Want to pick up this shift?" Of course, Remy was stressed about being short staffed, not about the fact that people like me had become an even more unwelcome presence in this country than before.

More than I wanted to visit Daniel, I wanted to feel normal, and the most normal thing I could do was pick up an unexpected shift at the Sinkhole.

I smiled. "Sure."

Remy slapped me on the back. "There's a uniform in the store." He considered my pants. "I wish you hadn't come in shorts. I don't think we have your size." He also commented about my shoes, and my hair, which wasn't combed neatly enough for him. Same old Remy. He had only closed the place once, when his little girl got married, and even then only for a few hours.

I almost posted a status with a photo of myself frowning, but I couldn't think of a line funny enough to accompany the image. I changed clothes, got an update about the day's specials, and started working. Two regulars walked in when they spotted me from outside with a Sinkhole T-shirt. When I served them their coffee, I maneuvered them just a little, just enough to get a smile out of them.

Two hours into the shift, my feet started aching because I wasn't wearing work shoes; excruciating bursts of pain shot up my back, and I finally felt normal again. I couldn't stop smiling.

Around ten o'clock, a man in a neatly pressed shirt and dark trousers walked in. He looked too formal for a sea-side café.

"You've got a coffee and pastry deal, right?"

"Sure!" I put on my nicest smile. "Want to hear about our cake selection?" I went over the list in my head before beginning to recite it.

"No," he cut me off. "Ice coffee and an almond croissant." His expression was utterly blank, as if incapable of emoting.

"Sure!" I said, suddenly realizing I was repeating myself. I retreated to the shelter of the countertop to fetch him his coffee and croissant.

He sat down at the bar and waited. The man was completely frozen inside. My hands shook as I poured his ice coffee into a tall glass.

Everything's OK. I'm home. Everything's perfectly fine. I shouldn't be stressing out just because a man I've never seen before is sitting at the bar, studying me as if I'm a caged animal at the zoo.

The loudspeaker was murmuring with the voice of the real boss who was born to run. I thought about Lee. About his smile. I took a deep breath, curving my own lips into a natural smile, and turned around to the customer serving him his order. My hands were no longer trembling.

I had no other customers in need of service, and Remy signaled me to stay behind the bar. I took out a dishrag to clean the countertop of drink rings.

"You're the sorcerer, huh?"

"Yup." I smiled at him politely. "Don't worry, I'm not–"

"I'm not worried."

The frost sheeting his words made me wince. I stopped mid-stroke, the dishrag going limp in my hand.

His lips tightened around the rim of his glass in a thin, flat line. "You should be worried."

No I shouldn't. I could crush his mind if I wanted to.

I swallowed. "I'm not," I replied in a tone more confident than I felt.

He took a sip of his coffee, and I hoped he was done talking. "The Sons of Simeon know what needs to be done. How your lot should be handled."

"I don't talk religion before my second cup of morning coffee," I said, trying to smile. Remy was busy with a table of four squealing teenage girls and wasn't looking at me. I could maneuver him, I thought. Just a little. Just to enough so he'd notice something was off and come over to help me.

I knew the customer wasn't about to attack. All I felt from him was that same internal, unmeltable frost. He only wanted to rattle me. To harass.

"Blind," he snarled, almost spitting the word out. His hair was neatly combed – certainly more than mine – and gleaming with gel. If anyone were to look at the two of us, he'd deem the customer better put together. More polished. "Or stupid. Which one is it?" He leaned in. "We'll get you too, don't worry."

"Get the fuck out of here. Now," I hissed.

The client let out a chuckle and tossed a bill on the countertop. A slightly torn note was folded around it. "Keep the change. Buy yourself something nice before they off you." He got down from the barstool and started walking away, half his croissant still sitting on his plate.

I unwrapped the note from the bill and opened it. 'There shall not be found among you anyone who burns his son or his daughter as an offering, anyone who practices divination or tells fortunes or interprets omens, or a sorcerer or a charmer or a medium or a necromancer or one who inquires of the dead.' The note wasn't signed. But I didn't need a signature to know who was behind it. I leaned against the bar. Breathe. Breathe. It's just words. Breathe.

Remy approached me. "Everything OK?"

"I need…" My voice came out croaky. I felt Remy's concern swelling. "Everything's fine." I took a deep breath. "I just need to make a call home."

One of the café's windowpanes suddenly looked darker. Someone had scribbled the verse from the note onto the left window. A small, rational part of me said it couldn't have been the customer. It was probably some pebble or pyro who warped the glass. Which meant he had an accomplice waiting outside, and that accomplice happened to be a sorcerer. Maybe it was even the same pyro who had hurt Daniel. I felt sick to my stomach.

Remy ran outside. The customer had disappeared into the crowd forming at the front of the building: a combination of people in swimsuits, parents in casual beachwear and businessmen in suits too hot for the Israeli summer. Someone had called the police.

The world was spinning around me in a swirl of noises and panic that jumbled the details. An oily trail of satisfaction drifted through the crowd. Too many of them didn't want me here. I stood near the boss, trying to make sense of it all. He put his hand on my shoulder. "Don't worry, it's just plain old vandalism."

I felt a knot in my stomach. We continued to stare at the window. Someone suggested cleaning it with water and soap. A woman quaked that there was no way of getting it off. Another man blurted out, "What do they expect when they hire those…" and fell silent when Remy shot him a menacing look. I felt stifled, trapped.

A squad car pulled up at the curb. Two officers got out. One was Sherry, her tablet already switched on. They were both wearing the same white ribbons on their lapels.

"There was no squad car when it happened at Haim's," someone in the crowd whispered. I got the feeling it was the same person who had asked what Remy could have expected when he hired me.

Sherry gestured at the squad car parked at the curb. "Let's start the questioning with you." She gave her partner orders and guided me to the car. She led me into the passenger seat, sat behind the wheel, turned to me and said, "Talk."

I told her about the customer. She typed in the information, asked a few guiding questions, and didn't admonish me for not calling her the moment he walked out of the café. When we finished, she looked at her screen and tapped on it with her pen.

"Does this have anything to do with what happened to Daniel?"

Sherry typed something else into her tablet. She then looked up at me and asked, "What do you think?"

"That it does," I replied, my voice tremulous.

"Why?"

"Because Daphne saw all of us wounded, and then he shows up here and–"

"When a seer gives you a vision, it's never accurate. The fact that Daphne saw everyone injured doesn't mean that it starts here, or that it has anything to do with what happened to you this morning. Instead of trusting a vision, try trusting your common sense. Why do you think the Sons of Simeon attacked an ordinary boardwalk café whose sole attraction is a sorcerer who hasn't done anything to anyone?"

"So assuming they weren't after me…" I started saying.

Sherry nodded.

"Then it means that the Sons of Simeon are trying… to distract you from what's really going on?"

Sherry arched an eyebrow. "Meaning?"

I started listing with my fingers. "First they strike at the Beer Belly…"

"They attacked at the rally first," Sherry corrected me.

"No, no, at the rallies they always attack only…" I suddenly paused, seeing it all clearly now. "They attack whoever doesn't matter. Whoever isn't important enough. Like me. They make sure their attacks won't attract enough attention to alert the police damuses, so they won't be able to see the attacks before they go down. That's how they manage to fly under the radar. They attacked the café because it won't affect any major change in police activity, but… but they can see how you react!" I snapped my fingers. "Learn who responds, and later use that information so…" I paused.

"So when they strike with full force, they'll already know all our weaknesses," Sherry concluded quietly.

"So I'm not significant enough to derail the course of events, but I'm important enough to Daphne, which is why she saw what your damuses didn't."

Sherry nodded.

I bit my bottom lip. "What now?"

"Now we continue as if nothing has changed," she replied, and flipped the cover of her tablet closed.

"Because as long as the Sons of Simeon think their plan will work, you can look for ways to bring them down?"

Sherry shot me a brief glance. "So you do take after Matthew."

I gave her a clipped smile.

Sherry drummed her pen against the cover of her tablet. "Let me know when you make it home."

"We're open till midnight."

Sherry's brow furrowed. "Any exciting plans today?"

"Not really," I said. "I'm working." I gestured at the café.

Sherry stopped tapping her pen and looked at me. "You're not. You're going home."

"Hmm, excuse me?" I straightened my back.

Sherry raised her hand and pointed her pen at me. "You're planning on going back to work at the same café where the bartender was hit–"

"Barista," I corrected her. "He makes coffee. It's a different profession."

Ignoring my remark, she continued, "Because they thought he was the sorcerer here. You were threatened. And now there's a death threat right there on the shop window. This is where you want to work till midnight," she said in a tone that made it perfectly clear what she thought of my idea.

"You said I'm not important," I said with a small voice.

"To the Sons of Simeon. You're very important to Matthew, and consequently, to me." Her eyes narrowed in suspicion. "Or maybe you're one of those people who think we should provoke confrontations with the Sons of Simeon so everything will blow up and 'that way we can finish them off'?"

I knew too many people who subscribed to that notion. Forrest, for instance. I shook my head.

"You go straight home, get it? And you let Matthew know you've made it there safely." She tapped her tablet again. "Otherwise I'm assigning two officers to keep track of your every move."

"I don't know whether my boss can do without me here," I replied, knowing that it was just an excuse. He could manage, just like he had been doing since I landed in the hospital. Maybe he could get his daughter over to wait tables. It would probably bring in all the customers who hated me; he might even see a profit from it.

Sherry nodded. "I'll wait."

I got out of the car and noticed the crowd had begun to disperse. Remy was offering people coffee on the house. He fell silent as I approached.

I gestured at Sherry. "The cop doesn't want me working today."

"If that's what she said…" Remy wiped the sweat off his forehead. "This thing isn't normal. It's not normal. You have to look after yourself."

It was only then that I realized how much I had wanted him to shrug the incident off, how much I depended on the pretense that nothing was wrong.

"I'll go home." The words came out of my mouth without thinking. "It isn't worth it."

"Daniel's in the hospital, you're leaving–"

"You'll manage perfectly well without me," I said, trying to affect a confident expression. "And Daniel will be back pulling shifts in a few days."

After a little moaning and groaning from Remy, intended to make me feel wanted rather than actually persuading me to stay, I went to inform Sherry that I wouldn't be working there anymore. I wanted to burrow under my blanket in bed and think about Lee, not about how the world had become narrow and menacing.

Remy promised he'd save a spot on the roster. "Once this is all over, I'm hiring you back." I wanted to believe him, but I felt the wave of relief rippling off him as I walked away. I didn't linger around to find out whether he really meant what he said.

I had already left the café when I remembered that I wanted to grab a sandwich and frothy milk for Daniel, and I didn't have the energy to go back. The thought of the empty house awaiting me, dim and locked up, made me miserable. I wandered the streets, letting my thoughts race in circles, looping around the conversation I'd had with Daphne that morning.

Her vision was becoming real, taking form in front of my eyes. I envisioned all my friends wounded, dead. I plodded along with no particular direction in mind, feeling the tension mounting inside me, permeating every crevice. I needed to unwind, to untie the knot in my stomach, but I couldn't calm myself down.

I stopped when I recognized where I was – standing outside Lee's building. I looked up. He lived on the third floor, a rainbow flag with six colors dangling from his windowsill. It wasn't there the last time I had visited. The shades were slightly different from the usual ones; the red too bold, the yellow too faded, the blue and green diffusing into each other. I wondered what emotion was attached to the flag's design, and whether he'd want me to help him inject that emotion into the fabric. I could weave it into the edges if he wanted, so that the emotions would only affect those standing beneath the flag.

"Want a ride?"

Lee's voice jolted me. He was looking rather official in his suit and carefully styled hair. The last time I had seen him he was in a pair of scruffy jeans and a T-shirt.

"What were you thinking about when you designed the flag?" I pointed at it, and added before he managed a reply, "Wait, is there a robot hiding there somewhere?"

"Nope," he smiled and gave me a once-over. "You don't look like you walked only a mile."

I bit my lip.

Lee's expression turned somber. "Come," he said, and gestured to the entrance of his building.

"I don't want you to be late on my account."

"I'm already late." Without waiting for an answer, he walked back into the building he had just emerged from a moment ago.

I followed him. I needed to think of an answer. An adequate reason for being there. I could say I popped by to pick his brain about the books I had to moodify for ArtDot. Or talk to him about making a change in the contract. Or…

My mind was racing again. I made sure my walls were high enough to keep my tension from leaking.

"Water?" he asked while opening the door to his dim apartment.

"No," I said and cleared my throat. "I just wanted to go over the books with you."

"Right," he said skeptically, locked the door behind him and took off his jacket. "Sit."

I hesitated. He peered at me. "You're here in the middle of the morning, and you're blocked as if I'm going to attack you. You need help. Let me help. Sit down."

I sat down. Lee brought two glasses of cold water and loosened his tie.

I picked up my glass and took a sip. I was trying to think how I could recount the story without having to mention the threat or the vandalism, or even the remarks about how Remy had brought it on himself by hiring someone 'like me.' I couldn't put it in words that wouldn't sound dramatic, and I didn't want to turn the threat into my reality. A pesky thought told me it already was my reality. I shooed it away.

My glass was long and narrow, with droplets of water condensing on the outer surface. I dragged my finger down the sides, trapping plump, perfect drops. Lee reached out and caught my hand with one of his long, delicate fingers, his touch gentle.

"There are a few things that could help," he said quietly. "We could try sage. Not what Oleander does, a different kind. It empties your mind of all feelings. Very calming."

"I don't smoke," I quickly said.

"OK, that rules out a few options. I have pills, a few of them aren't half bad. The only problem is that if you're not used to them, they'll wipe you out for the rest of the day. Sound good?" he asked with an arched eyebrow.

"No chemicals," I said. "Would you just," I faltered, my voice trembling, "help me dismantle a bit of my anxiety? Just a little."

"Are you sure? I'm not that good at it."

And it would have forced both of us to lower our walls to more than just a small opening, an idea I wasn't at all confident about. He suddenly seemed so fragile that I felt I was the one comforting him. "I trust you."

Lee took away my glass and lowered it onto the table, his hand perfectly steady. "Ever done this before?"

"A bunch of times. With Daphne. Whenever she has an upsetting vision, or after crowded rallies." When people got killed.

He looked at me and I could feel his tension. Something about how he held his shoulders, avoiding any touch. He even kept his knees pressed against each other, putting more distance between us.

"You just need to find the right knot and unravel it. I'll stop you if it's too much."

Lee nodded, his eyes dark in the dim living room. I slowly lowered my walls. He followed suit. I felt his touch, fluttering, almost imperceptible, snaking inside the curves and bends of my mind.

"Feels nice," I said. Partly to encourage him, but also because it was true.

"It's difficult," he said, smiling while staying focused.

When he reached the source of my tension, I recoiled. "There."

Lee nodded silently. He gingerly touched the knot. I felt him tracking the contours of my feelings, searching for a loose end in the tightly wound coil.

A smile suddenly appeared on his face, vast and unexpected. "Found it."

The sudden relief made me gasp. Lee retreated from my psyche. I closed my eyes and breathed slowly. Inhale. Exhale. Lee placed his hand on mine.

"Everything alright?"

I nodded with my eyes closed. "Terrific." My voice sounded as light as a feather.

Lee pinched me. I opened my eyes. "What?"

He grimaced. "I overdid it."

I brushed my hand across my face. "Yeah." I smiled. "It feels good when someone does it to you."

Once again he beamed with that giant, winning smile of his.

I scooted closer to him. "Keep that up and you'll get a kiss."

He didn't move. "Keep that up and I'll tell your brother that you're my dealer."

I stuck out my tongue. He smiled. I pulled away from him and leaned back on the couch. Lee got up, tightened his tie and picked up his jacket. "Come," he said, reaching out his hand. "I'll give you a ride home. You need some rest."

I took his hand and hoisted myself up. "I'm fine," I said, my head spinning.

Lee supported my weight and started laughing. I leaned against him and he helped me down the stairs and onto his motorcycle. Bright green, a little like his eyes. I wanted to share the observation, but I was flying too high to put a whole sentence together. We made it to my house and Lee walked me in.

"Are you going to tuck me into bed?" I asked as he stepped into my room.

Instead of answering, he swept his gaze across the orange-neon walls. "I've never seen such an ugly color in my life." He pointed at the picture hanging on the wall, a horse galloping against the sunset. "And what's this generic eyesore?" He looked at me, his eyes flickering. "Please tell me you didn't decorate this room yourself."

I held up my hand. "Sorry."

Lee shook his head. "And to think I almost liked you."

"Almost," I said, parroting his headshake.

Lee smiled and pointed at the bed. "You need some help?"

I removed my shoes, took off my shirt and pants and crawled into bed. "Lee?" As I pulled up the blanket I felt the exhaustion hitting me. "Are you doing that?"

"No, it's a side effect, I think." He crouched near the bed and stroked my cheek, brushing the hair off my face. "Thanks for asking for help." He kissed my forehead and I took in the delicate, subtle scent of his aftershave.

"Stay with me." I yawned.

"You need to get some sleep," he said, the softness of his tone suddenly stirring something inside me.

"It was a gift from Daphne," I mumbled and closed my eyes. "Don't think I chose…"

And I fell asleep.

22

Daphne woke me up by hurling a pillow at me. "Get up." She was wearing a tight-fitting outfit, and I faintly sensed her bra digging into her skin.

"Where's Lee?" I yawned. "He was just here."

"Six hours ago," she said, and bent over to pick up the pillow. "And if you don't get out of bed I'll kick you out of it."

I raised my hand in submission. "I'm up, I'm up!"

Once in full possession of my faculties I managed to take a closer look at the change Lee had affected. He really was inexperienced. While he had indeed found the root of my anxiety and disentangled it, he had also unraveled some of my normal tension – the driving force that made me get up in the morning, pull myself together and set off to work.

I wasn't sure how to recreate those knots. I knew they'd eventually fuse back into place even without my interference, and wondered whether it wasn't better to just leave things as they were. I was jobless now anyway. Lee had unraveled so much of my angst that I couldn't even regret that I had sort of gotten fired and my modification work had dried up.

I still felt slightly spaced out. Not completely rooted to the ground. The shower helped me wake up, but not land. When I got out of the bathroom, Daphne was standing there holding a pair of black pants. "Put these on."

"Is something supposed to get spilled on me?"

"Maybe." She winked.

I leaned against the wall behind me and crossed my arms. "What's going on?"

Daphne waited, and when she saw I wasn't moving she leaned on the wall in front of me. "We're going out." Her smile vanished.

"Where to?"

"A party," she replied, her fingers working the edge of her shirt.

"You have work tomorrow morning." Although no one would dare fire Daphne; she wasn't as expendable as I was. Her boss would readily build bunkers to protect Daphne if someone dared threaten her. The capital market couldn't survive without damuses, and Daphne was among the best in her field.

She was quiet.

"I'm sorry I didn't come this morning."

"It's OK. I…" she sighed. "I saw what happened. I also saw your conversation with Sherry. I'm not mad."

"Thanks for understanding." I was still standing with my arms folded across my chest, and realized it might come across as defensive or even aggressive. I lowered them back to my sides. "Why did you change plans? Did something happen?"

"No," she replied, and bit her lip. "I thought about… about afterwards. After the rally. Even if we pull it off, at some point I'll be lying in bed alone, thinking about you, and I want the image in my head to be one of you happy and laughing."

It was the first time I realized it didn't matter what present we were in, I was still going to die before her. A deep chasm of pain exploded inside my chest. I couldn't imagine what her life was like right now, seeing everything that lay ahead of us and still having to go through it, to experience it. I felt the sorrow rippling out of her, and the gentle thread she clung to in order to root herself in the present and not sink into depression.

I took my pants from her. "Are you going to tell me who else is invited?"

"Lee. Matthew. Sherry. Oleander."

"Sherry?" I raised an eyebrow.

Daphne tugged on the hem of her shirt. "I have to talk to her myself. It won't work if…" her voice trailed off.

I put my hand on her shoulder. "Thanks."

We went to a club I'd never heard of before. The sign on the door read 'Everyone is Welcome,' and yet there was still a separate door for us, a bell chiming as we entered.

A few couches were scattered inside, with typical dance music playing in the background. A handful of people were swaying to the beat on the dance floor, their emotions flat and faded.

Lee and River were sitting at the bar, drinking something disturbingly colorful. Blaze was standing next to River, brushing his fingers up and down her back. The bartender was serving a couple standing at the other end of the bar, who were radiating intense confusion. Oleander shot up from behind the bar, holding two bottles of Goldstar. "That's all we have left," he said to Lee. "You don't look like the Goldstar type."

Lee put his hand on my shoulder. "It's not for me."

Oleander glanced at me and shifted his gaze back to Lee. "You two need to have a serious conversation."

Daphne leaned over the bar and kissed Oleander. "Thanks for organizing this."

"You're a bartender?" I raised an eyebrow.

Oleander nodded. "But I'm not working right now, just helping out a friend."

Matthew walked in, Sherry close behind him. They both entered through the white door, and I was flooded by a wave of warmth, tinted with fear. He couldn't keep doing this, not as things stood. Lee tensed beside me. I noticed River was looking rather on edge as well, if not as much as Lee. I wondered if it had anything to do with the police's attitude towards sorcerers in the Confederacy. I wasn't sure how to raise the question. Everyone ordered alcohol. I ordered a Coke, but Lee slammed his fist down on the bar and said that if I wasn't going to drink anything stronger than a Coke, he was going to personally make sure I wouldn't be able to stand up straight by the end of the night. Matthew laughed, and I caved and told Oleander to uncap of one of the Goldstar bottles.

After we all received our drinks, Matthew raised his glass. "So," he said, straining his voice over the music, "what are we celebrating?"

Daphne lifted her glass. "That we're not dead yet."

"I never thought I'd meet anyone more morbid than me," Lee said, holding up his glass. "Here's to us not being dead yet!"

River looked at Lee and raised her glass. "Oh yes, baby!" They exchanged glances, and I felt a deep current passing underneath the seemingly innocuous toast. The memory flooded me all at once. The moment when Matthew walked into my room before I managed to hide the pill bottle, and sat down in front of me, and asked quietly whether to call an ambulance or let go, and promised not to tell our parents whatever choice I made. And I remembered his eyes, wet with tears, his pain submerging me, filling the parts inside me that were depleted of emotion. I swallowed the sadness and hid it where no one could see.

Oleander was the last one to raise his glass. He looked at Daphne, and drank in silence.

After the first round of drinks, Oleander and Daphne retired to a couch in the corner. I felt Lee starting to space out, although he hadn't drunk that much. I wondered whether he was on something. He mumbled something about changing the music and went off in search of the DJ's booth.

Blaze, Sherry and Matthew were deep in conversation about basketball. River and I were the only ones left standing at the bar. She was gazing at her glass. Like me, she had barely touched her drink.

Her silence was unnerving. "Thanks for coming," I said.

She looked up from her glass. "Happy to be here. You mean a lot to Blaze and Lee."

I wasn't sure how to reply to that.

River fixed her gaze back on her glass. "I'm sorry. I keep saying the wrong things." She was nervous, engulfed by a haze of exhaustion.

"Hard day at work?"

She nodded. "Hard day. Hard month." She paused. "It's not your problem. I'm sorry."

"Don't be," I said. "It's nice dealing with other people's problems for a change."

"Oh," she replied. "Like Lee's."

My heart fluttered, but I managed to rein in my emotions quickly enough so that Lee wouldn't notice.

She dragged her finger around the rim of her glass. "It's funny how you guys fail to comprehend such obvious things."

I took a sip of beer. "I comprehend a lot of things."

"You and Lee. You don't get body language. You don't understand what people think. If you can't read a person's feelings, you're lost." She straightened her back. "It's like what happened with Blaze. Lee was convinced everything was fine, that he had him wrapped around his little finger. Instead of pausing to think that maybe, just maybe, if a guy hasn't made a move in two years, he's just not interested." She stopped playing with her glass and pierced me with her eyes. "And you can't read what my brother's projecting in any frequency that isn't this one," she said, pointing at her temple with her index finger. It wasn't the American gesture. She just wanted to signal thought.

"I'm fairly sure that when Lee is interested in anything…" I said, trying to keep my tone lighthearted.

"I'm not talking about sex." Her eyes narrowed. "I'm saying that you're not thinking about your impact on others. You come to my brother, asking for his help, letting him into your psyche, without stopping to consider that maybe it's not good for him."

"If Lee hadn't wanted to help…" My bright and breezy tone had disappeared.

"He wouldn't have said a word," she said cuttingly. "He never does, to anyone. Ever. And I'm the one who has to find him afterwards with…" She paused, panting, and continued in a quieter voice, "I'm only asking that you think before you act."

Lee was swept up in the music. I felt him, calm and distant. "I understand you're worried about your brother…"

"I'm not worried about my brother," she interrupted me. "I'm far past worrying about my brother. I've moved continents, to this miserable humidity of yours, for my brother."

"I thought Blaze wanted to move back here."

River tightened her grip around her glass. "Is that what he told you? Apparently he forgot to mention that Lee suffers from a serious case of ants in his pants and has to move every few months, and that ArtDot was the only one willing to hire a graphic designer who's basically a digital nomad," she spewed all her rage on the empty beer glass in her hand. "So Blaze tells him, 'Move to Israel, it's a lot safer than the Boston Reservation,' and I can't leave him on his own for too long, otherwise…" She finally fell silent.

I tried imagining myself moving continents for Matthew. I wasn't sure I could do it. But if it were the other way around? Matthew constantly found ways to befriend my friends and hang out wherever I lived or worked. He created an entire network that watched over me when he wasn't around. River was also the sibling of an empath.

I looked her straight in the eye. "How many times had he tried to, you know?"

She wiped away tears I hadn't notice until then, and didn't say a word.

I picked up my glass and raised it. "I'll try to hear what he's not saying."

River held up her glass and said, "And not only what he's feeling?"

I nodded and clinked my glass against hers.

We drank in silence.

The music got louder. Lee approached us. "So who's dancing with me?" He had to yell to be heard.

Before I managed to say anything, River put her glass down on the bar with a thud, swiveled around to Lee and said, "Me!" with her giant smile. I knew Lee was picking up the same feelings from her as I was. Stress. Anxiety. Exhaustion. But she jumped off her chair, and he reached his hand out to her.

They were moving together to the beat of the music, exchanging silly gestures that looked like a revisiting of childhood dance moves. I was sure of it, judging by the amused feelings flowing back and forth between them. I tried looking at them without reading them. River's moves had more rhythm to them, smoother. Lee snuck me a glance every now and then, smiling. He wasn't dancing with her like he had danced with me.

Well, she was his sister after all, he wasn't supposed to pin her against him.

But he was looking at me. I drummed on my glass to the rhythm of the music. Lee wanted me to dance with him – a conclusion I had reached without reading him, although it would have taken me a lot less time if I had. I had no idea how people who weren't moodies were able to communicate with one another at all.

It was a nice exercise. I glanced around me. Oleander and Daphne were no longer huddled on the couch. They were dancing, pressed up against each other, Daphne's hands under Oleander's shirt, on the small of his back. I didn't need to feel them to know what they were thinking.

Across the bar, Sherry was keeping her distance from Matthew and Blaze, even though they were all talking to one another. Matthew's gaze wandered every now and then to Oleander and Daphne. He must have been worrying about her. Like me.

Blaze couldn't stop laughing. His glass was empty. It had been his second, maybe third; I had no idea how much was too much for him, but I had no doubt that his laughter was covering up for something. The attempt to figure out what he was feeling without reading him was more difficult than I thought. Every now and then he snuck a glance in Lee and River's direction.

Once in mine. I smiled at him, and he returned the smile. But his was the kind of smile that didn't extend to his eyes. It stopped at his mouth. And when he laughed he didn't slap Matthew on the back, but merely placed a nervous hand on the bar. And now I noticed that it was him keeping his distance from Sherry and not the other way around. He was standing close to Matthew and far from Sherry. Whatever had made Lee and River ooze with tension around Sherry was making Blaze recoil from her. So it was Sherry who was making Blaze nervous, and he was drinking as a means to cope with his anxiety. I had figured it out. Good.

I took a sip from my glass, deciding that being a normal person was too much work.

Lee waved Blaze over to the dance floor, and River shuffled back to the bar, reassuming her post beside me. I felt the tension sluicing out of Blaze; something about the way he held his shoulders, which slouched the moment he turned his back and walked away from Sherry. Sherry knew. I saw it. She was a cop, she must have been used to people not trusting her. And still, she was hurt by Blaze's visible relief when he removed himself from her presence. River was waving her hand in front of my face. I focused on her; she was sweaty, and her smile seemed bigger.

"You OK?"

I nodded. "I was playing at being like you."

"And…?" She focused on her glass, and it filled up with water. I didn't want to know where she had materialized it from. I hoped not from the tap. No one drank tap water in Tel Aviv.

"Exhausting," I remarked, gesturing at Lee and Blaze together on the dance floor. They were dancing at least an arm's length from each other. Now I understood River's previous comment. Blaze clearly wasn't interested in dancing closer to Lee, but Lee was oblivious to this, and persisted in his attempts to wrap his arms around him. However, Lee was already high as a kite, and I wasn't sure how much of his behavior was affected by whatever it was he was on.

"I'm thinking about joining them," I said to River. "If you approve, of course."

River downed her water in two big gulps. "You can dance with Lee. It's too late to try to break you two up even if I wanted to. I'm going to trust you to keep your promise." She sounded like Daphne, but she wasn't a damus. She was just more astute in matters of body language and gestures than me, whereas I had never needed to pay that sort of thing any attention. She lowered her glass onto the bar and smiled a thin, sardonic smile that looked just like Lee's. "But if you touch Blaze, I'll chop off all your limbs, toss them in a bag, bury them and make sure no one ever finds your remains."

"No touching Blaze. Got it."

"Good," she said, beaming with her usual wide smile.

Lee shot me a probing arrow. Instead of answering, I turned to him. He smiled and held out his hand. "Do I get a dance?" His pupils were dilated.

I stepped onto the dance floor, careful not to accidently brush against Blaze. "Depends, is your head still screwed on straight?"

Blaze laughed. He put his hand on my shoulder and said, "Lee can dance even when he's totally wasted."

Lee raised his hand in a saluting gesture. "I dance even better when I'm totally wasted."

I let out a chuckle and approached Lee. Blaze removed his hand from my shoulder and winked at Lee, who ignored him. I stifled a groan. Everyone in this club knew more about the relationship between Lee and me than Lee and me. Great.

Lee lowered his walls as I approached and sent me a warm, enveloping wave, tinged with slight confusion, probably a result of what he had taken. I sent him back an amused wave. It was our language, the only one we understood, and all the rest could keep settling for body gestures. Lee wrapped his arms around me. He was sweaty, singing along with the music. I stepped close enough to feel him breathe. I stopped thinking and let my body move on its own. Lee pierced me with his gaze and smiled, which made him miss a line in the song, after which he got mixed up when he tried to catch up with the rest of the lyrics. I laughed.

I felt the conversation behind me resume. River and Blaze started dancing, while Oleander and Daphne left the dance floor for another drink. Sherry laughed intermittently and flicked her hair back. It was short and black, cut just above her jawline. She wasn't pretty. Her nose was too big and her clothes drab, just a simple T-shirt and pants. And yet, as the evening progressed, Matthew stopped sneaking glances at Daphne and shifted his attention to her. Their foreheads almost touched as they spoke over the loud blare of the loudspeakers.

"You're wearing a plain T-shirt," Lee almost yelled into my ear, tearing my thoughts away from Matthew.

"Sorry," I replied, pressing into him. He smelled of aftershave and sweat and the faint scent of alcohol. "I don't have any robot shirts."

Lee smiled. "You want one?"

Standing so close to each other, I knew he could feel the wave suddenly spilling out of me. Before I could say anything he held up his finger and said, "But you have to show me what you did to my shirt."

I nodded. Lee smiled, and we trailed back to the bar. He pulled a double-tipped black marker from his back pocket, took a napkin, smoothed it out and looked at me. "What do you want?"

I shrugged. "I'm not really a robot expert."

Lee chuckled. "Neither am I." He sent me some of his lightheadedness. I felt my brain being swathed in cotton balls, muffling the outside. He took a deep breath and smiled at me.

I returned the smile.

He smoothed the napkin again and took the cap off the narrower edge of the marker. "I think…" he said slowly, "something pretty."

"Pretty would be pretty nice." My words came out slurred. I sat beside Lee, almost missing the barstool. He giggled and took back some of my floating sensation into himself. "If you can't handle it, don't take it," he said loudly. I put my head on his shoulder and my hand on his thigh.

Lee cleared his throat. "Something pretty it is," he said, and I felt the tension building inside him. "Something pretty for Reed, who's distracting me right now and I can't concentrate."

I lifted my head and looked at him.

He smiled. "Put your head back where it was, and don't disturb the artist." I could barely hear him over the music.

I laughed, sidling up closer to him and resting my hand on his shoulder. Dipping his shoulder to make me more comfortable, he began doodling on the napkin. The world was light and warm, and there was nothing I wanted more than for that moment to last.

"Should I take some more from you?" he whispered in my ear.

I shook my head. "I like it like this," I said, and hoped he heard me. The music had become louder. I let myself be swept up by the melody. The walls seemed to be moving. I wondered what exactly Lee was on, and how much it was affecting me.

I felt his hand moving as he drew, and his body gradually relaxing as his drawing took shape. I wanted to know what he was drawing for me, but I didn't dare look before it was finished. I felt someone entering the club. I looked at him. He was radiating calmness in soft waves, but it was too dark to make him out.

The newcomer didn't head to the bar, but kept standing at the entrance, surveying the room. Daphne and Oleander hit the dance floor again. River and Blaze were drinking and laughing. Matthew and Sherry sat at the bar, fragments of their conversation drifting in my direction between songs. There were others in the club, dancing to the music. The bartender was levitating paper balls, making a woman giggle. I couldn't count the balls. Whatever Lee had taken, it was certainly affecting me. I wanted to give him back some of the lightheadedness he had sent me, but I couldn't concentrate enough.

Something about the man who had entered the bar felt off. I straightened to examine his silhouette, dark against the red lights glowing around him.

His movements were incongruous with the waves drifting out of him. He felt calm, peaceful, but his shoulders were tense, and the gaze he swept across the room was full of intent. He was obviously searching for someone. I couldn't focus; no single thought stayed in my head long enough to be contemplated. I sent back the rest of my lightheadedness to Lee, and heard him curse when the wave broke his concentration.

"There!" Lee exclaimed and lifted the napkin. "What do you think?"

Lee's gesture caught the man's attention. He was looking straight at me. I blanched inwardly, and immediately reprimanded myself. I was being paranoid. If something dangerous was about to happen, Daphne would have alerted us. He stuck his hand in his pocket and smiled at me with thin, pursed lips. The lights flickered. Now I recognized him. I had seen him only this morning. It was the customer from the café. Daphne's knees buckled and she staggered into Oleander's arms.

He pulled a gun out of one pocket and a barrel out of the other, linked the two in one swift stroke and aimed it at me. No. He wasn't aiming at me. He was aiming at Sherry. Stop him. I have to stop him. I wanted to call out to her, to shout. The music was too loud. She wouldn't hear me.

I had to stop him. There was no time. Empaths don't maneuver sorcerers, but a stranger was pointing a gun at Sherry, and by the time she took notice it would be too late.

I maneuvered Blaze, full thrust. I felt his consciousness around me and stirred a feeling of panic in the gun's direction. I felt his fire sizzling before he himself had realized the cause. I maneuvered River in the same direction, and felt her bubbling in response, forging a puddle.

Last but not least, the bartender who was levitating paper balls. I maneuvered him towards the music, heightening his sensitivity until he could bear the volume no more and stopped the sound waves, at which point I yelled out, "Sherry! Gun!"

The customer fired. Sherry turned around. Blaze set fire to the bullets mid-air, and they exploded. River enveloped the bullets in water, giant bubbles that trapped the shrapnel.

Sherry was still rooted in her spot. Four bullets had been fired, and I was afraid more would follow. Daphne collapsed in the middle of the room, with Oleander barely able to hold onto her.

Empaths don't maneuver sorcerers, and certainly not other empaths. I was hoping Lee would forgive me. I extracted all the blurriness out of his head and planted it in the gunman. When enough of Lee's mind had cleared, he realized what I was doing. I felt him maneuvering beside me, numbing the stranger's mind into oblivion. He was more experienced in that particular emotion than me, and the shooter fell to the ground.

The gun went off again, the bullet hitting a chair; splinters flew every which way. A woman screamed. One of the people on the dance floor slumped to the ground, legs spread out, utterly pale. His two dance partners kneeled beside him, trying to calm him down.

Sherry got up, tense. Matthew stood next to her, clutching his arm. I ran over to him.

"I'm fine," he said in answer to a question I hadn't asked. I made him move his arm. "It's just a scratch," he said. But it wasn't. It was a big bloody gash where a shard of wood had torn into his arm. I dabbed the blood with a napkin from the bar, overcoming the temptation to take away some of his pain and absorb it myself. Someone had switched off the music. My ears were ringing in the sudden silence.

Sherry crouched over the unconscious man. She looked at me. "Your doing?"

"Ours," I said. Lee approached us slowly, still holding the napkin with the drawing on it.

Daphne was on the floor in the middle of the room, black waves drifting out of her towards me. A vision. She was trapped in a vision. I felt Oleander, calm and clearheaded. He was a damus, he'd know what to do. He'd take care of Daphne.

"I didn't feel anything from him," I said. "I don't understand it."

Everyone was looking at me. They knew what I had done. I was engulfed by a feeling of disgust. I didn't bother isolating its source. They knew I had maneuvered them. The *why* didn't matter. It made no difference that people would have died if I hadn't done it. They were angry at me anyway, and with just cause. At least this time it wasn't an entire bar crowd.

Blaze was standing beside me. "A moody must have dismantled him before he walked in." His voice sounded flat in the silence of the room. "After you dismantle them, it takes time for the feelings to regenerate. They come back slowly. It's not like with normal feelings. Don't you remember? How I always told you I felt safe around you?"

I nodded, the memory flitting before me. Blaze lying in my bed, in my childhood room at my parents' house, naked, smiling at me with outstretched arms. "Come here already!" he said when I tried to fashion an amateurish, makeshift barrier. "If anyone walks in on us, I'll burn him." I laughed so hard I could barely keep standing.

"So that's why. Because you always dismantled my fear, and it would take hours until it came back." There was distinct guilt in his voice, along with a faint note of longing underneath.

I had done no wrong by maneuvering him back then. He had let me. And yet, I shrank as he recounted it in front of everyone.

Matthew cleared his throat. "It never happened to me."

I looked him straight in the eye and said, "I don't touch you. Or Mom, or Dad."

"How come Daphne didn't stop him? Or Oleander?" Lee asked. He only sounded calm and rational; his fear was leaking through every crack in his walls.

River snapped her fingers. "Divergence!"

We all stared at her. "An unforeseeable divergence," she said, as if that explained it.

Sherry held up a hand. "Slower, please." Her voice was low, clear.

River wiped her hands on her skirt, her one telltale sign of stress. "A last-minute decision. If someone decides what's going to happen ahead of time, seers can pick up on the course of events and change it."

Sherry was nodding slowly. "And if he decides only seconds before acting, it would be too late to prevent the divergence. Brilliant," she said.

"There's no way they could pull that off on their own," Matthew said, folding his arms across his chest. "They probably have collaborators on the police force."

"There are no collaborators in my unit," Sherry remarked pointedly. "And yet, this shit is here." She kicked the shin of the passed-out stranger. She looked at me. "Good thing you didn't stay at the Sinkhole today. Who knows how it would have ended."

My head started pounding. I could barely think. I needed to lean on someone. The person standing closest to me was Blaze, but I could feel he didn't want me near him. I'd never maneuvered him without asking permission before. Poking around his feelings, I felt the deep sense of betrayal. The loss and distrust seeping into him. He took a step back, averting his gaze.

Sherry wasn't scared. She was filled with purpose, calm and collected. How on earth was she able to take in this information so easily? Or maybe she had already guessed it was so, and this was just another piece of the puzzle she had begun to put together. She kneeled by the stranger on the ground, flipped him over, took a photograph of his face and of the gun in his hand. "How long will he be like this?" She looked at Lee. "What did you take?"

Lee just stared at Sherry, crumpling the napkin in his hand.

"Let's try again. When this man walked into the room I clearly saw he was on something before he pointed the gun at me. What did he take?"

"Datura and belladonna," Lee replied, thrusting his chin in defiance. No one said a word. The combination sounded hardcore. I knew that for normies it induced hallucinations. I had no idea how Lee had fine-tuned the affect so that we would experience mostly a floating sense of calm.

Lee was avoiding my gaze. He walked over to the bar, stood beside Blaze and downed a glass of water. River went to hug him. Blaze stood quietly beside the two siblings, staring at the wooden surface of the countertop. I heard people murmuring around us. Matthew examined the stranger on the floor. Sherry started collecting information from the people who stayed at the pub. Names. ID numbers. Contact information.

"You get it?" River was saying to Lee, her voice loud enough to be heard over the crowd's murmurs. "We're talking monumental collaboration here. Like with the KKK."

"That makes no sense," Lee replied. "Back home it's a movement that sprang out of the craziness of '65. Here it's something new."

"So they're copying ideas that have already proven themselves," Blaze said, reason suddenly dissipating his fear. "Because I'm telling you, these Sons of Simeon weren't around when I left."

Of course they'd been around. But when we were young they were only active in the settlements, places where there was little to no enforcement anyway. They pervaded central Israel when I was studying at university. I had a vivid memory of my conversation with Ivy about them, when she spoke of a new, clean world, one that had true equality. She almost managed to convince me to join. "They're just trying to make the world better," she said, "just look at their vision, feel a bit of what they're offering." But Daphne had warned me that it was a decision from which there was no going back. The more I thought of Ivy, the angrier I became. If Blaze and River were right, the Sons of Simeon weren't only killing us in order to fulfill their damuses' vision, but also using moodies to make sure their murderers couldn't be found, as if we were in the Middle Ages.

A crushing wave of pain coming from Oleander broke my train of thought. I edged out the memories and rushed towards him, my temples beginning to throb. Daphne was looking at me, her eyes dark.

I reached out and brushed the hair from her eyes.

"I can't pull her out of it," Oleander said.

"You want to tell me what you saw?" I asked Daphne quietly.

Her worry condensed around me, as tangible as the room we were standing in. I felt her roiling wave drowning out the background noise. She was deep inside the vision, submerged by the pain it was inflicting on her. It was no ordinary vision. It was a flooding one. She seldom had those. Seers who had more than five a year were hospitalized in restricted wards, sedated into a stupor.

Daphne was there, with me, but she was also nowhere. She was the vision, and nothing more. She hated them, and I hated them for taking my soulmate away from me. My funny Daphne with the crazy curls. I needed help. I shot Lee a short arrow. He sent back a wave of shriveling anger.

But Daphne.

I shot him another arrow of pleading, and directed his consciousness to Daphne.

Lee approached and kneeled beside me. "Now you remember to ask?"

"Help me pull her out. Please."

Lee nodded.

I put my hands on Daphne's cheeks. "I'm going to help you out a little." I didn't know whether she could even hear me. It was impossible to stop a flooding vision. You could only deal with the aftermath.

I tore off a tiny, almost imperceptible piece of the blackness surrounding her and absorbed it into myself.

"Don't absorb it," Lee said in a reserved tone. "You won't be able to wake up tomorrow."

"You've got a better idea?" I asked him, stroking Daphne's cheek, unable to think of a solution, feeling her sadness increasing as the vision progressed.

Lee suddenly flashed his thin smile. "Shall we do this the American way? What do you say?"

That I'd maneuvered too many people already. That I was exhausted and sick to my stomach from maneuvering sorcerers. But it was Daphne, and the stranger on the floor had just injured my brother. I melted the piece of Daphne's depression into the mind of an unconscious man. My own psyche felt slightly lighter. Next to me, I felt Lee doing the same.

Oleander was gaping at us. "You're maneuvering him without consent."

"Then what do you suggest? It's either this or waiting until Daphne comes out of her vision in a day, or week, or a month, or however long it takes."

Oleander lowered his gaze silently.

Working in tandem to dismantle Daphne's depression was more effective. Lee and I toiled until my back turned to stone and my feelings diffused into Daphne's pain.

Daphne was focusing on me, and hadn't yet said a word. Tears were pooling in the corners of her eyes.

I was panting with effort. We were close. We could pull her out now. The psyche of the man sprawled on the floor was almost flooded. Lee continued to transfer chunks of Daphne's depression into him.

I put my hand on his arm. "Enough."

"No," he said, and clenched his jaw. "The motherfucker deserves it. Piece of shit. Trying to shoot our…" He wrenched out another piece, bigger this time, and sent it to the comatose man.

Matthew crouched down beside us and put his hand on Daphne's wrist. "What are you guys doing?"

"Maneuvering depression into the guy who got your arm all bloody," I replied, depleted of emotion.

"You're killing him," Oleander said with a horrified tone. I couldn't feel him over Daphne's whirlwind of emotions.

"Reed isn't killing anyone," Matthew said, shooting me a look, "right?"

Lee said, "This asshole is going to want to die when he wakes up tomorrow, and he won't quit trying until he pulls it off. And nothing's going to stop him."

"Because it isn't his emotion," I said, maintaining a clear, quiet voice. "So it doesn't change like organic feelings. It's a borrowed emotion. It intensifies and takes longer to get rid of without help."

Sherry approached and stooped beside us. "Want to let me in on what's going on here?"

"We're debating the hypothetical question of how this asshole's going to end his life tomorrow. Maybe slash his wrists?"

Sherry gave a smile that sent shivers down my spine. "He won't end it. He'll be in handcuffs, and whatever you guys are maneuvering into him right now will be dismantled by my officers."

Lee's smile withered. "That's a shame."

Sherry shook her head. "I didn't say when we'll start dismantling those feelings."

Lee's smile reappeared. Matthew stared at her with appalled silence.

Sherry looked straight at me. "We're going to need you to fill out a full incident report." She then shifted her gaze to Lee. "And it's a real shame you left when I wasn't looking, which is why we don't have any urine and saliva samples from you." She raised an eyebrow. Lee understood. He nodded silently. Sherry put her hand on Daphne's shoulder and looked at me. "Tell me when she feels better."

"I don't think I'll be feeling any better," Daphne said, her voice lucid, clear. "That's it. That's the course. It took me some time to figure out what I was seeing. Now I know what you did that got you killed."

"But I'm not dead," I blurted, choking back the panic. "Look, I'm perfectly alive. He wasn't even aiming at me."

"Now they're going to kill you."

Lee was breathing slowly. Panic was taking over me. Matthew silently tightened his grip around Daphne's wrist.

"I should have seen it beforehand, but I was with Oleander, and after the rally–" Daphne paused, shaking her head and closing her eyes. "I killed you. Lee and I killed you."

"You didn't kill me," I said, raising my voice. I held her hand and placed it against my chest. "Daphs, look. Look at me."

Daphne opened her eyes. Huge. Black. She was moving in a different world; a medium that slowed down all her movements. "It was only a few injuries, people wounded. Now it's just you. You want to be a hero, so you sacrifice yourself to save someone else." Daphne turned to Lee. "You get it, right? You know. Your reflections understand it, so you do too."

Lee cleared his throat. "What do you mean?"

Daphne looked at him. "That's not what you're supposed to ask. You ask what choice Reed made."

Lee didn't answer. Daphne shifted her gaze back to me. "When you met. And he asked for coffee. And you brought it to him. I should have warned you. I should have said something. But I was so absorbed in my own life, my own pain, and I wasn't looking. I didn't see. I see it now. But it's too late."

"That's not what I asked." Lee sounded choked up. "So you're wrong. Just like you're wrong when you say he gets killed because of me."

Daphne looked at me. "Now you ask me if I'm sure, and I say I am, and Lee starts crying." She turned to him, Lee's face an impervious mask. "That won't help, you know. We both know we killed Reed. All your reflections are saying it."

Matthew let out a stifled moan. His grief cascaded over me in a single gushing wave. Daphne's eyes were fixed on me. "Should I explain?"

I shook my head. I could see now the trail she was talking about. "If I hadn't brought Lee his coffee, I wouldn't have landed that job at ArtDot, and we wouldn't have connected, and wouldn't have ended up here, and I wouldn't have intercepted this guy's plan." I gestured at the man sprawled on the floor. "And now they've singled me out. Now I have a bullseye on my back. Up until now they were planning on hurting everyone at the rally, just general mayhem. Now they're going to target me specifically. That's what you're saying, right?"

"No," Sherry said, her voice as quiet as Daphne's, but where Daphne's had been steeped in depression, hers was distinctly determined. "You're not important enough. If they wanted to get you, they would have done it this morning."

"So why is Daphne seeing me dead?" I asked, proud of myself for managing a steady tone.

"Because you're going to try to get in their way, and they won't have a choice but to get rid of you," Sherry said. "You have a tendency to put yourself in the line of fire."

"So he just won't. Right?" Matthew asked, his grief crashing into me. "You'll stay home. That's it. Let someone else march, or… I don't know. Whatever it is." He looked at Daphne. "It's just a probability, right? It's not like it happens for sure." His eyes were welling up.

"So close? It's a high probability," Sherry said in a low and strangled voice. I felt an old pain resurfacing inside her.

"No. No," Matthew's voice cracked, "this can't be true…" Lee leaned in, narrowing the gap between them, and placed his hand on Matthew's shoulder.

"They're not targeting Reed," Lee said sternly. "You said so yourself. We'll protect him. Reed won't try to be a hero and I'll go in his place. That should do it." He looked at Sherry. "Right? You'll enlist your damuses, and you guys will find a way to fix this." He was clenching his jaw. I didn't need to read his determination.

Sherry shifted her gaze from him to Matthew and back to him. "Right," she said. "We'll find out what changed, and solve this." Lee and I were the only ones who could sense the pain inside her.

Lee lowered his hand from Matthew's shoulder, leaving him looking forlorn and dazed. Lee sent me a perfectly clear, round ball of calm and tranquility. "It's all I've got left," he said quietly. "I think you need it more than I do right now."

He got up and turned towards the exit. I wanted to rush after him, but Daphne grabbed my arm, stopping me. Sherry walked after Lee. I followed them with my gaze. The man was still passed out on the floor, his hands and feet cuffed. River ran after Lee; he said a few brief words to his sister, and she turned back.

Oleander was staring at me. I wondered how much of Daphne's vision he had seen.

Daphne held her arms open, and for once it was my head on her shoulder, comforted by her embrace, and not the other way around. Matthew touched my back, and then it was him hugging me. I felt the tremor of his sobs on my back, and then heard Blaze and River whispering to each other. River was saying something about Lee, and Blaze was silencing her. I closed my eyes, uncontrollable tears pouring out of them.

I heard Sherry in the background calling in her report. Something about the make of the gun, and the device the sorcerer had mounted onto the barrel. I was too flustered to listen, and couldn't gain my bearings. There were too many things going on and not enough time.

23

The following morning I couldn't pull myself out of bed. I felt the remnants of Daphne's depression swimming inside me, all those parts we hadn't transferred to the cuffed man. My mind was marred with dark blotches, and I had to remind myself that it wasn't my depression. That it was an external effect. It would pass. I'm fine. I'm not depressed. My head was throbbing so excruciatingly that every move shot bolts of pain from a different, unexpected part of my body.

I had a text from Gaia. *I heard nothing happened anywhere last night, expect for a little rioting. Were you involved in anything?*

There are sorcerers trying to kill us, and I'm going to die. *Everything's OK, don't worry. How are your neurons doing?*

I got a ninety-three on my physics summer term exam. It's going to screw up my avarage!

I had the feeling she misspelled the last word on purpose. *Sounds like you won't be winning any spelling bees either.*

What can I do. Maibe I go stody art.

I sent her a smiley. The app claimed she was typing, but nothing appeared. She must have reread her reply over and over before sending it.

Aurora said you'll be our counselor this year.

It's a shame no one had come up with a way to convey emotions in texts. I could imagine her impassive expression, the attempt not to betray her feelings.

Correct, I replied.

Good, she wrote, and after a moment added, *Just remember who called you a geezer first.*

I smiled.

My phone rang. Lee's name flashed on the screen.

"I wanted to see how Daphne was doing."

She was curled up in her room, dissolving into sobbing fits, flooding me with uncontrollable waves of pain. Every now and then Oleander would come out of his room to ask me to take away some of his pain, so he could support Daphne, which just exacerbated the depression that had already begun to settle inside me.

"She's fine." I rubbed my eyes. "And you?"

"Perfect." His sarcasm was leaking through the phone. "I also wanted to... check on you. Because yesterday... it's still affecting me."

I lay supine on the bed staring at the ceiling, at the border splotched with the color of the wall. "What would you like to hear?"

"That you're OK." He sounded broken down, beaten.

"Perfect." I tried to sound casual, unencumbered. Lee didn't laugh. I sighed quietly. "I'm coping."

"If you want–" he faltered. "I have a few..."

"No," I said, harsher than I had intended. "I'll deal with it without–" I was searching for words that wouldn't offend him. "Without external help. I'm used to it. This isn't the first flooding vision she's had." The last one had been over five years ago, and involved her mother's death. She knew the treatment would fail two months before her mother was even diagnosed.

"So it's business as usual?"

"Yes, please." Without drugging me up and without taking me to places where my brother gets injured. I quickly sat up. "Damn."

"What is it?" Panic filtered into Lee's voice.

"I need to go to the police station, give Sherry a report." It was ten am and hot, and I didn't want to schlep around on buses; I already felt sticky and gross enough.

"Is it safe for you to leave the house?"

That was one question I actually had an answer for. "What Daphne saw happens at a rally. Rallies only take place at the beginning of the month. So, it's not going to happen today." Daphne didn't know which rally it would be, or why I would find myself at a rally when I knew my life would be at stake there, but at least I knew it wasn't on the cards for me today.

"I could give you a ride to the station if you want," Lee said, his voice tapering off into a whisper. As if there was any chance I'd pass on a ride to a police station that was three buses away from my house.

"I'd really love that." Then I remembered another thing. "You still have that napkin from last night?"

"Yes."

"Could you bring it?" I was curious to know what he had drawn for me.

"It didn't come out that great, it's all crooked."

I shrugged, even though Lee couldn't see me. "Bring it anyway, OK?"

"Sure." I couldn't read his feelings over the phone.

Lee promised to be at my place within a few minutes, after he got ready. I was surprised he was still at home.

We were out of hot water again, and I grumbled and moaned from the moment I stepped into the shower until I shut the door behind me. Oleander and Daphne had fallen back asleep. I considered texting Matthew, but decided against it. Had I done so, it would have broken his concentration and he wouldn't be able to keep drowning his feelings in his work.

Lee arrived half an hour later. His migraine started pulsating in my head as he approached the door. So that's why he hadn't gone to work. I was wondering whether it was a belated effect of what he had taken last night, or of the depression we had dismantled.

My own head was throbbing, and I felt a lot weaker than usual. But I had maneuvered four people to his one.

He held out his hand when I opened the door. He was unshaven, and there was no print on his T-shirt for a change. I started searching for an emotional wave to send him, until I noticed the crumpled napkin in his hand.

"Let's get it over with," he said, eyes sullen and unyielding, and handed me the napkin.

I looked him in the eye. "This is the first time anyone has drawn me something. Even if it's just a crooked doodle, it still makes me very happy."

Lee exhaled slowly, his features softening. He slightly lowered one of his walls and sent me gratitude. I smiled at him and sealed my walls, blocking him out.

He raised an eyebrow.

"That way I can fake admiration," I said, and looked down at the napkin.

Lee had drawn me a small kneeling robot holding out a childish heart. It wasn't an anatomical sketch of a heart, but the kind kids draw, puffy and cute. I couldn't take my eyes off the drawing. I could make out the places where his pen had quivered, a result of the mush-like state of his brain last night. The emotion was clear and simple.

Any thought about Daphne's vision faded at the sight of this drawing.

I was conscious of Lee's shallow breaths beside me; I had to remind myself to breathe normally. I didn't trust my expression. If I showed too much emotion, it would scare him off. He'd bolt, or burrow behind his walls. I spread out the napkin and carefully inserted a little of what I was feeling. The paper was tissue thin, and the pen had nicked it in a few places. I had to work around the holes so that the feelings wouldn't drip through them. I injected gentleness, affection and tenderness into the frail paper, and tied the edges. The emotions were only readable on one side of the napkin; the paper could have disintegrated if I had tried injecting them into both.

Without looking up, I reached out and unclenched Lee's tight fist, then placed the open napkin in his hand. His breathing settled. I lifted my head and peered into his eyes, engulfed in their green.

He cleared his throat. "What do we do with this?"

Instead of replying, I took a step closer and kissed him. Slowly. Giving him every chance to run away, to retreat, but feeling his arms wrapping around me. He brushed his fingers through my hair and pressed me into him. I hugged him and slid my hands under his shirt. He was sweating, his skin warm beneath my fingertips. My feelings glided into Lee, and I felt him fusing his feelings with mine. His were centered around passion and need. Mine were a mix of warmth and tenderness.

I broke away from him and he whispered, "No," but released me from his embrace. We remained close. Lee mumbled to himself, "Why have I only found you now? It's not fair."

I wanted another kiss. I wanted much more than a kiss, but couldn't put my desire into words.

Stepping back, Lee opened the door behind him. "Come, let's go file a complaint, or whatever people do in this country."

He put on his helmet and handed me a light blue one. I scanned it, searching for a robot, but found only an illustration of a withered rose.

"Let's go. The quicker we get this over with, the quicker we can come back and get into bed. Or we could stay standing. Whatever you're into," he said, and winked.

"We could do both." I returned the wink and he laughed. Strapping on a helmet, I sat behind him on the motorcycle, holding onto his waist. He kept his walls lowered, and we exchanged emotional blasts throughout the ride. Not too strong, not enough to render him unable to steer, but enough to leave him flushed and panting when we arrived, like me.

Lee parked and pulled off his helmet. "You need me to go in with you?" The tension had crept into his voice all at once.

"You don't have to." I climbed off the motorcycle and stood beside him. "I can see it makes you uneasy."

"Cops…" He pursed his lips. "I'd rather keep my distance from them."

"I get it." I put my hand on his, and sent him a condensed wave of passion.

He narrowed his eyes. "It's not fair."

"I'm just thinking," I said slowly, dragging out the words, "that if there's a long wait, we might…"

"What have I gotten myself into?" Lee said, curving his lips into a little smile.

I smiled. "Don't worry, it'll be over before you know it."

A small wave of loss managed to make it across Lee's walls. He quickly raised them back up and said, "Good, I don't think I could handle too much of you."

I had to kiss him. In the middle of the street, while he was still on his bike and I already had my feet on the ground, to feel his breath caught in response to the wave I had sent him.

When we detached from each other, he got off the bike, locked it and stowed away his helmet in the seat storage compartment. He slid his arms around my waist. "You're too short," he remarked. "I've never dated anyone more than three inches shorter than me."

"How much would that be in centimeters?" We started calculating and from there got to size comparisons in general, with me trying to defend short men, and Lee easily dismissing me with examples of football players he knew.

In accordance with the Public Sector Equality Duty Act, the entrance to the police station wasn't segregated, but there were two guards standing at the gate, a normie and a woman who emanated sorcery. Her nametag stated that she belonged to the security department and that her name was Manny. I wondered if it was her first or last name. "Where to?" She lifted her hand, palm out, fingers spread upward. A pyro. To anyone else it would have simply seemed the gesture of a security guard.

I touched my temple with my middle finger, pretending to scratch my head.

"Sherry Yakov," Lee said, and I felt his body tense. He raised his hand and tucked his hair behind his ear, completing the intimation by turning his palm outwards. It was the American gesture. Manny shot me a look.

"Tourist," I said, and tightened my grip around Lee's waist.

The security guard gestured to a small side room. "Start there."

We walked into the station, arms still tucked around each other. Lee sent me a small but very condensed wave of fear. I pulled him closer to me.

An officer was sitting in the small room. His badge read that he, Shmueli – that had to be his last name – was also a member of the security department. He gestured towards the chairs in front of him, palm down, fingers mimicking a wave-like motion. A splasher. Or an ariel, as Gaia would have called him. His dark hair receded in two large tufts on either side of his head, turning gray at the sideburns.

This time Lee remembered the correct gesture. We sat down, and Shmueli handed me a long form in small print, exuding poorly executed sorcery. Instead of frightful or anxious, it just made me nauseous and dizzy. "You need a better moodifier," I said.

Shmueli shrugged. "Police budget." He handed a similar form to Lee, who didn't even pretend to read it, just stared at me.

The sorcerer leaned back in his chair. "It's a consent form stating that you grant us permission to administer a neutralizing substance, and that you won't do anything, and blah blah blah."

"Blah?" Lee raised an eyebrow.

Shmueli leaned in and said, "You want to be allowed in? This is what you have to do."

I took the pen and signed on the dotted line. Lee held his pen in the air, wavering.

The officer interlaced his fingers. "It's a standard form. You've got nothing to worry about." He was emitting a faint, menacing threat. I wondered whether sorcerers on the force learned to control the feelings they project. I'd heard rumors, but they were never corroborated. "Another option is assigning you a chaperone damus. Any funny business and he'll shut you down before you know it."

I put down the pen and looked at him. "Maybe you could give it to me first, so he'll see what it does?"

Shmueli opened his desk drawer, took out a rattling bottle and fished out one white pill. It looked a little like an aspirin. He handed me the pill along with a glass of water. I swallowed it, and a few moments later felt my sorcery draining, the feelings around me ebbing; first the officer's feelings, then Lee's. A thick gray partition stood between me and the world. It was temporary. It would pass. This wasn't what they used to do to us in the Middle Ages. This wasn't even what they said the Sons of Simeon wanted to do to us. It was just temporary.

"Are you neutralized too?" I asked Shmueli, trying to take my mind off the fact that the world had just been hidden from me.

"Are you crazy? I have to work."

Lee leaned back in his chair. "So what do they do to make sure…?"

"A damus." He didn't need to explain. The color was draining from Lee's face. The mere thought of a damus watching my every move sent a shiver down my spine.

"Why would you put up with that?"

"It's a living. You show up in the morning, do your eight hours, and go home. I make in one shift more than the two of you make in a week." Shmueli was playing with the pill box. "It's a job. Like any job." His voice trailed off.

It wasn't like any other job. I could only imagine what they thought about us on the force. How they treated us. The same as everywhere else. We were hated, and feared.

Lee shifted his gaze between me and the cop, and lifted his pen.

"Where do I sign?"

I looked at him. "You don't have to, it's OK."

He kept his eyes on the form, searching for the dotted line at the bottom. "I don't have to, I want to."

I didn't ask why. I felt a warm surge of gratitude, and Lee smiled without looking at me. After he took the pill, Shmueli handed us a green form devoid of emotional design; it was the pill's information sheet, including the duration of its effect. "Show it to anyone who asks. Don't get caught around here without it." This time there was nothing subtle about his threat.

We walked out of the room holding hands.

Walking with Lee without being able to feel him wasn't easy for me; relying only on his words and body language. Holding hands was a positive sign. The fact that his body was rigid and he barely said a word – not so positive.

A clerk led us to Sherry's room. It was on the second floor, behind a sign that read 'Interrogations.' We sat down on the bench in front of her room. The clerk knocked on the door, and Sherry stepped out to greet us.

"It'll take me at least another fifteen minutes." She glanced at her watch. "Can you wait?"

"Sure," I said, trying to sound nice about it.

She returned to her room.

Lee looked at me. "Fifteen minutes." He ran his hand down my thigh.

I put my hand on his. "Come."

We found the bathroom at the end of the corridor, a relatively clean room with two lockable doors. Our lips met even before I made sure the outer door was locked, and I felt Lee locking it while I reached for his zipper.

It started well, but neither of us managed to hold back for long, and it all ended too quickly.

Afterwards, I was leaning against the door, our zippers opened, my shirt slightly hiked up so I could feel Lee's skin against mine.

"That was nice," Lee whispered in my ear and kissed me.

"This is the first time I've been with someone without knowing what he felt in the process," I whispered into his shoulder.

Lee took a step back and looked into my eyes. "You're disappointed."

"No," I blurted out too quickly.

"Sorry, I… next time it'll be better," he said quietly, "if you want there to be a next time."

I shoved him and zipped up my pants. "You're an idiot."

Lee was pulling up his own zipper, avoiding my gaze. I held his chin and forced him to look at me. "It was perfectly fine." I kissed him. "From here we can only get better."

Lee kissed me back, a long, deeper kiss that lasted until I ran out of breath.

"OK." He smiled, his eyes twinkling. "Remember you could have run away."

I touched his nose. "Why would I want to run away?" I brushed my hand across his cheek, down the jawline.

He grabbed my hand and pressed it against his cheek. "Because I'm not much of a catch." He kissed my hand. I felt my heart shrink. He didn't believe I wanted him. How could he not see it, after I had woven so many emotions into his napkin drawing? I couldn't find the right words to say, and I couldn't send him an emotional wave.

We stepped out right into the scrutinizing gaze of some cop sitting in front of the bathroom. Lee flashed her his wide smile, held my hand and dragged me along. I giggled as we approached the bench opposite Sherry's office.

Lee sat down. "What?"

"Why would I want anyone else?" I sat down and put my head on his shoulder. He hugged me. I felt him pressing his lips to my head, his body going slack. I closed my eyes.

Almost half an hour went by before Sherry called us in. It was a drab room painted a sickly yellow, a color Lee would have surely pinned some degrading name to. Sherry's desk was green and piled with folders, documents, stamps, paper cups filled with coffee dregs and desiccated teabags, and one ancient computer screen perched in the corner.

"We were told to give you this," I said, sat down and handed Sherry the green document.

Sherry sighed. "I don't get these stupid protocols. I mean, really, what are two empaths going to do, make everyone high?" She didn't use the slang term. It suddenly dawned on me that she almost always used the official terms, and I wondered whether she was just the formal type or whether there was another reason.

"Empaths can cause harm," Lee said, and wove his fingers together.

Sherry picked up her pen and pointed it at Lee. "As history proves, whenever an empath caused damage – he paid for it." She started listing with her fingers, "Richard Laurence, Sergey Kirov, von Stauffenberg…"

"Samuel Byck," Lee interrupted her, "Griselio Torresola …"

"Never heard of any of them," I said.

Sherry looked at Lee. "They don't teach anything in today's schools."

"Sherry's examples are of empaths who tried to carry out an assassination and failed," Lee explained to me.

"And Lee's examples are of empaths who failed but managed to kill a few others in the process," Sherry said, leaning forward in her chair. "A few of them failed because of seers. Most because they radiated too many feelings right before attempting to carry out the deed, and the bodyguards detected and stopped them."

"That's why all the famous assassinations were carried out either by elementalists or normies," Lee contributed.

"And usually against people who didn't pay for the round-the-clock services of a seer," Sherry added.

Two history buffs. I had the feeling they could have spent the next few hours talking about obscure historical figures no one but them knew.

Sherry gripped her pen between her fingers. "The suspect we picked up yesterday killed himself an hour ago."

I felt a chill in my stomach. Lee tightened his grip on my hand. We had done that.

Lee straightened up. "How? You knew he…"

Sherry shot him a look and said in a level voice, "Last-minute decision, just like your sister said." She turned to me. "We managed to interrogate him and corroborate some of the information we already had. We know he was with the Sons of Simeon, but we couldn't get anything out of him about who he was targeting, who exactly he was aiming at yesterday."

"He was aiming at you," I said.

"Daphne said they're targeting you," Lee said to me, his tone reserved, his expression utterly devoid of feeling.

"You're both wrong," Sherry said, clicking her pen.

"Daphne said that…" Lee began to answer.

Sherry shot him another look and he fell silent. "Seers don't see the future. They remember backwards, and like any memory, they notice mostly the significant things. Daphne sees Reed dead because he's important to her, and close to her. It doesn't mean that's actually the main event." She kept clicking her pen. "People are so used to listening to seers that they forget to use common sense." She pointed her pen at me. "What would happen if they hurt you? Nothing. So why would anyone go after you?"

I shrugged.

"Think. Really."

Lee squeezed my hand. "You said it yesterday. That he tends to put himself in the line of fire."

"Correct." Sherry looked at Lee. "So…?"

"So he'll be close to…" His voice petered out. "They're not aiming at Reed. They're targeting someone standing next to him. And Daphne sees it because she cares about Reed more than she does about that other person."

Sherry nodded.

Lee balled his hand into a fist. "OK. So how do we protect Reed?"

"You're asking the wrong question." Sherry looked at Lee. "Think like one of the Sons of Simeon."

Lee slid his hand out from under mine and tapped on the armrest of his chair. "They're aiming at Reed, because Reed's

THE HEART OF THE CIRCLE

standing in the way of that other person. But… if you knew whose path he was blocking, you could protect… no… wait. It's something else." Lee bit his lip in concentration.

"They want to bring on a revolution, right?" Lee looked straight at Sherry. I had no idea he knew anything about the political happenings in the country. After all, only yesterday he hadn't even heard of the Sons of Simeon. He had probably spent the night catching up. Out of concern for me. I almost smiled.

Sherry nodded.

"So they have damuses telling them what to do in order to bring about this revolution, and putting Reed in the line of fire is part of their plan. Because otherwise, the person they're after will make sure to replace Reed with someone they can't kill. No, wait…"

"You're right," Sherry said, crossing her arms. "They know their target will surround herself with whoever can protect her, and the weakest link will be Reed."

"Precisely because he's insignificant. That's why they need him there. Which means… which means they'll do whatever it takes to make sure Reed is there when they need to strike, to bring him down to get to their real target." Lee accompanied his words with the drumming of his fingers against the table. "And that means they'll make all the futures converge into an unalterable state."

"Exactly," Sherry said.

I cleared my throat. "Meaning?"

They both looked at me.

"Meaning, they'll hurt you if that's what it takes to make sure you'll be where they need you," Lee said.

I was trapped in my thoughts, looking for a way out. I recalled Professor Yeshurun's exhortation: 'The community needs to do some soul searching, we must embrace those who are different from us.' I felt sick to my stomach.

"I have no intention of letting them lay a finger on you. I'll do all I can to protect you, but that's going to require your cooperation."

"Cooperation means I'm putting Reed on the first flight out to Boston," Lee interrupted her.

"No." Sherry shot him a look. "Cooperation means you two putting your trust in me."

"No," I interjected. They both shifted their gazes to me. "Cooperation means you tell us what you intend to do in order to keep me alive, and I decide what I intend to do."

Her smile reappeared.

"What? I'm reminding you of Matthew again?"

Instead of replying, Sherry interlaced her fingers and raised her hands to her heart. The symbol of sorcery, solidarity and reciprocal aid.

I couldn't read her, but I could look into her eyes. She seemed genuine. More than that. She seemed determined. Matthew trusted her, and I had seen her in action when the pyros burned those people in the pub. She did everything she could to protect me. No, to protect everyone. And now she was committing to help protect me with a gesture meaningful to us both.

"The Sons of Simeon envision a future in which people like us are enslaved to them, and in exchange, they can use their powers without restrictions. They claim that's freedom," she said. "I say that real freedom is the possibility to live side by side in mutual respect, that our society will prosper only if we truly accept one another. I believe you agree with me."

I peered into her eyes and put my hands on the table, side by side. "I promised Daphne that I wouldn't die as long as we're sharing the same apartment." I interlaced my fingers and raised my hands to my heart, mimicking her gesture.

"I'll do whatever I can to protect you," Sherry said, and then shifted her gaze to Lee, her fingers still linked.

Lee sighed quietly, leaned in and imitated our gesture.

I separated my hands and leaned back in my chair. "What do you need from me?"

"For starters, I need you to go to the rally."

"So the Sons of Simeon will think their plan is still working?"

Sherry nodded.

"But how are you going to identify their real target?" Lee asked her.

"Again you're asking the wrong question," Sherry replied. "Give it another shot."

He tapped his fingers against the armrest of his chair. "So you'll be able to find a way to intercept their plan without arousing their suspicion."

"And also…?" She asked, looking at me again.

I nodded towards Lee. "He's the genius here. I, apparently, am simply everyone's crash test dummy."

Lee snorted. "Genius, huh?"

I smiled at him, stroking his thigh. "Well, what's Sherry's 'and also'?"

Lee scratched his forehead. "You're not going to help out?"

I shrugged. "All I've been hearing is 'Reed's going to die according to their plan so that…'" And I stopped. They had chosen me because I wasn't significant enough, and yet I wasn't just a random choice. I was someone who put himself in the line of fire, like Sherry said, but only for friends. Or for a worthy cause. And someone on the Sons of Simeon's side knew this and intended to take advantage of it. Sherry didn't only want to find the Sons of Simeon and foil their plan. While she seemed to reject this hypothesis yesterday, she knew as well as I did that they wouldn't have been able to murder so many people at our rallies without collaborators. She wanted to find the collaborators within our community and root them out. Ivy? No. Ivy would never do something like that to me. Regardless of what happened between us. I knew her well enough to know that no matter what she'd gone through, or how much she had changed, she'd never betray me like that.

"You've got it," Sherry said quietly.

"You want to find the collaborators." I felt the tension building up inside me again. "This rally…"

"Blood soaked," Sherry whispered. "The seers working with the Sons of Simeon are hiding it well. I don't intend to let them hurt anyone on my force. If people get hurt, I'd rather it be people who don't think…"

"Like you," Lee interjected. "You'd rather have people who think differently from you die; you're just like them." His voice was shaken.

"No," Sherry said, staring at Lee. "I'd rather the people who get hurt be those who try to harm the innocent, who think people like us have no right to exist." She held out her hands. "This world is shitty. I think we can make it better for all of us. Including for people who don't agree with me." Her voice turned harsher. "It's a suicidal form of terrorism. These are people like us who're crossing the lines to hurt us. We have to stop it, any way we can."

I could hear Yeshurun's voice. I had to embrace them, to understand those who turn against the community. For a moment, I was on his side.

Sherry's voice softened when she said, "I'll do whatever I can to protect you. At no point will you be exposed."

"How?"

"A protective circle."

Protective circles only worked if the sorcerers who partook in them were united in their cause. The circles failed if the sorcerers sustaining them had conflicting intentions. The main difficulty was making sure all the sorcerers actually had the same goal. I could see what Sherry was thinking. A circle that contained her and everyone close to me. She assumed they'd all want me to live. And then the Sons of Simeon would try to carry out their plan, and she'd catch them and find out what they wanted.

Lee burst into a joyless laughter. "Maybe we should make a voodoo doll too? It's just as effective."

Sherry gave him an icy glare. "A circle of six sorcerers. Four elementalists, two psychics. We'll cast it on Reed. That's what we did with Rabin."

"Yeah, and we all saw how well that turned out," I smirked.

"It worked, the first two times."

Lee shifted in his chair and looked at Sherry. "Just so we're clear. If anything happens to Reed…"

"Threatening a civil servant is sufficient grounds for an execution."

"I'm not making any threats, just stating a fact."

"I'll pretend I didn't hear that fact." Sherry turned to me. "I'll assign you a police officer for protection. I won't let anything happen to you before the rally."

"And then you can kill me according to plan." I attempted a smile.

Sherry pursed her lips "I don't kill civilians." She leaned in and lowered her voice. "It's just going to be a few days. It'll be over soon."

Lee placed his hand on my back.

Sherry swiveled to face her computer screen. "So, about yesterday…"

After we finished with my report, Sherry called in a police officer named Dimitri. He was a tall, blue-eyed blond, arms sinewy and bulging with muscles. I noticed Lee's pleased smile. I nudged him with my finger, and his smile dissolved.

Dimitri turned out not only to be a damus but a three-time winner of the regional boxing championship.

After we left Sherry's office, the effect of the pill finally started to wear off. Lee looked at me and flooded me with a wave of affection and intense desire. I returned the wave. Dimitri trailed behind us, keeping a seemly distance.

Lee stroked my arm. "What do we do now?"

"Something that will help me keep my mind off *that*," I said, tilting my head towards the police station behind us.

Lee looked back and then fixed his gaze on me again. "Want to go catch a movie?"

I smiled. "That sounds really… normal."

Lee slid his hand into mine. "Normal can be nice sometimes."

At the box office, we wondered whether we should buy a ticket for Dimitri too. He whipped out his badge and entered.

The theatre was relatively empty. We sat in the front row, our hands all over each other, stealing the occasional kiss. I missed most of the storyline in the first half of the movie, and Lee didn't even pretend to look at the screen, his eyes resolutely on me.

"Is this normal?" he whispered as he slid his hands between my thighs.

I hummed and leaned back, closing my eyes. I felt Dimitri at the end of the row, his concentration popping my and Lee's little bubble of privacy.

Dimitri's constant scouting out threats from the audience was giving off an echo that kept jolting me out of my moment with Lee. I pulled away from Lee and gazed at the screen, trying to focus, but I was still engulfed in a cloud of Lee's scent and couldn't think of anything other than his hands and his lips, and the need to get back home already.

I edged out the fear and anxiety, burying it deep beneath the need for physical intimacy. 'Don't think about it' became my strategy.

Lee walked me home after the movie, with Dimitri taking the lead up the stairs and opening the door. Daphne was standing on the other side. They both stood there, motionless, eyeing each other. I felt the shift in their feelings, from suspicion to mutual acknowledgement to a certain affection. Daphne took a step back, letting the three of us into the apartment. Dimitri canvassed the rooms, sat down on the living room couch and heaved his legs onto the coffee table without uttering a word.

Daphne shuffled to the kitchen, took out a bunch of grapes from the fridge, rinsed them under the faucet and put them in a bowl. She burst into laughter, and Dimitri smiled. She walked out of the kitchen and into the living room, handing Dimitri the bowl. Lee and I remained in the entrance hall, Lee radiating mounting confusion.

I cleared my throat. "Anything you'd like to share with the rest of us?"

Daphne turned to me and bit her lip. "Oh, sorry."

Lee looked at me. "What's happening?"

I pointed at Dimitri. "They're communicating. She and Dimitri are choosing futures in which they've already spoken to each other, so they don't actually need words now."

Lee stroked his chin. "Would it work if I tried it?"

Daphne shrugged. I already knew it wouldn't, because Daphne and I had never managed to pull it off, no matter how hard I concentrated. Lee looked at her silently. After a moment, Daphne started laughing, and Dimitri gave off an uncomfortable feeling.

"What?" Lee said, looking at Dimitri. "I just thought that…"

Daphne raised her hand, still laughing. "It won't work if you're thinking about a few things at the same time, one of them being this person standing here, looking at me." She winked at me.

Lee sent me a small wave of embarrassment. I held his hand. "Come, I've got an idea for something we can do without words."

"Wait," Daphne stopped me. "Gaia was looking for you."

"Gaia?" Lee's brow furrowed.

"A cute moody chick, from my Yoyo group." I shifted my gaze to Daphne. "What did she want?"

"Just to ask if you're OK," Daphne said, then lowered her voice, "you know her boyfriend is a damus, right?"

I nodded.

"So she probably knows about how you spent your morning, but without context she can't tell why you've got a cop following you around."

"I'll call her. I'll calm her down."

"I've already calmed her down myself," Daphne replied, "but next time…"

I nodded. A moody with a damus. I knew how that relationship worked. I had to listen to her more, and remember she was only getting partial information that could worry her for no reason. I swallowed a sigh. She was only sixteen. The world was tough enough without her being exposed to all the information that came with having a damus by her side.

Lee caressed my shoulder. "Should I be worried?"

I winked at him. "Depends on how much you improve your game." I led him to my bedroom. The living room went quiet behind us. I locked the door and looked at him. He was running his hand up and down my jawline, and I felt him inside me, searching for the root of my fear.

"I can help with that." He leaned into a kiss, and I let him dismantle my anxiety and drown it with warmth. I heard music coming from the living room. Daphne must have turned it on to give us some privacy.

It wasn't amazing, but much better than in the bathroom at the police station.

24

A text from Aurora came in the following day, around noon. *Reminder – today at five. Yoyo.*

Daphne was at work, and Dimitri and I were standing alone in the kitchen. "I've got to go out," I explained to Dimitri.

"You've got to stay," he repeated for the third time. "Sherry's orders." He put his syringe back in its box and folded the tourniquet. I knew vaguely about how the Soviet Union kept its damuses loyal to the country, and that it had to do with addiction from birth. In one of her rants, Ivy told me about the different policies countries had regarding damuses. In the Soviet Union, kids diagnosed as damuses were injected with substances that rendered them unable to use their powers, and the older the kid got, the more injections he had to receive, otherwise his power would drown him. There was an entire movement dedicated to smuggling damuses out of the Soviet Union, and a lot of them fell apart after leaving their homeland, because the substances in other countries weren't as pure as those administered back home.

"Sherry knows, as do you, that I don't die until the rally." I tried keeping my voice steady and calm. I pierced my fork into the last piece of lettuce.

"No." Dimitri closed the box with a thud. "Sherry knows, as me, there are enough ways to hurt you before rally."

I chewed silently. I wanted to go out. I wanted to meet Gaia and see how she was coping. I wanted to feel like I was doing something meaningful, like I used to do.

"In five futures there is pyro waiting for you at bus stop." Dimitri raised a silencing finger before I managed to answer. "Each future, different bus stop. Even though you think you get away, he waits."

"Pyro," I mumbled at my plate. "What's their obsession with pyros?"

"Active force, quick strike, hardest to combat, effective deterrence, keep going even after pyro is neutralized." Dimitri sounded as if he were reciting.

Ages ago, during my military service, we attended a course in which we had to memorize the pros and cons of each force on the battlefield, but I was never in the mood, and Daphne kept choosing the future in which we managed to dodge the exam.

"And what do we do, other than sit on our behinds and keep me from meeting my commitments?" I pierced the last piece of tomato on my plate.

"We? You and me? Or we, Sherry and entire force, who for years been trying to prevent exactly what is happening now? You think is so easy to keep country safe? Ask Daphne how bad futures are we not in," he said breathlessly.

"Sherry's just one person," I muttered.

"One person with right vision, and many damus on her side." Dimitri drummed his fingers on the table. "I not flee Soviet Union for little sun and beach. I follow Sherry because I see what she doing, and I want be part of it." He was almost talking to himself. "If she do what she promise, if we help her, few more years and it all be better. Not just here. Everyone see what Sherry doing." He directed his attention back to me. "You understand what is growing up in Russia? What is like to be shot full of stuff that take your powers when you still baby? Then you have do everything country wants, or they not give you any more of it? You understand what is to see my children grow up, happy, not like

215

their father?" He balled his hand into a fist. "I see Sherry many years now. Sherry make country safe. Sherry make I go in street and no one yell 'fucking sorcerer,' and no one throw things on my children, and no one hit my children, and no one put my children behind fence and… and…"

"I'm sorry," I said quietly.

"This Sherry make. She make better world. Sherry make world of sorcerer and normie all live together. This is world I want to live in, not pass my time until dead." A mix of rage and adoration was pouring out of him. I bit my lip. Another apology didn't seem in order.

"She…" I hesitated, searching for the right way to ask the question.

Dimitri looked past my shoulder and turned his gaze back to me. "She not senior enough to change everything. Not yet. That why she still successful at staying under Sons of Bitches' radar. Until now. And she… she…" He pounded his fist on the table. "She not like us. She cannot see where we head, but she is only one who is thinking about shared future. Future safe for everyone." He sounded almost choked up when he spoke. "Society only rely on damus. No one imagining better future. Damus say something, everyone believe. Sherry not like that. Sherry has vision."

"We all have a vision. I, for instance…"

"Need not to die," Dimitri interrupted me, "and I not let you go to place where you draw attention."

"But they don't kill me on the way to Yoyo," I said, playing with my fork. "They get me at the rally. Until then I'm safe. That's what Sherry wants, for me to go on with my life as always so they won't suspect anything." I put down my fork and looked at Dimitri with as much confidence as I could muster. "And if they try anything… that's what I've got you for."

"What you do is good. Go outside? No good." He leaned in. "You not understand? You have do what Sherry want. I am enough to protect you here, home. Not out. At place with many people, you need combine powers."

Someone knocked on the door. Dimitri glanced in its direction and nodded. Apparently the Sons of Simeon weren't going to attack me in my own home.

I stood up and walked to the door. Blaze was standing on the other side, holding three books in his hand. Proof copies I didn't recognize.

"Odelia told me to bring you these."

"Thanks."

He lowered his gaze the moment I looked at him. "Lee said you need police authorization to leave your house, and Odelia wants you to take a look at these, do at least the first round of revisions. When you're done, tell me or Lee and we'll come pick them up."

Two days. It had been two days since I had maneuvered Blaze without his consent, and I had been so preoccupied with myself and with Lee that I hadn't even thought of reaching out to him, hadn't even apologized or tried to explain. Two days that he spent stewing in his anger and disappointment with me. I was searching for the right words to say to him. Any words at all really. All I wanted was to ask Dimitri to transport us to a present in which Blaze had already forgiven me. Instead I said, "Is River OK?"

Blaze's eyes were fixed on the floor. "We're all a bit rattled by what happened."

I knew he was searching for an excuse to leave. He wouldn't even look at me. I took a deep breath. "Sorry," I said, with a steadier voice than I had expected.

Blaze glanced up at me. Dark, black eyes I had spent hours on end peering into. Eyes that had smiled at me, had shed tears with me, had enveloped me with their warmth each time anew, promising shelter.

"I know it doesn't help, me apologizing."

"You can maneuver me into thinking it helps," Blaze said coldly.

"Sherry would have died if…" I said, my voice trembling.

"You could have yelled, could have said something, could have…" Blaze was flailing his arms. "I don't know. Your damus friend can probably tell you what you could have done that didn't…" He fell silent. "It doesn't matter."

"It does," I said, restraining myself from grabbing his arm. "It matters to me. You have to understand… you…"

"Do you really think saying 'sorry, I didn't mean it' makes up for what River's going through right now? What I'm going through? What Lee's going through?" He was clearly trying to keep himself from yelling on our stairwell.

I retreated into the apartment, and Blaze followed me inside without thinking. "Lee. Of all the people in the world, you don't understand… you…" He was waving his hands in the air again. "You don't understand what he's been through. You don't get how much…" He unclenched his fists. "I expected you to understand," he concluded in a dejected tone.

Dimitri had disappeared from the kitchen. I felt him sitting on the toilet, which he clearly didn't need; he was simply taking refuge behind a closed door.

What had Lee told them about me? About us? It couldn't have been much. It was Lee, after all. He wasn't one to share intimate details of his life. It suddenly dawned on me that Blaze wasn't really talking about Lee. He was using him as an excuse. He had obviously heard about Daphne's vision, and was worried about me, and angry at me, and that was one thing I knew how to handle.

"Remember the first time you let me maneuver you?" I asked quietly.

Blaze shrugged. Of course he remembered.

"I had never before…"

"I know," he said, his voice slightly thick.

"Nor since," I said.

Blaze's eyes flickered with surprise. "Not even with Lee?"

"With Lee it's…" I couldn't help but smile. "It's different with him."

"Different," he repeated, mimicking my tone. I forgot how good he was at making me smile.

"Lee's different." I felt my cheeks flushing. Great. I was supposed to be apologizing, not getting dragged into an entirely different conversation.

"Are you going to apologize again?"

I shook my head. "I'm going to tell you that you of all people should know that if I maneuvered you without permission, it was because I had no choice."

"You once told me there's always a choice," he said, his tone again reserved.

Back then I had been young. And no one was aiming his gun at a cop in a room packed with people. And my place of employment hadn't been torched.

"I'm sorry," I said quietly.

"I know you're sorry. I still feel shitty. River still feels shitty."

He was still there, hiding somewhere beneath his words, the Blaze I always knew how to talk to.

"OK. My head feels like it's exploding."

A faint hint of a smile crept over Blaze's face. "You're absolutely right. A headache is exactly the same as the nausea brought on by empathic penetration."

I nodded. "So is the self-loathing and the questions about what I could have done differently. Exactly the same."

"Could *I* have done anything differently?"

I wasn't expecting that question, but there was only one answer. "You could have not been there."

He slouched his shoulders. "Meaning, stayed away from you?"

"Yes." I bit my lip. "I maneuvered everyone, and it wasn't the first time, and I'll probably have to do it again. I won't have a choice."

"Daphne said you're going to die."

I choked back my tears and nodded.

"How much time have you got left?" His eyes welled up. Warmth, longing and loss.

I couldn't tell him about Sherry's plan, or even her promise to keep me safe. "I don't know. Not much."

Blaze stuck his hands in his pockets. "What am I supposed to do? Pretend we're just casual acquaintances? Take advantage of every moment we've got left?"

"I know which one I'd prefer," I said quietly.

"I know which one I'd prefer," he parroted, teasing me.

And once again, despite the tears, I couldn't help but smile. I reached out my hand to him. "Want to be my friend?"

Blaze's lips curved into a crooked smile designed to suppress his tears, and he shook my hand. He had come to a decision, and my hand was becoming painfully hot. Blaze knew me too well. He knew just when to stop. "You maneuver River one more time, and I'll burn you. And that's no threat."

"Got it," I said quietly. And I did.

The bathroom door opened and Dimitri emerged. "That took longer than I saw, and you still not call your blonde friend to say you not go."

"Go where?" Blaze let go of my hand.

"Yoyo," I said, and explained to him about the organization. Blaze let out a chuckle. "Still volunteering, huh?"

An idea flickered on the edge of my mind. I turned to Dimitri. "Blaze is a pyro."

"I know," he said. "I see what he do."

"Someone who can respond quickly, and all those other things you've mentioned before."

Blaze took a step back. "You're trying to sign me up for something?"

I nodded, my smile widening. "Come, it'll be worth it."

"I'm still mad at you."

"No, you're not." I tugged his hand. "You want to come with me to see kids trying to use their powers for the first time, and laugh at their miserable attempts."

Blaze raised his eyebrows. "Depends. Will I get any inside information to use against that annoying tall guy from my office?"

"Inside information?"

"You know, stories I can use against him next time he decides to bitch about a report."

"Depends. Will I get any inside information to use against him next time he decides to play hard to get?"

Blaze laughed. "Hard to get? You're dating the wrong Lee."

I looked at Dimitri. "OK?"

Dimitri shifted his gaze between us. "You not leave my sight. You not leave Blaze, no matter what happen." He pointed at Blaze. "And you watch over. Clear?"

Blaze nodded.

We took Dimitri's car. It had 'undercover cop' written all over it, but Dimitri wouldn't even consider taking Blaze's car and I was so desperate to leave already that I didn't try to argue.

I gave Dimitri directions to the community center. It was the only place the municipality would allocate for our meetings. The parking lot was spray painted with *Thou shalt not suffer a witch to live – let me help!* and graffiti of a naked woman, her head blown, her shadow with horns and tail. Blaze was oozing disgust. I didn't feel any intense emotions coming from Dimitri. I assumed he had grown accustomed to it, like me.

"You don't see these kinds of things in the Confederacy?"

Blaze shook his head. "We all live on reservations, and there's a special task force that prevents any run-ins with normies."

"Sounds perfect," I said quietly.

"These are people who prefer going through life with a blindfold over their eyes instead of facing reality. And it's been that way for nearly a hundred years." A streak of anger infiltrated his calm demeanor. "Better the shit over here. At least you get to see the truth."

Dimitri parked the car. "Shit here better than back home too."

Blaze and Dimitri exchanged glances in the rearview mirror.

The smell of urine hit us as soon as we stepped out of the car. Blaze scrunched his nose. I heard the sounds of vomiting somewhere close by. I put out my feelers and poked around. It wasn't a moody.

Just some drunk. Dimitri followed close behind us, pulling off the 'undercover' look almost as successfully as his car.

There was a guard on either side of the white-painted gate, directing the thin stream of teenagers filing through it. Dimitri gestured at them with two fingers, and was greeted with a similar gesture. I wondered whether Sherry was responsible for stationing these two damuses here.

"These kids look like us," Blaze whispered, and I knew what he meant. Clad in oversized clothes with their eyes fixed on the ground, they refused to make eye contact. A few of them had their hands in their pockets, avoiding touch, unaware this was exactly the telltale sign of damuses and moodies. Even fewer of them exchanged more than two words with one another.

I poked around. Terrified, twitching consciousnesses. Two of them were sealed off. Not one of them responded to the others, and there was no affection between them.

"No, it's much worse," I said to Blaze quietly as we proceeded towards the gate. "They have no friends."

Blaze squeezed my shoulder. "That's what you're here for, isn't it?"

Aurora was waiting at the entrance, Forrest beside her. They were handing out origami flowers, a different color for each teenager, and calling cards. The phone number was the same on all of them, but the names and addresses varied. Some were for dentists and florists and others for SAT courses. One calling card looked like an invitation for a modern poetry writing class.

The girl in line before me got a red flower, and so did Blaze. He smiled. Then Aurora handed him a blue flower and said, "And this one's for River. Tell her I said thanks for the help, OK? I didn't have time to call her."

Blaze radiated flickering happiness and stroked his flower.

Aurora handed me a paper violet. "I'm happy you came. I was afraid you'd bail because of all the…"

"Bail?" Blaze chuckled. "You think there's anything that could stop Reed from volunteering for something? You don't know each other that well, huh?"

I laughed. "I'm not that bad."

Blaze tugged on my sleeve. "I remember at high school I had to physically force your hand down when they asked who wanted to join student council, even though we were about to graduate."

Aurora smiled at me and pushed her glasses up the bridge of her nose. "I'm glad you're here." She gestured at Blaze with the rest of the flowers in her hand and asked, "Will you be joining Reed or taking on a group of your own?"

Now it was my turn to laugh. "Offering Blaze to volunteer for something is like..." I searched for an apt metaphor.

Blaze nudged me with his elbow. "*I'm* not that bad."

"I remember I had to physically force your hand up when they asked who wanted to sign up for college prep math courses, even though you were already planning to apply to do a MSc in math." I pretended to shiver in horror. "They almost picked me instead of you. It was awful."

Aurora laughed. "Now I understand why I had to do all your assignments for Statistics 101."

"Hey." I raised my finger. "I repaid that with interest in Structures and Spaces."

Forrest cleared his throat loudly. Five teenagers were standing behind us, eyeing us up with the belittling looks only adolescents can shoot at people a decade older than them.

Aurora gestured behind her back. "Room three is yours." She looked at Blaze. "And if you change your mind..."

I took the paper lilac from her hand and linked my arm with Blaze's. "Don't worry, he won't."

I led Blaze to the small room, Dimitri following our every step. A hot water dispenser stood on a side table with a pile of teabags, a stack of disposable cups and a plate of lemon flavored wafers next to it. The tables were pushed up against the walls, and the chairs were placed in a circle in the middle of the room. There were about eight teenagers in the room, including Gaia and Guy, holding paper lilacs similar to mine.

I sent Gaia an introductory wave. She turned around, purple-pink hair swinging. "Here, the geriatrics came to teach us the law of the land."

"Hey," I exclaimed, raising my hand. "I'm not that old."

Gaia blew a bubblegum bubble and popped it. "Yes, you are." She smiled at me. "But you're OK." She sent me a playful wave. It was more precise than the ones she had sent me previously. She was a quick learner.

A girl in jeans and a shaved head opened her hand, producing a tiny, flickering flame. Blaze repeated the gesture, and they smiled at each other.

"Two pyros," I said, and then gestured at myself and Gaia, "and two moodies." Then I waved across the room. "You want to group up in cardinal points so I'll know who else we've got here?"

Blaze and the girl with the shaved scalp settled in the southern side of the room, next to the hot water dispenser. They kept sending little flames back and forth.

A boy in a black faux-leather jacket, another in overalls and a girl in a basketball jersey stood beside the western wall. There really were a lot of splashers this year. A girl wearing giant glasses and Birkenstock sandals sidled up against the northern wall, hands on hips in a defiant gesture that reminded me a little of Sherry.

A girl in a red dress remained alone in the middle of the room. I reached out my hand to her, and she flinched.

"It's OK," I said, giving her my nicest smile. "I won't maneuver you, I just want to show you where ideally you should stand."

"I know where. I'm just …" She lowered her gaze without completing the sentence.

"She's on neutral," Gaia said.

I exchanged glances with Blaze. He shrugged. I didn't know how to phrase the question without Gaia calling me a geezer.

"It prevents sorcery," the splasher in the black jacket interjected. He ran his hand up his cheek. "Can't you tell?"

I looked at the girl in the red dress again and focused. I felt the cloud of sorcery engulfing her. The gentle tug at the pit of my stomach indicated another presence similar to mine.

The girl looked up and tucked her hair behind her ears. A gentle, almost invisible line was drawn in a skin tone colored pencil on her jawline. I reached out to touch her cheek and she blanched.

"It will affect you too. It passes through touch," she whispered and lowered her gaze again, her hair veiling her face.

I lowered my hand.

"They *say* it passes through touch," Gaia said. "It's not true."

The shaved-head pyro said, "You've never heard of neutral?" I felt the criticism in her tone, concealing a layer of fear.

The term rang a bell. Something Gaia had mentioned in the past.

"It makes us normal," the girl in the red dress whispered. She looked up at me again, and this time I noticed a fluctuation in her sorcery. It wasn't moving around her as it should. She wasn't using it at all. Something was blocking her. It wasn't depletion, otherwise she would have been drawing sorcery from everyone in the room.

She spread out her arms. "I can't feel the air. I can't feel you breathing. I can't feel the wind outside." A smile flickered on her lips. "It's perfect."

I sealed my feelings well, so that Gaia wouldn't accidently pick up on my criticism. "And it doesn't bother you?"

She shook her head.

I felt the pain in some of the teens, and the yearning in others. I swept my gaze across the room. "Anyone else on neutral?"

The boy in the black jacket pulled something out of his pocket and opened his fist. "I'm taking it later, before I go home."

The pill in the boy's hand reminded me somewhat of the one I had been administered at the police station, but its effect was different. Deeper. I still needed my power when it was blocked. The girl standing in front of me clearly wasn't touching her power at all. Not to mention that the pill from the station was a regulated substance. Neutralizers were always state regulated. More than they feared us, they feared substances that could prevent us from using our powers and then stop working all at once. No one wanted sorcerers draining everyone around them, accumulating power so as to pose a danger to their surroundings.

"Where did you get it from?"

"My dad gave it to me." He sounded defensive. "Because then I don't flood our house when I have a bad dream."

The splasher in the basketball jersey next to him giggled.

"And how long does the effect last?" I tried to control my voice, to sound genuinely interested and nonjudgmental, and not betray the horror I was feeling.

"Twelve hours," Gaia said behind me.

"But why would you want it?" The words flew out of my mouth.

"That's what you don't get," Gaia said, stepping forward and attracting everyone's gaze. She straightened up, slender and almost drowning in the long dress she wore. "You never had to truly fight." She waved her hands. "We don't even know if they're going to take our powers into consideration when we apply for college, like they did with you."

Blaze shot me a look. I clenched my jaw, considering my group. "OK." I sealed in my anxiety and glanced at Blaze. "You want to try it?"

He smiled. "Hell no. Our oven hasn't been working for a week. River will kill me if I can't warm up dinner."

The girl next to him smiled. He was ten years her senior, but had already won her over. Deep inside, I resented him for it.

I looked at the girl in the red dress. "What's your name?"

"Tempest," she whispered.

"That's a very pretty name." I smiled at her. "Could you stand near the eastern wall, just so I can get my point across?"

She shrugged and shuffled eastward, standing under the large windowpanes. I could feel the sorcery move inside the room, swirling into vortexes when it hit the barriers Tempest had erected around herself. I nodded towards Guy and Gaia. "You guys are with me."

They walked to the middle of the room. I turned around, gesturing at the entire group. "Circle." I lowered my hand. "Can you feel it? The waves flowing through us?"

Gaia put on her usual expression of indifference, but I could feel the wonder inside her. The splashers were feeling it too. The pebble perked up her shoulders, ignoring everyone. Tempest kept her eyes on the floor. Of course she wouldn't feel anything. She was detached.

"Good," the splasher in the jersey said, folding her arms across her chest. "Now we just need objects related to our powers, to get ourselves organized properly, and for Tempest's neutral to wear off…"

"And how's that going to help us?" the teenager in the black jacket asked. "We protect someone, and the moment someone else gets hurt, the circle collapses. That's what always happens with all the solutions these…" At least he clammed up before calling me a geriatric.

I pulled up a chair, turned it around and straddled it with my chest pressed against the backrest. "A partial circle, true. But a full circle will enable us to harness the elements and attack." I narrowed my eyes. "You have heard of full circles, right?"

"What's a full circle?" the boy asked in a derisive tone, but I could feel his curiosity piquing. Everyone's, actually.

"Should we start off with a round of introductions before I give you tips for something illegal?" It worked, as always. They dragged their chairs closer.

We spent an hour talking about the structure of different circles and power combinations, with me stressing more than once that a full circle was illegal nowadays. While it did enable the harnessing and integration of the elements for a short period of time, it was also unstable and could cause serious damage. I didn't tell them that full circles depleted us more than any other use of our powers, or that it could hinder their ability to draw in any sorcery at all.

They were taking neutral. Overusing their powers wasn't currently a risk. I held back from mentioning Houdini.

I got them talking a little about their fears, and manipulated them into agreeing to protect each other when they left the group. After two hours, we said goodbye, and I felt the hesitant buds of affection sprouting between them.

Gaia lingered behind after the session was over. Blaze and the pyro girl were tossing small fireballs to each other. Guy was standing next to Dimitri, and judging by their animated feelings I knew that Dimitri was showing him how to talk in reflections. Daphne had already known how to do that when we were in the army, but I never asked her how she learned it. I had always assumed it was something they just knew how to do, instinctively, although even I had to learn how to effectively maneuver others. It wasn't instinct, contrary to popular belief.

"Are you OK? Because Guy said that…" Gaia left the rest of the sentence hovering in the air between us.

I shrugged and stacked the white plastic chairs. "These are trying days."

"You don't say." She leaned against one of the chairs.

I reached my hand out, signaling to her to pass it to me. She picked it up and handed it over without bothering to stack it herself. Teenagers.

"How about you?"

"I'm OK. The algebra assignment was super easy. The literature paper, on the other hand…"

"What's with all the summer assignments?"

Gaia shrugged. She was more reticent than usual.

I put my hand on her shoulder. "You need to talk to someone?" I asked quietly, and sent her a sympathetic wave.

She shrugged again, shaking my hand off. "I need this world to stop trying to kill my friends."

I gestured at Guy. "He saw it?"

Gaia shook her head. "We're not close enough, or something like that. But…" She faltered, her eyes welling up. "Is it true?"

228

I sat down and Gaia plopped herself onto a chair in front of me.

"Daphne's never been wrong before."

Gaia sniffled.

"But," I said quietly, "she already saved my life once when it seemed death was inescapable. I trust she'll find a way again."

Gaia narrowed her lips. "Can't you do anything?" She sounded almost angry. "Instead of sitting here, talking to us about things we shouldn't do because we'd get everyone killed if we tried…"

"No one will kill you over a full circle. You'd just be tried and sentenced to ten years on the chain gang," I said, attempting an amused tone.

"Stop it," she hissed. "It's not funny."

I fell silent.

"You drag us all here, and Aurora keeps going on about how we can be more than what we were born into, and now you're going to die, and you're not even trying to fight it."

I lifted my hand and, after a moment's hesitation, placed it on her cheek. She was crying. Her sadness flowing in my direction, I pulled it into me, dismantled it and sent her a gentle wave of affection and security.

"I…" I began to say, and changed my mind. "We're doing all we can. Really. I have a police damus glued to my side, and Daphne won't rest until she finds a way to change the situation. Nothing's set in stone. I promise you."

Gaia was still sniffling.

"When there's a protective circle on you, I want to be part of it," she said, thrusting her chin out.

She was too young, and I knew I would prefer the older, more experienced Lee as part of my circle. I stuck out my hand. "Deal."

She shook it. "Good."

After we had finished tidying up the room, I said goodbye to Aurora at the gate. Blaze and the pyro girl were exchanging phone numbers. I edged out the petty desire to yell that he had a girlfriend.

Back in the car, Dimitri sat behind the wheel, engulfed in a gray cloud of discontent.

Blaze turned to me. "What's this neutral business?"

"It's a steroid combined with an antihistamine," Dimitri replied, looking at me in the rearview mirror. "And it stops harnessing of sorcery. More powerful than what we give at police station. Work differently." He sounded like he was reciting a police briefing. The anger bubbling beneath his words was bone-chilling. "Children pop it like M&M's. Only at school age. We cannot track down the dealers."

"Only school-age kids?" I asked, horrified. "But that's the most vulnerable age. If they don't experiment with their powers like they should at that age, then…"

"Then we'll get an entire generation of inept sorcerers, who'd rather not practice their powers because they simply don't know how," Blaze completed the sentence with a chillingly quiet tone. "Just as long as they don't have to cope with their abilities."

I exchanged glances with Blaze. "How could anyone…" I cracked my knuckles. "Why would anyone not want to…"

"You really can't imagine yourself at their age taking something that will stop you from feeling?" Blaze asked quietly.

"Shit," I blurted.

He put his hand on my shoulder and pulled me closer to him. "Totally."

We spent the rest of the ride in silence.

Back at my apartment, Blaze insisted on coming upstairs with me. Dimitri was busy on the phone, conveying brief reports.

Blaze walked into my room and gazed at the walls. "There's no way Lee didn't say anything about this color. Or about that," he said, pointing at the poster of the horse against the sunset.

I stood at the doorway, waiting for Blaze to leave. He finished his survey and looked at me. "What do we do now?"

"Look for some neutral. I heard that's what all the cool kids are doing." I felt stifled.

"You want me to call Lee?"

I shook my head. It would be too hard to pretend I hadn't noticed the sadness Lee was burying beneath his affection towards me.

"Want a Lost in Time marathon?"

I gave him a skeptical look. "You're joking."

Blaze held out his hands. "Am I?"

I shook my head. He was loaded with fear and concern.

"I just want to do what I promised you," he shrugged. "To be your friend." He placed his hand on my shoulder in a feeble embrace. "Let's watch some TV, you can keep wallowing in self-pity afterwards."

I let out a chuckle. "I've earned that self-pity fair and square."

"Totally." Blaze kept his hand on me.

I used to lean on him, and he'd hug me, and from there a kiss would follow. Instead, I shook his hand off, looked at him and said, "OK."

I had ten episodes downloaded on my computer. We holed away in my room, isolated from Dimitri's phone conversations and from the world that refused to let me come up for air.

25

As the weekend drew near, my feed was bombarded with posts and messages about the rally on Saturday. Gaia had sent me ten texts within thirty minutes, including a rambling voice message relaying the disjointed fragments of a plan. I sent Aurora a text asking how to make her stop, and she had sent back an emoji of a woman shrugging and some Zen quote about acceptance and letting go.

Daphne had arranged for Aurora to participate as an airhead, and Matthew offered to talk to Lilia, the pebble who worked in the ER at his hospital. Sherry was also a pebble, but we didn't want her to be busy with my circle instead of protecting everyone.

When Saturday morning rolled by, I couldn't get out of bed. Lee was at work catching up on tasks, and the fear I had successfully managed to edge out when he was around burst out all at once.

Daphne came into my room and sat on the edge of my bed.

"Tell me I'm going to make it," I said, just barely straining out the words.

"You'll make it. And you and Lee are going to have two gorgeous kids," she replied, caressing me.

I closed my eyes. "Shit."

"You don't feel like settling down?"

I managed a brief chuckle. "It's too quick. It's… I…" My voice cracked.

Daphne leaned in and hugged me. "I can't tell you it's going to be OK."

"I could just not go." I sniffled. "I could decide to stay home."

Daphne nodded.

"So there." I sniffled again. "I've decided. I'm staying home, and Sherry and her plan can go find some other victim."

"They will."

I felt her tensing. "Daphne?"

She tucked her hair behind her ears.

"Am I going to die today?"

Daphne bit her lip. It was one of those moments. My heart started racing. One of those moments in which the future diverged, in which Daphne couldn't tell me what to do, in which, if I made the right choice, I'd survive.

"If I don't go to the rally, someone else will?"

"Not exactly." Her voice was strained.

"Someone that's planning on being there anyway?"

She nodded. A lump began to form in my throat.

"And there'll be another murder?"

Daphne pursed her lips.

Gaia was going to be at the rally. My entire group of teenagers, Aurora and Forrest. And there was going to be another murder. A murder that I could prevent, that Sherry's plans could prevent. The world Sherry had in mind depended on me.

Daphne fixed her eyes on me. She didn't have to say anything. Her gaze softened as my thoughts came into focus.

"I'm going," I said. I wasn't asking.

Daphne squeezed my hand. "Thanks," she said, and got up. She couldn't say anything more than that. I realized now that all the other side's damuses were watching me.

"Any wardrobe advice?" I asked once she got to the door.

She smiled. "Something you don't mind dirtying."

I managed a small smile.

Lee and Oleander were the first ones on the scene. Dimitri cleared the way for Lee, but blocked Oleander's entrance. Oleander stuck his hands in his pockets, and stared at Dimitri. They didn't exchange a single word, but their emotions were shifting. Dimitri's concern made way for feelings of safety, and Oleander's humility shifted to an apologetic sentiment.

When Dimitri stepped aside to let Oleander pass, Daphne hugged him. Oleander held her and whispered something in her ear. She nodded.

Lee approached me and stroked my hair. "Is everything OK?" He sent me a delicate wave of concern.

"It's going to be." I nodded towards Daphne and Oleander, still in each other's embrace. "I've got a lot of damuses looking after me. And we have another hour until everyone else makes it here."

Lee hid a small smile. "I've got an idea how we could spend that hour, if you'd like."

"No! I've seen enough of you two," Daphne yelled out, and we both started laughing.

"You owe me, 'Miss I'm-just-bringing-over-someone-from-the-pub-for-a-bit,'" I retorted, and Oleander laughed.

Dimitri shifted his gaze between us. "I also need to find a woman in rally now?"

"Or a man," Lee said with an almost serious expression.

Dimitri rolled his eyes and turned his back to us, but I felt the amusement lurking inside him.

Blaze and River showed up at seven pm on the dot, just like we had scheduled. Matthew, Lilia and Sherry arrived together at a quarter past seven. Matthew apologized, saying he had gotten caught up at work. His bag looked full and puffy, and I felt his fear.

I had wanted Daphne to convince him to stay home, but I knew nothing could stop him from coming. He wouldn't let me leave the house alone. Aurora, the last to arrive, pulled me into a tight embrace.

"Forrest is already there with our teens," she said. "And don't even think about bailing from our meetings next week with the excuse of being dead. I don't have enough experienced counselors, and your group's already in love with you."

I returned the hug, and afterwards we did a round of introductions.

The prearranged objects were resting on the kitchen table. To an outsider, they would have looked like a jumble of unrelated items.

There were six spots in the circle, and as the one being protected, I had to stand in the middle. I took my spot.

"Wait," Matthew called out, looking at Sherry. "What about a bulletproof vest? Something?"

"Three seers," Sherry replied.

"Three?"

"One." She pointed at Daphne. Then at Oleander. "Two." And then at Dimitri. "Three. They'll keep choosing the present in which no one gets hurt."

"There were riots in every recent rally. I spent hours in the ER stitching up marchers, and in each of those rallies there were seers who were supposed to prevent it."

"Yes, but–" I began to explain.

"But what?" he cut me off. "What? In the goddamn pub there were two seers who were supposed to protect you, and it didn't work, right? So don't tell me everything's going to be fine."

Only then did I realize Sherry hadn't told Matthew anything. The only ones who knew about Sherry's plan were the damuses, Lee and me. How was I supposed to convince him it was vital I be at the rally if I couldn't tell him about the plan?

"Matthew," Daphne said, stepping forward and putting her hand on his arm. Matthew looked at her. She continued with a soft voice, "At the pub none of us thought anyone would try to hurt us. This time we're ready. We'll do whatever it takes. No one will get hurt."

"Remember the circle?" I placed my hand on his shoulder. "Hail? Fire? And nothing hit me? That was thanks to Guy. That's what it's like having a damus whose only goal is to protect you, and Guy's only seventeen."

"I don't like it," he said.

"Neither do I." I shrugged.

He raised his finger menacingly. "Don't you dare go die on me."

"OK."

"Which way is east?" Aurora circled the living room with a feather in her hand.

"Aren't you supposed to know that instinctively?" Oleander asked.

Aurora let out a brief chuckle. "No more than psychics naturally dress in purple."

Lee and I exchanged glances. I had purple socks on, and I knew the color of his underwear. We didn't say a word.

Lee pointed at the door. Aurora looked at him. "Really?"

"East," Dimitri said. Then he pointed in the direction of the bathroom. "West." Then at the kitchen. "North." And finally at the couch. "South." He rummaged through his pocket and fished out a compass. "You want to check?"

Aurora smiled. "Thanks." She stood in the middle of the living room.

Lee cleared his throat. "Maybe we shouldn't cast a circle on the carpet? We're going to need fire."

Daphne and I exchanged glances. Lee had used his nicest tone, though he couldn't hide his agitation from either of us. Aurora paced three steps forward.

Blaze stood to her left. He was holding the mound of ashes Lee had brought. I felt a tickle at the back of my neck. River joined the circle on Blaze's left, in front of Aurora. She unclenched her fist, revealing a shell. The tickle at my nape grew stronger. Before Lilia took her position, Daphne and Oleander stepped forward.

"No," Dimitri said, stopping them. "I'm the bodyguard. I will be inside." I had the feeling he said it loudly so we'd all hear, and so they wouldn't argue with him.

Daphne and Oleander remained outside the circle, with Lee and Dimitri standing on either side of me. Lee stroked my hand with his finger.

Lilia stood to River's left, in front of Blaze, closing the circle. She held a small clay pot in her hand, the kind toy stores sold for a shekel and a half for kindergarteners to paint on.

Lee and Dimitri turned to face each other, with me standing between them. Lee held his hands out toward my sides, palms upward. Dimitri looked at him and held his hands out, palms downward.

Standing outside the circle, Daphne counted out loud, "Three. Two. One."

Once her voice fell silent everyone dropped the objects they were holding and held hands, closing the circle. Dimitri placed his hands on Lee's. The tickle at my nape turned into incessant shivers. I wondered how I'd ever be able to thank them. This circle, even though they were all willing participants, was going to drain them physically and mentally. Over the next few days, none of them would be able to practice their power as usual, if at all. How was Dimitri going to function on the police force? At least we weren't casting a full circle that could actually harm them. There were enough people throughout history who had completely lost their abilities after participating in a full circle.

The four elements merged and created a ring around us. Fire, water, steam and clumps of earth swirled in a large circle, passing through the four elementalists who created its circumference. The air vibrated around me. I felt the sorcery flow between us, ossifying into an invisible shell, a cylinder of energy compressing and tightening around me, taking the exact shape of my contours. The elements whirling around us blurred the outside world, hindering its effect on us.

I shivered as I felt the force passing through us. If we stopped now, we could channel the sorcery into action. In the past, sorcerers used full circles to build giant structures, to move boulders around or change the courses of rivers. It came in handy when technology didn't exist. It was also used in wars, in more ancient times. No one dared practice full circles nowadays. The Confederacy was still paying the price for holding these circles in Korea, and there were entire areas in Africa where, due to the excessive use of powers during the colonial period, not a single sorcerer has been born in decades.

Everyone let go of each other's hands at the exact same moment. The elements dissipated but the sorcery remained compressed around me, blocking the outside world. I couldn't feel anyone. My psyche was dulled. I looked at Matthew, who seemed worried, his brow furrowed.

"It worked," Lee said, turning to Matthew. "Don't worry."

"How can you tell?" Matthew's voice sounded strained. He bunched his fists.

Sherry whipped her gun out of its holster and handed it to Matthew. "You want to check?"

"No," he replied, raising his voice.

Sherry secured the gun back in its holster. I assumed she hadn't intended to shoot me. I was hoping she hadn't intended to shoot me.

Daphne went to the kitchen while everyone in the circle remained still, looking at each other. River and Blaze were exchanging beaming glances.

Daphne returned with a knife. She handed it to Sherry. "Do us the honor."

Matthew grabbed Sherry's arm and yelled, "No!"

She shook him off. Daphne held Matthew back while Sherry stepped into the circle, looked me straight in the eye, and stabbed me in the stomach. I flinched, waiting for the pain.

Nothing happened. Sherry yanked out the knife. The tip was clean. I touched my stomach and looked down. There was not a single mark.

I looked at Matthew and attempted a smile. "See? Everything's fine."

Matthew wasn't smiling.

Lee looked at Sherry. "Can we open?"

Sherry nodded.

Instead of taking a step back, Lee hugged me and held my head against his chest. I could hear his heart racing. Blaze and River were talking to each other in their half-Hebrew half-English. I wrapped my arms around Lee and took in his scent.

I'm not going to die today. I'm not going to die today. I buried my head in his shoulder.

"I can barely feel you," Lee whispered.

I nodded and said, "I can't feel a thing." I looked up at him, meeting his gaze. His eyes were wet. "It's probably because of the circle," I said and touched his eyelids, his cheeks, wiping the tears before they rolled off his face. He leaned in and kissed me. I could barely taste him. There was a barrier between us, a kind of veneer preventing me from feeling the world properly.

I looked into his eyes. Surrounded in green.

"Time to head out," Sherry said.

I felt Lee's stomach pressing against mine as we inhaled together. We broke away from each other, but continued to hold hands.

"You don't need to maintain the structure," Sherry said as she opened the front door, "but you do need to stay close to one another."

We walked down the street together, Sherry in the lead. She was dressed in civvies, her gun tucked beneath her shirt. I assumed she had more weapons concealed on her body. Matthew was walking beside her, his bag dangling from his shoulder. They were talking to each other, but he kept his distance. I noticed the way she pulled back her shoulders, projecting invincibility. Matthew glanced back every now and then, considering me. I had the feeling that at the smallest sign, he'd call it all off and take me home.

Lilia was walking on Matthew's other side. She managed to insinuate herself into their discussion, and soon Sherry fell silent, Lilia and Matthew falling into conversation about the hospital and their patients, as if the two women had prearranged to distract Matthew. It seemed that Sherry had a plan for everything.

Dimitri, Oleander and Daphne shuffled behind them in silence. It was only the occasional nod and friendly pat on the shoulder that indicated they might in fact be communicating with each other. Oleander's arm was wrapped around Daphne, pressing her against him.

Lee and I walked in a half-embrace. I was hot, and my shirt stuck to the small of my back where Lee had his arm around me. I had a feeling he wasn't about to let go.

Blaze, Aurora and River ambled behind us. River was asking Aurora about the types of support programs for Israeli youth, the political efforts and even the popular meeting places. Their tone was friendly, and I wondered how many times they'd met after the circle I had first encountered River.

I couldn't focus on a single conversation. I was surrounded by people who were looking after me, engulfed in the most powerful protective sorcery one could cast. A protective circle could be broken only if one of the people who had cast it got hurt. I was entirely safe.

I marched to the beat of my thoughts. I'm not going to die today. I'm not going to die today.

There were already people at the Three Sons Intersection, the main point where the march was supposed to begin. Squad cars stood on both sides of the street, blocking the intersection. Two officers stopped us at the entrance. I couldn't tell whether they were normies or sorcerers.

"Security check," one of them said, and reached out for Matthew's bag. The other officer noticed Sherry and tapped his colleague's shoulder. The latter withdrew his hand, blurted out "Sorry," and gestured a brief salute.

We marched to the assembly point. I felt my heart racing, my breathing shallow. I glanced around, seeing only familiar faces; the same people who always marched with us, who called out for equal rights, who chanted with us. There were no traitors here.

Gaia squeezed her way to us through the crowd. "Look!" She tugged on my sleeve. "Look, they're all here!" She waved at my group behind her. Even Tempest was with them. She turned back to me, saying, "She's not on… on… Don't worry." Only then did she notice Lee's arm wrapped around me. "You're a moody," she blurted.

Lee nodded.

She shifted her gaze between Lee and me. I tried to think about what to say so that she wouldn't be offended. She had offered her help with a heart full of anticipation. Gaia stuck her hand into her pants pocket and took out a stick of purple gum, similar to her hair color. She peeled off the wrapper and shoved it into her mouth.

"Hello," she said, and extended her hand. "I'm Gaia."

"Hello," Lee said, smiling, and reached out his hand to meet hers. "I'm Lee."

They shook hands somewhat formally, then Gaia popped her purple bubblegum bubble and looked at me. "Anyway," she said, "we're here. All of us. We've got your back. Don't worry."

Lee pressed me closer against him. "Good. I'm having a hard time looking after him all by myself. He keeps getting into trouble."

Gaia smiled at Lee. "That's how they are at that age. Testing boundaries."

Lee laughed.

Forrest appeared behind us. "You'll be fine."

"Of course he will," Aurora said with a smile. "I'll give him hell otherwise. It would be a nightmare building a new counselor roster."

Gaia popped another bubble, winked at me and disappeared back in the direction of her group. My group. I took a deep breath. Everything will be fine.

We fell into lines. Lee wouldn't let me march at the edges like the rest of the empaths. He held my waist and led me to the middle of the line. I tried to explain that wasn't how we marched, but Daphne silenced me with her touch, her expression grave.

"What is it?"

She shook her head. "Something. I can't tell yet."

"You want us to look together?" Oleander asked her quietly, and I assumed he had asked the question out loud more for my sake than to get a real answer.

Daphne shook her head. "Not now."

The knot in my stomach tightened.

"We're going home," Matthew said, shouldering his bag. "Let's go."

Standing next to Lee, Dimitri said, "I don't see anything." He was looking over my shoulder.

Daphne bit her lip. "Neither do I."

"I won't have–" Matthew started to say.

"It's not your call," Sherry interjected. She looked straight at him, talking in a softer voice than I'd expected. "It's your brother's decision. I know you're only looking out for him, but he has the best possible protection."

They eyed each other silently, and Matthew backed down.

Blaze and River came and stood behind me; Lilia, Aurora and Dimitri in front of me; Lee stood to my left, and Daphne to my right. Not one of us was standing where we should have according to our powers. Matthew stood near Daphne, ignoring Sherry who kept trying to pull him out of the line and position him near the cops. I suspected that had been her plan all along, and that he was refusing to cooperate. From a distance, I heard Gaia and the others' hoarse, enthusiastic shouts. I wondered whether they had been among the high schoolers who got their asses whooped outside the Basement after the previous rally.

Matthew linked arms with Daphne. "Stay close to me," she said, her voice brittle.

"Sure," Matthew said sternly.

Lee pressed me against him. I felt his breath catching. "We can go home."

"It's too late," Daphne said, sweeping her gaze across the crowd. "They already know we're here. I can barely see anything. All I see is that your presence is vital here, beside me."

Matthew pulled Daphne into a half-hug.

Everyone was nervous, but the circle held. I felt its protection. Sherry got up behind me, between Blaze and River. Now I noticed the undercover cops she had stationed there; unfamiliar faces dotting the lines, creating a loose circle with me in its center. She had been serious when she said they intended to catch whoever tried to hurt me. Oleander had inched slightly away from me. I was surrounded by friends who were looking out for me, by the protective sorcery and by the protection of the police officers.

When the moon was fully visible above, someone in the crowd drummed seven quick beats, and another yelled, "Go!" and started shouting our slogans.

"And we're off," Sherry said.

Daphne reached her hand out to me. I held it, and we started marching.

Daphne and Aurora began to chant. Once she managed to make out the words, River joined in. Lee silently held me close to him.

We chanted our usual slogans, demanding the right to vote for parliament, the annulment of the oath of allegiance and the right to make our own decision regarding early detection in fetuses. There were other slogans, but with Sherry and Dimitri marching so close to me, I felt bad shouting about police corruption and coverups.

Throughout the march, the police officers shifted positions based on some logic only they were privy to. Sherry kept me at arm's length. She pulled me apart from Daphne when Daphne wouldn't let go of Matthew, and squeezed herself in between Lilia and Dimitri when it was her turn to lead. At no point was she more than one person away from me. The rest of the cops stood farther back.

Half the march passed uneventfully. I started feeling safer. Even Matthew began to smile, genuine smiles, and chant slogans he found amusing. He changed a few of the words so that the rhythm was the same but the meaning completely altered. I got swept up by his enthusiasm, and together we made up new slogans and shouted them with just as much gusto as the rest of the marchers.

Aurora no longer looked scared, and was now busy shooting us angry glares whenever we chanted, instead of 'equal rights in parliament!', 'Pluto is a real planet!' From a distance I heard Guy and Gaya shouting the distorted slogan along with us. Aurora's glares cut through me. I stifled my smile.

When we reached the intersection of Paula Ben Gurion and Shenkar Street, Lee tightened his grip around my waist. He was shaking his head. "Something. I don't know," he said in answer to a question I didn't ask.

Tension reverberated through the lines. Daphne's hand was covered in sweat. Dimitri was marching to Lee's right, looking at Daphne.

"I don't see anything," she said, shaking her head. Sherry placed her hand on her belt. The other cops in the lines around me mimicked her gesture. I tensed. Going home suddenly sounded like a great idea. I reminded myself that the previous victims hadn't been shielded by protective circles. That was precisely their mistake. I had three damus friends and police protection.

We switched places; River and Blaze now marching in front of me, chanting. With Lee's arm around me, I could admit they made a cute couple. Sherry was on River's left, scanning the crowd. Aurora to Blaze's right, glancing back at me every now and then.

We kept walking. Daphne let go of my hand and wiped her forehead. Aurora took a step back. Matthew grumbled something about her elbowing him, and that he wanted to be close to me but everyone was pushing him away, and then I heard a gunshot, and I froze.

All at once, everyone started moving.

Before I managed to react, Lee pulled me to the ground, shielding my head under his arm. I felt his breaths, shallow, rapid. I was hot, sweat dripping from my forehead into my eyes. Lee wouldn't let me get up.

A few more shots were heard from several directions, after which people began tripping and stepping on me. Lee arched his back every time I was stepped on. I heard someone running towards me. Matthew collapsed on top of me. I recognized the scent of his deodorant. He shielded whatever parts of me were still exposed. I heard their breaths, labored and painful. I didn't dare say a word.

I heard shouts, Sherry barking orders to the cops around us. She called each one by their name, directing them to their places. Someone fell to the ground next to me, and the protective sorcery snapped like a guitar string.

My ears popped, and everyone's feelings came crashing into me. Fear, anxiety, sadness, tension. A shooting current of pain was flowing next to me. Someone was hurt.

I felt the cops, all full of determination, and some tinted with fear. I felt the depletion of everyone who had participated in the circle, the anguish building up inside Lee from the moment it expired.

I dug deeper inside him. Footsteps running, and more gunshots, and Sherry yelling, "Disperse!"

"Did they get him?" Matthew asked.

Someone approached us. "Is Reed OK?" Sherry asked.

Lee finally let go of me.

I kneeled, trapped between Lee and Matthew, both pale and drenched in sweat. Matthew was panting. Sherry's brow crinkled. "We're on it." She looked at me and said, "Thank you." Her shirt was torn, a red blotch spreading across her abdomen.

Between everyone's feet I saw a body lying on the ground, four officers crouching on top of him. I didn't dare poke in his direction. I stayed on the asphalt, Sherry already disappearing back into the crowd, yelling more orders at the cops.

Lee hugged me, his face damp with tears and sweat. Matthew managed to settle his breathing. He wiped his face. None of us was able to speak. A wave of sadness hit me from behind Matthew. I moved a little to get a peek. Daphne was sitting on the ground, her hair veiling her in a dark cloud of curls. She was holding Oleander in her hands. Blood was everywhere.

"Matthew!" I yelled out, and pulled him over.

"He's been shot." Daphne was holding Oleander's face, her tears dripping on him.

"It's my fault," Aurora said. She was as white as a ghost. "I thought we caught all the bullets, but then another one was fired, and Oleander moved. He was so quick."

Aurora's hand was red with blood. She cradled it against her chest. I wondered whether it was Oleander's injury that had broken the protective sorcery, or perhaps there was something more.

Oleander was lying on the ground, his head in Daphne's lap. Around his left leg, his jeans were soaked in blood. Because he was unconscious, I couldn't trace the source of the pain.

I was struck by Daphne's sobs, and had to blink back my own tears. Matthew opened his bag, his steady hands betraying nothing of the panic rising within him. He handed me a pair of scissors and said, "Cut his pants," then turned to Lee and instructed, "Blur his pain."

Matthew called out to Lilia to come help, Aurora amplifying his cry, creating a tunnel between us. Blood was dripping on her dress. I wanted to ask her not to utilize what little sorcery was still left in her, not to deplete herself, but I couldn't put together a complete sentence. There was so much blood. Everywhere.

I crouched above Oleander's legs. I couldn't understand why Matthew didn't want me to help Lee, until I noticed my hands were trembling. I could barely hold the scissors in place. Daphne sobbed quietly.

Raising his voice, Matthew instructed her, "Choose the future in which he's OK," and proceeded to rummage through his backpack, fishing out bandages, a suture kit and antiseptic ointment. Now I understood why his bag looked so bulky.

Oleander's wound didn't look that terrible. Just a small hole on his shin.

"It's the entry wound," Matthew muttered while disinfecting the area. "The bullet is still lodged inside."

"It's my fault. It's all my fault," Aurora kept mumbling. "I felt the fluctuation in the air pressure inside the barrel and I diverted the bullet's course, but I didn't realize I had to stop two bullets."

Gaia ran over to us. "You're OK, right?"

"Aurora took a bullet, but… she's OK." I tried sounding confident, for her sake.

Gaia tore her gaze away from Oleander and stared at Aurora. She collapsed beside her. "Oh no!" Gaia squeaked, and I could feel her taking Aurora's pain away. She wasn't experienced enough not to absorb the pain inside her, and I was too overwhelmed to show her what to do.

Lilia finally made it over. Without looking up from Oleander's leg, Matthew told her, "Go check Aurora, please."

A police officer showed up and told Matthew there were more wounded and that they needed his help because there were only medics and no doctors in the ambulance escorting the rally. It turned out one person had sprained his arm, another had taken a beating during the frantic stampede, and another appeared to have broken his leg as the result of a fall.

I looked up at Gaia, who was pale and oozing horror. "Go with him," I said and gestured towards the cop. "Get your group to help out."

"Fire sorcerers to cauterize wounds, water sorcerers to wash them," Matthew said while disinfecting the wound. "And get the ambulance over here. Do you have air sorcerers?"

Gaia nodded, blinking.

"Get them to call the ambulance over," he said, shifting his attention back to Oleander.

The officer held Gaia's arm, and the two rushed off.

Matthew instructed me where to press, when to stretch the bandage, how to sanitize. He was entirely focused on disinfecting and treating the wound, his panic momentarily fading as he immersed himself in the familiar work. Lilia calmed Aurora down while dressing her wound. Dimitri disappeared into the crowd, presumably to help with the arrests.

We were all covered in blood, and then I heard the ambulance siren. Sherry appeared just as the ambulance pulled up next to us. She took one look at Aurora and shifted her gaze to Matthew. "How are the patients?"

"Mine will be fine," Lilia said.

"Oleander will make it," Matthew said, tying the dressing around his wound. I refrained from remarking that of course Oleander would make it. He wasn't supposed to die yet. But he could very well spend the rest of his life in a hospital, hooked up to machines, unconscious.

The medics emerged from the back of the ambulance and lifted Oleander onto a wheeled stretcher. One of them commented on the professional job we had done, and Matthew gave a joyless laugh. He slid off his bloodied surgical gloves, bunched them together and handed them to one of the medics to throw away. Another medic led Aurora into the ambulance.

Sherry looked at me. "We took care of it," she said, and I didn't tell her it was the second time I'd heard that from her. "Tonight you're safe. You can go home and get some sleep."

I wanted to ask Daphne if it had helped, if we had actually succeeded, but I didn't dare. She was entirely focused on Oleander. I saw her shift every now and then, moving her hand or her leg. It looked like a physical expression of the way I maneuvered people, when I clenched every heartstring to affect the desired result. She was probably transporting us to a future in which Oleander had regained consciousness and didn't spend the rest of his life bedridden.

Matthew got into the ambulance, and Daphne joined him. Lee and I stayed behind. Sherry patted my back. "I'll give you a ride home." She waved behind her and said, "Lilia and Dimitri are going to the hospital."

"Was Dimitri hurt too?" Lee's voice sounded thin and enervated.

"Just a few blows from one of the shooters who resisted arrest. It's fine." She smiled. "We're used to it."

Lee returned the smile. I felt his fatigue. I wanted to take a shower and go to bed. "Who's coming with us?" I asked; my voice sounded frightened and strange, and had a faraway quality to it.

"I'll stand guard at your place tonight. My people will watch the suspects. We've arrested quite a few women."

"Female suspects?"

"Yup." Sherry raised her brow. "Why?"

I returned the look. "I'm just used to having the women around me protecting me, not shooting me."

"You'd be surprised how close I came to shooting you myself on more than one occasion." Sherry smiled halfheartedly. "I don't think it's all behind us, but thanks to you…"

"Don't say it." The exhaustion crept into my voice. "Unless Daphne says I'm fine, I don't want to hear it." Sherry wasn't as depleted and hurting as my friends. I was hoping she would indeed be enough to protect me. She wasn't part of my circle. The reason Dimitri had entered the circle suddenly made a lot more sense. He probably wanted to keep the damus closest to me functioning and capable.

"How many were there?" Lee asked, steadying his voice.

"Five. At least two pyros. Soon we'll find out what the rest of them were," Sherry said.

Lee said, "When I pushed you down to the ground, I maneuvered Blaze towards the gun, like you did at the bar."

Sherry raised her palm in our mutual protection gesture. "It was justified." She looked at Lee. "If you want to join the police force…"

Lee let out a brief chuckle. Sherry smiled. I felt the camaraderie between them, something in the way they stood in front of each other.

Blaze and River appeared behind Sherry. River's ordinarily neatly styled hair was disheveled and Blaze seemed exhausted. He looked at me and immediately hugged me. I felt the sigh trapped inside him. "Sherry said you're OK, but I had to see for myself," he whispered.

I hugged him back. Once Blaze released me from his embrace, River squeezed in between us and hugged me. She didn't say a word. I felt her relief. Neither of them was completely depleted. I breathed a sigh of relief.

Gaia had sent me a text: *On our way to the hospital. We're all fine, but need to help the wounded.*

I leaned against Lee and typed *You all did great. Take care. See you soon.*

I was so tired by the time we got home that I could barely make it to the couch. Sherry canvassed the apartment, peeping into every room, like Dimitri had done when he first arrived at our place.

I let Sherry use the shower before me. Exhaustion radiated from her with every step she took. I offered her some old clothes of mine, sweatpants and a T-shirt that was too small on me and too big on her. She took them without protest, and after the shower went into Daphne's room and shut the door behind her.

My phone rang; Daniel's name flashed on the screen. I picked up.

"They said on the news there were gunshots at the rally," he said. I could hear the concern in his voice. "Are you OK?"

"Yes." I stifled a yawn.

I heard murmurs on the other end of the line, and Daniel said, "The boss is asking if you're OK."

"Yes, I'm OK." I was hot and sticky and wanted to get out of my sweaty clothes. There were blood stains on my shirt. On my pants.

"There's a neighborhood watch of… volunteers. They came over a few hours ago to make sure you weren't here," he whispered. "The boss kicked them out, but now they're back, and he had to sign a document promising you won't work here."

"Hand him over!" Remy yelled in the background, and after snatching the phone he said, "You hear me? There are a bunch of psychos here trying to tell me how to run my business. *My* business! That I built with my own two hands. You hear me?"

"I hear you."

"So I kicked them out, but they've got a cop with them, or someone who looks like a cop. I don't care. Anyway, they came over with this cop, threatening that if I don't fire you they're going to raise hell, so I've got no choice, you know? I've got no choice. I have to let you go."

I heard yelling in the background, and Remy saying to someone, "OK, OK, I'm doing it. It isn't easy. He's been working here since he was a kid."

My ears perked up. I'd been working at the Sinkhole for a little under a year.

"So you hear me, Reed? You're fired. I'm sorry, but I've got no choice. I'll transfer your severance package to your bank account. Severance for ten years, the duration you worked here. But that's according to the base salary, no tips. I don't want to hear about tips."

I gaped into the phone.

"One month salary for every year, so that's ten monthly paychecks of severance, you hear me?"

"I hear you," I stammered.

"What do you mean?" Remy yelled to the person next to him. "He's been working here since before he got enlisted. When he was just a kid I'm telling you. He worked for me." Remy shifted his attention back to me. "So that'll be going straight into your bank account, and I don't want to see your face here until things cool down, you get it?"

I could imagine the scene unfolding at the Sinkhole; Remy finding a way to pull one over on the Sons of Simeon or their messengers who had gone there to get me fired. What I couldn't imagine was how he had explained his plan to Daniel, and I was hoping none of the people currently there was going to rat him out.

"Got it, boss. I got it. Thanks."

He hung up.

"Everything OK?" Lee looked at me.

"Yes." It was too hard to explain, but at least I wouldn't have to worry about money anytime soon. My base salary at the café wasn't that great without the tips, but it was better than no income at all. Lee hugged me and we went to take a shower.

There was nothing sexy about that shower, merely a ritual of scrubbing off the dirt and then changing clothes. I shoved all our dirty clothes into the washer and turned it on, wishing for the memories to fade like the blood stains.

Lee changed into clothes that belonged to one of my exes. I couldn't even remember his name. It was the longest pair of pants I had in my closet, and they were still too short on him. He looked ridiculous.

"Music," Lee said. "We need music." He approached the stereo and began fiddling with the speakers.

"I don't want music," I said, plopping myself onto the couch and closing my eyes, "I want to sleep." And forget. The noise. And the crying. And shouts from every direction. And the protective circle collapsing. Gaia's pale face. Aurora cradling her wounded hand. The smell of blood and burnt flesh. I was supposed to feel happy I was still alive, but I was exhausted.

The first few notes sounded like heartbeats. I heard Lee's footsteps approaching. I opened my eyes. "Come, we're dancing." He reached out his hand. His walls were as shaky as mine. If I tried, I could peek inside.

"I don't want to dance." I looked into his eyes, trying my best not to examine how brittle his walls truly were and look behind them. He was the one who always guarded himself from me. I couldn't take advantage of the opportunity now.

"It's easy," he said and winked. "Like sex, but with our clothes on." He took my hand. "Come on. We're dancing." There was no joy behind his gaze. A facade of the right physical gestures without the corresponding emotional interior.

"I'm miserable, and I'm sad."

Lee looked into my eyes. "Me too," he replied quietly. "But if we go to sleep like this it will end in nightmares. We have to shake it off before we go to bed."

In the background, the heartbeats evolved into beating drums and wailing guitars. It wasn't happy music. The singer sang about pictures from a broken, joyless world that was dying, doomed to perish in five years.

I let him heave me up from the couch, and we stood facing each other. "And now," he said, holding up a finger, "a magic trick."

He stuck his hand in his pocket, smiled, pulled it out and unclenched his fist, producing a cigarette.

"I don't smoke," I said and shrugged. "And I thought you wanted to dance."

Lee held the cigarette between his thumb and index finger and stuck it in his mouth. "You don't have to smoke," he said, his voice muffled from the cigarette. "I'm smoking. You're just dancing with me, and I'm helping you with the sadness."

"You're not…" I searched for the right word. "I can deal with it on my own."

Instead of replying, Lee pulled out a lighter from his other pocket, closed his eyes, took a deep drag and exhaled two small jets of smoke through his nostrils. Daphne and I didn't allow smoking in the house, but I couldn't send him outside. Not now. I'd deal with Daphne tomorrow.

"That's not tobacco," I said once the smell hit me.

Lee opened his eyes, plucked the cigarette from his mouth and held it out in front of me. "You want some?"

I shook my head. "I don't like things that play with my mind." Sherry was in the next room. I felt her consciousness slip away as she fell asleep. I had the feeling that even if she had been awake, she wouldn't have done anything. She had reached some sort of agreement with Lee, and neither of them would violate it.

Lee smiled and took another puff. "You don't have to." He took a step forward and placed a hand on my waist. "Come, we're dancing." He swayed his hips, and I danced along with him. We were out of sync. I felt ridiculous, swaying all stiff and awkward when all I wanted was to lie down and not think.

Lee took another drag of his cigarette. He closed his eyes every time he took a puff, and opened them and smiled at me as he exhaled the smoke, his smile becoming increasingly lopsided. We danced three songs together, until his cigarette was finished, and he carefully placed the butt on the table.

He straightened and put his hand around my waist again. "And now," he whispered, his accent more pronounced than I had ever heard it before, "magic." He pressed his forehead against mine, and I felt him touching my psyche. Slowly. Giving me ample time to retreat. I didn't move. His walls were full of cracks, and he barely managed to hold them in place. He plucked part of himself and wrapped it around my consciousness. I felt his mental fog infiltrating every part of me. It was different from last time. This time he was using the blurring effect of the substance itself to cleanse the negative emotions, to leave nothing behind but the pleasant, positive feelings.

"You don't need to smoke," he whispered, "and you don't need to be sad." I felt the blurriness enveloping all the prickly, painful feelings and dissipating them. "You're alive, and I'm happy." How did he have enough sorcery in him to maneuver me like that? He was going to deplete whatever was left in him if he continued.

I should have taken a step back, broke the connection. I could have pushed him off me. But it felt nice. It was so easy to let go, let loose, let him veil my consciousness in haze. I noticed we were swaying together. Slowly. Not entirely to the music's rhythm. Both his hands were on my hips. I moved closer to him, into a real hug, pressing my stomach and chest against his. He moved his head so I could lean on him.

"More?" he whispered in my ear.

I nodded and closed my eyes, giving in to the feeling. He wrapped my entire consciousness, slowly, gently. I let myself be swept along. We breathed together, moved together wordlessly. I barely noticed when Lee led me to the couch and helped me sit down.

The fog started to dissipate around the same time the album looped back to the beginning. Lee lifted his head and looked at me. "I need more," he said, and slightly lowered one of his walls. I felt the misery pouring out. It was the accumulated misery of years of repression.

I couldn't put words together. I was flying so high I felt that if I attempted to talk only air would come out. I nodded.

He fished out another cigarette and extended his hand. I took it. "Want to dance again?" His voice sounded indifferent, as if my answer didn't really matter. There had been intimacy between us only seconds ago. He wanted to keep moving.

I pulled myself up with his help and smiled.

"You're gorgeous when you smile," he said, making my stomach shrink. He smiled too and put the cigarette in his mouth. "Together this time." He pressed me up against him. We stood face to face. He lit the cigarette. First puff. Now, instead of keeping it all to himself, he swaddled my thoughts once the sage started to affect him.

I didn't think. I rested my head on his shoulder and closed my eyes. I adjusted my movements to his; I listened to the air entering his chest, filling him up, and felt Lee transferring his feelings to me, his consciousness being tucked behind a blurring veil. I didn't want to resist. I was swept along.

26

Morning slowly seeped into my consciousness. I was naked under the light blanket. I liked the feeling of the fabric against my skin. Lee was lying in bed behind me, making the mattress dip on his side. He was caressing me. Long strokes. The back of my neck, my arm, forearm, lower back, shoulder blades and back to my nape. I took a deep breath, trying to remember last night.

The fog lifted, leaving a trail of warmness behind it. The pain had almost entirely subsided. No wonder Lee decided to smoke after the rally. Shoulder, arm, lower back.

"Feel good?" he whispered. His voice was hoarse. Gentle waves flowed from him to me. I leaned back a little. He was closer than I thought. My body brushed against him. He was probably leaning on one arm. I moved my pelvis, scooting closer.

He stopped stroking me.

"More." My voice was croaky, a morning voice. I cleared my throat. "Please."

I felt him moving behind me, lying down.

I touched his hand, lifting his finger and placing it on my skin. "More cuddling, please." This time my voice sounded like its usual self. He slid his finger down my waist, and stopped. Slowly, he dragged his finger along the border between my bottom and lower back.

My outburst of emotions took me by surprise. I didn't have time to block it. Lee's breath caught when it hit him.

"Sorry," I mumbled.

Lee didn't move. "What do you want, Reed?"

You. Now.

"For you to keep touching me."

I heard his snigger. I had a perfect mental image of him. Strained smile, amused look, aloof expression. "I think," he said, pressing up against me, "that you want something completely different."

I turned to him without opening my eyes. We were lying in front of each other. I felt his body against mine, stomach to stomach, chest to chest. He folded his knees, so that one of his legs was placed on top of me and the other was pressing against my thigh. I knew how his body felt. It wasn't our first time. And yet, something was different. There were almost no barriers between us. "We didn't do anything last night. Just so you know. I didn't take advantage of…"

I opened my eyes. He was looking straight at me, green eyes with brown flecks. So close.

"I just took off your clothes because I hate falling asleep dressed, and I thought you probably don't like it either." He was speaking rapidly, his words stumbling over each other. "And I stayed around to see that you're OK, because an emotional cleanse can be scary the first time, and I woke up before you, that's all. And I didn't want you to panic…"

I pressed my lips against his, to make him stop talking. I didn't want to listen to the apologies that were only meant to conceal his fear. I pulled away from him.

"It's over. The feelings will return soon. I…"

I kissed him again. His lips moved against mine, parting for me. This time the kiss was longer.

"You're not going to let me finish a sentence?" He curved his lips, his smile reaching his eyes, creasing the corners.

I pressed up against him and this time I didn't pull away until I felt his heart racing like mine, the sweat on his back, the movement taking over him. I lowered my walls, flooding him with warmth, with affection. Slowly. Like he had so caringly done last night, without drowning him. Or scaring him. To let him feel what I felt. He shifted in front of me, deepening our kiss, pulling me against him.

I detached myself from him. His eyes were closed, lips slightly parted. It took him a moment to open his eyes and look at me. He took a deep breath, exhaling slowly, like I do when I'm trying to pull myself together. So very slowly. He lifted his finger and brushed the hair from my face, then dragged it along my cheek and neck. I kept looking into his eyes. He stroked my shoulder.

"If I said…" he began, and I immediately shot up and kissed him. I felt him laughing into my mouth. It was a very crooked kiss.

This time he was the first to pull away. He looked at me silently. I felt his stomach pressing against mine with each breath. He lowered one of his walls. The emotion gushed my way. Passion, a deep, flooding need. I placed my hand on his waist, pulling him closer to me the more he lowered his wall. When he was done, he didn't smile, only looked at me with anticipation.

"More," I whispered.

"That's everything that has to do with you," he said, still looking into my eyes.

I gently touched one of his other, crumbling walls.

"Those are feelings that have to do with my parents," he said. "I don't want to think of…"

I didn't let him finish. I kissed him hard, deep, and he succumbed to me. I wasn't expecting him to give in so quickly, but his walls couldn't endure. He lowered them one by one, the kiss growing more intense with every one that collapsed. I wasn't as broken inside as I had been last night. I could handle his emotions. And he needed to unload. So much had been hidden. I merged his feelings with mine, dismantling his sorrow and loneliness, flooding him with passion and warmth.

He moved from my shoulder to the back of my neck and shoulder blades. His feelings were roiling around me. There was fear, and worry, and anxiety, mixed with passion and the need to lose control.

I flamed his passion and he let out a moan. In a remote crevice in the back of my mind I noted to myself that he was whispering my name, and that I was moaning even louder than him, and that it had been so long since I'd felt this good.

"Condom," he said, panting.

I rolled to the side of the bed, opening the dresser drawer. "I hope they haven't expired."

I heard him laughing behind me. He kissed my shoulder. "I have one, if we need."

I barely managed to whip one out of the drawer and read the expiration date on the wrapper before he lunged at me.

I held onto him, weaving our feelings together, lost in a soul that wasn't my own. Lee granted me access into every corner of his psyche, and I couldn't stop exploring. Touching, prodding, examining. To find out what made him get closer to me, what made him move faster. I didn't have to stop myself, I could let our waves coalesce until I was no longer able to tell us apart.

27

Once the final waves abated and I managed to settle my breathing, I could reassemble the room around me into a single, coherent image. It was already after midday. My pillows were scattered across the floor. The chair was upside down. One of Lee's legs was entangled in the sheet, and the blanket was twisted up between us, covering no one.

Lee was breathing slowly, deeply. He was lying on his back, his head propped up on his arm, smiling with his eyes closed.

"You OK?" My voice was croaky. I remembered shouts and began wondering whether they had been mine.

Lee nodded, the smile still plastered across his face.

I lay down beside him, sliding my hand under the back of his neck, and pulled him closer. He turned to me and nestled his head under my chin. "I think," he said, just as hoarsely, "my body's made of Jell-O."

I smelled him. His sweat. His skin. I entwined my legs with his, feeling him kicking as he tried to disentangle himself from the sheet. I brushed my foot against his, and he stopped. He simply stopped moving, and only breathed.

I didn't want to withdraw from him. I didn't want to stop feeling him. From the inside. To know what he felt when I touched him. How my every breath affected him. I hugged him, and he nestled up against me. We breathed. Slowly. In sync.

Someone knocked on the door. Lee managed to find the edge of the blanket and pull it over us.

"Yes?" I called out once we were partially covered.

Daphne opened the door and peeked inside. I felt her emptiness, her difficulty breathing. Happiness bobbed to the surface once she looked at me.

"We're ordering takeout," she gestured behind her. "You want anything?"

"How's Oleander?" I asked, heaving myself up while holding the blanket around me.

"He'll be OK," she said, tucking a stray curl behind her ear. "I was with him all night. He's sleeping now, so I came to save poor Sherry." She winked at me. "I warned her this would happen, but she wouldn't listen to me."

I admired her. I couldn't imagine what her night had been like, what she had been through while I was busy getting high and fooling around with Lee instead of being at the hospital looking after her.

I felt Lee retreating, preparing an apology, making himself smaller. I pinched him. It hurt me as well. "Don't you dare."

Lee raised his head, looking at me from below, an angle I wasn't used to. "It's OK. You two need to…"

Daphne stepped into the room and sat down on Lee's side of the bed. She patted his shoulder. "I'll translate Reed for you. He wants you to stay. I want you to stay. I just feel lost at the hospital anyhow, and it's a lot more fun here." She brushed her hair off her face. "So what do you want to eat?"

She was flooded with loss and sadness, it was just the top, brittle veneer that suggested lightheartedness. It was her way of coping. I couldn't deny her that.

I tightened my grip around Lee's shoulder. "Besides, you can't move."

Lee shook his head. "I'm trapped." He placed his head back under my chin, "I'll have anything vegetarian." He closed his eyes and breathed in.

Daphne pointed at me. "Don't let him run off."

"And what would happen if I ran?" Lee mumbled under my chin.

Daphne placed her hand on his bare shoulder. "Reed would be sad." She got up. "And we'd be left with too much sushi."

Lee laughed. Daphne winked at him and left the room. Lee kissed the base of my neck. "You'd be sad if I left?"

"Yes." I stroked his hair. It was longer than mine, and thinner, spilling between my fingers.

"You'll have more sushi." Lee slid his hand around my waist.

I cupped his face and steadied it in front of me. "You're right. Leave."

He laughed. His eyes flickered. "I feel guilty." He straightened up, and now we were at the same level. "I'm so happy. And I'm not supposed to feel that way. Everyone's miserable, and I'm the only one who's happy."

Small, warm waves were flowing out of him. Like when he had woken me up. Buried beneath was a small, almost imperceptible current of guilt. And suddenly I knew what to say to him.

"You're not the only one who's happy," I said and kissed him. He was flooded, and halted himself before the massive wave hit me. His every feeling was too sharp, unadjusted to reality. No wonder he had to keep blocking himself all the time. I kissed him more passionately, pulling his wave into me. I wanted to be inundated by his warmth, his affection towards me. Some of his guilt dissipated just because of what I had said.

I wondered whether Daphne had done this on purpose. Maybe if she had said something else, Lee would have reacted differently. And I wouldn't have said those words to him. He wouldn't have felt this flooding wave, and I wouldn't have slackened again, completely giving in to my feelings. Intertwined with him without the ability or desire to break free.

28

We ate the sushi and took a shower, which led to yet another round that we did our best to keep quiet. When we stepped out of the bathroom, ruddy-faced and engulfed in steam, Sherry made a comment about the stamina of empaths, and Daphne let out a joyless laugh.

Her feelings confused me. She was supposed to be happier. While Oleander was hospitalized, it sounded as if her situation was under control. Then again, Sherry was still here. Not at the police station, interrogating the suspects, but here on our couch. As if danger remained imminent.

Lee looked at me, sensing my confusion, and shifted his gaze to Daphne. She looked as if she was trying to shrink inside her skin.

"It's over," I said. Trying to convince all of us. "We're past the rally. It's over."

Daphne bit her lip. She had exactly the same expression as when she didn't want to tell me to go to the rally.

"You saw everyone wounded. That's what happened. Aurora and Oleander got hurt. We were all covered in blood, just like you saw. Sherry's plan worked. We're back in the timeline in which no one dies. That's it, it's over." I paced to the couch and stood above Sherry. "It's over. Tell her it's over," I said, raising my voice.

Sherry stood up in front of me. She had the posture of a person used to standing to attention. Her voice was much quieter than mine. "It's not over till we're completely sure no one's trying to finish the job." She pointed to her chest. "I'm staying here to make sure you're safe. Until we get final confirmation from every seer I know," she said, intoning the word 'every,' "I'm not leaving."

"But…" I mumbled. "It's over. Daphne said that if I go to the rally and…" But Daphne hadn't said that. Now I remembered. She only hinted that if I didn't go to the rally, someone would die. At no point did she say that if I went to the rally we'd be done with this, or even that this was the rally she had originally seen.

The world whirled around me.

"You can't change it," Daphne said, stepping closer to me. "I discussed it with Sherry. She has a plan, and it isn't half bad."

I was still going to die. That's what Daphne was saying. She wasn't being callous. She had simply accepted this future. I remember her reacting the same way when her mother quit chemotherapy. The acceptance of an imminent fate.

Lee took my hand in his. "Come. Now."

"Where?"

"Doesn't matter." He tugged my hand. "Divergence, like River said. We'll do something they can't foresee. Come with me. Let's go. We'll hop on a plane, go somewhere far. We'll hide. They won't find us. Let's go."

"I'm coming with you," Sherry said, taking a step forward. She folded her arms across her chest. "I'm not letting you out of my sight."

"No. We're going alone." Lee pulled my hand again.

We ran down the stairwell and stepped out into the street. His motorcycle looked completely intact. I was almost expecting to find a flat tire. Lee jumped on the bike first and handed me a helmet. I put it on.

The bike wouldn't start. Lee tried again, to the same effect. He cursed and got off the bike. I felt the helplessness swelling inside me. He reached out for my hand. "We'll take a taxi. Come."

I shook my head, choking back the tears. I'm going to die. I'm going to die and I can't escape it. I'm going to die.

Lee pulled out his phone and called a taxi stand. There were no available taxies. He tried the app. With each of his attempts, I felt my future hollowing out, reducing.

"We'll take Daphne's car." He dragged me back upstairs. Daphne and Sherry were still standing in the middle of the living room, and it didn't look as though they had exchanged more than two sentences since we left. Daphne's expression was grave.

"We need your car," Lee said to her.

"I left it at Matthew's," Daphne replied.

"This is my life we're talking about! You're just sitting here and—"

"We're trying to save your life, you idiot!" Sherry yelled at me. I fell silent. She was breathing heavily. "We have a plan. I can't discuss it with you. Neither can Daphne. What is it about the-Sons-of-Simeon's-seers-are-watching-us-so-we-can't-talk-about-our-plan that you don't understand?" She clasped her hands tightly.

Daphne took a deep breath and looked at me. "Please, we're doing all we can. I'm having a hard enough time with all the mixed up timelines."

"What would happen if we walked?" I asked Daphne in a calmer voice, trying to bottle up my anger, bury it where only Lee could feel it.

"You get stopped two kilometers from here, regardless of which direction you choose. The two of you get shot before you even notice the man with the gun."

"Bicycle?" I asked.

"A car runs you over. Kennedy Intersection." Daphne approached me and placed her hand on my left temple. "This is the only part of you that doesn't get crushed."

"They're targeting me specifically right now," I said.

"No," Sherry interjected quietly, "they want to make sure you get to the rally according to their plans."

Daphne wiped her eyes of tears I hadn't noticed. As long as I was here, she would see me dead. My reflections dead.

"Is there an edge?" I asked quietly.

"Maybe. Stop asking."

Lee looked at me. "An edge?" He sounded confused.

"A rare, extreme timeline," I explained, without taking my eyes off Daphne. "Events that are so far away on the fringes of the futures, they're almost invisible."

I sent Lee as soothing a wave as I could. I felt a decision taking shape inside him. When I looked at him, he managed a smile, burying the sense of loss deep beneath the waves of affection. "OK. But I'm not going to live as if you're about to die."

I hugged him silently.

"We're staying," Lee said, pulling me against his chest. "And you better get some earplugs."

I smiled through the pain and heard Sherry chuckling. "You want us to post a security detail outside your apartment? It'll afford you some privacy. Just let me know if you intend to leave."

Daphne's pain was still there. She had seen me die, and she couldn't take comfort by looking at the edge or else she'd draw the attention of the other damuses.

Lee glanced at Sherry and said, "Want to watch a movie?"

I sent him a wave of confusion. I thought we were just getting a bit of rest and going back to bed. Lee stroked my back and looked at me. "There are people I like here, and I want to get to know them."

There was something strange about Sherry's smile when Lee said he wanted to get to know her. Her shoulders slouched, and her posture became less rigid. She needed to feel welcome, and Lee had caught on to that faster than me.

I pulled away from him. "Potato chips?"

"Yes, please," Sherry replied, brushing her hand through her hair. "Can I help with anything?"

"You can choose the movie," Lee said, whipping out three DVDs from the dusty pile in the living room. "Action, espionage or science fiction?"

29

I checked my phone while we watched the movie. Everyone had sent texts asking how I was doing, and expressed their relief to find out I was fine with a lot of silly stickers and emojis. My group notified Aurora that they wouldn't accept any substitute counselor. "We'll come over to yours for a meeting," Gaia had written me. "If that's OK." I could imagine Daphne's reaction to a teen invasion of our house. "I'd rather have the Sons of Simeon skin me alive than host you hooligans here," I wrote in reply. She sent back a picture of a cat rolling her multi-colored eyes.

Lee peeked over my shoulder. "Is that the girl I should be worried about?"

I looked up from the screen and nodded. "She's cute, and smart, and seventeen."

Daphne stifled a giggle. "And she's a moody with a crush on you."

"Hey!" I shouted halfheartedly.

Daphne shrugged, feigning innocence. "Just calling it like I see it. You're the current subject of conversation between her and Guy."

Lee leaned in. "Do you peek into all of the private conversations between the people around Reed?"

"It's my number one way of keeping him alive," she answered quietly.

We fell silent and went back to watching the movie.

My mom called just when the lead character had crossed paths with the villain, and the girl lost yet another layer of clothing, for a reason none of us seemed to understand.

"Forgot about us?" Her voice wasn't shaky, or angry. It suddenly dawned on me that shots had been fired at our rally yesterday, and neither Matthew nor I had called to inform them that I was OK.

"No, of course not." I looked at Lee and Sherry. Lee was laughing at some joke Sherry had made. Daphne was sitting in the corner and, judging by the outbursts of affection flowing from her every now and then, texting Oleander. "I'm fine. Sorry I didn't call."

"I know you're fine." This time the rebuke in her voice was loud and clear. "I heard it on the news."

I recoiled. Lee looked up from the screen and glanced at me. I sent him a calming wave, and he went back to the movie.

"So when are you coming? The soup's getting cold." It was my mother's way of telling me she was worried about me. She fussed about details without ever discussing actual feelings. And she of all people had a moody for a son.

"I can't go outside. There's…" If I said I had a policewoman guarding my house, my mom would have freaked out. They didn't know about the future Daphne had seen.

Daphne stood up and reached her hand out to me. "I'll fix it." She flashed me a suspiciously wide smile.

"What's going on there that's more important than your parents?" My mother's voice rose. I felt like a kid again, trying to think up an excuse for not doing my homework.

I handed the phone to Daphne.

Daphne smiled and told my mother, "Reed's new boyfriend's here. They won't leave each other's sight." She winked at me. I felt a sinking sensation spreading through my body. Lee turned pale. He looked more shocked than last night at the rally. Sherry started laughing. Daphne turned to her and added, "And the girl Matthew has a crush on is here too. We're making sure she won't run off before Matthew arrives."

I snatched the phone from Daphne's hand. "Mom, it's not true. Daphne's just…"

I heard my mom laughing. "Oh, that Daphne," she said, and added a few words in Romanian. Some proverb about shoes always walking at the wrong time. Lee and Sherry were sitting perfectly still on the couch. I heard my dad scold my mother in the background. My mom's laughter calmed down. "We'll come over with dinner, don't worry."

"We don't need—"

"We'll just drop off some food and leave. I promise." She let out another chuckle and hung up.

"My parents…" I cleared my throat. "My parents are bringing us dinner," I said, just barely managing to strain out the words.

I looked at Lee, and felt the anxiety washing over him. "I'm not good with parents."

"You don't have to stay," I said.

"He's staying," Daphne interjected, and shifted her gaze to Sherry. "And so are you." With a somber expression, she looked at me and said, "You realize this is exactly what'll help your parents, right?"

I collapsed onto the couch between Lee and Sherry. "To come here? And I'll have to…" I couldn't organize my thoughts into clear sentences. Lee was something private. We were just beginning to establish intimacy.

"For afterwards," Daphne said. She wasn't smiling anymore. "After everything. Your parents will remember this day, when they came to check out your new, cute boyfriend. And they'll remember you were happy, and that'll help them. They won't suspect you tried to kill yourself."

"I don't…" I brushed my hand through my hair, trying to control my tone. "You know I wouldn't…"

Daphne snorted. "You really think they'll listen to me afterwards? They'll blame me for not stopping it." I felt the stifling tightness creeping up my stomach to my throat. My parents had in effect adopted Daphne after her mother's passing, and my mom had never stopped trying to be a surrogate mother to her. If I die, and they think Daphne had something to do with my death, they'll abandon her. I could see it with painful clarity. Daphne standing over my grave, and my parents snubbing her, leaving her to her own devices.

I felt Lee poking around inside me, dismantling a little of my anger. I nodded to signal him to continue. He understood without me having to say anything.

"OK," Lee said, stretching out on the couch. "So what do I tell Reed's mom when she asks about the wedding and grandkids?"

"She won't ask that." I buried my head in my hands. "She'll only talk about food, and ask what you like, and what your parents do for a living, and avoid any question whose answer might be construed as a conversation-ender." I peeked at him through my fingers. "You don't have to stay."

"You afraid I'll make a run for it?" He smiled.

I shook my head. "I'm afraid my mom will like you."

Lee laughed. "Don't worry. If your mom gets too close, I'll let the cop here pull out my entire rap sheet." He glanced at Sherry. "The federal bureau already transferred it over, I assume?"

Sherry rolled her eyes. "I never betray my sources." She stood up and straightened her shirt. "Am I supposed to play Matthew's girlfriend?"

"It's just so we won't have to talk about why there's a police officer around. If you're there because of Matthew, it will distract their mom, and she won't grill you."

Sherry nodded. Her expression was blank, unrevealing. She shot Lee a glance. "Looks like I'm the one who's going to have to deal with questions about marriage and grandkids."

"Thanks," Daphne said quietly.

Sherry shrugged. "No different than any other undercover work I've had." She patted Daphne's back. "Maybe you should bring Matthew over, just to make it more believable?"

I was already dialing before Sherry finished her sentence. If I was going to suffer, so was Matthew. It was childish and silly, and I knew he had spent the entire night in the operating room, and certainly wouldn't want to spend the next few hours in the company of our parents, but I couldn't face them on my own.

My parents entered the apartment carrying heaps of food. My mom made a beeline to Daphne, crushing her with a tight hug. She asked how Oleander was doing, and how she was managing, and whether she needed anything, and inquired into her grandmother's health, and finally handed her a stack of home-cooked meals in Tupperware containers for Oleander at the hospital. I didn't even know Daphne had told her about Oleander.

The next to be crushed between her arms was Matthew. She had bestowed upon him the title, "My brave boy." It turned out that during all those hours I had spent in bed with Lee, Matthew was being interviewed by every news outlet as the normie doctor who marched in the rally and saved a seer's life.

"He even talked about you!" My mom finally turned to me with a hug. "He said how much you had influenced him to help others."

Matthew rolled his eyes. "They shoved their cameras in my face in the middle of my morning round, inconveniencing my patients."

My dad patted him on the back. "And humble. That's my boy."

Lee was standing behind me. My mom could barely suppress her giant smile when she noticed him.

"This is Lee," I said, gesturing at him, my heart pounding. I prayed they wouldn't do anything embarrassing. Anything that would make him regret agreeing to stick around. Anything that would ruin what we were just starting to build.

My dad reached out his hand.

"I'm an empath," Lee blurted, his accent heavier than usual. He was oozing discomfort.

My dad shrugged. "So is my son." He let his hand linger in the air. Lee shook it. My mother was literally squirming with questions. Instead of letting them out, she simply smiled and shook Lee's hand.

A small wave of happiness crept out of Lee in my direction. I exhaled my trapped breath. I introduced Sherry, to save Matthew the embarrassment. Another round of handshakes ensued.

Daphne and my parents got busy in the kitchen while Matthew and I set the table. Lee and Sherry tried to help, but my mom shooed them out of the kitchen, arguing that we didn't put our guests to work. Lee sent me a small gloating wave. Instead of sending him a wave back, I looked at him and touched him inside the place he marked as mine. I felt his passion stirring. I flamed it enough to make him lean against the wall behind him, breathing slowly. I withdrew from him and turned back to the kitchen, still smiling.

Matthew elbowed me. "What did you do to him?" he whispered.

"Everything he wanted," I whispered back and winked. Matthew shook his head and mumbled something inaudible.

My mother turned from the counter and said, "Sit, sit, don't let the food get cold."

We sat at the table. Daphne stopped Lee as he was about to sit next to me, and directed him to the chair in front of Matthew. She crinkled her brow, pointed to me to sit next to Matthew. I followed her instructions without asking why.

My parents were sitting in front of each other, Matthew and I on my mom's side, Sherry and Lee on my dad's, and Daphne at the head of the table. My mom had made at least two versions of every dish. There was vegetarian pea soup and pea soup with chunks of sausage; a meat lasagna and a vegetarian lasagna; chopped vegetable salad without onion, another without cucumbers, and a third with everything. It appeared she had spent the entire day cooking.

I tried to think about a topic we could discuss, anything that didn't involve the rally or the murder. It was too late. My mother turned to Lee and asked him, "What do your parents do?"

Lee gave her his most charming smile. "My mother is a journalist and my father is a lawyer."

My mother hummed. "And are they sorcerers?"

"Mom!" I hissed.

Lee sent me a small wave of anxiety and replied with his unwavering smile, "Air sorcerers. Comes in handy with two teenagers in the house."

My mom was like a dog with a bone. "Do you have a brother? Sister?"

Lee put down his spoon, sending me a clear wave of rancor, gave my mother a giant, captivating smile and replied, "One sister, River. She's two years younger than me, a water sorcerer, and Blaze's girlfriend. It's through him that I met Reed. I work at a publishing house and do quality control for our books' designs, which includes moodification. I studied history and graphics in college, and I have a master's in graphic design. I make a decent living, but I made more back in the Confederacy. I moved here because things are pretty dismal back home, and Blaze suggested I join him. River came with him. She's not pregnant."

It sounded nothing like the story I had gotten from River. However, a mentally unstable person who couldn't stay in one place for too long wouldn't have made a very good impression on my mom. He paused to catch his breath, and before my mom managed to say anything, he lifted his spoon and pointed at Daphne. "Did I forget anything?"

Daphne shook her head.

"Good." Lee's smile disappeared. He looked at me. "Can you pass the salt?" On the face of it, he looked like his usual calm self, but his psyche was roiling. I shot him a well-aimed arrow of affection.

My mother brought her napkin to her mouth. "Thank you, that was very informative." She then took a deep breath, and I was scared she was about to ask Sherry something. The latter was concentrating on her plate, cutting up the lasagna into tiny slices.

She looked up, smiled at my mother as widely as Lee had, and said, "Four brothers. I'm the youngest. A police officer. I met Matthew at a vigil. Make a lousy salary. It's been that way since the Ministry of Finance decided to privatize the investigations department. Doing my bachelor's in history and ancient Israel studies, and it will take me at least three more years to complete it because of my job. I keep kosher and observe Shabbat, unless it interferes with my job. It has nothing to do with being half Moroccan. It's a compromise between the two sides of my family. Everyone on my dad's side is religious, and everyone on my mom's side is secular." She turned to Lee. "And that, I believe, means I won our bet."

Lee closed his gaping mouth. "Doesn't count. You didn't wait for the question."

My mom sat completely motionless at the end of the table, not knowing where to look.

I shifted my gaze between them. I felt a wave of glee from Daphne. I turned to her. She was covering her smile with her hand. I pointed at her. "What did you do?"

Daphne shook her head. "Nothing," she said, feigning her most innocent expression.

Sherry tilted her head towards Daphne. "I asked her what the fastest way would be to get through this stage of the meal."

My dad looked up from his plate, clearly intrigued. I wondered how many times he had searched for a way to end my mother's interrogations.

"She said I needed to know in advance what your mother was going to ask, and memorize the answers." Sherry went back to dissecting the lasagna on her plate.

Lee sent me an amused wave.

"So you memorized the entire conversation before it took place?" Matthew leaned in and smiled.

Sherry waved her finger. "No, we memorized different parts of five different conversations."

"I only had to memorize three," Lee said, smiling his thin, sardonic smile. "Your mom kicks me out of the house in the other possible futures." He leaned further over the table. "You want to know what I tell her?"

"No." My mom's voice gave me a jolt. I was expecting her to be mad. She just sighed. "I should have known," she said, pointing at me. "He's a smartass like you, isn't he?"

"Much worse," I replied, and sent Lee the warmest wave I could muster.

My mom gestured at the lasagna. "Well, eat up, it's getting cold."

Daphne laughed, and my dad chuckled. Lee smiled. Sherry and Mathew exchanged glances. And I felt almost normal.

30

"I need a beer," Matthew said after my parents left.

Daphne followed him into the kitchen to get the Tupperware. "I'm going to visit Oleander." She took three of the containers and placed them in a bag. "You want to come? We'll have the entire night together, and I'm sure he'd appreciate some company."

I wanted to go back to bed, but it was thanks to Oleander that I was alive right now. I looked around me. "OK, who's coming to pester Oleander instead of letting him recover quietly?"

Lee gestured towards Matthew. "Take the beers. They probably don't carry that brand in the hospital."

Matthew took a six-pack out of the fridge. It was something bitter Daphne had bought two weeks ago that neither of us drank. I helped Daphne carry the bags of food. It was only on the way down that I noticed Sherry was unusually reserved. I stopped on the staircase and waited for her.

"Everything OK?" I whispered.

Sherry pursed her lips. "I don't like the way you're leaving the apartment when I'm supposed to control the comings and goings."

"Daphne's a damus. If something could go wrong, she'd stop it."

"Exactly," Sherry whispered back. "If anything goes wrong, it means she planned it. Every seer has plans."

Lee sent me a small wave of impatience. I heard their voices at the bottom of the stairwell.

"I trust her."

Sherry didn't answer, but simply turned her back and continued down the stairs. I followed.

Daphne suggested Lee sit up front, so he'd have enough legroom. I sat behind him and stroked the back of his neck. He leaned back and purred with pleasure.

"Aww, aren't you two sweet," Daphne said, and smiled at me in the rearview mirror.

Matthew sat behind her with Sherry squeezed between us. He pulled Daphne's hair. "You want some of that? You won't regret it. It is a truth universally acknowledged that the Katz boys are experts in neck feathering."

"I never feather and drive," Daphne laughed. She started the car and pulled out of the parking lot.

I dragged my finger lightly up and down the back of Lee's neck, sending him warm waves to accompany my strokes. He amplified the warmth. We entwined ourselves into one another. I heard Matthew and Sherry talking, and felt the motion of the vehicle, and didn't care about anything other than the sensations Lee amplified inside me. Not even the fact that we would both pay for our mutual maneuvering.

The guard didn't notice that we'd entered the parking lot, and the parking spot closest to the building was unoccupied. Matthew led us through the labyrinth of corridors and elevators to the wing in which I had been hospitalized in what felt like ages ago. I carried the Tupperware boxes, Lee the beer; Daphne could barely keep herself from running to Oleander's room, and Sherry scanned every corner as if dozens of Sons of Simeon were about to lunge at me

The walls were painted according to the types of sorcery: red for pyros, blue for splashers, green for pebbles and yellow for airheads. We proceeded along the corridor until the color of the walls switched to purple. Psychics. I felt a heaviness spreading inside me.

Sherry looked at me. "Something wrong?"

Lee gestured at the walls. "Too many suffering people in one place. Feels almost like a sorcery fountain."

"Wow," Daphne mumbled. "It wasn't like this when you here, Reed."

"There's been a spike in attacks," Matthew said in a clinical, detached tone. "A lot of new patients admitted in the past week. More pain, more suffering. I assume it influences you the most."

"A lot of damuses in the same place, which means no one can look in and see what's happening here," Daphne said.

I shot her a look. "What do you see?"

"Tons of timelines," she replied and gestured to a spot near Lee. "Oliver? Lee's friend Oleander had mentioned? I can see him, he's almost solid. Even I could have gotten mixed up now."

Lee looked at the spot to which Daphne had gestured. "What's he doing?"

"He's annoyed that I'm peeking into his timeline." She waved at the man we couldn't see and continued to walk down the corridor.

A doctor in scrubs and pink Crocs emerged from one of the rooms.

"Lilac!" Matthew called out, and she turned around and approached us. They hugged, and Matthew introduced her to us. "This was the best intern in my class. I almost lost my position to her."

Lilac laughed. "Who even wants to do an ortho residency? Vascular surgery is so much more interesting."

It turned out she didn't work at Rabbeinu Gershom but at the Gates of Zion hospital, and was just here to look in on one of her former patients. She and Matthew soon dove into a conversation, chit-chatting about mutual patients and trading OR anecdotes.

Daphne cleared her throat.

"You go ahead," Matthew said, "I'll just pop by the nurses' station for a moment to make sure Lilac's patient is getting the VIP treatment."

Lilac laughed and patted him on the shoulder.

Lee sent me a ball of amusement and tugged my consciousness in Sherry's direction. I didn't feel comfortable reading her, but he highlighted one specific line. Jealousy tinged with feelings of inferiority. Not particularly intense, but enough so I'd make a mental note to mention it to Matthew later.

Oleander's room was at the end of the corridor. He was reading in bed, his bandaged leg propped up on a pile of pillows. Daphne entered first, almost hurling herself towards him. Lee and I followed her into the room, Sherry close behind us.

Oleander held his arms open and Daphne plunged herself into his embrace, a few inches shy of his injured leg. "I missed you," she said, and they kissed.

I put the stack of Tupperware on the bedside table. The book Oleander had been reading was splayed open beside him. "*The Decline of the West and its Possible Redemption*," I read the title aloud. "A light read?"

"I studied it in college in my History of Nazism course." Lee stepped past me to take a closer look at the book. "This is what you read when you're bedridden?"

"It gets boring with no one around." Oleander hugged Daphne tighter, and she put her head on his shoulder."Now my redemption has arrived."

Daphne giggled. "How very decadent of you." They kissed again.

Lee pulled a can from the six-pack and handed it to Sherry. "Beer?"

Sherry shook her head.

"Always on duty," Oleander remarked.

Sherry gestured towards me. "As long as that one's still alive."

"Thanks," I smiled at her.

"Come on," Lee said, handing me the can. "You're having a drink, and I'm neck-feathering you."

Daphne smirked. "Reed hates beer. Good luck trying to take away the taste of that one from him."

"Lee has no intention of alleviating Reed of the beer's taste," Oleander laughed. "He wants to get him buzzed." He gestured a thumbs-up at Lee. "I admire that ability."

"The ability of getting someone buzzed?" Sherry asked. Something about her tensed, even though she didn't show it outwardly.

Daphne met her gaze and nodded. "That's why I brought you here. The other damuses can't see what's happening in here, and you guys have to talk."

"If you're a moody, you can use substances to…" Lee began to say and cleared his throat. "To affect other people."

Oleander stroked Daphne. "Lee means he can use the substance himself to maneuver someone else. It's like amplification. An artificial enhancement to what they usually do."

Sherry looked at Lee. "What's the difference between that and a regular maneuvering?"

Lee hesitated. "When you maneuver someone, you have to feel the emotion," he replied. "And when you… when you use, you can… you can take whatever you're using and pass it on. For instance, you're not happy but you take something that fills your brain with serotonin, then you can pass that artificial feeling on. And then you can… feel together," he barely managed to finish the sentence. The tension inside him was mounting. I poked inside him and caressed the stifled feeling, to alleviate it a little.

There was anger in Sherry's voice when she said, "My empaths said taking substances to affect other people's consciousnesses is nearly impossible."

"Only if you're inexperienced," Lee replied with a hint of disregard in his tone. "Your empaths probably don't want to take the risk of being affected by the substances themselves."

"I thought you were here to visit me," Oleander said, leaning back on the pillows.

Daphne stroked him. "I am here to visit you. I brought Sherry and Lee so they can talk without the Sons of Simeon listening."

Sherry looked at me. "Can you do what Lee's talking about to me?"

I shrugged. "With a lot of practice, maybe. It's a little like moodification." Except for the fact that this was someone's brain we were talking about, not books or posters, and the mere thought of maneuvering her made me sick to my stomach.

Sherry turned to Lee. "Can you teach me how to protect myself against it?"

"Only after I get a signed guarantee that whatever happens, you won't throw me in jail and forget I ever existed."

"You enlist civilians to the police force?" Oleander's tone was too sharp. There was too much happening, and I couldn't read him clearly. He was probably stressed, like me, talking about illegal things with a police officer.

"I make use of whatever I can." Sherry pointed at Lee. "I need to take defensive measures against it. Against a Sons of Simeon's empath screwing with the minds of my cops."

"What?" Lee shot up. "Nothing of the sort happened at the rally. I would have known if someone…"

"She said screwed with the cops, not with you," Daphne replied on Sherry's behalf. "I've suspected for a while that someone's maneuvering them, but not the regular maneuvering, one that's amplified by substances, and it's only now that someone's willing to listen."

"You don't know for sure that's what's going on," Oleander interjected. "It's just a hypothesis. It's not—"

"It doesn't matter," Sherry cut him off. She looked at Daphne. "Thanks," she said quietly and turned to Lee. "Now explain it to me slowly, please."

Lee began, faltering at first, but picking up his pace halfway through. He told her about Morty, a cleaner, more polished version. I recognized the terms, I had used them myself when cleaning up my past for professionals.

I helped him by contributing a little information Sherry was missing about the abilities of empaths. No, I couldn't maneuver her like that, and certainly not as well as Lee could. Yes, I could maneuver an entire pub full of normies and elementalists, but it wasn't like maneuvering moodies. Lee and I explained to her that maneuvering another moody required a lot more effort, and the price you paid for it afterwards was much higher too. The more we talked about it, the more we agreed that whoever was maneuvering Sherry's cops probably wasn't touching moodies, but focusing instead on normies, maybe even on elementalists, causing the desired effect without being discovered or entirely depleted.

Sherry sank into her plastic chair and drummed on her knee. I could picture her behind her desk at the police station, tapping her pen on the table.

"And if you both took the same substance? Could you combine your powers and maneuver more people?"

"Maybe. I'm not sure. I've never tried." Lee's brow furrowed. "I'm also pretty sure that if Reed took some of that stuff, he'd have such a psychotic breakdown we'd have to rush him to the ER."

"But not you." Sherry continued to drum her fingers on her knee. "And how do I defend myself against it?"

I knew the answer to that one. "You need an experienced empath on your side, and then he can dismantle whatever they throw at you. Preferably more than one empath."

Sherry pursed her lips. "My empaths refuse to experiment with those substances. The Sons of Simeon don't have the same limitations as the police. We're losing the battle before we've even begun the fight." She shook her head. "Damn."

"I could…" Lee said hesitantly, then continued with a more confident tone, "I could show your empaths what to do. If you want, that is."

Sherry leaned forward. "I'd really appreciate it. Thanks."

Oleander started laughing. "I can't believe she manipulated you so easily, dude."

Sherry raised an eyebrow. "Excuse me?"

Daphne pinched Oleander's arm. "Come on, stop it."

Oleander pointed at Lee. "It's incredible, how long did it take, five minutes? She got you to switch from 'I'm not doing anything, what are you talking about,' to 'sure I'll help. I'll maneuver as many cops as you'd like.'" He looked at Sherry and stopped smiling. "You're worse than Linden."

"Excellent comparison." Sherry interlaced her fingers. "A cop whose only goal is to keep everyone alive compared to a lunatic prophet who's convinced the best thing that could happen is a tyrannical regime with him safely installed as tyrant."

"And I say you're both so gung-ho there's no reasoning with either of you. He won't stop talking about his vision for the future of humankind, and you won't stop running over whoever's standing in your way, including people who're supposed to be dead within a month," Oleander said.

I shriveled into a ball.

Sherry narrowed her lips. "I'm doing whatever I can to prevent Reed's death…"

"I'm not talking about Reed," Oleander cut her off. "I'm talking about the fact that Daphne finally comes to visit me, and you have to tag along. I have exactly five more weeks to live, and you're ruining them."

Sherry straightened up. "So?"

Oleander seemed baffled. "What do you mean, so?"

"So what if you're going to die? You've known that for… how long now? Thirty years?"

"Yeah, but it doesn't mean I'm happy about it."

"Before my sister passed away, she made sure to make an impact on the world she was about to leave behind her." I felt the tightness in her throat, but Sherry's voice didn't waver. "I'm sorry you're going to die. But I need help. The Sons of Simeon are steering our present, and we have to find a way to deal with it."

"Or we don't."

"Or we don't what?" The arrows of Sherry's rage punctured the air between them.

"Have you even considered that maybe the vision Linden's presenting everyone is a decoy? That maybe the Sons of Simeon are steering us to a better place behind his back?" Oleander sounded just as angry as she was.

"And maybe tomorrow morning we'll all hold hands and sing about peace and love!" Sherry raised her voice. "The Sons of Simeon are navigating us towards a very specific future, and they're targeting a very specific person, and I won't let that happen."

"You can't stop violence with violence," Oleander raised his voice. "Don't you get it? You're trapped in the social conventions you're—"

"Enough!" Lee blurted. We all looked at him. "Enough," he repeated in a slightly quieter voice, and turned to Oleander. "We'll go now. We'll give you some time alone with Daphne, OK?" He looked at Sherry and said, "And I'll prepare a list for you. Substances, emotional responses, how to stop things, the works. OK?" He got up and reached his hand out to me. "Come, let's get going. I have enough yelling back home."

I took his hand and stood up.

"I'm sorry," Oleander said in a calmer voice. "Stay. I didn't mean to flip my lid like that." He looked at me. "I've got that type of shouting at home too."

I stroked Lee's arm. "It's OK," I said, managing a smile. "I need to take Lee back and get some very different yells out of him."

Oleander smiled, making Lee smile. We said goodbye to Daphne. Still withdrawn into herself, Sherry followed us out of the room.

"He's not wrong, you know," Lee commented once we were in the corridor.

Sherry's head swerved sharply to him. "What do you mean?"

"If the Sons of Simeon have a lot of damuses, they can navigate towards a different future from the one Linden's aiming at," Lee said quietly. "Back home, about ten years ago, there was a faction of the KKK that managed to steer an entire group away from their plan."

"We can't rely on the presumably good intentions of seers who're cooperating with the most dangerous force our community has faced in the past two decades," Sherry replied, but she didn't sound as tough as when she was arguing with Oleander.

Lee held his hands out. "I wasn't suggesting we trust them. I'm just saying that maybe Oleander has a point. Maybe confrontation isn't the right way to go about it. Not now, anyway."

"Said the guy who comes from a world in which they dismember whoever turns against the community," Sherry replied.

Lee fell silent.

We walked towards the nurses' station, where Matthew and Lilac were still immersed in conversation. Matthew turned to us as we approached. "We're going," I said.

"And Daphne?"

Lee gestured behind him. "With Oleander. We'll take the bus home."

Matthew looked at Lilac, then back at us, and once again at Lilac. "I'll see you around."

"You don't have to change your plans on our account," Sherry said dryly.

Matthew smiled. "Don't need to, want to." He waved towards the exit. "Shall we?"

Lee and Matthew got to talking about the differences between the hospitals in Israel and the ones in the Confederacy, and Sherry got a phone call. I lagged behind a bit, echoes of the argument in Oleander's room still haunting me. Lost in thought, I almost bumped into someone, catching myself a second before the collision.

"Sorry," I mumbled, and only then realized it was Ivy.

In a dark dress, hair weaved into a braid and freckles gleaming in the fading sun, she looked sixteen. I used to joke with her that she could pass as one of my group at Yoyo.

Ivy balled her hands into fists and immediately relaxed them. "We don't need to talk."

"What are you doing here?" I asked before realizing what a stupid question that was.

"Daphne's still with Oleander," she said, a statement instead of a question.

I nodded.

She exhaled slowly. "OK, I'll go check if the cafeteria's still open."

"You used to time things better," I couldn't help but quip.

"That was when my brother wasn't in the hospital flooded with so many timelines that I had to walk with my eyes on the ground so as not to see people fucking everywhere," she groused humorously.

"I'm sorry about Oleander."

Ivy crossed her arms. "Not as much as I am."

I didn't reply.

Ivy waited, but didn't look past my shoulder. She never skimmed my futures next to me. She always made sure to address only my current timeline, and talk only to me. She wouldn't say anything unless I continued the conversation.

"Do you know what's going to happen to him?"

"Not cancer or anything like that. Probably an accident. He doesn't allow me to look," her voice trailed off.

"Death is a private matter," I quoted her. She used to say it to me when I complained that Daphne wouldn't tell me how long she was going to live. Ivy always took Daphne's side instead of mine.

Another silence ensued. "From what I hear from Oleander, Lee sounds nice," she eventually said. "More than what's-his-face."

"What's-his-face," I repeated. "I'm not even sure which of the what's-his-faces you're referring to."

She smiled, and for a moment looked like my old friend again, the same damus who sat at our table in the cafeteria and told Aurora and Forrest that the way they were staring at each other was ruining her appetite, and if they didn't go release that tension between them at once, she'd use them as a case study in her course on intimate relationships – and after they disappeared whispered,

"I just wanted Aurora's pudding cup. It was the last one," and gobbled it up.

"I'm glad you have Daphne. She… she was always better at looking after you than I was," Ivy said.

"I don't need looking after."

"No." She peered into my eyes, and despite the flood around us, I managed to feel her. She was full of hopelessness. "You don't need some deranged damus to make sure you aren't hurting yourself," she quoted me. The sadness in her voice almost made my eyes well up. She put her hand on my arm. "Take care of yourself, will you?"

Instead of shaking her off, I put my hand on hers. "You too."

It seemed as if she was about to say something, but then I heard Lee calling me, and she slipped her hand out from under mine and walked away.

All I could think about during the bus ride was Ivy. How she had come back from that first meeting with the Sons of Simeon, back when they were just a bunch of sorcerers seeking a better future. She was almost beaming with excitement upon her return, saying that she had finally been shown a future in which we were living true freedom. She held my hand and could barely sit still, kept asking me to come to a meeting with her. To come share the vision. She promised me it was entirely safe. "We'll just enter a sorcery fountain for a few minutes, in and out." But Daphne stopped me, and later Ivy betrayed us all, and the whole world fell apart, and there was no getting her back.

31

Gleaming teeth and arms twisting around me. Water filling my lungs. I'm choking. Panting.

I woke up in the middle of the night drenched in sweat. Lee sat up beside me, engulfed in the haze of sleep. "What happened?"

I rubbed my eyes. "Nightmare." The last images slipped away as my mind came into wakeful focus. A distorted face chasing me. Suffocation. Clutching, inescapable arms.

The room was dark, lit only by orange stripes spilling in through the shutters and painting the ceiling. I heard Daphne's door opening, then quiet footsteps in the hallway followed by a hesitant knock on my door.

"Everything's OK," Lee said loudly. "Just a nightmare."

Sherry opened the door a crack. She was wearing the same clothes I had given her yesterday. Or perhaps two days ago. The days garbled in my memory. Lee pulled the blanket over us both. We were barely covered, and Lee's feet poked out the end.

"What was the nightmare about?" she asked.

I shook my head.

She pushed the door ajar, stepped into the room and shut the door behind her. She stood above me, arms folded across her chest. "What did you dream about?"

The door opened again and Matthew appeared.

"You can't get any privacy around here," Lee grunted. He was feeling weighed down, but it wasn't reflected in his tone.

"Your brother thinks his dreams are meaningless," Sherry said to Matthew, pointing at me.

"His brother thinks he wants to go back to sleep," I replied casually.

Matthew yawned. "Want something to help you sleep?"

I patted Lee's thigh. "Already got it."

Lee hugged me and looked at Matthew. "I'll get him to sleep. Don't worry."

Matthew and Sherry exchanged glances.

I straightened up. "What?"

"Nothing," Matthew replied, a little too quickly.

I shifted my gaze between the two of them, then to Lee. He returned the look, his eyes dark in the dim room. "What's the problem? Everyone has nightmares."

Lee brushed my hair off my forehead. I waited. He let out a quiet sigh. "I don't think your dreams have some deep message. I think we're all worried the stress will do you in."

Sherry said, "I've seen people go to pieces over a lot less."

I stifled a yawn. "I dreamed that Linden gets one of your suspects out, and she comes after me." I felt Lee strolling through my psyche, smoothing out the painful edges, his touch a gentle flutter. "And she has splashers that drown me." That was the cleaned-up version of the arms reaching out for me and the teeth gleaming in the darkness.

"It's perfectly normal—" Sherry began to say.

I raised my hand. "I know. Trauma. Post-trauma. All that psychobabble." I sighed. "I'd really like to try and go back to sleep."

Sherry nodded. She looked at Lee.

"I'll take care of him," he said and hugged me.

Matthew yawned. "Give us a shout if you need anything."

I nodded. They left the room and closed the door behind them. I leaned back in bed, Lee pressing me tightly against him.

I listened, waiting to hear Daphne's door opening, but all I heard was the screeching of the foldout couch in the living room and quiet whispers. I vaguely felt Matthew's warm thread of affection towards Sherry. I felt twelve years old again, burrowing underneath the blanket while Matthew and whoever he was dating at the time were busy in the next room, entirely unaware of what I was going through. I knew Lee could feel him too, could sense Matthew's slowly uncoiling passion.

"Someone's going to have himself a good time tonight," Lee mumbled in my ear.

Instead of telling him that Sherry had already turned Matthew down, I edged my discomfort underneath my affection towards Lee and burrowed deep in the part of his psyche he marked as mine, in an attempt to erase the memory of my dream.

"I ran into Ivy when we left the hospital," I whispered to him.

He tightened his arms around me. "Want to tell me about it?"

"Have you ever had friends who crossed the lines?"

Lee shrugged. "I told you. Back home they have a way of dealing with those kinds of people."

I caressed his bare chest. His body was pressed up against mine, and some part of me wasn't interested in talking but in entirely different things. "Here it isn't like that. Free speech and all."

He stroked my back silently. I took in his scent. "Talk to Aurora for ten minutes and you'll understand."

"Aurora is…?" Lee asked quietly.

"Blonde. Glasses. From Yoyo."

He nodded.

"So she's really into the whole embracing diversity bit, and understanding everyone, and accepting everyone, and if we only listened to each other, we could find a solution that would work for everyone."

I was engulfed in a cloud of Lee's scent. I pressed my feet against his. "She and Ivy were really close. They both kept yapping to Forrest and me about how privileged our approach is, and how we have to listen, and accept and embrace diversity. It's practically

Aurora's slogan. *Embracing diversity*. When Ivy walked out on us, it was bad. I think Aurora took it even worse than me."

"Why?" His voice reverberated through his chest.

I closed my eyes. "I think she suddenly realized it was one thing to talk about accepting diversity, and quite another to actually do it."

He was quiet for a moment, and then said, "What exactly did she do?"

I closed my eyes. I didn't want to remember. I didn't want to think about that day. But I wanted Lee to know. It was important to me that he understand. I told him about how Ivy joined me at the meetings at Yoyo when I was counseling three groups a week, juggling work and my studies and volunteering, and I was happy. I had a moody member of the group who barely uttered a word during meetings, looking as if she was about to drown inside one of the oversized coats she wore. After every meeting Ivy would make her stay behind and talk to her for almost half an hour, sometimes more. I thought she was helping me support the most fragile moody in my group, that it was the first step towards taking on a group of her own.

Ivy gave her a false vision. She told her that she'd die if she didn't join her in a Sons of Simeon meeting. She led her into a sorcery fountain, showed her their shared vision and made her leave my group, her one and only source of support. When I consulted with Daphne about ways to remedy the situation, she warned me against interfering. Daphne said the girl wasn't supposed to die, but if I made her leave the Sons of Simeon, that's what would happen.

"How?" Lee asked, drawing gentle circles on my shoulder.

"Daphne said the Sons of Simeon had become her primary support group, and pulling her away from them would made her spiral into depression, and from there..." I fell silent. Lee knew that path. The swift pain surging inside him made me realize we were both thinking the same thing. "Are you proud of her?"

"Of who?"

"Ivy. Look." Lee stroked my psyche and highlighted a line that was hiding from me. Pride entwined with pain and disappointment over the separation.

I flipped onto my back and stared at the ceiling. Lee turned to me. "It's OK," he said quietly. "It's good you're proud of your friend for taking a stand."

"She joined a bunch of lunatics who were trying to kill us all and basically robbed the girl I was counseling of her only chance at a normal life."

"Right, but it's more complicated than that." Lee stroked my hair. "She acted on her beliefs, she did what she thought was right and tried to bring about a better future." He waited, and when I didn't reply, he said, "She was still your friend. Despite everything. And you're the kind of person who can see the good in everyone." He paused and smiled. "Even in me." He reached between my legs and kissed me, and we stopped talking.

32

The following night, my nightmare presented even more teeth and arms. This time the faceless people tattooed dots across my entire body. I caught fire wherever the tattoo needle punctured my skin.

Lee woke me up with a violent invasion of my consciousness. He pulled me out of the dream, and I roused with his pale face inches from mine, glowing orange from the streetlights outside. He was hunched over me, propped up on one elbow.

"You were shouting," he said, sweeping away the vestiges of my dream.

"Sorry," I said, my voice gravelly.

He caressed my head and brushed strands of sweaty hair off my forehead. "There are things you could take." He placed his finger on my lips before I could answer. "I mean, I could take for you."

I shook my head. "I can handle it."

Lee leaned back beside me. I felt the pain in his arm, the spot he leaned against to stare at me, and his overwhelming exhaustion.

"Why don't you want me to help you again?" he whispered.

Because I didn't want to lose myself again. "Because I trust you to pull me out if I have another nightmare." I kissed him and cuddled up against him. Lee wrapped his arms around me and kissed my neck.

"What's that?" he asked, kissing my shoulder.

"A shoulder," I mumbled in his ear.

"No, that scar," he said, and pulled back from me.

"It's from four months ago. They were throwing rocks at us and some pyro blew one up too close to me."

Lee's forehead creased. "All your scars are from demonstrations?"

I nodded and pointed at my right arm. "This one's from almost a year ago. It was raining like crazy, and they threw bricks at us. Matthew patched me up."

Lee caressed my arm, inched over and kissed it.

"This one," I said, lying on my back and pointing at the scar on my chest," is from some nutjob who charged at us with a knife. Daphne tripped, and the knife didn't go in, but still managed to graze me."

Lee hummed and kissed my chest, his tongue tracing the scar.

I lowered the blanket and pointed at the scar at the bottom of my stomach. "This one's from the demonstration in front of city hall, after they blew up two school buses full of…" My words turned into a deep groan when Lee kissed me. Down and down, and further below, and very soon I stopped talking and he stopped asking.

When I woke up the next morning, Lee was still asleep, lying on his stomach with his arm hanging off the bed. His feelings were quietly swirling. I caressed the back of his neck. I wanted his dreams. They felt much nicer than mine. All I could remember from my nightmares were the white shining faces chasing me and the sense of suffocation that stuck with me all night.

"Five more minutes, Oliver. We don't have to submit the project until ten," Lee mumbled in English, turned his head on the pillow and continued to sleep.

His clothes stood in a neat pile on the chair, folded like in a store display. I picked up my clothes from the floor and put together an outfit that would be deemed acceptable out in public.

Sherry was sitting at the dining room table, scribbling on a yellow legal pad, surrounded by light brown folders and a pile of papers. I took a closer look at one of them. It contained Forrest's full name, date of birth, military service, place of employment, family members, school and a full description of his ties to me. There was even a list of the Yoyo sessions he had participated in, including dates. I picked up the document, and found a similar one about Aurora underneath.

I placed them back on top of the stack. "What are these?"

"Almost everyone you know," Sherry said without looking up from her legal pad or putting down her pen. "Everyone you've ever worked with. Everyone Daphne knows. Everyone she's ever worked with." Sherry smiled her joyless smile. "Someone's garbling the timelines to keep everything hidden from everyone. The upside is that the only one who can see clearly what's going to happen to you is Daphne, because she's the only one who's close enough to you. The downside is there's no other seer who can tell me what's going on." She slapped the stack of papers. "So, back to the good-ol' investigation methods."

I felt a little joy lurking inside her. She was enjoying her work. I didn't want to ask how she managed to glean so much information about my life in such a short amount of time.

"Aren't you afraid some damus will see what you're reading and sway you to ignore important things?"

"A seer would have to actually be here to see accurately what's happening. Ask Daphne."

"Is Lee in the pile?" I asked, picking up a page that carried the name of some girl who had taken Introduction to Folklore with me at the university; we used to work on our papers together. Apparently she had gotten married, then divorced, and moved to a kibbutz with three dogs of the tiny, yapping variety.

Sherry pointed at a bunch of stapled papers. "That's the summary."

"And Ivy?" I couldn't help but ask.

Sherry pulled out another bunch of stapled papers from a different pile. "Here you go."

I skimmed over the words. How we had met, in two short sentences. Work. Current social circle. Her activity at the Sons of Simeon was underlined with two bold lines.

"You think she's… I mean…"

Sherry looked at me. "What do you think?"

"I wouldn't want to think someone who was so close to me would try to hurt me."

"You don't have to think that. That's my job. Your job is telling me if I missed anything in her evaluation."

I looked at the pages again. Under the title 'Mental History,' I found the description: 'Extreme mood swings. Underwent several emotional dismantling treatments. In psychiatric treatment for the past two years.' Beneath the description appeared a list of the meds she was on. I looked at Sherry. "So she's in treatment?"

Sherry nodded.

"And she's not dangerous anymore?"

"She was never dangerous." Sherry took the pages from me. "She's the kind of person who likes the vision and wants to feel meaningful, but not the type who'd die or kill others to promote that future."

"Do you know what they show in their visions?"

"Sort of." Sherry rummaged through the pile of papers on the table. "A vision in which sorcerers rule. No one's restricted. The more talented a seer you are, the more details you can see." She gave me a side glance. "You know they let moodies see it too, right?"

I nodded. "In a fountain of sorcery. Ivy tried to take me with her."

"They have to bring someone with them, a new recruit, if you will, if they want to stay part of the program. It's a little like a pyramid scheme." Sherry pointed at the bottom of the page. "Opal, 17, member of the Sons of Simeon for the past five years. Sleeper agent."

The moody. One of my Yoyo teens. "She's still alive," I said.

Sherry nodded and handed me another page. "Want to see Oleander's?" She pointed at a sentence on the page.

"Founding meeting of Hands Across Israel," I read, and grimaced.

Sherry took the page from my hand. "He fled after one meeting."

"He has good taste."

"More than his sister. He never attended a Sons of Simeon meeting. In fact, as far as I can see, even though he and Ivy are siblings, they seem to be polar opposites when it comes to ideology."

"Good to know."

Sherry scratched the top of her head and tucked her hair behind her ear. "I'm surprised you haven't asked whether Alder is in the pile."

I bit my bottom lip.

Sherry yanked a page from the bottom of the pile and read aloud: "Alder Bareket. Thirty-two years old. Married with three children. Resident of Herzliya. System analyst at xBit." She looked up from the page and handed it to me.

I pulled up a chair and sat next to her. I breathed in slowly and took it from her. "How did you even know about him? Daphne wouldn't press charges."

"He was on the list because of your military service. Whoever commanded you and Daphne is in this pile." She pointed at the short stack containing the page on Alder.

"Yes, but how did you know that…" Daphne never told me the details of what happened between them. One night she knocked on my door, even though she wasn't supposed to be in the men's barracks, and came in without saying a word. Her whole body was radiating pain. "You want to tell me what happened?" I asked, and she shook her head silently. "Want a hug?" I asked. She shook her head again. "Want me to dismantle it for you?" I asked, and she looked at me with dark eyes and said, "Don't you dare." "You want to just sit here?" I asked. She nodded. We sat together in silence for nearly an hour, after which she got up and left without the slightest explanation. The following morning, when Alder walked into our office, Daphne's body went rigid and her heart numb and hollow. She smiled at him casually, and I felt the blatant dissonance and couldn't do a thing.

"I don't know anything," Sherry said, taking the abandoned page from my hand. "There are no complaints. Not a single sanction or note on his personal file. That's what's so suspicious."

"That his personal file is clean?"

Sherry nodded. "Every officer in the IDF has something on his file. Someone who took offense and issued a complaint against him. Some female soldier who felt harassed. No one's perfect. His file is completely clean. Unblemished."

"He's a damus."

"Precisely." Sherry returned the page to the bottom of my military service pile. "He knows how to avoid things, or, which makes even more sense, how to make the evidence disappear." She turned to me. "I really don't know what happened, but he's the only person in the whole shared history between you and Daphne who looks truly suspicious."

"I never did anything to him," I replied. It was the truth. We barely spoke. He was only interested in Daphne, and after that night he hardly ever showed up at our office. "I only saw him at meetings and things like that, and I haven't seen him since my discharge. He doesn't even come to the rallies."

Sherry hummed. "OK, back to the drawing board." She picked up a folder from the stack to her left and showed me the title, "Kibbutz Horshim."

"God, that was a horrid summer."

"Certainly reads like it." She opened the folder and her attention drifted away from me. My gaze lingered on the pile that contained the document on Alder. A single page. There was a whole pile on Lee, and that was only the summary. I put the paper down on the table and went to the fridge. Coffee, and then I could face the day.

Lee emerged from my room when the coffee was ready, dressed in the worn-out sweatpants that barely reached his ankles. Sherry looked up from her legal pad. "Joining my force today?"

"Good morning." He looked at my cup. "Too much milk."

"This one's mine." I pointed at the cup on the counter with the coffee grains and two sweeteners inside. "That's yours. Waiting for the water to boil."

He kissed me, sent me a warm wave and approached the kettle.

"Lee," Sherry said, her voice slightly raised.

"What?" he asked, rummaging through the cutlery drawer.

Sherry stood up and approached us. She barely came up to Lee's chest. "You remember the promise you made me two days ago?"

"I remember," he replied, straightening up. "Do you remember that I gave you all my notes?"

"There's no substitute for an experienced man in the field," she said in a somewhat softened tone.

The kettle whistled. Lee filled his cup with boiling water, the sweetener fizzing to the surface.

Lee sighed and looked at me. "You do realize that if I make good on my promise I'm coming home high, right?"

I tightened my grip on my cup. "I thought you were only going to teach the police moodies how to do what you do."

Lee snorted. "They're idiots. Like every other cop." He waited, but it didn't get a rise out of Sherry. "I have to show them, or it won't work." He shrugged, his vulnerability reflecting in his eyes.

I lowered my cup onto the counter and stroked his arm. "I understand. It's OK." I attempted a smile. "You're cute when you're high."

He stuck out his tongue and took a sip of coffee. But there was no playfulness inside him, only a deep-seated fear, of which I could only feel the fringes.

The door to Daphne's room opened. She was dressed, holding a pair of sneakers in her hand. "When are we going?"

"Who's going where?" I looked at her inquisitively.

"Lee and I." She considered him. "You were supposed to have finished your coffee by now."

Sherry raised her hand. "I didn't give you permission to go anywhere."

Daphne gestured at the papers strewn across the dining room table. "You're working here. Reed has tons of episodes of stupid shows to watch with Blaze–"

"Blaze?" I interrupted her.

"Of course, I'm not leaving you without protection." She shifted her gaze back at Lee. "And I'm going with Lee to be with more damuses somewhere safe, to search for more timelines your cops are overlooking, and then to take Lee home."

Lee looked at her. "And nothing will happen to Reed while you're gone?"

"Not in the next three hours. And in any event, Dimitri's watching just to make sure." She held her hands to her sides. "Can we get going?"

Lee put his cup down on the counter. "We're going." And went to my room to change.

The doorbell rang just after Lee had emerged from my room again, this time fully dressed. Blaze was standing in the doorway, holding a stack of books under his arm. "Notes on the last bunch," he said.

I reached out and took the books. The first in the stack was about cities that manifest as spirits which influence their residents. In what seemed like a different life, I had begun working on it a little over two weeks ago.

Blaze pulled a small USB stick out of his pocket. "Daphne ratted you out, said you'd have plenty of time for a *Married with Children* marathon today."

"I'm out of here," Lee said loudly.

Daphne linked her arms with his. "Quick, before their awful taste rubs off on us."

Blaze laughed, and even Lee smiled. I got a kiss, and not a word about what was awaiting them outside.

I turned to Blaze. "Coffee? Tea? Water?"

"You don't have to play host with me," Blaze said and approached the fridge, "I can sort myself out."

I felt the tension bubbling inside him. I reached out and stopped him. "Don't worry. Daphne wouldn't have left if she thought an attack was on the horizon."

"I don't..." he faltered, and looked me in the eye. "I miss you."

I didn't know what to say. 'I'm with Lee' sounded silly, not to mention obvious. 'Me too' sounded corny. And I wasn't really sure how he meant it.

"I miss talking to you. I miss hanging out with you. Everything feels so strange between us. I can't find my place. On the one hand you look just the same as you did back then, but on the other, you're suddenly the undisputed leader of the revolution."

I let out a chuckle. "Undisputed leader, huh?"

"I don't want..." Blaze raised his hand. "I don't expect you to run into my arms and suddenly go back to being the person closest to me in the whole world. I just want to watch TV with you and joke around, without making bullets explode midair or getting our asses kicked in rallies, and without having to listen to news about..." He left the unspoken words lingering in the air. He wanted to escape. Just like me.

I put my hand on his arm. "Homework and then TV?"

He smiled.

I pointed my finger at him. "But this time don't burn my notebook!"

Blaze laughed. "If I burn proof copies, Lee will dock it from my salary."

I laughed. "I'm sure I could get him to show you some leniency."

Sherry lifted her head from her paperwork. "Can I get some quiet around here?"

We giggled and went to my room.

Blaze and I spent the afternoon sitting at a safe distance from each other on my bed, me cross-legged against the wall, and Blaze on the opposite side. He was typing on his laptop incessantly, while I worked on dismantling the emotions in the new book I was supposed to fix, about sorcerers who harness the energy of the power plant in Hadera to manufacture more sorcery in the world. I blocked the outside world so it wouldn't influence my work. When the door opened, I didn't even notice.

I vaguely felt someone entering the room. I couldn't stop in the middle of what I was doing, otherwise the emotions woven into the paper might scatter into the other pages, making it more complicated to unravel them. When I was done, I put the book aside.

"I don't know who worked on this, but he ought to be hung." I shook my head. "The guy doesn't know his job. In my first year at the university I didn't make as many mistakes." I massaged my temples and yawned.

"That's why we took you on," I heard Lee's voice saying.

I raised my head.

Lee was standing behind Blaze, smiling.

Blaze looked up from his laptop. "I've been listening to him bitch all morning. He says the same thing after every page."

Lee placed his hands on Blaze's shoulders and leaned over. "Yup, he's awful."

I put out my feelers and poked around. His consciousness felt blurry in the fringes, a bit disconnected, but it wasn't the deep change I was expecting to find. I sent him an inquisitive wave. He sent back a feeling of security and some faint glee.

They were both looking at me, one head above another, completely different in their feelings towards me, representing a totem pole of my relationships. I rolled my eyes. "Should I call my mom? She'd be happy to help you criticize me."

Blaze pulled a panicked face and exclaimed, "Anything but that!"

Lee laughed and straightened up. "Come on, take a break."

Sherry was still sitting at the dining room table in the same position we had left her in hours ago. Only the piles looked different. Taller. Daphne stood next to the counter, oozing pain. Lee put his hand on my arm, keeping me from approaching her.

She straightened up and turned around, her expression masking the pain inside her.

I took a deep breath. "*Married with Children* marathon?"

"No!" Daphne yelled, feigning horror.

"Yes!" Blaze called out, slapping my back.

Lee shot me a look. "You cannot be serious."

Sherry looked at Lee. "Want me to arrange for him to get shot now?"

Blaze laughed. "Don't listen to them, we know what's good."

"I have a far better idea," Sherry said, pulling a USB stick out of her bag. "I could use a break myself. You choose the first movie, we choose the second. Deal?"

I made popcorn while Lee and Blaze went out to fetch drinks. By the time they got back, Daphne had convinced Sherry and me that we should start with some indie animation movie no one liked but her. She said something about it being the only thing that helped her ignore the timeline leaks, but wouldn't elaborate.

By nightfall we had watched four episodes and three movies and competed twice for the title 'champion of the stupidest thing you can do with popcorn.' I even managed to send Gaia a text about exercises I wanted her to do by our next Yoyo meeting, with Lee teasing me about her, eventually spurring on Blaze who started taunting me as well.

Blaze and I parted with a hug I initiated. It took him a moment to return it with an awkward pat on the back. When I pulled away from the embrace it seemed as though he was about to say something, but he just nodded and left the apartment silently.

Only then did it dawn on me that it had been his way of saying goodbye. He hadn't come because he missed me. He came because he wanted one last memory of me. I turned around to Daphne who was standing in the living room. Sherry and Lee were talking about the movies we had just watched. They were their causal, happy selves. No one was acting as though I was about to die. The thought struck me with such force that I had to lean my weight against the wall. Daphne looked up and met my gaze.

She walked over to me and said, "Ask."

"How was it?"

"I saw…" she said and hesitated. "I saw the main timeline clearly. The edge almost doesn't exist."

I felt the air leaving my body. Lee shot me a look. I sent him a calming wave.

"Who knows?" I asked. I was avoiding the real question, and Daphne knew it.

"Blaze and River. They figured out by themselves that if Sherry is still here it means the threat hasn't been shut down, and they made me tell them what I saw. Lee told me he doesn't want to know how much time you've got left, and that he'd make himself forget it even if I told him." She was talking slowly, quietly. "He also said that if I told Matthew, he'd make him forget as well. Matthew didn't want to know. He's scared he'd accidently blurt it out near your parents."

And not one of them told me. Not one of them even hinted at it. She lowered her hand. "And now I'm telling you."

I nodded, feeling the knot in my stomach threatening to swallow me whole.

"Four weeks," she said quietly. "I can't see the exact day clearly yet."

I gritted my teeth to keep myself from making any sound. I felt Lee stroking me from afar. I wouldn't let my feelings flow out towards him.

"You'll tell me when you know?"

"You're going to ask me to tell you, and it will be right before it happens."

"How long will you live after me?"

Daphne sniffled. "Does it really matter?"

My mind was racing. "I want to know that you, and Matthew, and Lee and Blaze and Sherry – that everyone is going to live a long life after me."

Daphne wiped her eyes. "I have forty-seven years, three months and two days left. Matthew has between forty and fifty-five years, I can't see clearly. River and Blaze are going to have four children, and they aren't going to name any of them Reed because Lee won't let them. I see only flashes of Sherry and prefer not to dig too deep because she'll be staying on the police force for a few more years. Aurora gets a PhD in international relations, and Forrest returns to the army. Daniel has another pair of twins."

"You didn't tell me what's going to happen to Lee," I whispered, edging out my fear.

"You're sure you want to know?" Daphne asked, her words strangled with tears.

I nodded.

Daphne wiped her eyes again and looked straight at me. "It won't matter. Just so you know. Your knowing won't change what's going to happen to him. His path is already set."

"Tell me," I said quietly, feeling the lump in my throat. It couldn't be anything good.

"Overdose. A year and four weeks from today."

"Because of a goddamn cup of coffee," I croaked with effort. I peeked past her shoulder. Lee was laughing at something Sherry had said.

"Because the man he loves will be six feet under, and he won't be able to find a reason to wake up in the morning." Daphne didn't move.

"What do I do now?" I asked in a cracked whisper.

"You go to him," Daphne replied, putting her hands on my arms. "You go to Lee, and you love him for all the time you have left and all the time you don't."

"Lee doesn't want to live as if I'm going to die any moment."

"And you believe him?" A tear glistened in the corner of her eye. "You practically live inside his head. You know what he wants."

"No, I know what he feels. That's not the same thing." I looked at Lee again. He and Sherry were quoting lines from the movie we saw. I shifted my gaze back to Daphne. "I'm sorry I'm going to die while we're living in the same house."

Daphne smiled, and her tears streamed out. I held her, teardrops dampening my shirt.

33

Four days later, Daphne came home alone around midnight from a visit to the police station, mumbling something about Lee preferring not to meet today. When I tried questioning her, doing my best to keep my expression from betraying the insult, she wouldn't say a word.

"But..." I held my hands out to my sides, aware of how ridiculous I looked in my silly pajamas. I chose them only because they were easy to slip out of. "I can help him, I can..."

She put her hand on my arm. "He knows."

He knew and yet chose not to be with me. I wondered whether the overdose Daphne had predicted had anything to do with what Lee was going through, but I didn't know how to put it in words.

I managed to fall asleep only after extracting some sleep out of the girl living on the floor below us. She had been to basketball practice and come home exhausted.

The shrill ringing of the phone woke me up. Strips of orange light filtered in through the shutters. I rubbed my eyes. It wasn't my phone. I heard Daphne talking in her room. She was oozing angst. I sat up in bed and waited. The conversation dragged on, Daphne's pain intensifying.

I got out of bed and went to her room. She was sitting on the bed, holding her phone in one hand and drumming her fingernails on her knee with the other. "I'm telling you that… but you… so listen!"

She looked up when I stepped into the room. "Everything OK?" I whispered.

"It doesn't help if you whisper," she said loudly. "He's peeking in here even though he's not supposed to." And after a moment she said into her phone, "Yes, you…"

Someone who was peeking in here even though they weren't supposed to. It had to be a damus. I mouthed "Oleander?"

She nodded. "He thinks what I need is support when what I need is…"

The voice on the other end of the line spoke, and Daphne fell silent. She listened, and after a few moments said, "Then stop yelling and listen! I'm right here. I can see what's happening from up close. You can look four hours back and see for yourself."

She waited. The voice on the other end sounded less furious.

"So look at me, ok? If that's what's–" The other voice cut her off.

"So that's that," she said in a slightly calmer voice. Her interlocutor said something, to which Daphne responded, "See you when I see you," in a quiet voice. She hung up and looked at me. "What?"

"Why is Oleander calling you in the middle of the night?"

Daphne's fingers worked the edge of her blanket. "He's worried about me."

I waited.

Daphne stretched her legs and scooted over to make room for me on her bed. "He sees what I'm going through, and he's worried because he can't see beyond the point of his death."

I sat down next to her. "It's good that you're talking to someone who understands."

"It would have been much better not to fall in love with someone when our time together is so limited."

"One-night stand, huh?"

She nodded silently. Only another damus could hide from her what was going to happen between them.

I stroked her hair. "Believe it or not, I totally get what you're going through."

"You want to stay here a bit?" she asked quietly.

I crawled under the blanket and hugged her. "Tell me the truth. You made Lee go home so you could have me for yourself tonight."

Daphne let out a brief laugh. "You've got me."

I tightened my grip around her. She shivered with stifled sobs. I ran my hand over her hair, questions wrestling inside me, none of which could be put into words. I dismantled her sadness and scattered it among the neighbors. Her breathing steadied, and she fell asleep. I waited until I was certain she was sound asleep, turned to face the dresser and picked up her phone.

Hesitating only for a moment, I dialed the last incoming number. "It's Reed," I said straight off to avoid any confusion.

"I know," Oleander said. "How's Daphne?"

"Sleeping. How are you?"

"A wreck," he said.

"I'm sorry."

"That I'm going to die?"

"That because of me you're lying in a hospital bed instead of Daphne's bed."

Oleander laughed. "I'd rather you be in bed with her than someone else."

I smiled in the dim room. "Reed-hot-water-bottle-Katz at your service, always."

"In the middle of the summer? What an awful friend. You should have brought her a bag of ice cubes."

I giggled quietly. "I wanted to say thanks for being here for Daphne. I know it's difficult for her to accept support."

"It's a shame you aren't here," he replied. "I would have loved having someone to help me fall asleep."

"What's keeping you up?"

"Life. Death." Oleander sighed. "You know. I want to do something important. Meaningful. Change the world."

"Doing something meaningful hasn't even crossed my mind," I said quietly. "I just thought… you know… I'd pass the time." And wait for Daphne to save me.

"It's different for you," Oleander said. "You don't see it as clearly as I do. You can repress it."

"Lucky me, such a privileged person," I said. "How does it feel? Knowing that…" I paused.

"An enormous relief," he replied quietly.

"You're not…" I wasn't sure how to phrase the question. Had he been near me, he would have been able to see my other timelines asking it, and answer without me having to sort my thoughts. "You're not scared?"

"A little. And I would have been glad to live longer, you know. But… I always knew when I was going to die. It gives you an advantage. You can prepare yourself."

"Daphne once told me that it changes you guys. That…"

"Yes, yes. The illusion of omnipotence," he said disparagingly. "I told Daphne she should spend more time reading philosophy and less time worrying about my moral fiber."

I almost smiled.

"The best thing about knowing when you're going to die is that makes planning a lot easier. I know exactly when I'm going to see my parents for the last time. The last time Daphne and I are going to see each other. The last time I'll see Ivy…" He paused. "Sorry."

"It's OK."

"She was happy to see you," he hesitated. "She… she misses you a lot, you know."

I wasn't sure what to say to that.

"I'm not justifying what she did or what… well. Everything that happened between you two. I'm just saying. You were there for her during a really difficult period. If you decide you want to renew your relationship with her…"

I fixed my eyes on Daphne's computer. The heart stickers glittered in the dark. "I'm not going to renew our relationship," I said, keeping my voice quiet. "She betrayed me. She betrayed all of us. I'm sorry, I know she's your sister, but I'm never letting her anywhere near me again."

"You're going to die," Oleander replied. "Don't you want tie up loose ends before it's all over?"

I tightened my grip on the blanket. "I tied up that end a long time ago."

Oleander didn't say a word. Neither did I.

"Thanks for being there for Daphne," I eventually said.

"I should thank you as well," Oleander said.

We hung up.

I stared at the dark ceiling, replaying our conversation in my mind. My thoughts kept wandering back to Ivy. To getting closure before I died. But I wasn't going to die, because Daphne and Sherry were working hard to make sure I stayed alive. But what if they failed? What if I died?

I thought about our last conversation. Ivy had told me to take care of myself, and…

I sat up. Daphne was mumbling in her sleep. I knew Ivy could see what was going on with me. She was with the Sons of Simeon. She knew what they were planning. And she had asked me to take care of myself because she was no longer around to look after me. And Oleander said she had been happy to see me. She was still my friend. Maybe she was trying to hint that somewhere, at some point, there would be an opportunity to get myself out of this mess. But the Sons of Simeon were convinced they'd succeed in killing me. They had me in their sights. Whatever path I paved they would immediately find out. Whatever plan I made, Daphne would notice, and the Sons of Simeon damuses would see what she was focusing on and make out the timeline.

I lay back in bed, staring into space. I had to beat them at their own game. I had to wait for an opportunity, and the moment it presented itself, seize it. I had… I had to pull one over on everyone. Even on Daphne.

I fell asleep, edging out any shred of hope.

34

The second time I visited Sherry's office at police headquarters, I went without Lee. Dimitri drove. Unlike my rides with Daphne, it seemed as though he was intentionally getting stuck behind every red light and in every traffic jam.

"Can't you arrange for a smoother ride?"

Dimitri tightened his grip around the steering wheel. "Easy to make out damuses if you look for person who hit only green lights. Keep you hidden also mean hidden in traffic."

I sank into my seat. "And…"

Dimitri raised his hand from the wheel. "Not good time for talking. Many timelines bumping into each other."

We proceeded to ride in silence.

A phone call from Oleander saved me from mind-numbing boredom.

"I need to surprise Daphne, and I need you to help me do it," he said before I managed to say hello.

"I can't block her out completely, and…" He paused. "Am I talking too fast?"

"You're talking too out of context."

Dimitri made a turn into a traffic jam on Ha-Nevi'im Street.

"I can blur Daphne a little, but she keeps looking at me," Oleander said. I didn't hear any background noises on the other end of the line. "And I want to do something nice for her. You know. Something that… that'll remind her of me. For later."

So he had found something meaningful to do after all. "What were you thinking of?"

"I can't tell you," he said, and I could hear the smile in his voice. "She's too close to you. She'll see."

I smiled in response. He really was looking out for Daphne. "OK, so what do you need?"

"I can vaguely see there's a damus close to you."

I glanced at Dimitri as he cursed all the Israeli drivers in raving Russian. "I'm not sure he'll go along with it."

"Not that one. A young one. He's not close enough to Daphne for her to see what he's doing, not unless she's actively searching, and he's experienced enough to hide himself."

"Guy," I immediately said.

"I guess. Could you give him my number? I'll explain to him what I need."

I didn't have Guy's number, but I certainly had Gaia's.

I called her. "Can I use you for something secret?"

"Depends," Gaia replied in a sleepy voice.

I passed on Oleander's message. She said, "Are you sure?"

"What do you mean?"

We were already quite close to the police station.

"A damus tricking another damus is… they have codes. Like we do. Like you wouldn't maneuver me without consent, they won't hide things from each other without consent."

"It's fine. He's Daphne's boyfriend. He just wants to surprise her."

"Are you sure?" she asked again, sounding hesitant.

"Sometimes in a relationship we do things to each other that… that we wouldn't do outside a relationship." I tried sounding as vague as possible. She was underage after all. Dimitri parked and turned off the engine.

"OK, fine. But just know it's weird."

"If he asks anything of you that sounds immoral, tell me. I'll report him to Aurora, and she'll punish him by forcing him to serve as a counselor," I said, trying to sound lighthearted. "And in any event, don't accept candy from him."

"God, you're a geezer," she giggled.

"We go," Dimitri said, gesturing at the front door.

"I have to get going," I told Gaia. We said goodbye and I hung up.

Dimitri got me past security. This time I didn't have to take any drug. His escort was enough.

The pile of papers on Sherry's desk seemed taller than on my last visit, and Sherry looked paler. Dimitri remained fixed in his post next to the door, his hands crossed on his chest. He looked like a model bodyguard. "Alder's abroad," she said the moment I walked in.

"Good." I sat down. "Can you make his plane crash?"

Sherry nodded towards Dimitri. "I'll ask my people to get on it." A hint of a smile flashed on her lips and quickly faded.

"Information we do know," she said, picking up a document and handing it to me. I took it. It was a list of names. "All these people met with either you or Daphne and had some form of contact with the Sons of Simeon, directly or indirectly."

I scanned the list. Half of the teenagers in my group were on it, with Tempest's name topping the list. "Why are these kids here?"

"They're on neutral." Sherry's voice betrayed none of the emotions whirling inside her. I could only sense a few of them, vaguely. I blocked her out.

"And...?"

"And they might be passing on information. They might be divulging things without even knowing it. They might..." Sherry held her hands up. "I don't know. That's why I need your help."

"They just don't want to practice their powers. That's not a felony." I refrained from mentioning that the police administered a substance of similar impact.

"No, that's not what they want." Sherry drummed on the desk. "What they want is to not be sorcerers anymore." Her expression turned grave. "They're sick of being different. Sick of having to struggle all the time. They're looking for a way out, and neutral is their form of escape." She sounded as though she believed what she was saying.

"Ever tried it?"

She shook her head. "It wasn't on the street back in the day. But I can totally understand them. I can also understand why a kid, in exchange for a pill, would tell someone things that don't seem very significant to him. For instance, who his youth movement counselor trusts, who he hangs out with."

I handed Sherry back the list. "What do you need me to do?"

"Use your brain." She leaned in. "You know the community, you're kept in the loop."

"I don't know every sorcerer in the country."

"Start thinking on a different level. Someone's trying to hurt you, and there's a chance it's someone you know. We're not talking just people who get into fights at the pub after an attack. We're talking people who truly cross the lines. It's a small country. You probably know such people."

"What, Ivy? We've already talked about her. You said she isn't a threat."

Sherry tapped her pen on the table. "Will you focus? Please? Instead of playing dumb?"

I looked at the list again. None of the people on it seemed like someone who'd want to hurt me. It looked like a list of all the people who wished me no harm.

"I'm not looking for someone who obviously, visibly, flipped sides. I'm looking for people who are capable of understanding the Sons of Simeon, of accepting them. Maybe who even agree to run errands for them in the name of some ideal."

Like Aurora.

Sherry leaned in closer. "I'm looking for people who think freedom from sorcery is true freedom."

Like most of my teenagers at Yoyo. I couldn't sic Sherry on my group, though. And Aurora was solid. She'd never truly cross the lines.

I put down the paper on the desk. "Maybe Daphne will have a useful idea."

"Daphne..." Sherry sighed and leaned back in her chair. "I let her go. Told her I didn't need more help."

"You told her what?"

"She was taking on too much. She and Lee. They were very helpful, but..." She sighed again. "Sometimes it's easy for me to forget that even though you guys volunteer to do something, it doesn't mean you've got proper training. When I send out our empaths or seers, they know how to isolate themselves."

I bit my lip. Lee was alone in his apartment, refusing to see me. Daphne was overwhelmed with pain she wouldn't let me dismantle.

"So, enough," Sherry said. "Enough. I won't put them in harm's way anymore. We've got all the information we could get from them, and any further move would..."

"Put them in danger," I completed her sentence.

"No," she said. "Would take from the time they have left. With you. With Oleander."

A sharp pain shot through my chest. "None of those kids would hurt me. Most of them don't know me well enough to volunteer information, and the ones who do..." I said, thinking of Guy and Gaia, the only ones close to me, "are doing all they can to protect me."

Sherry placed her hands flat on the desk. "And yet. Give it another try."

She brought her hands together and gestured sorcery and protection.

I mimicked the gesture and buried my fear beneath every other emotion.

35

Sherry put me on a 24-hour protective detail again; every morning a different cop reported at our door, and the same ritual ensued: I took a photo of the cop and sent it to Sherry. She sent confirmation; the officer entered the apartment and relieved the previous officer from his post. None of them exchanged more than two consecutive sentences with me.

One day, unable to find a reason to go out into the living room, I spent hours in bed. The officer stationed at our house at the time was busy on his phone and didn't look up from his screen even once. He was a damus, and every time I tried to initiate a conversation with him he only said I'd make him lose the round, and went back to playing his game on his phone. When I asked him about the situation with the Sons of Simeon, he exclaimed, "Motherfuckers, I hope they burn," without elaborating. A Yoyo meeting was to take place that evening, and I had the feeling Daphne wouldn't let me out of the house. I couldn't find a single lead for Sherry, and was resigned to shuffling from the living room to the kitchen, to my room, restlessly opening and closing cupboards and closets.

That afternoon I suddenly remembered my and Blaze's list. After we had received our IDF postings, we made a bucket list. It was stuck in the bottom of the same drawer where I kept our photo from my seventeenth birthday.

I rummaged through the drawer until I found it, beneath a pile of letters I had received at the end of the training course, an empty water bottle with the signature of a singer I used to admire scribbled with a felt-tip marker, an unopened deck of playing cards, and the journal I thought I'd keep but eventually gave up on after writing only one entry. Both photos of Blaze and me were faded. My face was riddled with acne and smeared with chocolate, and my smile enormous. Blaze looked so young in those photos. Long hair, the same smile, and his arm wrapped around me in a suggestive manner. We looked like my kids at Yoyo. I picked up the photos and found the list.

It was a sheet of grid paper torn out of a math notebook, the list scribbled in blue ballpoint pen. The same pen that had run out in the middle of my final civics exam.

I smoothed out the paper. First item on the bucket list was 'Finding true love,' and it was crossed off. I remember how Blaze had kissed me when he saw me crossing it off. I sniffled. I was so young. So stupid. No, not stupid. Naïve.

Second item: 'Attend a *ThunderCats* concert.' It made me smile, just like it had done back then. Blaze reminded me that animated TV shows didn't go on tour, and I explained that it was a list of dreams, so I could write whatever I wanted. It was an argument that ended when he added 'Marry Brian May' to the list, and we began bickering about that item.

The third item was 'Backpack through South America." I picked up a pen from the dresser and crossed it off. Daphne and I had traveled there together right after we were discharged from the army. I had been planning a surprise visit to the Confederacy, showing up unannounced on Blaze's doorstep, but when I looked into getting a visa I discovered their immigration laws stipulated that sorcerers who had served in a foreign military required a special security clearance to enter the country. To this day I wasn't entirely confident Daphne hadn't manipulated me to agree to the trip she had proposed. I never asked her what would have happened if I had succeeded in obtaining the special clearance.

Item four was crossed off: 'Eat nothing but chocolate for a whole day.' There was that class trip I had spent throwing up from a stomach virus, and the only thing I managed to eat was one square of chocolate for dinner. Blaze had crossed that item off for me.

Item five was a list of seven books, three of which were crossed off. I looked up from the page and stared at the wall in front of me. I could spend my last few weeks on Earth reading dead Soviet authors. I toyed with the idea of convincing Lee to let me do some erotic moodification to one of those books, and then have an underground edition printed and distributed. I imagined literature students getting off on reading it.

I got back to the list. Items six through nine included 'See the northern and southern lights,' 'Cycle through Europe,' 'Learn to make soufflé,' and 'Participate in a full-on sorcerers battle outside the military.'

I crossed out item nine, and arrived at ten. I'd forgotten all about that one. 'Weave myself fully into another empath.'

I considered crossing it off the list. I remembered the explanation I'd given Blaze. That it was like when he stepped into bonfires on *Lag BaOmer*, or how pebbles go spend entire days in the desert. The boy I'd once been was convinced that a full weaving of consciousness with another moody was the closest I could get to pure sorcery. But it wasn't like that. It wasn't similar at all. Lee and I didn't feel as one, even though there were no walls between us anymore. We were still two separate individuals.

I held the pen hovering over the paper. I wanted to add another item. Something meaningful. Something I could do, and be remembered for. Like Oleander. 'Change the world.' That was something seventeen-year-old Reed would have written. Not feasible, but meaningful. Maybe 'Not die.' Also a good item.

I didn't write any of them. I put the pen back on the dresser, folded the paper and stuck it back in the drawer, beneath the water bottle, card deck and journal. I wasn't seventeen anymore. And I wouldn't live long enough to cycle through the radioactive craters in Europe, or see the northern lights, or any of the silly things that seemed so significant when I was with Blaze and the world was our oyster.

I'm going to die. I'm going to die, leaving no mark on the world. Nothing but a few books better moodified than they had been, and one sad Lee.

My phone beeped. It was a message from Aurora: *Meeting at the ditch. We have visitors.*

The ditch was an open, derelict lot in the eastern part of town. We used it for big get-togethers during the summer. But Yoyo met at the dank community center, not at the ditch. Odd.

I got out of bed and left my room.

Daphne was sitting in her room going over stock exchange listings. "No," she said before I even asked. She had dark bags under her eyes, and a few unruly curls had slipped out of her hairband. She was still in the same chafing bra she had worn to work, and I could feel how much her legs hurt after an entire day in high heels. Underneath it all were the same sadness and loss that wouldn't abate, no matter how much she tried to immerse herself in work.

I waited.

"No, you're not going to the Yoyo meeting. I'm not letting you out of my sight, and I have work to do here so we're staying in. Tell Lee to come over if you can't calm yourself down."

I didn't reply.

"Don't tell me you guys got into another fight," she said, without looking up from the screen.

I didn't tell her. Our last argument had ended with both of us screaming at each other, me hurling all my pain and frustration at him and he in turn blocking me out and shouting that if I was incapable of behaving like a normal human being he didn't want me anywhere near him. In response, I yelled that he had nothing to worry about because I'd be dead soon enough, and from there we found ourselves at an unbridgeable impasse.

"There are five reflections of you yelling at me right now," Daphne mumbled into her computer. "I can hear you even with

319

your mouth shut." She looked up at me. "You're going to meet Lee tonight, and you'll make up, and he'll dismantle your depression. You'll feel better tomorrow. I'm sorry there isn't more I can–" She stopped midsentence, tilting her head, her gaze wandering to the right.

"Oh," she said, and turned her gaze back to me. "I'm tagging along." She turned off her computer and stood up.

I raised my eyebrows. "To Yoyo?"

Daphne pulled off her hair band and redid her ponytail. "You lecture me for ten whole minutes about the importance of nurturing our youth, all while climbing the walls here with boredom and depression. I explain to you that our youth can bite me because your survival is much more important to me, and I have to talk to Sherry about the last-minute change of plans, and Sherry calls to tell me we're meeting at the ditch, so we're going." She straightened her shirt and slipped her feet into her sandals. "Come."

So I did.

The circle convened in a different place this time, between dilapidated houses uptown, near the shelter that was bombed in '97.

A homeless man lay on the curb across the street; next to him was a sign scribbled in black: *Traumas for a meal.* I poked towards him. Blurry walls, like something brought on by one of Lee's substances. The homeless man sent me a pleading wave. I sent him back some childish glee. I didn't have enough emotional reserves to share much more. He tugged it into him, opened his eyes and waved in gratitude. Lee told me that in the Confederacy they called moodies 'emotional vampires.' I edged out the horror and kept walking in the direction of the circle.

There were a lot more people than I had expected, divided into two distinct groups; Forrest, Aurora, a few of our mutual friends, and all the kids from my Yoyo group, opposite a group of people I didn't recognize huddled together on the far end of the lot. The cop that came with us took one look around and joined the second group. Daphne and I began to follow the cop once I felt a wave of recognition reaching me from across the lot. I turned around. Lee and Sherry were standing there and seemed to be instructing people.

Lee sent me a small, surprised wave. I returned the surprise. Sherry was standing beside him, talking. Lee said something to her and started walking towards us.

Daphne was massaging her neck. "Lee was planning on coming over to our place after he's done here. And at least one of your reflections disappears with him behind there." She pointed to the brick wall behind me.

"We do other things together too, you know."

Daphne sighed dramatically. "Unfortunately, I know exactly what you two do and when."

Lee had made it across the lot, followed by Forrest. "What are you doing here?" he asked, and quickly added, "I mean, I'm glad you're here." He sent me a small wave of happiness, but didn't apologize. I was still mad at him for his outburst from yesterday.

He was hiding something from me. I dug deeper. He was concealing shame and a slight measure of aversion beneath his affection, which was currently dotted with residual anger. He didn't want me there.

"Forrest invited me."

Lee shot Forrest a look. The redheaded sorcerer returned it and said, "You said you needed help. You said bring people. These are the people I know. I would have invited River and Blaze as well, but you said you didn't want them here."

Before I managed to question him, Gaia ran towards me and almost crushed me with her hug. "You're here!" she squealed.

"And I'm now deaf!" I yelled into her ear.

She laughed. Guy ran towards us, radiating happiness. "Wow! You're here!"

I shifted my gaze between the two of them. "What's with all the excitement?"

Guy skimmed over my futures, looked at me and winked. Gaia sent me a wave of secrecy. The surprise for Daphne. Of course. I had almost forgotten about it. I sent her a wave of anticipation, and she shot me back an arrow of confirmation. It was ready, or almost ready.

"I'm starting to regret that you two weren't born ariels like the rest of your class."

Gaia made a show of gaping at me in astonishment. "Wow! The geezer got the slang right!"

I waved my finger at her. "If you don't stop, I'll turn you into a toad."

"You can't do those kinds of things," Guy said, and put his arm on Gaia's shoulder, her hair spilling under his arm.

"I can maneuver you into *thinking* you're a toad." I folded my arms across my chest, trying to look threatening and stern.

Gaia giggled again. "Bring it on."

Sherry cleared her throat, and Gaia immediately turned serious.

"Lee, over there," Sherry said and pointed at the distant part of the lot. "Gaia, you're with Forrest." She glanced at her and added, "Reed thinks you're good."

Gaia blushed and lowered her gaze.

"Reed's with me," Sherry concluded. She looked at Daphne. "Are you synchronizing?"

Daphne nodded.

Sherry led me to the edge of the lot. The groups divided into two clusters.

"What exactly do you need from me?" I asked when we began walking off. I thought we'd be forming circles, but there was no way Gaia could hold a circle by herself.

"Lee promised to help with my cops."

"Those are cops?" My voice went up half an octave. Two men standing on the fringes of her group were looking at me.

Sherry nodded. She pointed at a half torn-down wall at the edge of the lot, which offered a good vantage point.

"But we're not allowed to attack–" I didn't even know how to begin to phrase my objection. More than I was scared of dying,

I was scared of participating in a battle with cops. And in such numbers. I had no idea there were so many cops like us.

"It's not a sorcerers versus cops problem," Sherry said, putting her hand on my arm. "It's our problem. People who believe we have a right to exist versus a bunch of extremists who want to murder every last one of us." Something about her tone suggested she had already given this speech more than once. With a softened expression, she added, "Really, Reed, do you think Lee would have been here if there was any chance it would end in jail time?"

She was right. I balled up my panic and edged under my fear of death. Lee withdrew himself from me, focusing entirely on the goings-on in the other group.

The teams stood on either side of the lot. Sherry led me to the half wall and climbed it. I followed suit.

"I need you to explain to me what's happening," she said, once again her usual driven and focused self. I sat beside her on what was left of the wall. It was warm outside, the faint smell of blossoms wafting through the air. Just another ordinary summer evening. Just an ordinary summer evening practicing assault and defense. Practicing assault and defense against a group of cops. Nothing more. "How are your suspects doing?"

A pyro in the cops' group produced a small fireball, and thus the battle commenced. The elementalists were moving slowly, as if just practicing the movements and not really trying to strike.

After a time, Sherry poked me with her finger. "Explain what's happening."

"Your splashers aren't very good."

"I don't care about the elements. I need you to be an empath, not a sports commentator."

I put my feelers out into the distance, groping after the sorcerers' awareness. On Forrest's side they were all nervous and scared, yet focused on their attempt to break up the lines. The feeling on the other side was different. Blurry.

I retreated.

"What…?" I mumbled.

"Lee," Sherry replied.

So that's why he hadn't wanted River or Blaze here. Now I also understood the shame he radiated when he saw me. He didn't want me around when he was using. No. He didn't want me around when he was maneuvering people while using. I swallowed my sigh. He could have just told me.

I pulled my knees to my chin and instead of focusing on Lee and 'our' group, looked at the group of cops, ignoring the elementalists. A fire wall sparked up between the two sides. I was searching for moodies on the cops' side. They had three. One of them managed to stir nausea on Lee's side. Another lay on her back and gazed up at the sky. I felt his consciousness drifting away. Now I could recognize Lee's fingerprints. The third was still standing, directing his thwarting efforts at his own team out of sheer confusion.

I explained to Sherry what I was feeling. She pursed her lips and drummed her fingers on her knees.

"We're never going to win if this is how they behave," she mumbled.

"In the rally?"

"In general." Sherry wasn't listening to me. Her narrowed gaze was fixed on the group of cops. "The rally is only the beginning."

"Lee's focusing on your last moody, and he's also slowing down your pebbles' movements," I said, pointing at the other side of the lot. The rally was only the beginning. What would follow? What would happen after the Sons of Simeon got me? Me and the person next to me. The rally would turn into a bloodbath, and then what? Martial law would probably be imposed, and then… and then they'd take over every position of power. And after that?

"Need to talk to someone? I'm here." Sherry placed her hand on mine.

"After–" I cleared my throat. "After I die, I want you to look after Matthew." She seemed as though she was about to object, so I kept talking before she could say anything. "I don't mean romantically. Just… be there for him. You know what it is to lose a sibling. He's going to need someone to talk to, and Daphne won't be in any position to support him."

Sherry bit her lip. "OK," she said quietly.

I turned my gaze back to the battlefield. Our teens were doing an impressive job of resisting, creating whirlwinds of fire and mud on the cops' side. Guy was hopping around, and I assumed he was moving between futures so that no one could hurt Gaia. There were other damuses on 'our' side, but I wasn't familiar with them. When the last moody on the cops' side sat down to stare at an ant crawling on the ground, the battle was over.

Sherry got up, wiped the dust off her pants and climbed off the wall. I bounced off after her. I felt Lee alleviating the cops of their blurriness, along with Gaia's help. I joined them, and together we rid them of any remnant of their daze.

We grouped around Sherry, the teams breaking up.

"That was disappointing." She turned her gaze towards her cops. "A group of twenty civilians can knock you down?" Not a shred of her inner turmoil reflected in her expression.

Lee sent me a little ball of satisfaction. I wondered whether he had put 'getting cops high' on his bucket list.

One of the cops, an airhead, took a step forward. "Chief, that was nothing like the rallies. You said it would be just the same."

A wave of agreement passed through the lines. Lee and I exchanged glances. What had they been thinking? That Lee wouldn't try to challenge them?

Sherry looked at Lee. "Care to respond?"

"You said sorcerers were slowing down your cops, inhibiting their movement. That's what I did." He shrugged. "You want me to do something else?"

"Yes." She smiled. I felt a wave of tension coming from the cops. They knew her better than I did. "Let's see how fast you respond when your movement is stimulated instead of suppressed."

She gave Lee a number, and he smiled his thin, sardonic smile.

We divided into two teams again. I felt his enjoyment, and a similar, smaller wave in Gaia. We were all happy to get another chance to aggravate the cops, and with such explicit permission.

When Sherry and I hopped back onto the wall, I asked, "You numbered Lee's list?"

Sherry nodded. "It saves me time. I already know your boyfriend's good at memorizing things quickly. He's very analytical."

I glanced at Lee, who was squatting in the distance, rummaging through his bag in search of a substance I could only assume was illegal. Or borderline legal. There was a lot of things I'd call him, but analytical wasn't one of them. A wave of sharp pain came over me. I didn't know him well enough, and now I never would.

I edged out the pain along with the fear. I couldn't focus on that right now. I hadn't even noticed I was no longer angry at him.

"I wanted to ask you…" I said, trying to distract myself, "Why do you keep using the official terms instead of our slang?"

"Because words matter," Sherry replied without taking her eyes off the teams repositioning on the battlefield below. "And if we ever want to be acknowledged as equal members of society, we must remember what our powers are. If I call myself a pebble, I'm sure to be met with disrespect."

"And calling yourself an earth sorcerer would make them less scared of you?"

Sherry looked at me, her eyes narrowed. "I don't want people to stop being scared of us. That would be impossible. I want them to appreciate and trust us. Like Matthew appreciates and trusts you."

"I'm not everyone's brother."

"God, sometimes I just don't get why you insist on playing dumb."

I shrugged. "I truly don't understand."

Sherry smoothed out her shirt. "Matthew appreciates you because he grew up with you, and he knows you'd never hurt him. He doesn't for a moment suspect you might maneuver him against his will or that Daphne would force a future on him that would benefit her. He's not afraid that I'd maneuver elements near him."

"Matthew's very special," I said quietly.

"Matthew grew up with you and saw what you do and don't do, and he knows you hold back when you're around him." Sherry held her hands out and gestured at the battlefield below us. "I want these kids to grow up in a world in which everyone knows that. I want them to be free to have whatever job they want, study whatever they want, marry whoever they want." She pointed at Guy and Gaia who were huddled together. "I wish that they'll never have to know what a shredder or a gorger mean."

I'd never heard either term before, but I could guess by the insult she was radiating.

"Don't you get it?" She looked at me. "The Sons of Simeon are able to win public opinion by convincing the normal people that we want to take over the country; at the same time they're gaining traction with sorcerers themselves since we have it so bad, that the utopian vision of sorcerers ruling the country actually sounds like a *good* idea. No one is using common sense anymore." She put her hand on her chest. "We have to convince everyone that it isn't true. That we can all live together, peacefully, quietly. Respecting one another."

She started listing the necessary steps with her fingers. "That means we, the community, have to understand the normal people. We have to make sure everybody's on the same page, take neutralizers if need be, make sure whoever breaks the law is punished. The thought that in the name of some wacky notion of camaraderie the Cash Splasher got aid from the community makes my stomach turn. We can't stand for that. No. We must remember that our true allies are the normal people, and we have to obey their laws. In return, we'll receive meaningful, real integration, a cohesive, free society." She was panting by the time she was done talking.

I whistled quietly. "If you're running in the next elections, you totally have my vote."

She flashed a brief smile. "If you want to live to see the next elections, you better start paying attention to what's happening here."

We turned to the battlefield, Sherry's words still resonating inside me. I imagined Gaia working toward her PhD in the classroom with everyone else, instead of sitting in the corner marked in white designated for people like us. No. More than that. I imagined parents not crying when they found out their kid was like me. Someone like Ivy not getting swept up in visions of a utopian future because the present was good enough. Myself walking down the street without being cursed and spat at. All of us sitting at a pub without separate entrances, in a world in which we no longer had to hide, or hole out in cellars or risk fresh scars at rallies, because true equality had been achieved. I finally understood Dimitri. I would cross continents for something like that.

The battle started up again. This time Lee afflicted the cops with an itching sensation. I absentmindedly scratched the back of my hand. My skin was tingling all over. I shut Lee out and focused. The pyros were creating little explosions around them in an attempt to edge out the itchiness. The splashers drenched their clothes. They invested so much effort and concentration in avoiding the itchiness that they failed to notice the airheads creating dust devils all around them, making it harder for them to breathe.

"Have you arrested anyone else?" I asked Sherry, more to suppress the itchiness than to actually get new information from her.

She laced her fingers. "Another five. They were hiding in a cave down south, planning to infiltrate Masada. We're trying to make out their power base, but they're scattered in unconnected cells."

"Like any terrorism network."

Sherry nodded.

I nudged her with my elbow. "See? I do know something."

Sherry shot me a side glance. "I'll tell Lee."

This time their moody managed to block out the itchiness from a few cops, who were starting to fight back. The battle was finally becoming interesting. The cops created small mushrooms of fire, surrounded by clumps of earth that exploded between the lines on Lee's side. The pebbles in Lee's group were crushing the clumps faster than the cops could produce them.

The itchiness intensified. One moody stumbled and fell, and the two moodies next to her tried to make up for it by absorbing the itchiness inside them, until one collapsed onto the ground and was almost injured. The other kept the lines intact, drawing more and more of the tingling itch, enabling the elementalist cops to create whirlwinds of earth and fire. Gaia took advantage of the moody's tumble and amplified the itchiness Lee had created. I could anticipate her cries of joy a few minutes later.

The airheads on Lee's side dissipated the whirlwinds, and the splashers launched a concentrated barrage of hail on the cops. The moody cops prevented Gaia's access to them. She couldn't penetrate the barrier they erected, and after a few moments she gave a shout and one of the splashers on our side raised a ball of ice into the air, the symbol of surrender.

The battle was over. I looked at Sherry. "They're quick learners."

"Not quick enough. They broke up their lines. There were four breaches assassins could infiltrate through." Sherry waved over an airhead from our side. He stopped a few steps from us. Sherry got up and started shouting. The airhead amplified her voice so that everyone could hear. She declared a ten-minute break, followed by a rematch.

During the break, Lee and I took advantage of the wall Daphne had pointed at earlier. When we returned, Daphne rolled her eyes before going back to discussing humor in children's TV shows with Sherry. Gaia sent me wonderment and excitement. She probably wanted to tell me more about what happened on the battlefield, as if I hadn't witnessed it myself. Lee was following the trail of emotions and looked at Gaia, who was standing across the lot.

"Tell your admirer you're taken."

"I think she picked up on that all by herself." I kissed him. Gaia sent me an embarrassed wave. I sent her back an apology.

During our short absence, the two groups had mingled and it was difficult to tell the cops from the civilians. I heard Aurora launch into one of her "accept, understand and support" speeches. This time she was lecturing the cops about the importance of understanding the Sons of Simeon, of accepting their motives and working to integrate them into society. When one of the cops remarked that it was hard to accept murder as a legitimate form of resistance, Aurora said, "Think how desperate someone has to be to go to such extremes. You understand? We mustn't respond with violence. We have to understand and contain their pain and show them a different method of coping."

I was about to intervene when Daphne suddenly turned her gaze to someone limping towards us.

"Is that Oleander?" Lee asked.

Daphne rushed to him with me in tow.

She wrapped her arm around him, letting him support his weight against her. "What are you doing here? You need to be resting!"

Oleander kissed her curls. "What I need is to be with you."

A victorious wave surged from Gaia's direction. So that was the surprise they'd been planning.

Despite her anguish, Daphne smiled. Oleander looked at me. "And how are you?"

I shrugged. "Could be worse."

Lee caught up with us and stood behind me. He wrapped his arms around me, the smell of his sweat engulfing me. We stood there, two couples staring at each other.

Oleander straightened up a little, and Lee winced when the pain in Oleander's leg radiated to both of us. "So what's going on here?"

Lee smiled. "They're letting me make the cops high."

Oleander smiled back. "Sounds great. What are you giving them?"

Lee pointed his thumb at Sherry. "Whatever the boss tells me to."

Oleander looked past Lee's shoulder. "You think she'd let me join?"

"No," Daphne said sharply. "You have to rest, you can't be running around like this when you're so…"

He looked at her, his pain reflecting in his smile. The deep pain of an imminent parting. "I just want to be with you."

"I can totally relate," Lee said, pulling me tighter into his embrace.

Daphne bit her lip. "Fine, but not on the ground with us." She pointed to the spot where Sherry and I had been sitting earlier. "You're with Reed. Far from the rest. Safe."

When Daphne helped Oleander trudge across the lot, Gaia hopped towards me with Guy. "Did you see? Did you see? It worked, we did it!"

I sent her a wave of genuine admiration. "I can't believe you managed to hide it from Daphne."

Guy looked puffed up with pride. "We did it together."

"Excellent work." I patted his shoulder. "Daphne's happy."

"Did what together?" Lee asked, shifting his gaze between us.

Gaia launched into one of her incessant rambles. Apparently Guy had focused on timelines in which Oleander wasn't with us in order to draw Daphne's attention, and Gaia tried to distract Daphne while Guy sent Oleander a text asking when was the most convenient time for him to arrive. Looking quite lost in her babble, Lee smiled politely and paid the successful duo a few compliments of his own.

"Round three!" Sherry called out, using the airhead as a megaphone.

The battle resumed, and I took my seat between Sherry and Oleander. He stared intently at the field and didn't comment when I explained to Sherry what Lee was doing, or what I sensed from her officers. Every so often Sherry stopped the fight and gave Lee more instructions. The battle became more complex, entangled by conflicting orders, and Sherry kept halting them whenever she detected a breach. I mainly followed the teenagers. They were clearly getting tired, but were so full of good intentions that you couldn't get mad at them. The cops tried to avoid hurting them, creating small breaches in their force, which Lee's side failed to take advantage of.

After the fifth round ended, Sherry stood up. "I can't take it anymore," she grumbled. "They're completely ignoring everything I told them to do," she said and walked away.

I wondered whether I had enough time to steal a few minutes with Lee.

"Not really," Oleander said. "She'll be back in two minutes."

"You're reading me, and what's worse, you're reading a cop."

"What are they going to do, execute me?" He wasn't feeling angry or lost. He was feeling whole, having come to accept his fate.

I searched for the right words to say. "How weird is it, knowing you're about to die without even being sick, huh?"

Oleander nodded. "I was always sure I'd go in a mountain climbing accident or something. The last thing I see is the earth coming closer and I can hear people shouting." Oleander touched his leg. I could feel the bandage under his pants. "But I guess that's not it."

"Can I ask you something personal?"

Oleander nodded. "Sure."

"How much do you see?"

"I can see more details the closer we get to it." He turned to me. "You want me to look and tell you how it ends for you? I'm close enough to Daphne to see her timelines."

I let out a short chuckle. "What I really want is to crawl into bed and never get out. I want everything to be over and done with." I looked at Sherry, furious at her cops. "I have no idea how you two can handle it. For real."

"Remember Silman? The guy who set himself on fire during the welfare protest?"

"Sure," I answered quickly. It was the summer when we were sure change was finally coming. That this time they were really going to listen to us.

"In some timelines they actually do get him a heater like he asked for before the protest started. A small one, and his blanket catches fire during the night. He always dies in a fire. He simply chose the timeline in which his death had the most impact."

Oleander straightened his leg. I recoiled when the pain shot through me.

"Sorry," he said, stopping mid-movement. "I didn't take anything before I left the house because I thought I'd be able to handle it."

"It's OK. Want me to take some of your pain and pass it onto Sherry's people? I've got permission to maneuver cops."

He started smiling. "Yes. Enough so I can walk."

"And then you and Daphne will bail on me?"

He chuckled. "We'll bail on this together. Want to go to the amusement park? I heard they give great discounts to dying people."

Before I could think of a smart reply, Sherry turned to us and walked back up the hill, her rage blocking our attempts to carry on with the conversation.

She waved her hand, and the battle resumed.

This time Lee made each one of the cops feel something different. It was a complex hallucination, and it took me some time to describe it in detail to Sherry. She drummed her fingers on her knee.

"Come on, figure it out," she mumbled to herself, her tension radiating to me and Oleander.

Maybe we really could go to the amusement park? Matthew could probably get us a wheelchair. I could imagine Lee and me pushing Oleander along the paths. And Daphne would be happy.

The pyros aimed at the ground in the middle of the circle of cops and set it on fire, and the cops' splashers struck back. Hail formed in the middle of Lee's side. I could feel the chill seeping into my clothes.

"I'd love to be there right now," Oleander mumbled, his leg sweating inside the bandages.

"Me too," I whispered back.

"Quiet," Sherry scolded us, pointing at Lee. "What's he doing now?"

"He's continuing to drown the–" I started to say, when a flame burst out inside our side of the lot.

"Yes!" Sherry exclaimed excitedly.

I felt the pyros struggling to extinguish the fire, pushing the teens back in order to shield them. Our damuses, led by Daphne, protected them. Everyone was responding too slowly, starting to deplete after such prolonged fighting. The pebbles joined forces with the splashers and created little lakes of mud under the cops' feet. Lee bolstered the hallucination he had inspired in them earlier, and they slipped. I followed the twists and turns of their emotions. Gaia was maneuvering them, adding some gentleness into the motion. She was inexperienced, but knew enough to support Lee's efforts.

I sent her a small wave of satisfaction. She was too focused to respond, but I felt the wave seeping into her. She'd understand later...

Guy screamed. A sharp pain cut through me. I couldn't feel Gaia anymore.

I froze, and after a moment ran across the lot faster than Sherry. Someone had put out the fire that was burning in the middle of our side of the field. I heard people yelling, talking, someone calling out for help. I pushed people out of my way, I didn't care if they were cops or not.

Guy was crouching in the middle of a circle of people, Gaia in his arms. An icicle was sticking out of her stomach, darkening from the blood pouring out of her. She was unconscious.

"I didn't... I..." Tears were running down Guy's cheeks.

One of the cops standing next to us had turned completely pale. "I... I thought she was protected. I didn't even see her."

I put my hand on her chest. She was still breathing. What did Matthew say? What had he done after Oleander was injured?

"Pyros." I looked up. "I need pyros!"

I called Matthew's instructions to mind: pyros to cauterize the wound, splashers to sanitize it, then call for help. I didn't remove my hand from Gaia's chest. Every breath she took was a small victory. Every trickle of blood a failure.

"Choose the present in which she makes it," I heard myself say. I sounded composed. Confident. Nothing like the frenzied clusters of fear I actually felt. I pretended I was Matthew, and sealed my expression. Like Lee. Masking my emotions.

Lee.

I put out my feelers and tapped into him. He was blurry, trying to rid himself of all remnants of the concoctions he had taken. I withdrew it all from him and deposited it in Gaia. To alleviate her pain. He quickly sobered up, and I felt the lightheadedness overwhelming him. Dizziness and nausea, and early traces of the headache that would attack him full on in a few hours. Not my problem. I blocked him out.

"It's going to be OK," I said to Guy, my expression conveying nothing but compassion and assurance. "It'll all be OK."

Three pyros were crouching beside me. I passed on the instructions as I remembered them. One of the pyros was from my Yoyo group. Keep my expression composed. Look confident. I'm still their counselor. The splashers sanitized the wound, the pyros cauterized it. I trusted Daphne to help Guy choose the present in which Gaia survived. She wasn't near us, but she was good. The best damus I knew. She'd pull it off.

Gaia's chest rose with breath.

The icicle slowly melted thanks, in part, to the pyros' cauterization and the splashers' efforts. Guy hugged Gaia so tightly I could feel the tension in his biceps.

She exhaled.

The residues of Lee's blurriness spread inside her. I could feel her pain, followed by silence.

"No," I whispered.

And she ceased to be.

36

After Daphne got stuck in traffic, and mumbled "Sorry," and started crying behind the steering wheel; after I let Lee fog up my mind, stopping just before I'd no longer be able to stand; after Sherry arrived in official uniform and approached the family, and I heard her speaking but couldn't make sense of her words, and hugging Guy at length; after the look on Gaia's parents' faces when her mother told me, "She thought the world of you," and her father said, "She was grateful for everything you taught her," and her brother, a ten-year-old in a stiff suit, shook my hand...

After the shrouded body and the hole in the ground and the quiet murmurs and the shovels; and after I couldn't stop trying to poke into her, to feel her, and no one sent me a wave of amusement with unrefined edges of boredom, or called me a geezer or popped pink bubblegum in my face...

After all that we stood in the parking lot. Sherry's gaze followed the line of cars forming at the exit. "We can go to the *shiva*."

Matthew was on call, and I had no doubt that if he had been here Sherry would have leaned on him like I clung to Lee. All her arguments about maintaining boundaries and the need to devote herself to the cause would have gone up in smoke had he been here right now.

"No," Daphne said with a shaky voice. "I'm not... in her house, it's..." Her voice trailed off. We all understood. Gaia's house, where her life had unfolded, would be full of her reflections.

Daphne's phone rang and she picked up. "Oleander's suggesting we meet at the beach. He'll bring food and drinks and meet us there."

"How will he carry it all?" Sherry's voice was reserved.

Daphne listened to Oleander for a moment and then turned back to us and said, "Ivy will bring it. He says he'd love to come, even though he didn't know..." her voice choked. "Because it's important to him to support us, and he..."

Sherry raised her hand and looked at me. "You want to go to the beach?"

I wanted to take some of Lee's concoctions, and make the thoughts go away until it stopped hurting. "OK."

Daphne settled the specifics with Oleander and hung up. We walked to the car, and Sherry stepped in front of Daphne and snatched the keys out of her hand. Daphne didn't even protest.

It was hot, and the breeze from the shore wasn't enough to dry the sweat on my back. It wasn't yet the time of day when the sea worked its charm. There were people on the beach, but no one came near the circle around Oleander and Ivy. I could picture him saying, "Why do you think you've got two damuses here?" if I'd asked how they managed to pull it off.

Ivy stood up once we approached. She looked at me. "I'm sorry, I know how much..."

"Enough," Daphne said, her voice soaked with tears. "Not now."

Ivy seemed as though she was about to tell me something, but instead she just said, "You'll give Oleander a ride home?"

"Sure," Sherry said, and Ivy walked away without looking back.

We sat down. Oleander and Daphne talked, and Sherry interjected a remark every now and then, and all I could think about was the tight lump in my throat, and why we didn't just go home, and how everyone managed to talk to one another and seem interested, and I wanted to scream, and cry, and instead I stared silently at the sea. Three children were burying a jellyfish with sand, and a woman behind us was yelling at a kid to finish his grapes, and someone was swearing and laughing at the same time.

Lee touched my hand. I had no doubt that if I asked him to, he'd maneuver me more, but I could feel his pain exacerbating. Soon he wouldn't be able to do anything. He had worked harder than all of us in the circle yesterday.

It was only yesterday.

I sniffled, and Lee tugged me closer to him, and I couldn't let the tears out and couldn't push the aching lump deeper down my throat, and the woman behind us yelled at the boy not to throw his grapes in the sand.

"It doesn't make any sense," Daphne said with a cracked voice. "I don't understand how it happened."

Sherry opened her mouth and closed it without saying a word. Her hair was disheveled, and she looked paler than ever. Not just because of the formal uniform. She seemed... hollowed.

Oleander stroked Daphne's hand, but she didn't lean into him. She remained stiff in her spot, staring into the horizon. "I don't understand how it happened," she whispered to herself.

"Stop looking over there." Oleander's voice was the only one that didn't sound strained with tears. "Nothing good can come out of–"

"Guy was right there next to her. Guy was protecting her." Daphne blinked, and the tears rolled down her cheeks. "I specifically remember making sure Guy was near her, and I told him–"

"Enough, honey, enough." Oleander caressed Daphne's shoulders, her shirt glued to her lower back.

"Oleander's right," Lee said, leaning closer to Daphne.

She looked at him. "What?"

"Oleander's right," he repeated quietly. "It's not your fault. None of us is at fault."

Sherry bit her lip. Daphne bowed her head. Oleander and Lee exchanged glances.

"You need to take your mind off it. Let's look over there," Oleander said, pointing at the horizon. "There's a tyrannosaurus over there."

"No way," Lee said, elbowing him. "It's too deep, and there were never any tyrannosauruses here anyway."

"Enough," Daphne whispered, and the two fell silent. She looked up at Oleander. "I can't. You understand that, right? I can't look at anything else. I can't fast forward and rewind water reflections to soothe myself. I can't do anything other than look at what happened at the ditch or what's going to happen to Reed and look for a…" She paused, and turned all of her focus on me. "You don't take the edge," she whispered.

"What?" I jolted.

"Before Gaia… before the ditch. We found an edge and we've been working our asses off to sustain it, and you won't choose it," she panted. "What's your problem?"

"What?" I repeated, unable to make sense of her mumble.

"You won't take the edge," she whispered, gaping at me. "I can see it so clearly now. Lee's there, and Sherry's there, and you move. You just leap into harm's way. Just like… I'll never forgive you for it. Just so you know. Even years from now. I'll stand over your grave and I won't forgive." Daphne was clutching Lee, her fingernails digging into his skin. "You tell him. Tell him you won't forgive him if he doesn't choose to live."

"I don't understand…" Lee said, staring at me, then turning his gaze to Daphne.

Daphne closed her eyes. She took a deep breath, exhaled slowly and opened her eyes, looking at Lee. "You have another week and a half together."

I felt the pit in my stomach deepening. I blocked everyone out. Lee turned pale. "I don't want to know."

"Too late. You know. A week and a half." She pointed at me. "You're going to spend every minute of it together. And now you need to convince Reed that you deserve more than a week and a half with him. That you'll suffer if you don't get more than a week and a half. If he changes his mind, it'll only be because you managed to persuade him." Her voice petered out. "He won't listen to me."

"Daphne," Oleander said, stroking her forehead, "what do you see? Show me."

Daphne looked him in the eye. "They're trying to kill some girl who's standing next to Reed, and once he realizes it he deflects the shooter. He picks up on his intention and tries to do what Aurora did, make him aim at the feet. But he's not as skilled as she is. The bullet hits him in the stomach. It ruptures the liver and severs the aorta. It tears him up from the inside. Reed dies before any of us manages to reach him."

Lee's hand was sweating inside mine. He wasn't moving. "He can't be there."

"No," Daphne said.

Lee looked at me, and shifted his gaze back to Daphne. "Why is he there?"

She took a deep breath. "Because he's part of the circle that's protecting Sherry."

I felt the sadness flooding me. I didn't know if it was Lee's or mine. It might have even been Daphne's. "Me in exchange for Sherry? That's the edge?"

"No," Sherry whispered. "That's not what happens." She turned to Daphne. "That's not what you said was going to happen."

Daphne looked like a character from a black and white film. Flat. Her edges were too sharp, too bright. "They changed something. I warned you that edge wasn't stable."

"You're both wrong," I raised my voice. "That's not what happens."

Daphne looked at me. "If you're not there, Sherry will die."

"I won't die," Sherry said, her voice puncturing our bubble. "Even if the edge you saw won't work, it doesn't matter. We'll find another edge. It can't be that—"

I felt the knot in my stomach turning into a rock. I knew for sure that Lee would die a year after me. I could imagine his corpse, pale and lifeless, tossed in some alley with a needle stuck in his arm.

"They closed it all. There's no other edge. Because the Sons of Simeon have to kill you." Daphne clenched her jaw and looked at Sherry. "They see your impact. In four more years you're elected to parliament. In fifteen years, you're elected prime minister. There will be no more murders. No more movements calling for the segregation of sorcerers. No more Sons of Simeon. That's why they're trying to kill you at the rally." Daphne paused and looked at me.

My mind was racing. We'd cast a protective circle around Sherry. And then they'd kill me. And then her. No. Not her, otherwise the future Daphne and Dimitri talked about wouldn't come into being. They'd aim at her, I'd move. They'd kill me, and then aim at her in the hope of eliminating her before she came to her senses, and then… and then she'd be Sherry, and lead the battle even though she wouldn't be protected, and everyone would follow her. The certainty was frozen in my stomach. It was obvious to me that I had to die in order for her to live.

I felt the despair overwhelming Lee.

Daphne looked at him. "It's funny. How our world is falling to pieces right in front of us."

"Hilarious," Lee said, his voice cracked.

"Enough," Sherry interjected. She looked at me. "I won't accept it. You don't die. I don't die. Enough of that." She looked at Oleander. "Tell Daphne she's wrong. You know that's not what happens."

Oleander shook his head. "I'm not close enough to Reed to see it."

"But you can see the rally!" Sherry raised her voice. "I'm not the person that gets Reed killed!"

"No. He dies because of who he is," Daphne said quietly, and we all looked at her. She had her eyes fixed on me. "I see it so clearly. Reed tries to be a hero. You try to be a hero. In the end, I'm the only one standing there, over my best friend's grave, and my flowers aren't enough to cover it."

"I've heard enough." Lee stood and tugged my hand. "Come."

I stopped. "I'm not done yet. We have to think about it. There must be a way."

"No," Lee cut me off. His words rapidly gushed out of his mouth, "You or Sherry. Just like you said. And I know you well enough to know what's going to happen." He clutched both my hands and pulled me up. "We're going to my place now. And we'll do whatever you want. Anything." His voice was trembling. "Now, Reed. Now. I have a week and a half with you. Come. Now. I need you. You can go save the world in a week and a half. Now, I need you."

His tears were pouring out uncontrollably. He wasn't trying to hold them back. My eyes welled up on their own. I looked at Daphne. Sherry collapsed on the sand. For a moment, she looked like a damus in the middle of a flooding vision.

"Go," Daphne urged me.

We left.

37

The sun was almost up by the time we fell asleep. Lee was burrowing under the blanket, hugging me. His body was limp, giving off the scent of soap and shampoo.

"Don't die," he said, the pain pulling at the corners of his mouth. "I know that–" He paused. I reached out to caress him. He grabbed my hand and held it flat on his chest. "I know you well enough to know why you choose what you choose. But…" He took a deep breath, and I felt his overwhelming anguish. "Please, try not to die."

I kissed him, dragging out the kiss as much as I could. When I pulled away from him, tears were trickling out of the corners of his eyes. He sniffled. "I've cried more since we met than in the past ten years."

"I haven't been as happy in the past ten years as I've been since we met," I replied. It wasn't accurate, just close enough to what he needed to hear.

Lee bit his lip, sobbing in quiet whimpers. I lay down beside him and pulled him closer to me. He rested his head in the crook of my neck, drowning out the world in my shoulder. I felt him shiver in my embrace.

I slowly took his pain and absorbed it into my veins. As I extracted it, his crying abated. I took the tenderness I felt for him and planted it in the part of him that was filled with softness. Lee realized what I was doing. He pulled away from me, his cheeks shining with the tracks of his tears. He looked me in the eye. Slowly, together, we entwined our feelings. I was still able to tell us apart, but the boundaries blurred.

He started moving above me, his body accentuating the veins I highlighted. I wasn't searching for the boundary between us, didn't even try to parse how much of what I was feeling was mine, and how much of it was his. I sank inside him, yearning for his touch.

38

The hours turned into days that melted into one another. I didn't bother to glance at the clock or check the calendar. We switched off any device that could remind us of the existence of time. The only connection we made with the outside world was a message Lee had sent to Blaze, saying he was sick as a dog and expecting to recover in a week and a half. I perused all his books, trying to fix those I found lacking in emotional design. We compiled a list of my favorite episodes of TV shows and saw them in alphabetical order. I went over his music collection and catalogued it by 'songs Reed really hates' and 'songs Reed despises.' Our musical taste couldn't have been more different. We ate when we were hungry, showered when we wanted to feel each other under the current of water. Our conversations turned into emotional waves, combining words only when we wanted to be more accurate. Our feelings flowed in unison. I couldn't tell us apart when we were awake. It was only when we slept that our emotions sprang back into place.

One morning I woke up in my bed with an urgent need to pee. The surroundings made no sense. The sheet was purple instead of white, there was no wardrobe, just a clothes rack, and a pile of books rested against the wall.

Lee. I was in Lee's house. In Lee's bedroom. In Lee's empty bed. It only seemed like my bed because our feelings were so intertwined that it felt so snug and homey. I didn't know what time it was. The days had blurred into each other. I couldn't remember what had happened when, only the tears that turned into passion and fits of laughter. I poked around and felt Lee, slightly far from me. I managed to get myself out of bed and stagger down the hallway. I could barely remember last night. Lee had drowned me in his emotions, and I was only vaguely aware of what was happening inside my own body.

Now I was paying the price. I felt the tension in tendons I hadn't even known existed, and my neck was stiff. I wondered what position we had slept in last night that left my neck so unbearably rigid. I heard a trickle of water and opened the bathroom door. Lee was standing in front of the toilet. He turned to me and blushed. "I had no idea our relationship had already reached this stage."

He spoke, so I spoke too. "What are the chances you have another toilet hidden in this place?"

"Wait a sec," he said, turned around and sent me a very clear wave of embarrassment.

I left the bathroom and leaned against the wall. Don't think about peeing. Don't think about peeing. Don't think about…

I heard Lee flush the toilet and then wash his hands. He stepped out and said, "All yours."

When I got out of the bathroom Lee was already in the kitchen, mixing pancake batter, wearing pants.

"I don't get it." I walked up to him. "I throw all my fantasies at you and you don't even blink. I go into the bathroom while you're there and you turn into a tomato." I slid my hand between his pants and the small of his back. I focused my passion on him. Lee froze mid-movement. "And I also don't get why you even bothered getting dressed."

Lee turned to me. He looked different. He had a light shadow of a beard and his cheek was creased from the mattress. "I have work to do." He held the whisk in one hand.

"Really?" I asked, reaching out and snatching the whisk from his hand. "Or are you just looking for a reason to avoid me?"

Lee took the whisk back and turned to the kitchen counter. "If you want food, don't get in my way." There was something different about him. He was distant, and wasn't immersing himself inside me as I'd expected.

"I'm not hungry." He was avoiding me. Now it was clear. What had I done wrong? Why…

I put my hand on his back, between his shoulder blades. "Lee." I tried to imbue his name with softness. To utter it with tenderness. To calm him down. It didn't work. I felt his wave swelling. Underneath the insecurity was the unequivocal knowledge of our imminent separation. The thing we wouldn't discuss.

"I'm still here," I said, maintaining a calm, steady voice. "I'm happy here. I'm happy with you."

"You're in pain," he cut me off without turning to face me. "And before? That was me, not you. So…"

"So I woke up because you needed to pee? Great. It was really stupid of us to intertwine ourselves like that."

Lee shrank into himself. Just a little. The guilt inside him was surfacing right in front of my eyes. Instead of talking, I caressed and dismantled it. Lee finished flipping the pancakes. I sliced two tomatoes. He took the maple syrup out of the cupboard. We moved around the kitchen in silence. When I wasn't thinking about it, we acted as two bodies with one mind.

But he was still half-dressed and scared of the moment I'd leave, and I was still naked and aching, and all I wanted was to crawl back in bed with him and feel whole.

Lee dished up the food. I followed him into the living room and sat down beside him on his frayed couch, leaning half my body against the armrest.

"I'll dismantle it," he said, talking into his plate without looking at me. "My feelings will stop getting in your way."

I cleared my throat. He wouldn't look up from his plate. I cleared my throat again, loudly this time.

He finally looked at me. The green of his eyes struck me. A thought had crossed my mind. There was something I was going to say before he looked at me. "Your eyes are so beautiful." I moved in closer to him.

Lee lowered his gaze. "You're just saying that because we're entwined. Soon you'll–"

"You're an idiot." I remembered. That's what I wanted to say. "You really think I'm mad at you because our feelings our intertwined?"

"Noooo," he intoned. "I think you're hurting because of me, and I'm mad I didn't realize it in time."

"Yes. I'm hurting. And yes, your feelings affect me." I put my plate down on the floor and held his hand. "Now let's see how much my feelings affect you." There was a moment when I decided I wanted to be with Lee. I remembered the moment vividly. I focused on it, bundling up all the warmth and need I had felt, and sent them to Lee. He closed his eyes and took a deep breath, his expression softening.

That's what I wanted. That was the Lee I needed. I took his plate from him and placed it next to mine, sending him another wave. It was easy when we were so immersed in each other. I scooted closer and tilted him back. His lips parted.

"What I need," I said, making sure my voice came out clear and confident, "is you." I straddled him. He needed me just as much. "And I need you not to get dressed when I want you so bad I can barely think."

I fumbled with his zipper. Of course he had to put on proper pants, couldn't have worn pj's or sweatpants. "And I need you to stop being afraid of what's going to happen to you after I'm gone, and I need you to be m–" I was going to say 'my Lee,' but that would have made him break down in tears. I couldn't finish the sentence. He opened his eyes and touched me. He was gentle, familiar. His touch had become so familiar.

"Who do you need me to be?" His voice was low.

I bent over and kissed him. He helped me undress him. "The Lee who reminds me where he keeps his condoms."

One of us tossed Lee's pants onto the floor, and the other propped himself up on his forearms and flooded us both in an endless wave. I was utterly lost. We were one consciousness trapped between two bodies, swaying to a rhythm that made us groan at the same time, completing each other.

I hadn't noticed when one of us suddenly recalled that we had forgotten something, and I couldn't tell which one of us burst into laughter when the other accidently tickled him.

When our waves ebbed, Lee took advantage of the opportunity and started to retreat, to disentangle the ties between us. I took in his scent. "I don't want us to part."

Lee held me in his arms. He didn't reply, only kept breathing slowly. I felt how my scent affected him. He was filling with longing and a deep need to stay together.

"Then don't unravel us," I answered what he didn't say. "This feels so good right now."

Lee tightened his embrace. I buried my eyes in his neck. I was starting to get angry. At him. At the world. It wasn't fair. Nothing that had happened to me was fair. Until I found him. Until we found our rhythm.

Lee sniffled, and I was flooded with his loss. "It's going to hurt like hell, it's going to hurt so bad when you're gone." His voice cracked. He blurted it all out, all at once, as if these words had been piling up inside him, pent up for months, and now he had to let them all out. "And after you die, if we're this close, I won't... I won't..."

He was crying. I felt his body trembling. I didn't dare look up from my hiding place. I wrapped my arms and legs around him, hugging him tightly.

"We're too close. I need to be less close. I need to be myself a little before..." He barely managed to finish the sentence without pausing for air. "Tell me what to do. I'll do it. OK?"

He was overcome with helplessness. I tried to imagine him. To separate myself from him and imagine what would happen to him. After I was gone. What would happen to me if the tables were turned. If he suddenly disappeared. Despite all the preparations. Despite Daphne's warning.

Not to hear him whisper my name. Not to sway along with him. Not to feel him inside me, touching every spot in my soul. I recoiled. Just imagining his absence hurt. A pressing, all consuming pain that crushes every other feeling until there is nothing left but the pain itself, and that's the only thing that will be left, until you can take no more. That's what will be left of me. That's all Lee will have left of me after it's all over. Blaze will have the day we saw movies until late at night. My parents will have our last lunch. Daphne will have ten years' worth of shared memories. Lee will have nothing but the pain of the absence. Of the part of the soul that vanished.

Breathe in. Breathe out. Open my eyes. Look at his skin from up close, so close it's all a blur. Take in his scent. Sweat and soap.

Pull back. A little. To know he has been crying and his face will be wet, and still be surprised there's so much emotion in his expression. Caress his face. Wipe away the tears. Kiss him. A salty kiss. Taste him, really taste him, and commit the taste to memory. And the feeling of his lips against mine. And his tongue. The morning, and maple syrup, and he still hasn't brushed his teeth, and I don't mind. I don't mind at all. And to know that that's it.

And to pull back. A little more. Enough to look into his eyes, that were still wet, and still red, and still so green and breathtaking. Physically. I felt my breath catching every time I looked at them. I needed another kiss. One last kiss. To feel him moving in front of me, pressing up against me with all his weight. To drown in him. But it wasn't fair. It wasn't fair to him. He was right. He needed to be himself to diminish the pain, and as long as I was with him we couldn't separate.

To pull myself out of him. To hear his moan, faint, pained, when he realized what I was doing. To feel him brushing his fingers through my hair, flicking it off my face. Touching my cheek. My right cheek. I made a mental note of it. He touched me for the last time on my right cheek.

And to pull away. Truly. To not touch anymore. Not breathe him anymore. Not smell him anymore. Not step on those stupid pants he had to put on to get away from me, because it hurt. It hurt so much. And it would only hurt more the longer I lingered.

To pick up my clothes from the floor. To make sure I had everything. Underwear. Pants. Shirt. All scattered in different locations around the apartment. Remnants of these final days, when neither of us was able to think. Sandals. To know, with certainty, that he was still lying on the couch, naked, wanting me to return and knowing I won't, that it was the better choice, and not look back, and leave the apartment, and not wait.

And to sever the last thread that had tied us together.

And to walk away.

Ten minutes. That's all. A ten-minute walk from his place to mine. To go up the stairs. Not to think. Not to think. To open the door. To step inside. Daphne's in the kitchen making herself coffee.

To avoid her gaze. To go to my room. To not think about how it all hurts. About how my body can still feel him, still breathe him, and he's not here. To not think. To hide inside my own head, alone.

39

I didn't say a word when Daphne knocked on my bedroom door, and I didn't answer my phone. I lay beneath the blanket, fully dressed, breathing in the darkness. Every breath hurt. My skin still had Lee's smell on it. I couldn't tell how many times I broke down in tears. Every time the wave slightly abated, and the pain resurged.

I needed to go to the bathroom again, and this time I knew it was my need and not his, and it hurt even more. I held it in for as long as I could, until I realized I still couldn't edge out all my bodily needs.

I walked out of my room. Daphne was sitting in the kitchen, staring into the hallway. She rose the moment I emerged from my bedroom. I had a pee and washed my hands. Slowly. My stomach was rumbling. I didn't know what time it was. The light from the window had a yellowish glow of dusk. Four, maybe five in the afternoon.

Daphne waited. I felt her nervousness.

I bit my lip. "It's going to hurt him," I eventually said.

Daphne walked past the table and approached me. I lifted my hand. "Don't..." I didn't want to touch her. I didn't want to touch anyone.

She nodded.

"He's going to be in so much pain," I said. She didn't know what he felt. Only what he would do. She had saved me once. She had to do that for him. "When I die, here," I pointed at my temple with my middle finger, making sure she understood I was talking about Lee's psyche, "he's going to be so lonely. I can't hurt him like that." The tears began to pool in my eyes again. I wiped them with one hand. I didn't want to break down in front of her.

Daphne didn't move. Didn't try to come closer. I didn't know if she saw me dodging her, or simply chose the one future in which I stayed put and talked to her. I knew that if she made the slightest move, I'd go hole up in my room again. I couldn't face the world. She just stood there, looking.

"It's not fair." My tears burst forth despite my efforts. I wiped them again.

Daphne shook her head. I leaned back against the wall behind me, the tears blurring my vision, and collapsed onto the floor.

Daphne took a step forward. I recoiled.

"I'm not going to touch you," she said, her voice so lucid, contrasting with the haze of my thoughts. "I know you don't want that."

She crouched before me, without getting closer, without touching. "That's not what I saw," she said quietly. "I saw the two of you together until the end."

"This will break him." I looked straight at her. "You have to help him get through this." I wiped my eyes again. This time the tears remained trapped where they were and stopped trickling out. "Promise me."

"I promise," she whispered.

I stared at the ceiling. There was a crack above me. The landlord had promised to fix it two months ago. "I know you saw him die. But he doesn't have to die right away. Make him stay in Israel. Talk to him. He's going to need someone to talk to."

"OK." Daphne's voice was brittle.

The crack snaked above my head. A single ant was following its trail. My hands hurt. I realized my fingers were clutching each other. I shifted my gaze back to Daphne. She was sitting on the floor, cross-legged, keeping her distance.

"Is it going to hurt him anyway?"

Daphne nodded.

"But it'll hurt him less now, right? Because I'm still alive, and he'll cope with the separation gradually." I felt the tension in each muscle in my body.

"Yes," she finally answered. I suspected she was lying, but didn't dare ask.

I took a deep breath. "OK."

She kept looking at me, her smile gone. "Reed?" she asked, a slight tremor in her voice. "Remember how you once asked me what it was like to see the future?"

"You said it was like transparencies. That they pile on top of each other, and when they merge, you know it's the path that's going to happen."

Daphne nodded and bit her lip. I scratched my cheek. Where Lee had touched it. My right cheek. I had a few days' worth of stubble. I had forgotten to shave.

The knot in my stomach popped.

Daphne's sadness was infinite. She was going to pieces right in front of me, her sobs gushing towards me. I rushed to close the distance between us. She was hurting. She was hurting bad, and I was too messed up to help her. I hugged her, grabbing onto her curls.

"I'm sorry," she whispered. "You were supposed to be happy. You were supposed to be happy, and I was hoping that it might, that maybe you'd change your mind… I'm so selfish…" She faltered, unable to complete the sentence.

I didn't know what to say. I hugged her. Tightly. She couldn't stop crying. Something she said. Something small that lingered on the edge of my consciousness, linking into what Ivy had said. It wasn't supposed to happen like this. I had run out of options, but the options weren't supposed to unfold like this.

I opened my eyes and swept my gaze across our apartment without actually seeing it.

I replayed our circle in my mind. The protection coiling around me, the elements roiling around us when we had cast it. They were going to aim at Sherry. I would leap in front of her to protect her.

My mind was racing. There was a solution here. Something that eluded all the damuses. Including Daphne. I just had to think hard. We'd cast a protective circle around Sherry, and they'd aim at me to break the protection and create a breach, like when Aurora's injury shattered the circle that was protecting me. But Sherry would know that, and so she'd demand that we cast the circle on me, and they'd aim at her, and she'd go down. Or we'd cast the protective circle on her, and they'd aim at her, but the circle's protection would deflect the bullet and it would hit me.

The damuses on the Sons of Simeon's side had manipulated us into this current situation. They knew everything, but had failed to take Lee into account. Lee who knew how to simply not feel. How to block out all emotion. He knew what to give me. I mustn't plan things. I mustn't decide. I mustn't think, because the other side's seers had to keep thinking their plan was going to work. Sherry would die, and they'd take over every position of power, and all the sorcerers would be free to do as they wished as long as they cooperated, otherwise they'd be executed, and they'd finally realize their utopian vision.

I held Daphne in front of me and looked into her eyes. "I need you to tell me how much time I have left. In hours."

Daphne shook her head. "Don't make me, please."

"Now," I said, raising my voice.

"Four and a half," she said, her voice strained from crying.

I straightened up. Four and a half hours. "We're going to organize a rally."

"No," Daphne said and got up. "Absolutely not."

I raised an eyebrow. "I'm the one who's going to die. I get to decide how." I turned away and picked up my phone. "You call Aurora and River. I'll call Sherry and Lee." Uttering his name pained me. But if I was right, soon it wouldn't hurt anymore. It wouldn't hurt at all.

I turned to Daphne. She still wasn't moving. I approached her. "We're going to initiate a rally. We're going to cast a circle, again, and this time we're going to find the motherfuckers who're trying to kill me and Sherry." I focused on that. The other side's seers would have a field day with that plan. I'd call it 'Reed's Moronic Plan.'

"You're going to die." This time there were no tears. She was completely numb.

"I'm already dead." I looked her in the eye. "I'm dead because when Blaze came to the Sinkhole I brought Lee coffee instead of telling him to get lost. You said so yourself."

I didn't dare develop my plan any further than the initial glimmer of an idea. If I made any decisions, she'd know. I had to play by the rules the other side had set. Not make any decisions. Not commit to anything other than the timeline everyone saw. I had to actively not think of the timelines that became clearer and clearer in my mind.

"Lee is going to die in a year," I said, clutching Daphne's shoulders. "I want him to die thinking of how I saved the world, and how I was busy having sex with him." Lie. It was a downright lie.

I erased that thought, and focused on one thing. I was going to initiate a rally. We would tell everyone to come. We would cast a circle on Sherry. The Sons of Simeon would attack me to break the circle. And I'd die. I forced myself to picture it, to make peace with it. Not to think about a plan, or a getaway route. To think about the bullet Daphne had predicted, eviscerating me.

"And I don't want Matthew there this time," I told Daphne and took a step back. "I don't want him waking up from a nightmare about how he tried to save me."

Daphne didn't move. Her face was frozen. "You're going to die."

"Yes," I said and gazed at her. "And you're going to help me." She leaned back against the wall behind her. "We're going to organize a rally. We're going to call everyone we know, and we're going to cast a protective circle on Sherry."

That was the plan. A pesky thought in the back of my head said this was a bad plan. That I was trying to get myself killed. That I should run, hide. I ignored it. I had no plan. That was the important bit. I had no plan at all.

I called Sherry and told her to get herself over here ASAP and brief all her cops to meet us at the rally's usual starting point.

"There is no rally today," Sherry said. I heard the rustle of papers in the background and wondered whether she was at work.

"There is." I took a deep breath and looked at Daphne who was supporting all her weight against the wall behind her as if she'd collapse if she moved. "I'm going to cast a protective circle on you, and let those fuckers who want to kill you show their faces."

Sherry was silent. I heard her breathing. "It's a bad idea. They'll kill you." She knew. She knew exactly what was going to happen. She figured it out on her own, and knew that she'd demand that we cast the circle on me again.

I looked into Daphne's eyes. "No. They'll try to kill you. I'm not going to wait around for them to do that. I'm going to initiate it myself. Bring all your cops and we'll catch them."

"We have enough people in lockup and we're close to figuring out their plan…" Sherry began to say.

"And that's still not enough. I'm still going to die." I didn't raise my voice. I was calm and collected.

Sherry sighed on the other end of the line. "What do you need?"

"Lee's pages. You said you had a list detailing what he did to your cops." She said she had them and would bring it over herself. I suspected she wanted to talk me out of my plan.

Daphne finally picked up her phone and dialed Aurora with shaky fingers. Her voice failed her when Aurora picked up. I put my phone in my pocket and reached out for Daphne's. She handed it to me.

"You're coming, we're casting a protective circle on Sherry. I die," I said.

"Are you out of your mind?" Aurora yelled.

"We're meeting in four hours at the Three Sons Intersection. Round up the guys."

"No way. Forget about it," she said. I heard Forrest in the background, and Aurora repeated what I had told her. Forrest yelled, "Tell him to stop talking nonsense. We've lost enough good people." Then she told me, "I'm not going along with this. There are better ways of resolving disputes. You know that, you've seen it yourself. We'll organize roundtable discussions. We'll invite them to march with us in the next rally, we'll explain to them that–"

"Enough!" I cut her off. "The world isn't filled with unicorns and fairies. You know I'm going to die. You know how accurate Daphne's visions are."

"No," she said and sniffled. "We're all mourning Gaia. That's no reason to throw away everything you believe in…"

"You can have all the roundtable discussions you want after the rally. Today, I need you."

"Please," she said, her voice trembling. "Don't make me be part of this."

I pounded my fist against the wall. Tears were rolling down Daphne's cheeks. She wasn't going to help me. She wasn't going to volunteer the argument that would convince Aurora.

"You remember when we met at Structures and Spaces?" I asked.

"Of course." Aurora sniffled again on the other end of the line.

"You remember the first thing you said to me?"

She mumbled something unintelligible. I didn't wait for an actual response. "You said, 'Great, you're a moody, just what I needed today,' and then you told me how Yoyo was going to change my life."

I heard her incessant sniffles.

"I'm going to die today. I need my death to be meaningful. What I need is that twenty years from now you'll look back and say, 'I'm so fortunate to have met Reed. He truly changed my life.'" I closed my eyes, avoiding Daphne's dejected gaze. "I'm going to die, but thanks to my death the world you want, we all want, will come into being. Please, come."

Daphne wiped her tears. After a moment of silence, Aurora quietly said, "OK."

I hung up and handed Daphne her phone. "River. Blaze. I'll talk to Lee."

She took it without saying a word and dialed.

I called Lee. It took him forever to pick up, and when he did he could barely put a sentence together. He didn't sound sleepy. He sounded high. It didn't bother me.

"I need you to come," I said with a clear, sharp voice.

"Sure," he said and paused. "Come where?"

"Here. To my place."

Silence. And then, "You left."

"I'm here, and I need you to come. It's urgent." I drummed my fingers against the wall. Either he didn't want to come, or his brain was too slow to grasp what I was saying. Too fogged up with his drugs that took away who he was and left only an empty shell.

Another silence. I thought he might have nodded off.

I raised my voice. "I'm going to die in four and a half hours. Daphne just told me. I need you to come, and I need you to bring all the things only you can find."

"I'm coming," he said and hung up.

My heart leaped in my chest. Without having intended it. Without having prepared for it. It just started racing, and wouldn't stop.

Sherry was the first to show up, in uniform. Apparently she indeed had been at work. She simply looked at me and shook my hand.

Lee arrived soon after.

He seemed disheveled; unshaven, his hair a mess, eyes sunken. I felt his walls and the faint scent of sage as he walked up the stairs. There was nothing inside him. No pain, no sadness, no loss. Only the emptiness of the sage. I opened the door. He leaned against the doorframe and held up two fingers.

"I had two months with you." His speech was slurred, and he was swallowing the ends of his words. It sounded like the last sentence in a conversation he was having with himself. I wanted to kiss him. Hug him. Carry him off to my bed and forget about the world.

"Two months, Reed," his voice cracked. "And now I have four hours."

I touched one of his fingers, extracting the emotional cleansing out of him and dispersing it among our neighbors. I needed him focused. His eyes cleared as I did it. I felt his emotions gushing back into him all at once, a physical, debilitating pain.

"Don't go," he whispered.

We stepped inside.

Stage one of 'Reed's Moronic Plan': pretend I'm stupid. String everyone along. Even myself. Don't think about the elements in the protective circle warping everything around them.

I reached out my hand to Sherry. "I need the pages Lee gave you."

She handed them to me. His neat, round handwriting explained how to create any sensation I wanted. I pointed at a sentence beginning with "Present Progressive."

"That." I showed Lee. "Can you do that to me?"

Lee took the page. "It's not too complicated."

I raised my fingers. "Three hours. I want a three-hour trip. Without thinking. Without planning." I pointed at Sherry and Daphne. "And in three hours you two wake me up. We go to the rally, and we cast a protective circle on Sherry."

Daphne bit her lip. "No."

"My death, my call."

"No," Lee raised his voice. He stepped between me and Sherry. "I won't. I…" He brushed his hand against his face. "I won't be there if you're…" He threw it all at me. Loss, cavernous need, physical yearning.

My heart fluttered.

He folded his arms across his chest. "I won't help you die."

I wanted to shout at him that thanks to me no one was going to die. "You don't get it," I began, carefully choosing the words as I continued. "We're going to cast a protective circle—"

"Really?" Lee tilted his head. He sounded disparaging. Condescending. It was a show intended for everyone else. He didn't raise his walls. He wanted me to feel his pain. His sweeping sadness. He sent them to me without filtering them. "I'm not going along with this," he said, intoning every word. "It's going to kill you."

Stage two, the truly painful part of my Moronic Plan. To hurt Lee. The tears I had choked back were entirely genuine. I was fulfilling the role I had taken upon myself.

"I'm already dead!" I exclaimed. Lee turned pale, his aloof demeanor finally cracking. "I'm already dead. Daphne sees me die, and I've had it. I've had it up to here with everyone looking at me like I was some kind of ghost." Part of it was the rage Lee had projected on me. But most of it was mine. The inability to rebel against the fate I'd been dealt. The zero options I had. I no longer knew who I was shouting at. "All I want is to crawl into bed with you. That's what I want."

"Then let's go," Lee said quietly, his eyes deep pools of need.

"But I don't do that," I said, turning to Daphne. "Right? I don't go to bed with Lee, and we don't spend this entire fucking week in…" I paused.

Daphne shook her head. She was standing with her shoulders slouched, the tracks of her tears drying on her cheeks. "You've made your decision. None of us can change your mind. There's not a single reflection that…" Her voice cracked.

"So that's that." My voice didn't crack. You could hear the tears, but not see them. I turned to Lee. "That's that. We don't. We… we don't." I was searching for the words, desperate to find the right sentence that would convince him. "I'm going to the rally today," I clenched my hands. "And I'm going to find the people who decided to kill Sherry, and we're going to catch them before they manage to pull it off, and Sherry's going to lock them up, and they'll never hurt another person again. And if you don't want to be there, that's your choice. But when you smoke yourself into oblivion starting tomorrow and to the end of time, remember this moment. Remember you could have had four more hours with me, and instead you preferred to get fucked up."

I fell silent. I could barely breathe.

Lee just looked at me. I felt the pent-up breaths in everyone else. The anxiety, fear, sadness, pity. I couldn't tell what belonged to who, and I didn't care. My thoughts were swirling inside my head, colliding into each other.

"OK." Lee went blank. His fighting spirit had disappeared. His rage, and fear, and anger. He looked at me, filled with nothing but sadness and resignation.

I turned my gaze to Sherry. "Three hours. In three hours you pull me out of the trip. We go to the rally. We cast a protective circle on you. I die. And don't you dare think that by stalling it will change anything."

Sherry nodded. "I know how foresight works."

For a moment, just a fleeting one, I was hoping she was thinking the same thing I was. But she wasn't. She sighed. "Three hours."

Daphne looked at Lee. "And what about you?"

Lee returned the look. "Ask me later."

Lee led me to my room. I lay down in bed, fully dressed. I didn't dare take my clothes off. I knew I wouldn't be able to go on with my Moronic Plan if I was totally naked with Lee. It would be too big a temptation. Lee sat down beside me.

"I need to not think. I want something pleasant, and soft, and warm, like what you did to me last time." I touched his thigh. "And I want pretty colors, and to feel loved and safe."

Lee stood up, went to his bag and took out something that looked like a crushed herb, and sat back down beside me on the bed. He brushed my hair off my forehead, radiating loneliness. "It makes pretty images."

"How pretty?"

Tears pooled in the corners of his eyes. "Beautiful."

I was hurting all over, and didn't dare entwine my feelings with his.

Lee lay down next to me. We turned our heads until our eyes met. Just like back then, when he said he felt guilty for being so happy when everyone else was miserable, and I knew just what he meant.

He placed the herb on his tongue and kissed me. Slowly, methodically. He put his hands on my lower back, drawing me closer. I felt the bitterness dissolving on his tongue, and his consciousness groping his way into mine. I went completely slack, allowing him full access. My consciousness melted into a million shiny particles.

40

Daphne woke me. Lee wasn't in the room. My limbs were floating, and it took me a minute to figure out how my legs were attached to my pelvis. I sat up and rubbed my cheek. My beard was prickly.

"Three hours," Daphne said. She was oozing loss. "Like you asked. We talked to everyone we could get hold of. They'll all be waiting at the square."

I nodded, unable to pull myself together. I sent out my feelers and poked around. Lee was in the living room. I sent him a wave of urgency. After a moment, he appeared at my door.

I pointed at my forehead. "Some help? Please?"

My words were a garble of syllables. Lee poked around inside me, dismantling any leftover fog. My sight cleared, the walls condensing before me.

I shook my head. "I don't understand how you deal with this every time." I got up and walked carefully towards him, pressing my feet against the ground with every step.

Lee hugged me and held my head against his chest. "You do this so you won't have to deal with it."

Pain was surging towards me from Lee and Daphne. I raised my walls, and felt Lee's breath catching when I blocked him out of me. I pulled away. "It's painful enough."

364

We entered the living room.

I pointed at the kitchen. "Salt, pepper." I yawned. "Lee has tons of herbs in his bag, I'm guessing, so…" My thoughts evaporated the moment I tried to hold onto them.

Sherry straightened up. "You're serious. About the circle."

I nodded. "We'll bring the stuff with us. We'll cast the circle when we're there. There will be a lot of sorcerers there. When the circle takes form, it'll draw the sorcery out of all of them." I didn't use explicit descriptions. I thought it best not to clarify my intentions.

Lee's brow furrowed. "You need consent for that."

"No, you don't," Sherry said, clenching her hands. "If there are enough sorcerers around, their powers are automatically drawn into the circle. But if someone resists, the first circle collapses." She stuck her hands in her pockets. "That's how they broke Rabin's circle."

"I didn't know that," I said.

Lee snorted. "You don't know your history."

I managed to swallow my smile. He was still Lee. "So that's it. We get everything together, and we're off." I nodded. "Come on, off we go," I said, took one step, staggered and tripped.

Lee caught me and leaned me against him. "You need to drink. You need water, and a painkiller. We'll organize everything."

He sat me down in the kitchen. Daphne and Sherry collected all the items. I felt Daphne's pent-up anger. She wouldn't look at me. Wouldn't talk to me. Just kept shoving groceries into bags.

Lee stroked my hand and made me drink and take a pill. I looked at the small pill in my hand. White and innocent looking. It reminded me of something. "Neutral," I mumbled.

"You want?" Lee asked, raising an eyebrow. "I can get you one if you need."

I shook my head. It was the last thing I needed. I swallowed the pill and channeled its effect to the places that were still blurry inside me.

Daphne straightened up after bagging all the items. She looked at me. "You know there's another edge?" Her words were cutting.

"Damuses can't make out a clear image of people's faces in visions. Most of them see you as a moody with brown hair and light stubble." She looked at Lee. "He's not only willing to die. He's willing to get you killed in the process."

She picked up a bag and walked out of the apartment. The pesky thought had returned. There was some truth to what Daphne had said.

"I don't care," Lee said, his face empty of emotion. He raised his walls, looking into my eyes in the process. It burned in every part of me that he detached himself from. "Worse case scenario, the other moody with brown hair and stubble will die."

And suddenly I knew that he truly didn't care, and that hurt. Lee stepped around me and walked out of the apartment. I was engulfed in numbness. Sherry put her hand on me without saying a word. I locked the door behind me. Outside, a warm, humid end-of-August evening awaited us. It was a terrible night to die.

What if I'm wrong. If Lee dies today. If I stay all alone. I couldn't think about it. Breathe in. Breathe out. Start walking. The intersection was a thirty-minute walk from my house. We walked in silence. My funeral procession.

41

The square was swarming with people when we arrived. I recognized the cops who had guarded my apartment over the past few weeks. Dimitri and Lilia were standing side by side, radiating mutual affection. I tugged on Daphne and gestured towards them. "What will happen to them?"

"What do you care?" Her voice was harsh, accusatory.

I forced her to turn to me. "What will happen to them?" I didn't touch her pain. I needed those emotions for stage three of 'Reed's Moronic Plan.' Make everyone mad at me.

Daphne took another look. "Two kids. They get divorced in twenty years. Lilia remarries."

Aurora and Forrest spotted us and made a beeline in our direction. Aurora straightened her glasses, avoiding Sherry's gaze. "Thanks for helping me in Structures and Spaces." She sniffled, removed her glasses and cleaned them, even though the lenses were spotless.

I poked around, feeling Blaze and River approaching. I looked at Lee. His face was a mask. "Which way's north?" I asked.

He pointed at City Hall behind us. I pointed east, saying, "Aurora, you stand here." She took a few steps back.

"No," I said, grabbing her arm. "Closer. Here." She gave me a confused look.

"Don't get too far. Let's form a tight circle this time. It'll be easier." A silly lie. Everyone was too worried to think, and it was only a small change, swallowed in the masses around us. I felt the people crowding the square. The sorcery hovered in the air above us, heavy and oppressive.

"You need me?" Forrest asked. He wasn't angry at me. He was steeped in fear and the need to protect Aurora. He knew how my death would affect her, and he needed something to focus on.

"Are our kids here?" I asked.

He gestured with his head across the square. "Once the messages about the rally started pouring in, they all showed up." Had Gaia been here she would have run towards me, full of excitement, explaining how hard they were trying to protect me.

"You better stay close to them. Watch over them."

Forrest nodded, hugged Aurora and walked away. Blaze shifted his gaze between me and Lee. He didn't say a word. River sniffled in silence.

Daphne opened her bag, and River and Blaze took out the things they needed. An old mug for River, a chili pepper for Blaze. Lee took a small plastic bag with herbs out of his backpack and handed it to Aurora.

I pulled Lee and Daphne closer so that they stood on either side of me. "You're standing here."

"We're too close," Lee remarked. "We can't cast a circle like that."

"It's not that we can't," Daphne grumbled, "it'll just hurt like hell." She was still angry at me.

Aurora took the salt out of the bag. "Should we call Lilia?"

I took the salt from her. "No." I moved Sherry, positioning her north of me. I gave her the salt. "We have an earth sorcerer here."

Lee looked at me. A wave of understanding poured out of him. Sherry was right. Once he was in his right mind again, he grasped what I was trying to do. A tight, full circle, in the middle of the city, in violation of every law and taboo. Let them sue me after I'm dead. I turned my back to Sherry. Lee stood in the middle of the circle, and we huddled. I held my hands out to Lee's sides, palms up. It took Daphne a moment. She held her hands out. We needed to bend sideways because of Lee's height. "Three. Two. One," I said.

They got it. I felt their wave materializing all at once. The objects evaporated before they hit the ground. The sound of the circle forming around Lee was deafening. This time I was one the sorcerers casting the circle, and not the one in the middle. I felt our sorcery coalescing, creating a protective ring around Lee, cutting him off from me entirely. If anyone around me changed their mind... if any of them decided not to risk losing their powers and to break away from the others...

They weren't my kids from Yoyo. They knew the implications of a full circle.

No one broke away.

The circle of sorcery swirled around us. Fire. Clods. Steam. Too close. The fire scorched me. Clumps of earth hit my face. It didn't matter. Nothing mattered anymore.

The final stage of Reed's Moronic Plan.

Staying alive.

The sorcery roiled around me. Through me. Daphne's sight poured into me. I knew she could feel what I was feeling. We were united. The circle was too close. Too cramped. We wouldn't be able to keep it up much longer.

I felt the sorcery of the others in the square gathering, pooling into me. I was seeing through Daphne's eyes. I could see the timelines she saw.

I saw fragments of visions, shiny images that barely came together. A man in a baseball cap handing a much younger Lee a bouquet of herbs and patting him on the back. The same man, older, talking to Lee with his head bowed over a hot beverage. The images faded and reappeared.

I couldn't follow that timeline. I had to focus. To see how the Sons of Simeon would maneuver us. It would only take them a few more moments to deal with the change. They knew it was impossible to sustain such a cramped circle for long. They knew the elements swirling around us were wounding me and Daphne. All they needed was to wait. I could see that timeline. They'd wait, our circle would break up, they'd aim at Sherry, and take her down. I was saving them work by not casting the protective circle on her.

The circle was becoming more erratic. More elements struck me in every round. I felt Daphne's pain. We weren't enough. We needed more sorcerers.

Lee straightened up. He cupped his hands around his mouth and yelled, "The murderers from the rallies are here!"

I felt the attention of those close to us turning to him. They passed on the message, a human microphone.

"We can find them!" he yelled in a hoarse voice. "We need your help!"

As the sorcerers closest to the circle passed on the message it took on slight variations, but the gist of it remained the same – a call to all sorcerers to get closer to our circle and amplify the sorcery. Daphne tightened her grip on my hands. I felt her fear growing.

Through her, I saw people I didn't know gathering. They were moving from different directions across the square, far from us, synchronizing their movements. Lilia and Dimitri spotted us first. They began moving towards us, drawing the crowd after them. I felt their sorcery being sucked into the circle. Guy wasn't at the square, and neither was a pink-haired moody who had her heart set on a PhD when she grew up popping bubblegum in my face, feigning bravery. I blinked back the tears.

Blaze's power was the first to build up. Pyros were always the most active. River, then Aurora. But I needed more moodies around me.

Empaths don't maneuver sorcerers, and certainly not other empaths. Unless of course we're all about to die.

I drew from the circle's sorcery and put my feelers out until I found another moody. I stirred the sense of urgency inside him, directing it at us. He sent me back consent, and after a moment pushed a damus standing next to him. Because of my connection with Daphne I could see the choices the damus was making in order to clear a path. He moved to the right, bumping into a normie woman who was holding a grape slushy. It spilled on her. An airhead dried her shirt for her. The airhead's movement forced the woman standing next to him aside, clearing the way for the damus.

The sorcery of those who joined us condensed, amplifying the circle of elements and the combination of powers between me and Daphne. I felt through other moodies, saw through the damuses, felt the consolidating elements among all those who integrated their powers into the circle.

I poked around after the Sons of Simeon.

Whenever we talked about them, I pictured isolated sorcerers sitting in a dim cave, rubbing their hands together. Or a few armed sorcerers standing on a roof overlooking the square, peering down their scopes, choosing their victims. I never thought there would be dozens at the square wishing us dead.

The center of the square started emptying out. On one side stood the sorcerers that were with us, on the other, the Sons of Simeon, getting ready to cast circles of their own. There were two cops with them. I felt Sherry's hatred when she recognized them through me.

We needed more force. More sorcerers. But these were all those who could make it on such short notice.

The timelines Daphne was showing me were starting to jumble. If she couldn't see what was happening, they couldn't either. Reed's Moronic Plan in action. If I hadn't been so terrified, I might have been able to smile.

The Sons of Simeon started casting one circle after the other; first on their leader, then on members of the first circle, and so on until they were all protected. In order to strike the members of the circle, we had to get past everyone standing in the way. Their one weakness was that they didn't have enough sorcerers. They used a few of them for casting. The advantage was the protection of every circle participant. The disadvantage was that the elements weren't combined, which prevented them from creating a significant striking force. I was thinking like Dimitri.

It was the best way to protect the people in the middle of the circles. That's what we would have done had our goal been to protect me or Sherry. But Sherry and I didn't want to guarantee our own safety. We wanted people not to have to be afraid anymore. That's all. And for that, we were both willing to sacrifice each other.

I was missing something. I closed my eyes, ignoring the elements hitting me, ignoring the intensifying pain.

"Reed," Blaze said, his voice almost drowning in the blaring waves that surrounded us from the circle of elements. I looked to my left, blinded by the fire engulfing him. "Show me where to aim."

"We can feel you looking," River said from my other direction. "Show us where. We can steer the power of everyone who's with us."

Daniel had joked that I drew from his sorcery. The tempest in her red dress and on neutral. The pill I had been given at the police station, which kept me from touching my power.

That's it!

I opened my eyes. Sorcerers merely steered the power. It wasn't ours. We were standing in the middle of the biggest city in Israel, surrounded by normies full of sorcery. I remembered how it felt being depleted at the hospital. And how it felt to be slowly replenished from the people living around me.

I searched for the exact feeling, tracing it back to its source. Through the circle, I could do it voluntarily. I could draw the sorcery from the normies living around the square. Thousands of them, and all I had to do was maneuver the sorcerers around me to draw their power. I groped into the consciousnesses of the normies. One formless mass. A reservoir waiting to be utilized. I pulled instead of pushed. I felt a knot uncoiling, followed by a flooding turbulence of power. I maneuvered all the sorcerers around me that I could feel. The moodies were first. They understood what I was trying to do, and helped me squeeze out the rest of the sorcery from the normies around and transfer it to our elementalists.

There hadn't been so many sorcerers gathered in one place to crush an enemy army since Joffre and Falkenhayn in the Battle of Verdun. They were the first to try to bring normies to the battlefield in order to exploit them. And even they didn't dare completely deplete the normies.

I blinked. It wasn't my knowledge. It was Lee's, who was still connected to me in some distant form, still immersed in me enough for his knowledge to seep into me.

I focused on Blaze's fire, searching for its matching fire on the opposite side. It was a tall female sorcerer with a buzzcut. She was standing next to a pair of short twins, both pebbles.

"They're mine," Sherry croaked behind me. I felt her stability, the steady connection on the ground we stood on, echoing in the pebbles on our side. A fire flared next to me. Daphne's hands almost slipped from mine. I squeezed them tightly. She was sweating more than me. I could feel her pain. The clumps of earth in our circle attached themselves to small stones. The flames rose higher. The air condensed. I could barely breathe.

I needed to steady myself. Daphne and I were standing in the center, carrying the entire circle. If we collapsed, the circle wouldn't hold. I searched inside me for that small part of Lee. The one that remembered the dates of battles and number of casualties on both sides during World War I. I traced it back to its source, a thin thread that still bound us together. Lee was protected inside the enveloping sorcery of the circle. He couldn't support me or dismantle my emotions, but he could absorb them into himself. I started steering my own and Daphne's pain towards him. I kept her rage for myself. I could use it.

I felt Lee on the other end of the small tunnel connecting us, pulling into him everything I had sent him, helping me.

I tightened my grip on Daphne. Now. Because later it would be too late.

I pushed all the fear, insecurity and self-doubt on to Lee. I pulled in Daphne's anger, the anger of everyone around me, of everyone who knew I was planning on killing myself today. I felt the elements in the circle spiraling into a frenzy. But they were focused. I dumped it all on the moodies on the other side.

A single flooding wave of pain and helplessness. I needed to flood them until they collapsed. I showed our moodies how to go about it and, bolstered by the sorcery of all the normies around us, we extracted all the doubt and fear still left on our side, and hurled it at the other side.

They threw up barricades, walls, fortifications. But they couldn't handle hundreds of raging sorcerers, enhanced by thousands of normies.

The current was picking up. I heard battle cries, roars I didn't recognize.

On our side of the square, dozens of sorcerers caught fire. Some of them were pyros who managed to extinguish themselves, others airheads and splashers. The pyros managed to put out the flames, but not fast enough, not before they burned and scarred their flesh. I gathered the pain of the sorcerers on our side and steered it to the other side's sorcerers, bolstering the attack on their walls.

Blaze was busy cursing every branch of the family tree that led to the inception of the pyros on the other side. I was about to scold him, until I noticed that swearing helped him focus. He was steering all the pyros' powers. Like for us moodies, small changes necessitated less power than the creation of a big propellant wave. Instead of setting only a few chosen enemy sorcerers on fire, he preferred attacking them all. One after the other, the clothes on their backs started to melt. Their shoes turned into puddles of plastic and rubber. Those wearing canvas shoes screamed when they caught fire. Their pants were glued to their skin, blisters rapidly forming and popping. I felt their empaths trying to alleviate their pain.

River didn't curse. She didn't make a sound. She merely smiled, and I recognized that smile. It was Lee's thin, sardonic smile.

A sharp pain shot through me. From my legs to the back of my neck. I felt my spine catching fire. I clenched my jaw, to avoid screaming and diverting River's attention. Daphne's fingernails pierced my hand, and I felt her pain. No one else felt the pain. It was a well-aimed attack on both of us. I tugged on Lee's consciousness. He noticed our pain and took it into himself, releasing me from it. Daphne loosened her grip on my hand. I felt her and the other damuses garbling the possible timelines, preventing the other side's damuses from seeing us. The pain abated.

When I regained my bearings, I noticed lakes had formed on our side. We were all standing in puddles, some of them frozen. I was drenched. My feet became numb.

River's smile tightened. "Now," she whispered, and our splashers launched a synchronized attack. She had grown up in a world of barbwires and sorcerers who learned to focus their sorcery from the moment they were born. Her effect on the other side was dazzling. She didn't bother creating puddles or downpours. She steered the collective power of all the splashers to freeze the water in the cells of the lower body, and boil the water in the cells of the upper body. She evaporated the urine of the sorcerers who were participating in several protective circles, turning it into steam and causing them to double over in paralyzing pain. She made the blood thicken on their heart valves, and the sorcerers dropped like flies. She was effective and deadly.

Our side was flooded with a stuporous daze; a long, dizzying wave of lightheartedness and affection. I recognized the feeling from the emotions Lee had planted in Sherry's cops. Someone on the other side had duplicated the substance and was using it against us. The attack from our side weakened as our sorcerers' concentration muddled. I had no choice. I put out my feelers and reached into Daphne, pulling out the emotion that was buried deep, the pain I had never touched, and I hurled it at the moodies on the other side. The feeling of lightheadedness faded, and the other side was filled with guilt, pain and shame. Daphne groaned as the pain left her. It would be back, I had no doubt of that. But at least she would be free of it for a short while.

Aurora and Sherry launched a coordinated strike, crumbling the earth beneath the people in the main circle, creating gaping holes. They were protected by the sorcery of the circles around them, and

I felt their disparaging contempt. Their pebbles opened cracks on our side of the square, which soon deepened into pits under our feet. A few sorcerers on our side fell.

I suddenly realized that the small holes Sherry and Aurora had created were merely an experiment. Now they crumbled the facades of the buildings on the other side of the square. People began fleeing from the shattering walls. Rocks and bricks fell on the sorcerers who were already on the ground. Their airheads suspended a few of the flying rocks midair, but not all of them. The rest crashed onto the sorcerers who were holding the main circle, followed by an outpour of blood and shrieks. Their defense collapsed, and the man standing in the middle of their main circle was exposed.

I was about to rally our side. To strike him. This was our opportunity. But I was flooded with a vision. Crystal clear down to the last detail.

Children playing with fireballs in a playground. Two girls skipping in the fountain in Meir Square, splashing water all around them. Moodies sitting in a circle, smiling at each other.

Freedom. We're all free. It wasn't the freedom Sherry had suggested. Freedom from the mountains of restrictions. From using neutrals so normies wouldn't fear us. No. This was true freedom. I could see the moodies floating feelings into each other. Damuses sharing a vision in the middle of the street. A pyro and a splasher pushing a double stroller with two babies inside it, creating a rainbow above them. Water created from the air itself. It wasn't just any pyro. My sight sharpened. It was Blaze, with River. And no one was afraid. No one was hiding. No one was apprehensive about using his powers in public.

It was so clear, within arm's reach. No fences, no restrictions. I just had to make it in time. That's all. I had to break the circle. I knew, deep inside the vision, that they wouldn't hurt me. I would talk about how I helped them. How thanks to me, we were all free. I just had to let go of Daphne's hand, and I'd never have to pay the price for what I was about to do.

"No," Daphne said. "Look closer."

She led me to other places. Buried bodies. Timelines severed to prevent the birth of those who might undermine the government. Moodies sedated into a stupor in mental institutions, their minds too fogged up to rally their powers. Damuses tied in small rooms, calling out to people who weren't there, unable to move to timelines in which they'd be free. Elementalists forced to establish the new government, and tossed aside once they'd been drained of their powers.

I returned to our present. The world was exploding around me. The wounded's shrieks of pain filled the square. I focused on a man on the other side of the square. I couldn't see him clearly, but I felt his pain seeping into me, the sudden fear from when it all came crashing down. The pain, the wounded soul marred by failed suicide attempts, the trademark loneliness of every psychic I'd ever met. With no sharp and shiny teeth or menacing tentacle-like arms trying to grab me. Walls crumbling under the force of our attack.

I dug deeper and recognized the psyche in front of us. The sense of omnipotence mixed with mounting despair, so incredibly familiar.

Oleander.

"No." The wail trapped inside Daphne burst out. "No!"

I didn't understand what Oleander was doing on their side. Why was he with the Sons of Simeon? We had to get him out of there. He must have been pushed across the square by the mob.

Daphne pulled me into her. I gazed through her at the intersecting timelines.

He had used my anger at Ivy to hide himself from me. From all of us. He was a true believer. I could see his meetings with Linden, timed so that none of the damuses could see them. Timelines that had been set years ago and now intersected. He had pulled one over on all of us. From the moment Ivy met me, Oleander saw the current timeline and did everything he could to preserve it.

I saw Sherry saying no one could see into our apartment. That a damus had to be next to me to see what was about to happen. I saw Oleander offering Daphne to go out with him, so she wouldn't be beside me when I fought the pyros at the bar. Suddenly it dawned on me that all the flooding visions Daphne had had were in his presence. He was trying to make her lose her mind. "Blasted be the bones of those who foretell the endtimes." The Sons of Simeon were targeting damuses more than any other type of sorcerer, and none of us thought it was possible.

Because of him Daphne hadn't warned me before I met Lee.

He had used us to get to the ditch. That's how he knew how Lee intended to protect Sherry's cops.

He had prevented Daphne from protecting the Yoyo kids, and Guy from…

Gaia. He had gotten Gaia killed.

"No," Daphne said again, and I was blinded by the rage inside her. She grabbed my empathy and steered it herself, flooding Oleander with the mounting misery, her fear and sense of abandonment.

"Now." Daphne's voice sounded cold and detached.

One small stone was hurled directly at Oleander. The first damus who joined us found the right timeline and showed it to Aurora. She followed it, combining her power with Sherry's. Blaze set it on fire. There was no way to get a stone to burn, but Blaze wrapped it in fire. River added a barrage of hail, resistant to Blaze's spellbound fire.

"No!" I yelled. It was too late. They were overcome with revenge, and wouldn't stop. I felt the stone hitting him. The shooting pain of a cracking skull, the brief moment of relief, and the silence that immediately followed.

The damuses screamed together, their pain echoing from every timeline, flooding all of us. Daphne's hands dropped to her sides. The circle broke the moment she let go of my hand. Aurora caught her, and they both fell to the ground, stumbling into the pit behind them. I felt Aurora's wound, the gash in her ankle. The protection from Lee faded with a slight rustling sound. I looked at him.

"I'm not dead yet," I said, and passed out.

42

I woke to the sound of sirens and honks. People were yelling and running in every direction. I was more depleted of sorcery than ever before. For a fleeting moment, I wondered whether this had been the last time I would be able to harness my power, but the thought evaporated when the pain surged through every part of my body. I couldn't trace its sources, couldn't isolate the pain or alleviate it. I heard medics and doctors passing instructions. Sherry was barking orders. I couldn't understand how she was still standing.

I lay on my back. The stench filtered into my nostrils. Burnt flesh, ash and melted rubber. I managed to open my eyes. Green with brown flecks. So close he was a blur. Lee's tears trickled down on me. I blinked.

"It burns," I whispered.

Someone squeezed my arm. I felt hands all over my body and tried to push them off.

Lee stepped back and put his hand on my forehead. "Don't move." Another teardrop slid down his face.

"Where's Daphne?" I didn't feel anything other than myself.

"She's fine." Lee wiped his tears. "Everything's fine." He smiled at me. I couldn't read his expression, and I couldn't feel him.

Something was pressing against my neck, keeping me from moving. Matthew's face filled my vision. I saw the edge of his neon vest, yellow and green stripes under the Red Star of David emblem.

"Since when are you a medic?" My voice came out hoarse, strange.

Matthew ignored me and looked at Lee. "Can you maneuver him a little more? I have to set his leg."

Lee nodded. "Just give me a heads up."

"Wait," I managed to raise my voice.

Matthew looked at me. "Your leg's shattered, and you have serious contusions on both your hands. You have second degree burns covering half your body, and I don't think you'll be able to avoid an exploratory laparotomy. The only reason you still haven't been evacuated to the hospital is because there are people here in worse condition, and you've got a brother who can keep you alive until an ambulance frees up. Shut up and let me treat you."

I kept quiet. My pain subsided. Matthew disappeared from my field of vision. Above me was cloudless sky and Lee's hair falling on his forehead. He had long, thin hair. I knew how he felt when I ran my fingers through it. I saw every hair separately. Some were lighter than others, almost blond. I wanted to brush them off his forehead.

"Matthew," Lee said, his voice strained, turning his head. "You want more?"

"Knock him out. It's more complicated than–"

And everything went dark.

43

I woke up nauseous. Light attacked my eyes when I opened them.

I heard Daphne saying, "He's awake," and two heads appeared. Daphne's black curls pressed against Aurora's blonde.

Aurora said, "He doesn't look too hot."

"He's going to throw up," Daphne replied, looking at Aurora.

She was right. I felt my stomach churning, the acidic fluids burning their way up my esophagus. Aurora helped me turn to my side and I vomited into the bucket I was handed.

I tried to get comfortable. I blinked, my mind trying to piece the world together into a coherent image. Machines were beeping and humming around me, and I smelled the distinct scent of antiseptic and medication. My leg, set in a partial cast with screws sticking out of it, was elevated and suspended in a complicated-looking contraption above me. I lay with both legs facing the wall and my head facing the hallway.

As Aurora leaned over to cover me with the blanket, a lock of her hair caressed my forehead. "It's just the effect of the morphine and anesthetics." She tightened the blanket around me. "It'll pass soon." Only then did I notice the cuts around her eyes and the bandage on her forehead.

"Are you OK?" I whispered.

"Very minor head injury." She wiped her forehead of invisible sweat. "I'm better off than the others."

I glanced to the side. Daphne was sitting in a wheelchair, both her legs in plaster. Behind her was a row of beds, all occupied by people either in casts or hooked to an IV or a ventilator or some other beeping device.

"What happened to you?" My voice sounded rusty from disuse.

"My legs? A combination of a bad fall and a few stones that hit me, and your brother insisted they operate on both legs, which is how they found out they froze my veins in my left one." Daphne placed her hand on the cast. "Matthew says the damage is reversible, so I'll walk again."

I turned my head and looked around the room. Beds to my right and to my left. A light pink curtain was suspended above me, folded.

Aurora looked at Daphne. "He's about to ask about that guy. You know, what's his face."

Daphne's face contorted with confusion. "What guy? You don't mean the one who wouldn't leave his bedside or stop hugging him?"

"I can't believe I can't remember his name." Aurora snapped her fingers. "My head injury is probably worse than I thought. God, what's his name, the one who wouldn't leave, and slept on that horrible folding chair until the nurses physically kicked him out of the ward."

Daphne's smile widened. "The one who's going to kill us both when he finds out Reed woke up when he wasn't here."

I laughed. "Where's Lee?"

"In the staff dorms." Daphne put her hand over mine. "Matthew made him sleep in a real bed for a change." Her smile disappeared. "You feel anything?"

"Pain," I replied, "mostly in my back, and a little in…"

"That's not what I asked," Daphne interrupted me. Her eyes were fixed on mine. "I can barely see things. It's worse than when I was a kid. The change you made…" her voice trailed off.

"Barely," I said. "I can feel your and Aurora's presence. Nothing more."

Aurora and Daphne exchanged glances. Aurora looked at me. "All the sorcerers who were at the rally are completely depleted. They say it's going to take months until everyone's powers regenerate. Lee was the only one who didn't get depleted."

Daphne nodded. "He held your pain until you were evacuated, and then put you in a daze for days. He wouldn't leave your side."

"And there aren't enough normies around," Aurora added. "And all those who were close to the battle were also depleted, so…"

"He's depleted, and there isn't any sorcery to replenish him in the center of the city," Daphne concluded.

Someone approached me from behind. I felt only the angst of his presence. "There, I slept four hours." It was Lee. He walked around the bed's headrest and moved Daphne's wheelchair, standing with his back to me. He was wearing jeans and a crinkled T-shirt. "So no more pestering me."

I cleared my throat, barely, producing a strangled sound.

Lee turned to me.

"Good morning," I said, doing my best to smile.

He froze, sat down on my bed and touched my face. I managed to decipher his expression. Sadness mixed with hope. He leaned in, his lips soft and dry, and I couldn't lift my hand to draw him closer.

"No," I whispered when he pulled away. It was too short.

His eyes were closed. He leaned back and opened them. Green with brown flecks. "Good morning," he whispered.

"How is everyone?" That's not what I wanted to say, but I couldn't ask him to take off his clothes and come into bed when I couldn't move.

"I'll call Sherry," Aurora said, "she demanded we update her once you woke. She's already in the hospital so it won't take her more than a few minutes to get here." She took out her phone and dialed.

"And Matthew," I said. "I need…"

Lee put his hand on mine. "Matthew's in surgery. I'll leave him a message."

"I'm sure he'll step out of surgery for me." I sounded selfish. I wanted to see him and knew it would be important for him to see me.

Lee stroked my hair. "He's operating on Blaze."

I recoiled.

"A rock hit him and crushed his liver and spleen. He was among the first evacuated from the square. They operated on him straight away. Now that the operating rooms are less busy, they're performing a second surgery on him."

"And River?"

Lee sighed.

"Perforated lung," Daphne said. "The Sons of Simeon's airheads started blowing up lungs on our side. Luckily, our airheads caught on pretty quickly, so only five were severely injured."

Sherry's head appeared above me, pushing Lee out of the frame. "I was told Reed woke up." Her face was swollen and bruised. Red and purple blotches created an intricate, almost beautiful web across her face.

I smiled at her. "You're alive."

"So are you." She beamed in return – a genuine, teeth-baring, eye-squinting smile. She looked gorgeous when she smiled like that.

Lee looked at her. He didn't flinch when she approached him, considering his face from up close.

"How many hours?" She looked at him.

"Four." He held up his fingers. "Like your boyfriend ordered. So you can't send me back to sleep again."

Sherry sighed, walked around my bed and sat on the other side. "He's not my boyfriend. And he said you needed ten hours. The bare minimum to function is four." She looked at me. "Your boyfriend's crazy."

"I know." I reached out and took Lee's hand.

"We were just giving him a damage report," Daphne said. Aurora leaned against the wheelchair armrest. Only then did I notice the bandage enveloping her waist, peeking out from her hospital gown. Her forehead was dotted with beads of sweat and her inner elbow was stained with purple and blue patches, remnants of IVs.

"There's not a single sorcerer who was in a two-kilometer radius of the square who has any sorcery left." Sherry brushed her hair off her forehead, revealing another bruise. "All the normies living in a five-kilometer radius of the square are depleted." She peered into my eyes. "You created a sorcery storm, casting a full circle in the middle of built-up area without officially declaring war; we suffered three fatalities, two of them were Sons of Simeon's. There are dozens of severely wounded people. All the hospitals are crowded with sorcerers, even hospitals that aren't equipped to treat them. You maneuvered cops, and it's going to cost millions to renovate the square." She looked at Lee. "You're a bad influence on Reed."

Lee smiled and stroked my hand.

Sherry looked at me. "The seers' vision is completely blurred. No one knows what's going to happen now." She tilted her head slightly. "Mind explaining what you did exactly?"

"Reed's Moronic Plan," I said, trying to keep a serious face.

Sherry pursed her lips. "Sounds like a brilliant name."

I tried moving. "I knew that if I was protected by a circle I wouldn't be able to do anything, because the circle's protection prevents the person it's cast on from exercising sorcery."

"Not completely," Lee interrupted me. "I was still able to take away some of your pain."

"We'd been intertwined for days before the rally," I said. His hair fell back in his eyes. He needed a haircut. And a shave. "And it doesn't matter. If you'd been outside the circle, I wouldn't have had time to explain the plan to you, and they would've killed you." I turned my gaze back to Sherry. "That was the whole point. Not to decide on the plan until right before I carried it out."

"Doesn't sound that moronic," she replied.

"Wait until you hear it," I said, and took a deep breath, the mattress pressing into my back.

"Let's see what I can guess," she said, shifting in her spot. "You needed to cast a full circle, and it had to be tight enough so that nothing could penetrate the elements."

"It hurt like hell," Daphne said quietly.

I looked at her. "I know."

I shifted my gaze back to Sherry. "Lee was close beside me on one side, and the elementalists on the other. Even if they had aimed directly at us, the distortion from the elements combined with the smaller distortion created by the protective field around Lee would have deflected the bullet, or whatever they'd throw at us. That's the thing. If we'd cast the protective circle on me or you, they could have penetrated it by striking whoever was left outside the circle. But this way, the elements protected both of us equally."

Lee caressed my arm. "You think pretty quick for someone who doesn't want to think at all."

Sherry tucked her hair behind her ear, and it immediately bounced back. "I know what to say to every crook, victim or lawyer who steps into my station." She bit her lip. "You saved my life, and I don't know what to say. I have no idea how to thank you."

In movies, the hero always has a brilliant line, a sophisticated way of making everyone feel good about themselves. People died, got wounded, burned, frozen, and all because of me. Everyone was going to be in pain for weeks, if not months. Some would be left disabled for the rest of their lives. I couldn't come up with a witty one-liner.

"Oleander is dead," Sherry said. Daphne pursed her lips.

"I know," I replied.

Sherry drummed her fingers on my leg. "Ivy introduced him to Linden. That's why Oleander only showed up for one meeting. Linden shared his vision with him. All they needed was that one meeting to convince him to help them bring on the future they wanted. He was at peace with that vision from the first time he was exposed to it. A damus up north just found that timeline, now that the Sons of Simeon's damuses are no longer hiding it."

That's why Oleander had always felt so calm to me. He was using us all to get what he wanted, with no qualms or regrets. I looked at Daphne. "I'm sorry," I said quietly.

She bit her lip. "It's time I learned not to date damuses."

"What about Ivy?"

Sherry glanced at Lee and then looked back at me. "Disappeared."

"It was thanks to her that I understood what I had to do." I looked at Daphne. "I think she was trying to give me a hint."

Aurora leaned in. "What did she say?"

"She asked me to take care of myself." I coughed. "She must have seen the edge."

"I wish I was as optimistic as you," Daphne said, shaking her head. "It makes more sense that she realized the words she had to say to get you to the square."

I shrugged despite the pain. "Good advice is good advice, regardless of who gives it." I looked at Sherry. "What do you think?"

"What's important is the future," Sherry looked at Aurora. "Right?"

Aurora cleaned her glasses. "And that Reed's alive."

"Agreed," Lee said and smiled at me.

Sherry's phone rang. She glanced at the screen and picked up. "One minute," she said into her phone and turned back to me. "And now for something completely different. Filling in reports."

Lee burst into laughter.

Sherry hugged me and got up. "Yes, commander?" she said into her phone as she began walking away.

Daphne cleared her throat. I looked at her.

"My turn," she said. "Everyone else got to hug you. Now it's my turn."

Lee helped me turn to my side, and Aurora helped Daphne lean in. My hands barely made it around her back. She pressed her cheek against mine.

"I told you one day your beard would tickle me," she whispered.

I held her tighter and buried my nose in her curls.

ACKNOWLEDGMENTS

You can't write a book on your own. Parts of everyone you've ever met find their way into the pages, sometimes consciously, sometimes creeping in through invisible cracks, spotted only in hindsight. It was no accident that Aviel's shower curtain found its way to Reed and Daphne's shower, but his support and encouragement are part of what got me writing, and they are there, invisible, throughout the entire book.

In the list of invisible acknowledgments are Michael Gardos, my adoptive grandfather who asked me to write another book; Rami Shalhevet who wrote me that he wanted to read a full-length book of mine, and has edited short stories of mine for years; Ehud Maimon who put up with my agony and moaning for years and hasn't stopped encouraging me, conducted research for every question I asked him, big or small, wrote terrorist movement announcements, edited my stories and never complained even once; Iris Bosco who supported and encouraged without fail; Daryl Gregory who spent an entire afternoon convincing me that I could write a book without ever having read a single word I wrote; Yael Furman who taught me about characterizing villains and building plots, and contributed invaluable comments when the book was merely two thousand directionless words; Rotem Baruchin who taught me how to write about relationships and conflicts and read an early version of the book, back when I thought it would be a short story; Daniella and Boaz Karni-Harel, Dorit Tamir, Nimrod Aizenberg, Sivan Kotek and the rest of the Zarchin bunch who provided weekly space to create; Edva Lotan and Adam Levin, who every time I said, "This is the final draft!" laughed and took another chore off my hands; and of course – my family, who for months put up with me missing meals, slinking off into another room in order to write, and cutting conversations short to frantically jot down meaningless words onto scraps of paper.

Luckily, there are also more visible acknowledgements. Eran Katz, a clinical psychologist who explained to me about empathy, psychopathy and everything in between; Rika Graziani Teicholtz who taught me about sorcery and contributed excellent comments about the book. Hila Benyovits-Hoffman who taught me about wicca and its connection to gender and feminism. Aviel Tochterman who initiated our writing group and created a respectful and supportive space to sit and write at least once a week, loved Reed and Lee as much I do, and left an indelible mark on my life; Itay Landsman who contributed Monty Python jokes; Roni Gelbfish who read the manuscript, made excellent comments, held my hand as I revised and supported me when I sent the book onwards; Ester Wine Yaron and Shlomi Ben Abu for their help in explaining police activity in Israel and shaping Sherry's character; Maayan Eshkoli who came up with the Sons of Simeon's name; Uriel (my dad!) for helping to design the gun of the customer in the bar; Aliza (my mom!) who taught me how mothers react when their children are in crisis; to the Tweeter dwellers who answered research questions at bizarre hours, in depth and at length to help me make my characters more real; and to Sophie, the owner of my local café, who made sure I was eating, drinking, and amped with enough coffee to sit and write in peace. And to everyone else who supported, encouraged, commented, sent chocolates and pictures of cats and scolded me to get back to my writing, I extend to you my love and gratitude.

A special thanks is owed to Noa Menhaim, the perfect editor. Apart from everything I learned from her about writing, character development and scene characterization, motives and conflicts – her humor, optimism and empathy kept me sane. To quote Stephen King: "To write is human, to edit is divine." He was right.

Another extremely special thanks is for Daniela Zamir, the translator who turned my sultry Israeli summer into cool, crisp English.

To Yoav, Barak and Keshet, who for years have been living with a spouse and mother who stares into space and scurries off to her computer even in the middle of a conversation, and drills them about the details of their day just to gather material for stories, testing scenes and dialogues on them and making their lives especially chaotic – I hope to be worthy of you.

Last but not least, I extend my gratitude to you, who have finished reading the book (or just started and immediately turned to the last page to see who I chose to thank) – thank you for the faith you placed in me when you picked up the book and decided to read it.

ABOUT THE AUTHOR

KEREN LANDSMAN is a mother, a writer, a medical doctor who specializes in Epidemiology and Public health, and a blogger. She is one of the founders of Mida'at, an NGO dedicated to promoting public health in Israel. She works in the Levinski clinic in Tel Aviv. She has won the Geffen Award three times, most recently for the short story collection Broken Skies.

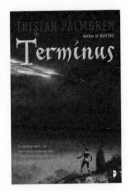

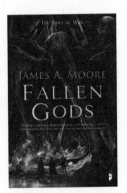
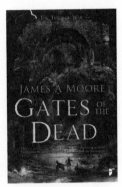

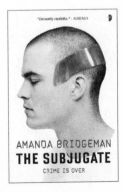

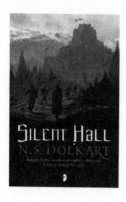

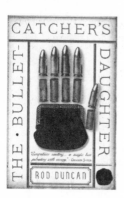